The B

N V Peacock (Nicky) lives in Northamptonshire. She has a degree in creative writing, loves True Crime, and has a darkly devious mind. In her spare time she runs a local writers' group. Nicky appreciates every review she receives and thanks all her readers in advance for taking the time to put fingers to keyboards.

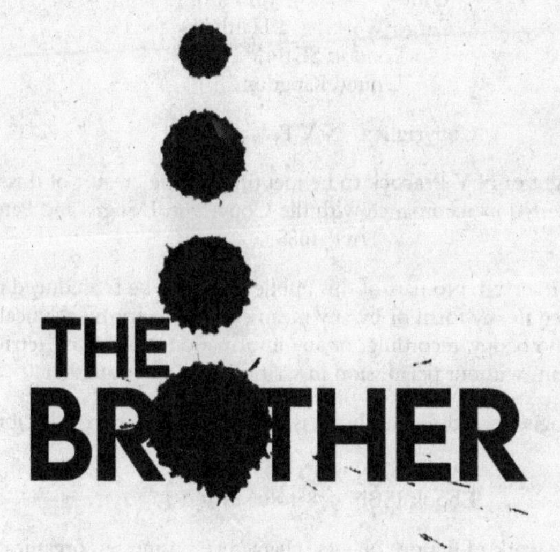

The Brother

N V
PEACOCK

hera

First published in the United Kingdom in 2023 by

Hera Books
Unit 9 (Canelo), 5th Floor
Cargo Works, 1-2 Hatfields
London SE1 9PG
United Kingdom

A CIP catalogue record for this book is available from the British Library.

Print ISBN 978 1 80436 461 1
Ebook ISBN 978 1 80436 460 4

Look for more great books at www.herabooks.com

Printed and bound in Great Britain by Clays Ltd, Elcograf S.p.A.

1

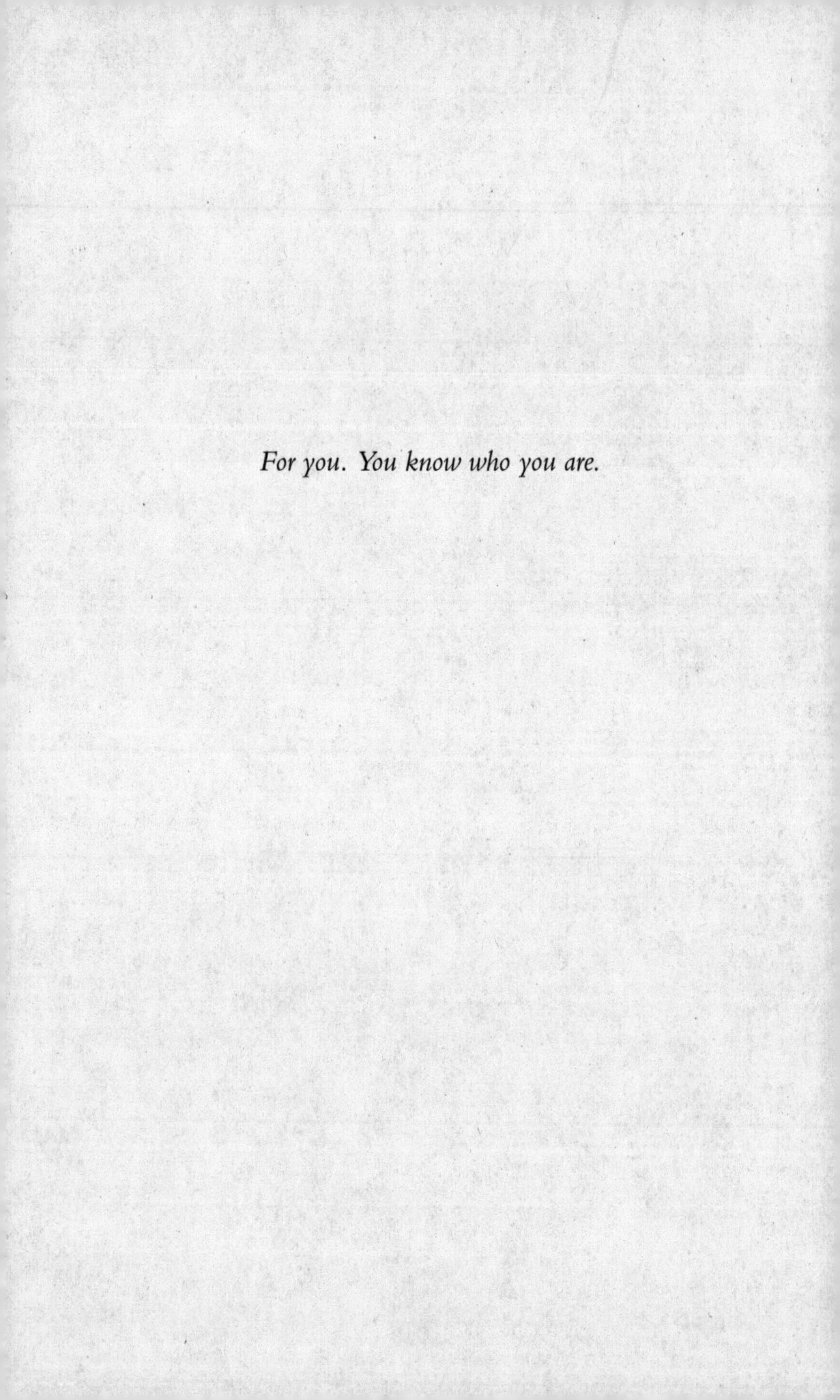

For you. You know who you are.

Prologue

I found my calling at school. It was when all the other kids were outside on their break. They called it playtime, but really it was mandatory exercise; like the kind prison inflicts on people they catch. To avoid it, I concealed myself in the stationery cupboard and waited. After eating the contents of my *Dukes of Hazzard* lunch box, I peered through the crack in the door and noticed another boy who'd had my idea. Not nearly as clever as me though, as he only hid beneath a desk. When the coast looked clear of teachers, he slid out. I opened my cupboard door and we regarded one another the way different species of animals do. A smile told me he thought he was my pal. When I mirrored the sentiment, I saw my new friend's shoulders relax.

'Want to do something fun?' he asked.

I nodded towards the door. 'We'll get caught.'

'We'll be quiet. Come on.'

Ducking low, he shuffled to the door then, on tiptoes, stole a glance through the glass top. 'No one's around, let's go.' He could have easily been spotted from his vantage point, which made me hate him a little; he was braver than me. He reached for the handle. We both held our breath as he opened the door wide enough for us to weave through.

Voices came from down the hall.

'It's coming from the teachers' lounge,' he explained. Already aware of this fact, I snorted at his knowledge. He thought he was better than me, but I silently followed him anyway.

Looking back with a grin, he said, 'Let's check out the science room.'

Science bored me, and I'd already endured my lesson that day, but he seemed so happy with his plan that I felt obligated to go along. I didn't like that. It made me feel as if my actions were not my own; as if I were a servant – less than him.

A twisted metal staircase sat dead-centre of the school. A frightening feat of architecture, with sickly thin rails and the imprints of a thousand plimsolls. I felt queasy when we climbed it on the first day. I swore it swayed beneath my weight as it creaked like something from a haunted house.

'Can't we just stay here?' I asked.

'No, let's go up.'

He scurried up the stairs, and I tried to do the same, only I took longer as I held on to the banister. Once at the top, my friend led me into a room. He didn't check this one for stray teachers, instead just slammed open the door like an explosion. Fortunately, no one was there, save for three rows of benches with uniform Bunsen burners; all lined up like good little soldiers.

'Want to turn on a burner?' he asked, his eyes already alight.

'No,' I replied.

'Why not?'

I shrugged. 'I have to do that in the lesson.'

'Yes, but there's no teacher here. We can burn anything we like.'

His idea ping-ponged about my brain. No rules, even though I was following *his* rules.

Without waiting for my answer, he reached over and switched on the nearest gas tap, making it hiss like a snake. He then pressed a button to ignite it. 'Do you have a pen?'

Dad bought me new pens for the start of the term; I didn't want to see them blacken and die. Especially as I preferred to gnaw on the tops, slowly mutilating them beyond recognition. 'No.'

'Wait, I think I have a pencil.' He rustled in his pocket, then produced a 2B. His eyes flashed with violent delight as he shoved it straight into the blue flame. Two things annoyed me. One, the smoke coming off our unofficial experiment was settling in my throat, making me cough. Two, if he had a pencil in his pocket, why ask me to sacrifice something of mine?

Carefully, I swatted the pencil from the fire. It tumbled onto the counter. Immediately, its odd-coloured flame died.

'Hey!' he said.

'Do you want to get caught? There are smoke alarms, you know.'

I wasn't sure what I'd said was true, but it must have sounded convincing as he mumbled, 'Whatever,' then left the room. I followed like a puppy.

Back in the corridor, I realised break would soon be over, and I needed to steal outside before anyone realised I'd stowed away.

'Shall we hide in the cloakroom, then join the rest of the class as they come in?' he asked.

It was a better idea than mine. My hatred for him bloomed brighter. He was braver, smarter, and therefore ultimately better than me. And if I could see that, then everyone else would too. As we stood together at the top of the twisted stairs, I motioned for him to go first. Not that he took any notice of my polite gesture; he had already started down the steps before I even lifted my hand. With the adult voices downstairs now louder, he was more cautious as we descended. Pausing on the third step, I almost collided with him.

'What's wrong?' I asked.

'Teachers are coming back to the classrooms.'

Braver, smarter, and better than me. Cautious only when he needed to be. Hatred didn't cover it. Extending out my hand, I softly placed it on the small of his back.

One push.

Unlike me, he wasn't holding the banister, so my touch easily propelled him forward. Down he went, his limbs smashing against each step. The sound of bones cracking and flesh tearing was like music I'd never heard before. He didn't yell or scream; he was plucky. On the final step, he twitched, then shuddered. A stream of piss escaped from beneath him. Teachers flooded in. Stepping back, I hid at the top of the stairs to watch the scene unfold.

'He fell. Call an ambulance!' screamed a teacher.

Another shouted, 'Don't move him.'

My teacher, a small fawn-headed woman, leant over to put her finger on his neck. Teary-eyed, she looked up at the staircase. Her stare sent me further back into the shadows.

It was then I knew my dark thoughts didn't have to stay locked in my mind. I could cast them into the world, like a fisherman throwing out a spikey net, excited to see his catch of the day. I'd crossed a black line in the sand, yet I didn't care. Looking down, three words replayed over and over – I did that. The power of life and death lived in my little fingers. My hands ached to do it again, and if there had been another *friend* standing next to me, I'd have pushed him too.

With a wonderful feeling building in my belly, I crept the long way round to the cloakroom. By the time I arrived, it was filled with children fresh from their play, yet to hear about the incident on the stairs.

The ambulance came and took the body away. Police interviewed the teachers. The school took out the staircase and a new, more boring one was erected in its place. Although my pal's name was often mentioned, I don't remember it now. All I remember is thinking, if he was better than me, and I killed him, then that makes me the best – doesn't it?

Chapter 1

Fallon

An intruder is outside my home. I've heard five heavy creaks on the decking in the last three minutes. They are circling, like a predator testing for vulnerabilities. Quickly, I pull a coat over my nightgown and pad from my bedroom to the living room. Living alone in a residential woodland lodge felt like a wonderful idea in the daylight; night is a different story. Suddenly, I wish I'd chosen a flat in the city, somewhere surrounded by people I could call on for help – but even that is wishful thinking. Strangers don't help you. No one risks their life for someone they don't know. I didn't.

I creep to the window. Christmas fairy lights hug the banister of my deck, faintly twinkling on and off against the dark, giving me only snippets of light. Still, I can't see anyone.

Not wanting to go back to bed, I sit on the sofa. The clock tells me it's three in the morning – Christmas Day. The thought of spending it with my family this year is both comforting and devastating. No one wants to be a single thirty-something sitting around their mum's Christmas tree.

My head snaps towards the window. There's the creak again, louder this time, taunting me.

On bare feet, I run to the kitchen. I grab a knife from the block. The handle is made of cheap plastic and it has a long, rigid vein, which digs into my palm as I grip it.

There's movement by the window. A hot jolt of fear spikes my limbs, flushing my body with adrenaline. I know I should call the police, but what if I'm wrong? It could just be a duck from the lake who waddled over to keep warm.

I can't live like this.

A combination of frustration and vigour fuels me. I march to the front door and, without giving myself a moment to hesitate, I yank it open.

The wooden slates of my decking are cool against the soles of my feet as I step into the night. I look to my left. No one. I look to my right… creak. But there's no one there either. Knife clutched to my chest, I move towards the sound. As I round the corner of my lodge, a shadow darts out. On my deck, in the twinkling Christmas lights, is a fox. Its eyes glow a fierce shade of yellow against its sleek red fur. I breathe a sigh of relief. Not only is my intruder not dangerous, it's beautiful. For a moment we lock eyes, it examining me as I admire it. Then, with a snarl, it races past me to disappear into the darkness.

It's not until I'm back in the lodge and putting the knife safely back in its block I realise how light-footed my furry visitor was, and how the creaking I heard before sounded heavier. *Get a hold of yourself, Fallon*. The mind can conjure all sorts of false fears if you let it run riot over common sense. But, seeing as I'm now wide awake, I get dressed and head off to Mum's early.

–

Last year, I was happy. I had a house, a boyfriend, and an illusion of safety. What a difference a year makes. Today, my ex, Grant, is happily sitting around our Christmas tree with his new girlfriend. And I now have a horrible certainty the world is dangerous. Bad things happen, without respect of time of year, whether you're naughty or nice.

'How long has the turkey been on, Mum?' my brother Ollie asks, snapping me out of my thoughts.

There's a scuffle in the kitchen. 'An hour, so good to carve.'

'Still looks pink to me, let's leave it longer and open presents first.' Ollie emerges from the kitchen, grinning. 'I think she's trying to poison us,' he whispers to me.

'Again?' I say, laughing.

'It's not truly Christmas until we're all puking glazed parsnips.'

Mum joins us, brandy glass in hand, and settles in her chair by the tree, ready to pass out the gifts. Ollie and I are on the sofa. Without asking, he puts a Christmas cartoon on the TV and suddenly we're kids again. Although there's only three of us, Mum runs a well-organised Christmas, ensuring no tradition is missed and no effort deemed too large for our tiny family. There are always perfect decorations hanging from every wall, along with proudly displayed Christmas cards from family and friends. Glittery pictures of trees, stars and reindeers are all carefully lined up on the mantel. Apart from one card, which I spot tucked behind another: an odd one out. It has a thin, papery appearance and depicts a religious scene of the baby Jesus in his mother's arms. Curious, I lean forward to find out who it is from.

'You're first, Fallon,' Mum suddenly says, throwing a large yet soft parcel into my lap. Abandoning the card, I unwrap my present to find a huge pile of homemade jumpers.

'They're not all my handiwork. I had friends knit them too. All one of a kind. You might say they're designer.'

I hold one up and discover it has pockets. 'I love them.'

'Thought it might get cold in that lodge-thing of yours deep in the woods.'

'It's not deep in the woods,' I reply. 'Foxglove Lodges is only a fifteen-minute drive from town.'

'Well, I just want to keep you warm and cosy in case you can't start a fire one night.'

Ollie leans over and grabs the nearest jumper, then holds it against himself for size. 'Fal has an electric fire, Mum.'

Snatching the jumper back from him, I gently lay it on my lap. She's not really worried about my warmth, but not wanting to start a family debate over my safety, I just hug the jumpers to my chest. 'Thanks, Mum.'

'Glad you like them. Happy Christmas, love.'

As amazing as my jumpers are, the gift I'm really looking forward to is from Ollie. This year, the box he holds is chunky and carefully wrapped.

'Merry Christmas, Fal. I know you've gone through a lot this year, so I wanted to get you something to make you feel safer. There's another part of the present, but I'll drop it round in a few days.' He hands me the box.

'How cryptic,' I say, then unravel the silk ribbon and pull apart the foil wrapping. Hidden beneath is a black velvet box. When I open it, I find a plastic pink lump that looks suspiciously like an electric razor.

'What is it?'

Moving forward, he takes out the present. 'It's a personal protection device. A stun gun.' He hands it to me and I find the side button.

'Careful,' my brother says, but it's too late, I've pressed it. A sudden crackle of electricity shoots from one end to the other. Gasping, I almost drop it.

'It's not as powerful as some others, but it'll get the job done.'

'Is that legal?' Mum asks, her eyes wide.

'No, but neither was what happened to Fal.' Ollie sits back, shrugging his shoulders.

I press the button again, this time bracing myself for the jolt. 'I love it.' No more having to grab a cheap knife when I hear my deck creak at night.

'What's the second part of the gift?' Mum asks, her eyes still fixed on the stun gun. 'I hope it's something significantly less dangerous, Ollie.'

'I promise nothing,' he taunts.

Mum inches towards me. 'Careful, Fallon. You could lose your job if you're caught with the electric thingy.'

'Don't be ridiculous,' Ollie tells her. 'Fal will only need it if she's in danger. I highly doubt the Health and Care Professions Council are going to get all mardy about one of their psychologists protecting herself.'

Before it starts another argument, I quickly put away Ollie's present and move to give out my gifts. This year, I decided life is short, so bought experiences rather than physical things. A spa trip for Mum goes down well, and I get an approving nod from Ollie when I give him a birds of prey day.

Once all the gifts are opened, I step into the garden for some air.

'You liked your present?' Ollie asks from the door.

'It's just what I needed. Thank you.'

Nodding, he opens his mouth, then quickly closes it again.

'What were you going to say?'

He moves to stand beside me. 'It's just, you're still not back to normal.'

I've self-psychoanalysed myself too many times to not know the answer; all the same, I ask him, 'What makes you say that?'

'Sometimes it's like you're… not you anymore.'

He doesn't mean it, but the words still hurt. To avoid his stare, I focus on a loose thread on my jumper, picking and picking with my nails until it unravels. 'I went through a lot,' I mumble.

'I know.' My little brother holds up his hands, then gently lays one on my shoulder. 'Just remember, you survived.'

Rolling my lips together stops my reply. The thread from my jumper is now long enough to wrap around my index finger; as I do, I pull it so tight blood pools to my fingertip, bulging it red.

'What are you doing?' Ollie nudges me and the thread falls away. 'You better not do that with Mum's jumpers.'

I try to smile.

'Hey, can I ask a favour?'

Glad for the change of subject, I reply, 'Of course.'

'I'm seeing this new guy.'

'What's he like?'

Ollie has the best taste in men. Blushing, he looks down at his feet. 'Amazing.'

'Then why isn't he here?' I ask. 'Are we that embarrassing?' then slips out, making me cringe.

'No, there's just a lot going on.'

My cringe morphs into unease. 'It's not because of what happened to me, is it?'

'God no!'

'Then why?'

'He wants to keep our relationship on the down-low.'

'He's not come out to his family yet?'

Ollie nods. 'When he's ready, will you be there with us to lend a therapist's ear?'

Lunging forward, I hug him. 'Try and stop me.'

'Thanks. Hey, I bought you this too.' After a quick glance over his shoulder into the house, he hands me a thick envelope.

'Is this the second part of the present?'

'No, it's something a friend at work recommended. It came a few months back, but Mum kicked off when I told her about it. I've been sitting on it ever since. Today, as I was leaving, I just thought *fuck it*. 'Tis the season for gifts and all.'

'Oh, what is it?'

'An ancestry test with DNA Hooray.'

'I don't understand.'

'My friend did one when they first came out and discovered she was something like forty-nine per cent Viking. Gave her this whole new inner strength thinking she could go berserker on people, or something like that.' Ollie blushes. 'I don't know. Seemed like a good present at the time. Especially after, well, you know.'

'How did you get my DNA?'

With a boyish grin, he replies, 'I did the cliché thing and stole your hair from your brush.' Cocking his head, he then adds, 'There was quite a bit to choose from. Stress is getting to you, baldilocks. Can I pick you out some wigs?'

My hand springs to my head and I run my fingers across my scalp.

'I'm just kidding! Look, I posted off your hair, and they sourced your DNA profile from it, and there's the results.' He motions to the envelope clutched in my sweaty palms. 'I've already seen my mine. I downloaded the app a while ago.'

'Ollie! You paid for two tests?'

'Yeah, I couldn't let you have all the ancestral fun,' he says.

'We're siblings! We'll have the same DNA, dumbass.'

My brother grins. 'Not exactly. We get fifty per cent DNA from Mum and fifty per cent from dearly departed Dad, so there can be a little molecule shuffle here and there.'

'But it won't be enough to have warranted a second test.'

'Oh, fuck,' he says, bringing a hand to his mouth. Then he shrugs. 'Oh well, good job I'm rich.'

'Not for long with a brain like that,' I say, laughing. I go to open the envelope, but am stopped when Mum yells, 'Dinner's ready!'

'I tell you what, how about you check them out when you get home then we can talk about our shared heritage over beers and steaks?' he says.

'Sounds like a plan.'

Dinner is hard roast potatoes, pinkish turkey and lumpy gravy. Reminding me of past family celebrations – it's wonderfully comforting. That is, until Mum begins to quiz me about Grant and why we can't get back together. She means well; she thought he was 'the one' too. Patiently, I repeat the sordid story of our break-up. When you stop being surprised at finding unknown underwear in your house, it's time to call it a day. After what feels like hours of questioning, she eventually turns her attentions to interrogating Ollie about his love life.

Christmas Day continues with more awkward conversations accompanied by too much rich food and sugary drink. All too soon, we are playing a terrible game of charades and I'm glancing at the door.

'Well, look at the time. I need to get home to log on to Hawk,' I say, grabbing my coat.

'Dr Hawk has you working on Christmas Day?' Mum asks. I've worked for Tina for years, but Mum still uses her formal name.

'I conduct online therapy sessions. The internet never shuts, and today can be difficult for some.'

'That's no excuse. She's working you to the bone, Fallon. I can't believe you're therapizing on Christmas Day.'

'Therapizing!' Ollie laughs.

Mum's cheeks redden.

'Don't be awful,' I say to him, looking up from packing my bag.

Then in the worst Arnie impression I've ever heard, my brother says, 'I am a therapist from the future, prepare to be therapized, mother fuc—'

'Ollie!' Mum butts in.

'Happy Christmas,' I say, then make for the door, Mum at my heels.

'Fallon, wait.' She reaches out to touch my arm. 'Are you all right?'

I conjure the best smile I can. Fearing I've only managed a grimace, I hug her instead. 'Course,' I lie.

Back at Foxglove Lodges, my memory skips back to last night. I see myself as if through someone else's eyes; wielding a cheap kitchen knife, and double-checking I locked all the windows and doors like some deranged fool. Steadying myself, I exhale out the dark thoughts and appreciate my beautiful home.

My lodge, Poppy Fields, sits between a man-made lake and a private wood. It's beautiful, with two bedrooms, two bathrooms, an enormous open-plan kitchen and living room, all on one level. It even has a fireplace, and a deck sweeping around the front and ending in a semi-circle big enough for a rocking chair. I bought the place in late autumn, then spent three days painting the decking pastel pink. When Ollie saw it, he said it looked like a giant penis curled around the front of my house, so bought me two large potted bushes for one end. I drew the line at a water feature for the other. When the weather is better, I'm going to repaint it grey.

Ollie found Poppy Fields for me. I wanted somewhere quiet, and with it being surrounded by nature and elderly neighbours, it seemed perfect.

Finally alone, I light the fire and get used to the feel of the stun gun in my hand. I read the instructions, then set up its charger by my bed. With the device being illegal in the UK, I wonder where my little brother got it from. I do worry about him sometimes.

Plucking my mobile from my bag to send Ollie a text, I notice I have two unread messages. The first is from Tina, thanking me for working tonight. The other is from Grant with a long-winded invitation for coffee. Clicking into my photo library, I swipe through old pictures of us together. Tight hugs that gradually loosened. Twinkles in our eyes which slowly dimmed. Smiles fading to frowns through the years. If I were the Fallon of four, or even two, years ago I wouldn't hesitate to accept his offer. But too much has happened. I delete my ex's message without replying. I need to keep reminding myself that in all the time we were together he never apologised for any of his heart-breaking mistakes, or stopped making them. To free up some emotional space in my mind, I delete all but the last photo we took together. I then print it off and slip it into a frame to sit above the fire. A constant reminder that when the bad times outweigh the good, there's no going back. With as much ruthlessness as I can muster, I then fill a box with all the gifts Grant bought me along with all the random things of his I couldn't part with before. When I'm able, I'll drop it all off at our old house.

Settled in my most comfortable chair, laptop before me, I log on to Hawk Therapy's website and wait for a chat request from a client.

After last year, Tina set it up so I could see clients online rather than in the office. She reckons it's how the therapy industry is going anyway. People nowadays want everything instantly, so being available twenty-four seven for those who need to talk has been a boon to Tina's business. Hawk is now the number one online therapy site in the UK, and through the wonders of search engines is always the first listing when someone in need searches for online help.

I've retained a select amount of regular clients, all of whom I trust as much as they trust me. They have fixed session times through the week, but sometimes, like tonight, I fill in with the general chats. When someone new wants to talk, their username appears in the virtual waiting room. Once I accept a client, they choose whether to join video chat, or just see me and direct message. Talking to text on a blank screen is never fun, so I prefer a two-way face to face chat, plus I then get to see something I usually wouldn't: a glimpse of my client's home. Behind them can be mountains of books, children's toys, and photos; even their wallpaper can hold clues to their psyches.

Tonight, everyone has the Christmas blues. They're lonely and looking to change their lives. This kind of therapy is like slapping a plaster on a broken limb. It irks me when our time is up. There's always so much more help needed than what fits into forty-five minutes, so I go over my allotted hours free of charge, giving advice where I can.

Although wishing for a white Christmas, Mother Nature decided on rain. The water striking the top of the lodge sounds like a drum, making my new home feel hollow. As I finally clock off Hawk, I close my eyes and listen to the rhythmic twang of the drops as they collide with the roof, then tell myself three things: 'I'm warm. I'm healthy. I'm safe.'

Tired, but not wanting to go to bed, I make a coffee. It's then I remember the DNA test. With my dark hair and hazel eyes, I could come from a myriad of cultures so it should be an interesting read. I fetch the envelope. From the postmark I can see it arrived over three months ago. How odd to think details of our heritage have been gathering dust in Ollie's house. I open it to find two pieces of paper. My results on one, Ollie's on the other. I scan my own page first and see a colourful pie chart made up of my places of origin. The biggest slice is Great Britain, then there's a sliver for Eastern Europe. The biggest shock is a percentage for Arabia. As a child, I loved the book *Arabian Nights*; the daring thieves, the tricky genies, the princesses in palaces made of gold and jewels. For a moment I imagine my ancestors on flying carpets clutching brass lamps and dressed in dazzling silks. Knowing my little brother, I bet he had the same vision. But when I read his results, I find they're completely different to mine. Origin countries not belonging to me, with different percentages. This has to be a mistake. According to DNA Hooray, my and Ollie's DNA are not just slightly different, but wildly so. I read it several times, hoping to discover they mixed up the results, but find nothing. We're not even listed under each other's family sections.

There's only one answer: I'm not related to my little brother.

Chapter 2

The Brother

Tick, tick, tick. I watch the clock in the corner of the screen as it counts down to zero. The bidding is almost over. Soon I'll claim my prize.

Millions of people use the Starsellers app to auction off their precious treasures and I often wonder about the stories behind each sale. Why would Lady45 sell her granny's wedding china? Why would Groucho69 sell his high-speed mountain bike? And why would 500Goldigger buy them both? Fascinating.

The necklace I'm selling today is an Art Deco paste with gold trim. It mischievously sparkled when I snapped its picture, as if it was about to tell me a shadowy secret. Its providence was a fashion student building an antique accessories collection for his first show. It was why he bought the fabric from me, why he so eagerly invited me in when I delivered it, and why his final pose was draped in vintage satin tie-dyed with his blood.

The bidding for the necklace is busy. Tootsie31 kicks it off, but is soon superseded by Geordielover52. I watch as bidders frantically scramble to stick their oar in before the time is up. Today's winner needs to be more of a challenge. I'm just too good. I remember when I started my game. Knowing I was better than all the other killers who have gone before me, or would come after me, I felt I had to test myself. When choosing your own victim you stack the deck in your favour, so I thought, why not let fate decide? It was an extraordinary thought on an ordinary day. Crammed into a car auction, I was bidding on an Austin Mini Mayfair. The car was nothing special and I only wanted it for fun, but there was another bidder. A man in his forties, a young vixen hanging on his arm; he was buying the car for her. Every price I offered, he matched. Each time I almost had him beat, he rallied. Every warning look I gave him, he ignored. Sadly, for him, he won. Jumping up and down and drowning in pretty kisses, he celebrated his victory against me. The celebration didn't last long. I followed him from the auction. And unlike his impatient win, I took my time and waited until the vixen had gone to ground and he was alone. He didn't see the knife in my hand until it was too late. It was from his home I took the first item I sold on Starsellers: a rich brown leather wallet which led me to my next victim. Admittedly, it took time to perfect my murder chain, but now, with thirty-three sales under my red belt, the thrill is the only thing that escapes me.

As the clock falls on zero, Hope&Storey11 wins, paying £67. Instantly, I'm gifted the name and address. It's supposed to be for a parcel label, but I don't use the post.

I read that Hope&Storey11 is really Nicole Stewart. She lives in Manchester, probably with her family or a significant other. They usually do. This time, to make it more interesting, I'll add an extra element to my game. A one-day time limit, echoing the auction itself. Within twenty-four hours, Nicole's hard-won necklace will be hooked around her lifeless throat.

The drive from Northants to Manchester is long so it affords me time to imagine what the new rule might add to my hunt. More danger? More excitement? More of a chance to get caught? Glancing at the clock, I see I've already lost an hour stuck on the M13 thanks to an accident a few miles in the distance. As I finally crawl past it, I'm momentarily blinded by emergency lights, then spot the lorry's huge front tyres on top of a little pink Beetle. Bonnet flattened and glass, like sparkling confetti, is strewn across the tarmac. The little car never stood a chance.

As I pull into Nicole's street, I work out my time limit. Four hours to get here, that leaves twenty for the hunt. After some brief reconnaissance, I find the perfect spot in her shadowed garden to watch my prey. There's a sturdy-looking man stuck to the sofa, who neither senses my presence, nor seems to care when his Nicole, all dolled up, leaves his house. I prefer to kill in my prey's home, but it doesn't look like the lump of a boyfriend is moving any time soon, and the clock is ticking. With a lovely tingling feeling in my belly, I follow Nicole to The Green Man pub, an un-impressive newbuild sitting by one of Manchester's canals. With its dark wood walls, beer stains, and cheap curry smell, I feel as if I'm in the stomach of a lad on a night out.

Nicole is a semi-pretty blonde in her late twenties. Tonight she styles her fawn-coloured hair in a childish ponytail and wears a skirt so short it vanishes when she sits down.

With the scent of stale beer in my nostrils, I sit with my back to Nicole in the next booth. I play with my mobile, as everyone normal nowadays does, and I wait. Whoever she's meeting is late. Why can't people just be on time?

It's rude to keep another person waiting, sucking up their precious minutes of life; something even more poignant to dear Nicole who doesn't have long left. She should be out doing something she loves, but instead her last hours are spent staring at an expensive watch.

Half an hour later a man slips into her booth. He's skinny with sharp features and wears knock-off Nike trainers.

I learn quickly that they met online and she is angry he not only kept her waiting, but doesn't look like his photo. Clumsy. This is the type of man who would be caught within seconds if he chose to tread my dark path.

He calls her shallow for only judging him on looks. I want her to spit back at him, to show some lady balls. Instead, her disappointment leads to uncomfortable silence.

Annoyed on her behalf, I get up and slide into the booth. Nicole looks worried, so I smile at her and say, 'You're too pretty to have to put up with this prick.'

'Hey!' he says.

I place my hand under the table and squeeze his kneecap in just the right place. If I yank it, it'll dislocate. 'You owe this lady an apology.'

'Yes, sorry. I should go,' he squeals.

I free him and he scrambles to the door.

'Wow, thank you,' she says, staring at me.

I'm good-looking. My brothers and I all are. In my calling, it's both a blessing and a curse. Symmetrical, sexy features may charm open all sorts of locked doors, but beautiful people also naturally get noticed. And when you do what I do, it's better to be forgettable. Every day, and with every kill, I meet my attractiveness as another challenge to overcome.

We chit-chat for a while, and she admits to living with a boyfriend called Roddy, but claims their relationship is all but over. I buy her another drink, and too soon she's dangling off my arm as we leave the pub to walk along the canal. With today's rain, the water appears dangerously high. As I peer in, she says, 'Careful, don't fall. In this temperature, you'd catch hyperthermia and be dead before you could swim to the side.'

'Interesting,' I reply.

It's cold, so when I pull on my expensive leather gloves, the act doesn't look out of place. I buy them in bulk and after each crime donate them to charity shops. It tickles me to think how many people are currently smothering their innocent digits with evidence of my murders.

After glancing around to check we are alone, I drop the charade. My hands find her throat and I squeeze. Unlike in the movies, it takes minutes rather than seconds to strangle another person. Her dull, doe eyes are on me the entire time. Does she think I'll stop just before her final breath? That we are playing the game together? Curiosity gets the better of me. I pull my hands away and she staggers back, gulping for air.

'What are you thinking?' I ask.

She tries to speak, but I've damaged her vocal cords so only a wheeze escapes as she drops to the ground, unconscious. Disappointing.

I crouch down and place the necklace around her rosy throat. The catch is delicate, so I have to remove my gloves to lock it in place. It looks good. Shiny, even in the shadows of the dim canal path. I slip off her watch, then lift Nicole into my arms. With one splash, the water finishes her.

And I feel nothing.

A quick hunt didn't quicken me. I was the lorry. She was the Beetle. She never stood a chance.

'You okay over there?'

I turn to see a man stumbling towards me. Clutching a half empty bottle, he waves as if we are old friends. It's dark and he's drunk, so I avoid an interaction by jogging up the embankment and disappearing into a nearby club. Heavy bass and the smell of a hundred sweaty humans hits me as I blend into the crowd.

It's not the first time I could have been spotted. After all, the UK has sixty seven million bodies crammed into its borders. But I still feel it: the thrumming tickle tiptoeing across my skin. It's not the fire of excitement I'm craving, but it is an ember. I scan the dance floor, then the bar. No police, no one meeting my stare. My fledgling excitement dribbles into nothingness. A realisation then settles in my stomach like a knotted noose. By playing the perfect murder game, no one will ever know my greatness. Catching the eye of the bartender, I order a beer. As he pours my pint, he asks if I'm having a good Christmas. I nod and imagine his reaction if I confessed what I just did. Would he be frightened or intrigued? Maybe that's what I'm missing, someone to play my game with. An opponent who can appreciate my skills. Perhaps a policeman with a mind like Sherlock Holmes and a Van Damme body could spice up my hunts?

Beer in hand, I sit in a dark corner and upload Nicole's watch to Starsellers. When the DJ plays Wizzard's 'I Wish It Could Be Christmas Everyday', I leave.

During the long drive back home, I imagine what it would be like to play my game against someone worthy.

Chapter 3

Fallon

The interloper in the family is definitely me. I remember Mum being pregnant with Ollie. How her belly swelled until I could see my brother's tiny fingers pushing to get out.

If pictures are worth a thousand words, what does my family photo album say now? The sun has only just begun to rise, so by the light of a candle I flick through my captured memories and edit their meaning against this new piece of information.

I don't belong.

Birthday parties crammed with presents and cake I should never have attended. School plays and Christmases where our smiles all looked the same, on the surface. Only now, as I examine those images more closely, do I notice how different I am to Ollie: hair colour, eye colour, and the way we hold ourselves. Each page in the album is a piece of evidence I simply glossed over every time I looked at it. These images used to tell me I was loved, that I had a family, and that I was part of something. Now they tell me I'm a stranger, I'm unobservant, and – above all – I'm an idiot.

After having a coffee, I think through what I'll do with this information. I could try to hide it from Ollie, but he has the login details for DNA Hooray, so is bound to be curious enough to look at mine at some point. And even if I did manage to conceal this bombshell, then I'd be as bad as Mum.

I need to know what happened. Who I am.

Eye-wateringly early on Boxing Day morning, I pull up at Mum's house, then bang on the door. I'm about to ask a question I already know the answer to, but it won't seem real until I hear the word *adopted* from my mother's lips.

'Fallon? Whatever's the matter?' Mum asks. She's wearing the fluffy dressing gown I bought for her birthday.

'We need to talk,' I say, waving the DNA Hooray envelope.

'Of course, love.'

Stepping into the house I grew up in suddenly feels odd, as if I'm in a stranger's home.

'What's going on?' She asks, staring at the logo on the envelope in my hand.

'Am I adopted?' The words spring out before I can sugar-coat them.

'Pardon?'

'Am I adopted?'

Her face contorts in surprise, or maybe anger. 'Why would you say that?'

'Because Ollie has completely different DNA to me!' I wave the evidence in her face.

Mum grabs the envelope from my hand, rips it open and reads. 'Let's sit down.' She ushers me onto the sofa by the Christmas tree. Tightening her robe around her, she perches on her favourite armchair. 'They've obviously made an error. They're not the most reputable company.

I told Oliver not to do this silly thing, but he never listens to me. I'll call the Hooray people, have this cleared up tomorrow. Feel better?'

Mum's a terrible liar. 'No.'

'Fallon, I don't know what else I can say. You are part of this family.' She looks determined, but shifts in her armchair.

'But I'm not biologically part of it, am I?' All my training tells me not to ask closed questions. Yes and no doesn't birth conversation, but my psychological skills have abandoned me.

Mum hangs her head. 'No, you are not biologically a Hurley.'

A sudden intake of breath chokes me. Childhood memories flicker through my mind like scenes from an old home movie. It can't have all been lies. I felt loved. I felt I belonged. I felt safe.

'Are you okay?' Mum asks. 'I'll get you some water.' She gets up, but I reach out and stop her.

'Tell me everything, right now.'

Sitting back down, Mum throws her hands in the air. 'How would it help?'

I've no idea, but if my entire life up to this point has been a lie then I need to know the truth. 'Please.'

'Is this really the best time? You've so much on your plate.' She reaches out to me, but I jerk away.

'Tell. Me. Everything.'

Mum gropes for a cushion to hold on her lap, then reluctantly begins. 'My first pregnancy was fraught with complications. One thing after another. I was in hospital for most of it. Scan after scan, test after test. It was a nightmare nine months but then I gave birth, and it was all worth it to see her beautiful eyes.'

'Her eyes?'

At my question, her reddening fingers grip harder onto the cushion, making it bulge out in a grotesque shape. Tears gather in the corners of her eyes and she opens her mouth to answer, but then suddenly frees the cushion to cover her face with her hands. 'I'm so sorry, I didn't tell you,' she whispers.

My instinct is to put an arm around her shoulders and say everything is okay. But something stops me. I've too many questions. 'Did Dad know?'

'Your father wasn't at the birth; he was away with work all month. But there was another mum I met at the hospital who helped me. She was having issues too. Too many days in those hospital beds, both of us waiting to go into labour, both of us only having each other as company. She was a little rough around the edges, but she had lots of kids, so was a dab hand at it all.' Mum looks away for a moment. 'I was so jealous when her husband and four little boys came in for the visiting hour. How they all held their little arms out for hugs, and crawled across the bed to reach her. She had her little girl on the same day. After I left the hospital, I called her to come round. But I was so exhausted that, before she arrived, I fell asleep with my daughter in my arms. When I woke up to the doorbell, she felt so heavy. The first thing I noticed was her colour. It was… her skin was…'

As I watch Mum mentally fumble for the words, I try to put myself in her shoes. I've not had the chance to be a mother yet, but I can imagine how earth-shattering this would be. I offer, 'She'd stopped breathing?'

'My friend called for help, but it was too late.' She throws me a look, as if to say we can stop this at any time. I lean forward and she continues. 'Devastation doesn't cover the feeling. I still remember it now.' She shivers. 'But before the ambulance arrived, the other mother took my dead girl and gave me her live one. She told me she could barely handle her boys, and money was tight. As awful as it sounded, she needed to lighten her load. When she put you in my arms, I knew it was the right thing. I'd so desperately wanted a daughter, and I didn't know if I could even have another child. When you touched my face with your little hand, I just agreed to everything she said. Anything to keep you. We promised never to tell anyone which baby died that day. From then to now, you were my daughter.'

'No one noticed you swapped babies?'

'You were both just days old. Most babies look alike at that age. The paramedics never questioned it when she told them it was her baby who died.'

Rolling around this new information in my head, I get up and pace. 'Seriously, you didn't even tell Dad?'

'I promised I wouldn't.'

'Am I legally part of this family? How did you do it?'

'I just carried on with the paperwork, but with you rather than my biological daughter. The other mother buried her. We were all at the funeral. Things were easier to conceal back then.'

'Even stealing a child?'

Mum's eyes glaze. She looks wild, as if she's about to run for the door. 'Just because something is illegal, doesn't mean it's not for the best. Everyone was happy. If I'd have been able to keep you both, I would have. God saw fit to take my first daughter, but my friend gave me a second.'

Too many words crowd my mouth, so many I have to close my eyes and control my breathing.

'Fallon?'

'Is that even my real name?' I seethe.

Mum cocks her head. 'She hadn't named you yet, and I'd already named my girl Fallon.'

'I have a dead baby's name?'

Mum gets up. She reaches out to hug me. 'Lots of people have family names. I'm named after my Great Aunt Heather. It's an honour.'

'Great Aunt Heather lived to ninety-three,' I whisper as my mum's arms encircle me. Wrestling free, I ask. 'What was the woman's name, the one who gave me to you?'

'She's not your mum.'

'Tell me the name of the woman who passed me over like a used tissue.'

'Please, Fallon. I promised,' she begs, tears gliding down her cheeks.

I don't want to make my mum cry, seeing it breaks my heart, but I need to know. 'You have to tell me.'

She purses her lips together as if to stop the name escaping.

'Tell me,' I press.

Mum shakes her head.

'Tell me!'

'It's Siobhan Kaplan!' She all but exhales the name. 'We still send Christmas cards.' Her eyes dart towards the mantel.

Springing forward, I grab the baby Jesus card concealed at the back and open it. There's her name. No heartfelt message. No checking up on her daughter. Just, *All the best, Siobhan.*

'Do you send her one back?' I ask.

'I always return Christmas cards.'

'Then you have her contact details.'

Mum promises to give me Siobhan's number, but only after she contacts her first. A vengeful part of me wants to just turn up at my bio-mum's door without warning and blow up her happy family – it's what's happening to me right now. But seeing the despair in Mum's eyes makes me agree to wait.

As soon as I'm back inside Poppy Fields, I call Ollie and blurt out the whole story. It's rare I stun my brother into silence, even rarer he can drive between his town house and Foxglove within ten minutes, yet today both things happen.

'Who the hell is Siobhan Kaplan?' he asks, a glass of wine in one hand, his mobile ready to Google her in the other.

'Calm down. I only just found this all out.'

'I've never even heard Mum mention her. But they were good enough friends for her to give a child to?'

Nodding, I stare at the fire. The metal bars glow so bright they birth little dots in my vision. If I'm not Fallon Hurley, who am I?

Breaking my thoughts, Ollie asks, 'Could Mum go to prison?'

I shake my head. 'I don't think so. It sounds like it was amicable, they just didn't do the adoption paperwork.' Even as I say it, I'm unsure whether I believe it.

My brother sits down next to me. 'Do you really want to meet Siobhan?'

'I have to confront her. Find out why she did it. It couldn't just be to save money.'

'When it comes to money, I wouldn't put *anything* past *anyone*.'

'I need to hear that from her.' As I say this I imagine her staring into my newborn face and, knowing that one day I'd bring shame to my family; a prediction that would easily unstick me from her arms.

I grab my phone to call Mum and push her for Siobhan's contact details sooner, but Ollie stops me. 'Wait, you've enough going on now, what with your…'

I finish his sentence: 'Testimony.'

'Yeah, maybe park this mess until you have the time to process it. At work we always say deal with the nearest fire first. When you're on more even footing, emotionally, I'll come with you to confront Siobhan. Deal?'

I hate that my little brother is right. Yesterday, he told me I'm not yet back to myself, and although I might never get back to the Fallon before, I shouldn't meet my bio-mother while still buried under so much stress.

'Deal,' I say. 'She had thirty plus years to contact me, and didn't. She can wait a few months until the court case is done.' I turn to Ollie. 'How are you feeling about all this?'

He hangs his head. 'I'm afraid I have some bad news for you.'

'What is it?' Both my heart and mind race at a thousand miles an hour. How much more devastation can I take?

'No matter what,' he says, then pauses to take my hand, 'I'm still your brother.'

Unclenching in relief, I point at Ollie. 'Don't scare me like that, you little…'

Laughing, he puts his arm around me. 'And hey, you know what this family revelation means?'

I raise an eyebrow.

'You can't blame us anymore for your high blood pressure and shellfish allergy.'

'Well, not the shellfish, but you're still responsible for my blood pressure.' I punch his arm. After chatting for another hour, Ollie leaves. Often in these situations, I try to think what advice I would give a client. I could dissect both mums' actions, twist them until I feel pain, but I could also look on the bright side: if Siobhan had four boys that means I have at least four other brothers. Ollie is my best friend. I feel safe when he's around. Having more siblings in my life could be a boon.

I spend a few hours catching up with clients. Listening to how their Christmases went, and talking through inevitable family fall-outs, forces thoughts of my own drama to the back of my mind. That is, until a hawk icon appears on the screen, announcing I have an internal call. It's Tina. I answer and my boss's face appears in front of me. Although in her sixties, her style is of a much younger woman. Today she's wearing a pale paisley blouse against her dark skin and big silver hoop earrings. I've known her over fifteen years, and she still looks the same as when we first met.

'Hey, pet. How's tricks?' she asks.

'Fine thanks. How's yours?' I reply with a smile.

Pursing her lips, she examines my face and body language. 'Anything you want to talk about?'

I do want to talk about it, but Tina is a 'by the books' professional, and I'm unsure how Mum stands legally on the whole situation. 'It's nothing.'

'Sure,' she says, suspicion lurking in her eyes. Tina thinks I'm upset because I don't want to talk about what happened last year. And she's halfway right. Running through that evening with my boss and mentor before my testimony seemed like a sensible idea, but now the first session is here, I realise how hard it's going to be. But regardless of my feelings, I have to do it.

'I'm ready,' I say.

'Try for as much detail as possible. You're going to be asked a lot of questions from both barristers, and you need to be able to carefully articulate each answer.'

Closing my eyes, I take a deep breath, then recall the most horrifying experience of my life.

Chapter 4

Fallon

Being winter, the night had drawn in quick. At six o'clock, without working streetlights, it was almost pitch black when I arrived at the half-built Cat Hall Estate.

When I climbed out of the car, I thought how weird it was that the place looked like a building site and yet there were no builders. The estate agent I was meeting, Rosie Howe, wasn't anywhere to be seen either. I pulled out the postcard she had sent me for the new estate. It showed a kitsch fifties family in front of a big ol' house and large red letters asked, Cat Hall, wish you were here? *I flipped it over to check the time and meeting point. There it was in big, black writing, right time, right place, but no estate agent in sight.*

The wind had picked up since I'd left work. It pushed at my back and stung my ears. And when it whipped about the nearby buildings, it sounded like distant screams.

I walked to the show home and found it locked. No lights. I knocked on the door, then cupped my hands on the window to peer in. It was lovely inside, but like everywhere else, deserted. I called the estate agent and Rosie apologised for being late; she was stuck in traffic.

'Do you want to reschedule?' she asked.

Looking at my watch, I replied, 'How long do you think you'll be?'

'Another fifteen minutes.'

Wanting to see the houses tonight, I replied. 'No worries. I'll wait.'

I messaged Ollie to tell him I'd be late coming home. He came straight back saying that we'd go together tomorrow, and I was welcome to stay with him as long as I needed. But staying at my little brother's house, sleeping in his spare room, was all a little too sad for a thirty-something. I had broken up with Grant, yet somehow it felt as if I had been dumped. Tears swelled my eyes, so I wrestled a tissue from my pocket. If I couldn't even successfully see a house, how could I buy one, move in, and then maintain it alone?

No, this wouldn't defeat me. If I had fifteen minutes to kill, I could simply look around on my own. There were no gates or fences. All the houses were being built around a massive square of man-made parkland, so nothing was stopping me from having a sneak peek. After I locked the car, I headed towards the park. A silly thought of getting dirt on my tan suede boots almost made me turn back. Almost.

Cat Hall was a ghost town. Diggers and large pieces of machinery sat haphazard amongst exposed foundations and the skeletons of buildings. With no lights coming from the houses, the night was blacker here, and oddly colder. The button had fallen off my favourite grey wool coat earlier, so I had to manually hold the flaps together for warmth against the wind.

No one had moved in yet. Why would they? The construction noise must have been awful during the day. I got so lost in staring at it all I didn't realise someone was behind me. I turned around expecting to see Rosie, but instead found a man in a dark padded coat. He was taller than me by at least half a foot. Handsome too. Plastered on his face was a broad smile, and the cool air had made his cheeks boyishly ruddy.

'Are you okay?' he asked. 'You shouldn't be here alone in the dark. It's dangerous with all the building stuff.'

'I'm looking at buying a house. Are you with the builders?'

'Yeah, there's some electrical bits we needed to sort out tonight.' He paused, his eyes lingering on my face. 'If you want to see inside a house, you're welcome to come and have a look around the one we're working on. I can make sure you get back to your car safely.'

'That would be great. Thank you.'

The man didn't stop smiling throughout our conversation, and when he offered me an arm, in an old gentlemanly gesture, he asked, 'I haven't offended you, have I? You're not one of those women who don't like men opening doors for them, are you?' He moved nearer to me to punctuate his point, his outstretched arm brushing against my own.

'Course not.' I took his arm without thinking, to prove he was wrong about me. As if being a feminist was an insult.

'Glad to hear it,' he said and chuckled.

Before I knew what I was doing, my forearm was nestled next to his bicep and we were walking towards the house furthest from the road. A silence stretched between us. I looked down at his hands and saw he was wearing thick, black pleather gloves. It was cold, so they weren't out of place yet still made me uncomfortable.

In the hope he would offer me his name, I said, 'I'm Fallon.'

'Nice to meet you,' he replied, the smile still playing on his lips. The man with no name, I thought. It's somewhat romantic. 'You know,' he continued, 'I could get in trouble for this, showing you around.'

'Oh, I wouldn't want you to get in trouble,' I said.

'You're worth it. But if anyone asks, we both work here.' He winked like we had an inside joke.

A tingle tightened in my belly. 'You do work here, right?'

'Of course. I've been on this site for two years now. I always wanted to work with my hands.'

Without both hands to hold it together, my coat flapped open, exposing my body to the bitter wind. Shivering, I instinctively leaned towards his warmth. I'm not sure what made me look down then, acting coy, a pathetic attempt at flirting, but when I focussed on his shoes, I noticed he was wearing trainers. Odd footwear for someone in construction; surely steel-capped boots were more safety conscious.

He'd said we, *so there must be other people around, I thought as I headed where he wanted to take me. My arm trapped by his.*

I knew meeting a strange man in the dark, in a quiet place such as this, should be cause for concern. But any fear I might have felt was blotted out by the thought this could be it: mysterious No Name could be the man I'd spend the rest of my life with. The story we tell our grandchildren was happening right now. Suddenly, I was living in a Mills & Boon novel. He was tall, good-looking. Perhaps a little younger than me, but not enough to make people talk.

And No Name wore a smile too. One which said he'd also found something he'd been looking for.

–

Trembling with anger, I stop speaking to stare at my slippers – pink fluff dusted with grime that will never wash off. They fit me well.

'Let's leave it there for now and unpack everything.' Tina's voice is measured, calming, and as she speaks she shifts her face closer to the laptop camera.

'I was an idiot to go with him.'

'No, you weren't. How many interactions do we have on a daily basis with people? Those we know and strangers who become those we trust. And how many end in… well, only a fraction.'

Shaking my head, I mutter, 'Doesn't help when you're in the fraction.'

Tina sighs. 'I understand. But people are much more likely to be hurt by someone they know than a stranger. You're looking back now with hindsight. Don't let it frame your memories.'

'But No Name…'

'And I think we should now use his proper name. Give him ownership over what he did.'

'Tyler Baker.' I hate the way my lips form around his nouns.

'Baker used every trick in the book to gain your trust. Distraction, referring to you as *we*, doing you a favour which could get him in trouble to make you feel guilty. He even slipped in the insult of, "you're not one of those women", making you want to prove him wrong and go against your better judgement.'

'*I* should have seen those signs.'

Shaking her head, Tina says, 'They're techniques for a reason. You need to stop beating yourself up, pet.'

'How can I? I did everything wrong.'

'Come on, let's not go down that road. I wish I could wave a magic wand and you be…'

'The Fallon I used to be?' I say echoing Ollie's thought.

'Don't put words in my mouth. And let's get this straight. You will never be *that* Fallon again, and it's okay. Because you're coming out the other side stronger.'

I know she's right, but I still can't bring myself to agree.

'The case started over two months ago, have you heard how it's going?'

'I can't attend court until after I give evidence. And I'm the last witness on the Crown Prosecution's list.'

'Understood. I'll text you another time for us to continue with your memory of events.' She stares into the camera, unblinking, until I nod my agreement. 'Take care, pet. And happy Christmas.' She logs off before I can return the sentiment.

After a glass of cold water, I check my phone to find two messages. One from Mum, the other from Grant. I look at Mum's first and see a long, heart-felt note of apology. She tells me she's made contact with Siobhan and told her I know about their baby pact. I reply with a thumbs up emoji, then see the moving dots to indicate another message being typed. They stop and start for what seem like forever, until I receive: *I want to show you something important tomorrow morning.*

Grant's message tells me he misses me. I don't love him anymore, and yet I can't help but soften as I see his words. To have his support at this time would be wonderful. But, then again, he never was any good at that. I stare at the photo on the mantelpiece and remember the day we took it. The night before he didn't come home, claiming he'd been playing Xbox at his mate's house all night. Another lie. Throughout our relationship he created more drama than he healed. I delete his text.

It's been cold today and even one of Mum's Christmas jumpers doesn't stop me shivering. Without thinking, I walk to the hall cupboard to grab a blanket.

There it is.

Still missing its button, only now the material is patterned with ghosts of blood stains. Deemed as unusable evidence for the trial, the grey wool coat was given back to me. I should have thrown it away, but it had been a gift from Ollie and before Cat Hall was my favourite piece of clothing. Beautiful and stylish, it went with everything. Now it goes with nothing. Even after having it dry cleaned five times, I still can't bring myself to wear it or get rid of it. I touch its sleeve. Soft wool tickles my finger and I swear I hear a screaming wind.

'I'm warm. I'm healthy. I'm safe,' I say, then slam the door shut.

–

In the morning, I put the address Mum gave me into the satnav and see exactly where I'm going. St Maude's Graveyard sits in the middle of the next town over. Surrounded by houses and shops, it's the centrepiece all else was built around. When I arrive, Mum is already waiting.

Silently she takes my arm and walks me, head down, towards a small piece of land by the entrance of the church. We stop at a tiny grave. The headstone is a small concrete angel weeping over a crib. The inscription reads, *Baby Kaplan*.

'I paid for her grave,' Mum whispers.

In death, the baby girl didn't even get to keep her name. I stole it from her.

'I asked Ollie to join us, but he's not speaking to me after you told him what happened,' Mum says.

'Are you mad at me for telling him?'

She snorts. 'No, but I'd have liked to have been there to soften the blow.'

I never even thought about that. Too wrapped up in my own drama, I didn't consider how it would affect Ollie's relationship with his mum. Now we're here at his real sister's grave without him. 'Sorry,' I say.

Mum puts her arm around me, and we stand together staring at the angel guarding the overgrown grass. Six feet below us is a tiny coffin that should have been mine. One which has my real surname etched on to it. How different would the world be now if I was in the coffin, and she was free to live her life?

'I thought you should know where she was in case you wanted to stop by. She's a good listener, like you,' Mum says.

'Thanks,' I reply, unsure what I'd talk about with a baby whose life I'm leading.

We stand in silence together for a few moments. Mum doesn't cry, but her eyes adopt a hazy focus. There's something so intimate and sad about the look on her face that I can't bring myself to speak. A minute later she surprises me with a question: 'How is your testimony prep going with Dr Hawk?'

'Good, I think.'

'Tell her everything. When you hold a secret back from those you care about, it rots inside you. I should know.'

I lean my head on her shoulder. 'Do you feel better now Ollie and me know about what happened?'

'Better than I thought I would.'

And I can see it on her face – relaxed cheeks which can easily form smiles, and a lightness in her eyes no longer dreading her secret will be exposed – the burden she's carried for decades has vanished.

'I'm happy for you,' I tell her.

'And at least she'll have a few more visitors now.'

'Do the Kaplans not come?'

Shaking her head, she laughs. 'I doubt they're that sort of family.'

'Oh, what sort of family are they?'

She rustles in her pocket and pulls out a piece of paper. 'You can find out for yourself. This is Siobhan's home number.'

I take it, then stare at the paper. Eleven digits lie between me and the answers I never knew I needed.

'Just don't overload yourself. I hate seeing you stressed.'

'Ollie thinks I should get in touch after the case.'

'Sensible,' she says. With a last look at the angel and a soft sigh, Mum turns back towards the cemetery gates. I follow her.

As we walk, I spot a new grave. Fresh flowers spelling out *Ryan Preston*. Without consciously agreeing, we veer off the path to pay our respects.

Mum reaches the headstone before me. 'Poor thing, just nineteen years old.'

My curiosity gets the better of me, so I Google the name plus Northamptonshire. An article from a week ago pops up. 'He was murdered.'

Moving to see my phone screen, she reads the article with me. 'He was a fashion student at the university,' she says.

There are photos of his designs; modern interpretations of Art Deco, they're beautiful. 'They think it was a robbery gone wrong.'

'What a stupid waste,' Mum adds.

I know what she's feeling, sympathy for his family for losing their loved one, sorrow for the world who lost a talented person. Me, I feel the terror which would have found him in those final moments. The blind panic that another person was trying to snuff him out of existence. The utter horror at his time being up and how he'd give anything, do anything, to slip death's noose.

'Do you think the police could do that forensic genealogy thing to find his killer?' Mum asks.

'Forensic what?'

'You've not heard? My neighbour was telling me about it the other day. Some clever detective in the USA submitted a killer's DNA to an ancestry database and found a relative he could track the killer back from.'

'And they arrested him?'

'Hung about until they found a discarded source of DNA, it matched, so they knew they had their man. He's standing trial soon.'

I mull this news around in my mind.

Mum interrupts my thoughts. 'You're so pale, love. Let's get back in the warm and have a coffee at yours.'

I nod, but don't move from Ryan's grave.

'I suppose with Cat Hall, there's one thing to be grateful for. They caught the bastards,' Mum says.

'And I'm going to help keep them in prison where they belong,' I say.

'That's my determined girl.'

–

Two coffees later I remember I should have logged on for a session with Tina five minutes ago. Mum says a hasty goodbye and I fire up my laptop. My boss then pops up on the screen.

'How's every little thing, pet?'

I went to visit my dead self's grave. I was illegally adopted. And the worst experience of my life is about to be aired across a court room. 'Good. How are you?'

'I'm great. Right,' she says, looking at her notes. 'When you were walking with Baker, what did you talk about?'

Chapter 5

Fallon

'Do you know much about serial killers?'

The question jarred me. Why would he bring something like that up?

'Some, I guess,' I mumbled.

'They fascinate me. I read all about them online. Do you think they all get caught?' He leaned into me to ask the question, my arm still locked in place by his.

'I hope so,' I replied. Maybe he was just a little macabre in his tastes. When I'm introduced as a psychologist, conversations usually flow towards sick minds. But then, I hadn't told him what I did for a living.

'I doubt they do,' Tyler said. 'Even now with all the forensics stuff and CCTV.'

I looked around us, hoping to spot cameras angled onto the street. There were none.

He saw me and smiled knowingly. 'We're putting the cameras up tomorrow.'

'Let's hope we don't encounter any Hollywood slashers tonight then,' I joked with the worst fake laugh I'd ever conjured.

'Interesting. You assume all serial killers are American. What about Fred West, the Suffolk Strangler, the Yorkshire Ripper. Not all the good ones are from the US.'

The good ones?

Before I could reply, he then asked, 'What do you think it's like to be a serial killer?'

His tone was as if he were discussing last night's football match, so maybe to him this was just making conversation? I remember thinking how popular the true crime industry was, and rationalising that he could just be a fan. I'd had similar discussions with others in the past. Following his lead, I replied, 'The majority of serial killers are impulsive. All the ones you just mentioned certainly were. They choose victims when the opportunity arose.'

'Is that why they killed whores and hitchhikers?'

I shuddered at the word whore. *'Yes. But with impulsiveness usually comes regret, and mistakes.'*

Tyler stopped walking. He then took his arm from me. 'Psychopaths don't regret anything.'

Unable to supress my psychologist know-how, I replied, 'Psychopaths have no empathy, but if it interferes with their needs and plans, they can regret an action, even obsess over it. And in life, things rarely go as we imagine.'

'I see.' He gently nudged my shoulder. 'Hey, I bet you never imagined this.'

'Imagined what?'

Winking again, he said, 'What's about to happen.'

–

'I should have run right then and there,' I say.

Tina purses her lips. 'Fight or flight? Do you know why you didn't?'

I shake my head.

'Because the psychological research on fight and flight was all done on men. A man's response to an aggressor is to either beat him down or outrun him. We women can rarely do either. It's why our brains tells us to do something else.'

I cock me head. 'Freeze?'

'And comply.'

'Really?'

'Instincts tell us if we comply with an aggressor, we'll survive.' Tina sighs. 'It's why I'm being called as an expert witness on so many rape trials. All these poor women being bullied and blamed on the stand because they didn't fight back or try to run. Compliance is not consent.'

Interesting. I make a note to research this later.

'Can you continue, pet?'

I nod. As hard as this is, I need to push through as much as I can to ensure justice is served.

-

We walked in step towards the skeleton of a large house on the outskirts of the site.

In an attempt to make more normal conversation, I asked, 'Have you worked here long?'

'Not really. You're very pretty,' he said, staring down at me.

My stomach flipped as the wind screamed past me once more. Was that the wind? I was about to ask him if he heard it too when his grip tightened on my arm. The small hairs on the back of my neck sprang up, and I blurted, 'I have a boyfriend.' Then tried to step away. His arm dropped suddenly and his hand latched onto the small of my back, pushing me towards the lonely house.

Even though, on first impression, it appeared the same as all the other houses, I knew this one was different. There were no windows or doors fitted yet, just sheets of flapping plastic in the holes; sheets being sucked in and out by the wind as if the house were breathing. As we got closer, I saw scarlet stains on the front brickwork.

'Through here,' he said as he pushed me into the plastic covered door frame. Dust smacked me in the face. Licking my lips, I tasted it – foul, like old bones.

The plastic momentarily distorted my vision, but when it cleared, I saw two men in the front room, their eyes widened with surprise.

'Who's she?' one asked and jabbed a finger at me.

As I was pushed further into the house, Tyler replied, 'Our new party guest.'

–

'We should stop there.' Tina says.

Wondering why she halted the session, I open my mouth to speak, then taste tears. That's why. Frustrated, I wipe my face with my sleeve. 'Sorry.'

'Don't be sorry for feeling the trauma. With these kinds of memories, the only way out is through.'

I know she's right, but my body and mind are not seeing eye to eye right now, no matter how much common sense is thrown at them.

Tina's stare darts to her notes. 'I noticed you've got appointments booked later.'

'Regulars mostly.'

Shaking her head she says, 'You should be preparing for court. Don't push it. Or distract yourself with too much work.'

'My clients need me. I won't abandon them,' I snap.

Tina puts her hands up. 'Wasn't suggesting it. Just carve out some time for you.'

Turning to hide the blush in my cheeks, I mumble, 'Thank you.' Then click off.

I don't doubt Tina's advice, but it doesn't stop me replaying my conversations with Tyler over and over in my head. Each time, I say something differently, act differently, react differently, and each time it ends the same; the rest of the story I'm going to have tell Tina, the barristers, the judge, and the jury. The events which even now leave me breathlessly ashamed.

When Cat Hall happened, I clammed up. Every ounce of my education and training told me not to, but I did. My theory was, if I didn't tell the people around me, parts of what happened that night wouldn't be cemented in my memory. And if I didn't remember them, they didn't happen. How many clients have I worked with who'd had this same denial theory; ones who tried to ride it into the sunset like the pale horse we all know it to be. I won't let my stupidity ruin the case.

Needing to get my head in the game, I call my CPS barrister. Every time we've spoken in the past, he's been supportive. He's fighting hard to win the case. He deserves to know… everything.

After two rings he answers, 'You've got Joel.'

'Hi, do you have a moment to talk? It's Fallon.'

'Good to hear from you! Of course.'

'It's…' I don't know where to begin.

'What's bothering you?' he prompts.

I open my mouth to let free all the Cat Hall memories, along with Tina's wise words regarding my actions, but the only sentence to escape is, 'How's the case going?'

'We shouldn't discuss it in detail until you've taken the stand. We've had a few bumps in the road, but it's mostly going as expected.'

I nod, then, realising he can't see me, say, 'That's good.' The words I should say are glued to my mouth. With effort, I try to unstick them. 'I really need to tell you something.'

'Okay.'

I imagine his smiling face on the other end of the phone. He's always been so sweet and protective whenever the case was discussed. What I am about to tell him will change his opinion of me. Would that alone damage the case? Stop him from trying so hard after finding out I don't deserve his help. My conscience isn't worth it. 'Oh, just wanted to say happy Christmas.'

'Thank you, happy Christmas to you too. Now, are you sure there's nothing else you want to tell me? I'm here for you.'

'You're great at your new job,' I say offhand.

'Thanks. I'm not afraid to admit it, but this case has been overwhelming. Of course, it's nothing compare to what you went through.'

I manage to whisper, 'Thanks.'

'Okay, we need to all meet up and have a chat before you take the stand. Your family liaison officer will call with the details.'

'Sounds like a plan,' I say.

We chit-chat a little, then hang up. Joel has been a rock, and with it being his first case here in a new job, the responsibility of giving him such a prestigious win weighs almost as heavy on me as getting justice.

Frustrated, I say aloud, 'You're such a coward.' Then rake my fingers through my hair. 'Oh, and now I'm talking to myself. Great.'

To stop myself from going mad, I text Ollie. Within the hour we're eating pizza and discussing the mess that is my life. He's not forgiven Mum for her secret, and when I tell him where he can find his real sister, he just rolls his eyes at me. *I* am his real sister, he tells me. Feeling awful about my part in their quarrel, I try to broker peace with an exercise I do with clients. I tell him to write a letter to Mum; a letter which he can pour all his thoughts and feelings into. He then has to edit it, subduing the hard words. And after digesting everything he has left, he must then put himself in Mum's place, and cross out what he now understands. Once every word is scored through, he will put it someplace safe, never to send it, but to look at when his feelings return. He agrees to write the letter, but I suspect it's just to placate me.

I should tell Ollie about what happened at Cat Hall. Mum said revealing her long-kept secret helped her. But we're down to the last slice of pepperoni and he's already throwing on his coat to meet up with his new boyfriend. My little brother leaves, none the wiser about what his 'real' sister is capable of.

Chapter 6

The Brother

If I could kill the festive period, I would. This time of year, there are far too many family obligations to meet to retain my mask of normalcy. Although worming my way out of some, I'm still uncomfortably tied to a number going forward. One of which is the 'It's almost the New Year' buffet.

Already, there are quite a few bidders for Nicole's watch. On a normal day, I'd be sat in my favourite chair, a beer in my hand, watching the race for who will be my next victim. But not today. Mum is hosting this year, so I arrive early to appear helpful. It's utter torture. And not just because of the people; I've never liked her house. Stuffed with multi-coloured nonsense, gathered through a lifetime of car boot sales, it feels as if the whole bloody lot could come crashing down upon me at any moment.

The buffet attracts flies from all over. Relatives who Mum only sees once a year squirm out of the woodwork to stuff their faces with sausage rolls. Neighbours who barely register her living on their street stop by to eat and be merry. Friends who ask after 'her family' when they bump into her in town, but mentally grope for names when they shake hands, flood the house. Jokes are made, stories are told, and lies are aired. All eerily similar to the ones I caught last year, and the year before. I have stories I could tell them, ones which would make them splutter their drinks and upchuck the turkey curry. I imagine gathering them about me, like cavemen crowding around a fire, and regaling their mundane minds with my game. How I play. The rules I play by. And how I always win.

Could someone already in my social circle be the person to play against me? Looking around the room at the pedestrian drunks giggling and boasting about their pathetic exploits, I cringe. None of them could even comprehend me, let alone compete.

After I've moved furniture and placed paper plates and plastic forks on the dining room table, I pluck wet wipes from my bag and absent-mindedly clean the items I've touched, then balance on the arm of a nearby chair to check my phone. The watch is up to £50. There's only an hour left on the clock now.

Hungry, I swoop in and gather a plate of food. I engage in some banal chit-chat with random guests, then wave at a couple who live next door to Mum. Greedily, they corner me and suck up my time until I extract myself and retreat to the kitchen. Straddling a stool, I reopen my Starsellers app, then scroll down the items I've sold. From the leather wallet which started my game, to Nicole's necklace, I lovingly remember each bloody link.

'Everything okay?' Mum asks from the doorway.

'Just feeling a bit nostalgic,' I admit.

She opens her mouth to say something, but shuts it quick when the neighbours tap her on the shoulder. Before giving them her full attention, she looks back at me. 'Be a dear and pop some more sausage rolls in the oven. We're getting low.'

Putting my phone away, I comply. And while Mum blends back into the party, I watch the pastry brown to perfection, then free the snacks from the heat and display them on a serving dish. When Mum sees me placing them on the buffet table, she smiles at me.

'They look good, right?' I ask.

'Perfect,' she says.

My brothers stagger round and begin devouring my offering, and I retreat back to my kitchen corner. Bored, I search online for Nicole Stewart. Her body has been found. She didn't float and bloat her way too far from the crime scene, and the police are urging anyone with information about the tragedy to step forward and call the special tip-line. To keep myself in the loop, I set up a Google alert for Nicole's name and Manchester.

Suddenly, Mum appears at my side.

Dryly, I ask, 'Are we light on sausage rolls again?'

'Look, I need to talk to you,' she whispers, 'meet me upstairs in five minutes.' Without further information, she saunters off, a fake laugh in her wake.

I rise ready for the clandestine meeting but as I do, my phone pings. Flossy32 has won the watch.

A flush of adrenaline grips me. The clock starts now.

As I head for the front door, the address pops up on my screen. Anna Gould in Cambridgeshire. Not far at all. I jump in the car and drive straight there, all the while imagining what it would be like to pit my extensive wits against a challenger, a fleshy obstacle intent on revealing my bloody secrets to the world. Maybe Anna will have a father like Liam Neeson or a *Die Hard* husband like Bruce Willis – either one might prove a semi-worthy avenger in my game.

–

Upon arrival at the Gould residence, I park across the street and wait. Anna's vixen-red hair is the most interesting thing about her. Even though she looks over forty she still lives with her parents, who, although no action stars, are still spry for their age. With deflated shopping bags, they are off to the sales. Anna waits behind, no doubt glad to get the house to herself. I'm glad we get the house to ourselves too. I'll knock on her door and say I was in the neighbourhood so decided to drop the watch off in person. I'll tell her I have more for sale, and can show her photos on my mobile. She'll invite me in. They usually do.

My phone announces a text from Mum. Have I not spent enough time with her today?

I have to tell you something.

I text back.

K.

Then see four words appear on my screen, plus an emoji.

You have a sister.

The emoji is a Shh face.

Narrowing my eyes, I text back a question mark.

I wanted to tell you in person earlier but you left so suddenly. She found out though DNA Hooray. Her mum called me the other day.

Intriguing. I text back.

Who is she?

You and your brothers need to leave her be until I figure stuff out.

Mum's command irks me.

What's her name?

At first, Mum tells me to drop it, but the more she insists the more insistent I become. Eventually, she relents.

Dr Fallon Hurley.

Mum must have been holding this secret for decades. How will my brothers react to this bombshell? I can't imagine well; they are predictable, not adaptable like me. A lot will depend on her, and who she is. I look up my sister online. The first result is her work profile with a company called Hawk Therapy, but the second is a news report about an incident last year. I read the article, then reread it. I have a sister. And she's a survivor. Considering our shared genes, this doesn't surprise me. I'm so entranced I only notice Anna has left the house when she jogs past my car, red ponytail swinging.

The clock is ticking, but I can't stop reading. I Google and Google Fallon Hurley until Anna reappears in my peripheral vision. Out of breath, my prey stretches her tired limbs on a nearby fence. Feeling a familiar darkness click into place, I climb out of the car.

Slowly, I approach, then expertly deliver the planned introduction. Flirting, just enough to be charming, but not sleazy, I smile at her – making an effort to push my cheeks up to my eyes to create those truth-telling crinkles.

Encouraged by Anna's nods, we walk to her house and I pluck out my phone to show her the photos of my imaginary pieces for sale. But instead of shiny watches, I accidently display one of the news articles about Fallon.

'Apologies,' I say. 'Wrong page.'

'Oh, I remember that story. Why were you reading about something so awful?' Anna asks.

'The victim is my sister.' The words skip out of my mouth before I have the chance to edit, so I fake a sad smile to go with them. Suddenly, I'm a wounded animal in her eyes. My beloved sister has been hurt. To seal the deal I add, 'I wasn't there to protect her.'

'You poor thing. Come in,' she says opening her front door for me.

Once my feet are over her threshold, my smile transforms from phoney to genuine.

Sweaty, she strips off her tracksuit jacket and says, 'You don't think things like that can happen in real life.'

'No, you don't.' My fist clenches around my phone.

'I remember when the case hit the news. The papers weren't kind to her.'

'We haven't spoken about it.' Not a lie.

'Oh, you should let her know she's got your support.'

'My mum won't let me contact her,' I admit. Carefully, I watch her reaction.

Rolling her eyes, Anna says, 'She shouldn't believe everything she reads. No one knows how they'll react when faced with a horrific situation.'

Oh, maybe that's why Mum is being cagey. She's mad at how Fallon dealt with her brush with danger. If she only knew about my deadly deeds, how proud she'd be.

'So you think I should talk with her?' I ask.

'Course. Family is everything.'

Hearing her empathic words makes me unfurl my fingers. 'I will, thanks. But first things first.' I headbutt Anna, slamming my forehead into the bridge of her nose. She falls backwards onto the floor, gasping. I kneel on top of her chest, curl my gloved fingers around her nose and cover her mouth. Even after she shudders unconscious, I continue my grip until her chest neither rises nor falls. The whole thing is over within minutes and, just as with Nicole's murder, I immediately feel deflated.

After unwrapping the watch, I fix it around Anna's wrist. It looks good, sparkly and solid, camouflaging her lack of pulse. As the body cools, I look around the house for my next bait. There are photos. Anna's parents, brown and wrinkly on a beach. Old and flabby, I'm guessing neither has the skill set to realise their daughter's death was part of a larger picture, let alone to track me down. Still, they could be back any minute, and I hate the mess of multiple murders. Looking up, I spot her pink tracksuit top, still damp with sweat. I take it and hurry from the house. With practiced calm I drive away, taking a different route from the one that took me into the estate.

Nicole met her end in Manchester, Anna in Cambridgeshire; counties work separately, so even if I choose a police opponent there'd be no connections to my crimes without a little help. Maybe I should pull a Zodiac and send a piece of Anna's jacket to the Manchester police? That could be fun, although selling a jacket with a hole would ruin my Starsellers standing as a top seller, and I have a reputation to maintain.

Once back home. I craft an advert for Anna's jacket: *Used generic tracksuit jacket. Has some miles on the clock, but can still run. Needs a new warm body to fill it. Cheap price for quick sale.*

The jacket is pink and pretty, and still smells of Anna's deodorant. When I snap its photo, I imagine a woman in it. Dark hair and eyes. Lean like me. Cheetah-fast. A quick doctor's mind to match her pace. I put a longer auction deadline down to afford me enough time to still attend all the festive family fun. Anna said that I should offer Fallon my support. All my other brothers are too chickenshit to go against Mum. Unlike them, I have the smarts to find a way around our matriarch's demands.

A Google alert announces itself. An update on Nicole's case. A man was spotted by the canal around the time Nicole fell in – police want the witness to come forward. Witness indeed; they're fishing. Throwing out a clever little lure, but it won't put a hook in my mouth. Baiting a trap is a clever idea. Enticing the person you want to meet to you, rather than having to hunt them down. Interesting.

Chapter 7

Fallon

First thing in the morning, I contact Tina. I need to get through my sessions as fast as I can; ensure I'm stand-ready when the time comes. A witness Joel can be proud of. After three cups of coffee, I feel awake enough to call my boss.

'Hey, pet, glad to see you're keen,' she says, then narrows her eyes. 'Do you want me to prescribe something to help you sleep?'

Images of me helplessly unconscious, as a shadow looms over my bed, flash through my mind. 'I'd rather not.'

'Your decision. Okay, Baker took you to the house. Tell me what happened next.'

-

Fight or flight. Neither was an option as I stood in front of three strange men, fully aware that there wasn't another person within screaming distance. The room had four wooden crates gathered around one big one, like a makeshift dining table. On the middle box were glasses, a cheap whiskey bottle and cans of beer, some half-finished and strewn on their sides to leak like dying victims. Other cans, completely drained, were piled in elaborate, wonky structures.

'I need to get home,' I whispered. I tried to walk away, but my body wouldn't listen to my mind.

The other two men were shorter and younger than Tyler, who was now standing between me and the door.

'Where'd you get 'er from?' asked one, holding a cricket bat.

'Plucked her right off the street,' Tyler replied, tickling me. Fortunately, his fluttering fingers didn't make it past my thick coat, so at least I didn't involuntarily giggle at his touch. Not getting the reaction he wanted, he encircled his arms about me like a snake. Struggling in my captor's grip, I tried to kick out at the other man now shuffling towards me, cricket bat firmly in his hand.

'Stop it, or else Ropey's gonna get yer,' he said.

I looked over at the third man.

'No, he's Ropey,' said my captor, motioning at the thug in front of me. Talking in the third person was not a good sign. He was distancing himself from what he was about to do.

'Maybe we should just bounce, eh?' said the third man, his posture slouchy.

'Why? You pissing yourself again, Streak?' asked Ropey. He then struck him in the arm with the bat.

Flinching, Streak stepped backwards; his height visibly shrinking by inches.

'Streak?' I asked.

'Yeah, coz he's a streak of piss.' Tyler laughed, then punched Streak too. As he did, I slipped from his grip. Gravity took me and I dropped to sit on the nearest crate.

'Why'd you tell her my name?' Streak whined, his eyes on me.

Tyler, beneath his breath, whispered, 'Like it matters.'

Edging towards the door, Streak said, 'I gotta go home now. My sis needs picking up from her friend's house.'

Not even looking his way Tyler's finger leapt up to point at his friend. 'Don't move! You're in this already. Your little sister is safe where she is.' He then added, 'For now.'

Rolling his lips beneath his teeth, Streak nodded his agreement.

'See, we're all the best of friends. Told you, it's these memories that'll stay with us all forever,' Tyler said with a grin.

Chuckling, Ropey added, 'Can't wait to make those memories.'

As the men laughed together, I tried to take in every detail of the room. Front door behind Tyler, blocked side door to a hall. Tools of varying degrees of terror laid haphazard on the floor, ready to trip up my escape. It was the very definition of a death trap.

Suddenly, the laughter stopped. Ropey moved closer to me. I recoiled, my hand jerking out at a box to steady myself. They laughed again, then all sat down to relax.

Sitting next to me, Tyler nudged my knee with his like we were old friends. 'Drink?'

I didn't reply to his offer. Instead, I scanned the room again, searching for potential escape routes and weapons. But after only a few seconds, I knew that faced with three grown men, I'd never make it more than a few feet to freedom. My only hope was to stay alive until an opportunity presented itself. My eyes lingered on Streak. Nervously, he pulled at the fleece on his jacket. He didn't want to be there either.

A glass was shoved into my eyeline. It was one of the half empty ones and a pink stain clung to its edge in a perfect lip print. Another woman was here.

I stared back at the now quiet men. They were all watching me. Women are taught, in the company of strangers, never to drink something you didn't pour yourself. But with all their eyes on me, I had no choice. Moving the glass to find a clean edge, I took the smallest sip I could.

'La-de-da,' Ropey said. 'What a lady.'

'Lift your pinkie up when you drink again,' Tyler ordered, then giggled with glee.

'I'd like to leave now,' I said, my eyes on a drill lying on the floor.

'Not yet. We're being social.' Watching me, Tyler got up, bent and scooped up the drill. He laid it heavily on the box before me, knocking over the glasses. Two fell and broke, and the sharp sound of the splintering glass made me jump.

All three men laughed. Lifting my cheeks, I forced my mouth into a smile and quietly laughed with them. It was then I thought, if I could show them I was a real person rather than a victim, they might end their games. I asked, 'So, what do you all have planned for the weekend?'

'I'm gonna watch that new monster film,' Streak replied.

Tyler groaned. 'TV is all you ever do. You should live life, not watch it on the screen. I'm right, aren't I, Fallon?'

'Yes, but there is a therapeutic benefit to TV. It's been proven to lower blood pressure.'

'Fuck's sake. You nabbed a boffin!' Ropey said.

'So,' Tyler said crouching down to my level. 'What did you have planned for the weekend?'

The word did *choked me and I spluttered.*

'Have another sip.' One of them pushed the drink at my face, and I felt the cool glass part my lips. As it was tipped up, I clenched my teeth, sending the liquid down my chin and chest.

Tyler's hand found my knee. 'How wasteful, Fallon.'

'I have to go,' I muttered.

'No you don't,' Tyler said. 'You're gonna regale us with your thoughts on TV.'

Ropey let out a deep cackle, then pointed his bat at Tyler. 'You're the best.'

I opened my mouth, but I couldn't release the words I wanted; only a soft whimper fell out.

'I love horror films,' Tyler then interjected. 'Especially ones about real killers. Wanted to buy some murderabilia stuff: John Wayne Gacy's paintings, and the Son of Sam's letters, but it costs way too much for the likes of little ol' me.'

At the mention of serial killers again, I rose and, holding Tyler's gaze, edged away from the boxes. 'If you want money, I can give you it. You don't need to do anything you'll regret.'

'Did you hear that, Ropey? She doesn't want you to do anything you'll regret,' Tyler said.

Smirking, Ropey stood and reached out his hand to pull my bag from my shoulder. All my valuables were in it: credit cards, keys, phone, even a present for Ollie's birthday. He flung those belongings into the corner of the room where the bag tumbled open. Seeing a collection of my most intimate things scattered on the dusty concrete brought a tear to my eye. I knew then if they didn't want money, then they wanted something worse.

–

After another uncomfortable conversation with Tina about my bravery, I log off and shuffle into the kitchen to make a sandwich. As I peel a slice of cheese from its wrapper, my mobile pings and I grab it, ready to delete Grant's latest message. But this time, it's not a text from my ex-boyfriend. It's an email. Weird – the title reads, *Your Brother*. What has Ollie done now? Weirder – the sender is a Lindsay Cross. Who is that? It reads:

Hi Fallon, I found you here on DNA Hooray. I'm your brother. I'd love to meet up. Can you come over to mine soon?

Ollie's wise words about emotional bandwidth bungee through my thoughts. I should listen to him, yet how much better would my life be right now with more Ollies in it? I may not understand Siobhan's and Mum's actions that day, but my brothers are in the same new sibling boat as me, and maybe it'll be better if we sail the waters together. Not replying now might upset him, and I could miss my chance to make a connection.

Wait, that's odd, his surname isn't Kaplan. Perhaps Siobhan remarried so all the boys took the new father's name? I've only known one other man named Lindsay; he was a poet. Maybe my brother will be the same? I'm not assuming people with the same names are identical, but I do know the importance of the name you give a child, and the affect it can have on their life. Perhaps Lindsay is an artistic free-spirit and we can talk for hours about our lives over a glass of brandy. Or maybe he isn't any of those things, but it doesn't matter, whatever he is, he's my brother, and he reached out to me.

Using my login, I sign on to DNA Hooray and check my profile. Where there used to be a blank space under family, there's now Lindsay's name beneath the heading of brother.

DNA doesn't lie.

I can't waste this opportunity.

Excitement makes my fingers clumsy, but I eventually manage to type out an acceptance to his invitation. Barely ten minutes go by before my new brother responds. The email is short, saying he lives on the outskirts of the county and to come over to his house as soon as I can.

It takes me an hour to craft a reply. Deleting, editing and overthinking every word I type adds to my nervousness. I message I'll come over tonight, then make a note of the address on a Post-it.

-

In a few hours, I find myself outside Lindsay's house in the countryside, so remote the satnav has a blank space where it sits. Although looking nothing alike, it reminds me of Cat Hall. What am I doing? We may be biological siblings, but I didn't grow up with this man. What if he's some weapon-wielding maniac?

Dusk is falling in around the car. I instinctively switch on the headlights to illuminate the house before me. Bathed in halogens, it looks quaint, almost picturesque. It even has an old-fashioned bicycle with a charming pink wicker basket chained to a nearby fence.

As I watch, a light flashes on in the living room. He's seen my car. Not going in now would be impolite. My stomach rolls at the familiarity of this situation. I should have asked for us to meet at a coffee shop, somewhere neutral teeming with potential witnesses. But I'm a stranger to him too and he's invited me into his home.

Normal people don't think like this. Suspicious of everyone, imagining shadowy monsters lurking in their periphery. For the vast majority of people, these thoughts never enter their heads. I so want to be in the majority again.

I switch off the engine and get out of my car. As I lift my hand to knock on the door, it opens inward, so quickly I almost fall in.

'Hello?'

With no light on in the hall, I don't see the shadow in time as it snaps out an arm and pulls me inside.

Chapter 8

Fallon

The shadow steps back and flicks on a light switch. After momentary blindness, I make out the figure of a young woman, barely in her early twenties, dressed in jeans and a thick argyle jumper. My heartbeat slows when I see a frightened look pass across her features.

'Oh, I'm sorry. I was looking for Lindsay Cross,' I tell her.

She's tall and has wispy blonde hair. Her eyes are wild, darting over me, taking me in.

'Perhaps I don't have the right address,' I offer, stepping back.

'Dr Hurley?' she asks.

I nod.

'You have the right address,' she mutters.

'Are you his wife?'

'I'm Lindsay.' She smiles a little, then ushers me into her dining room. 'I'll explain everything.'

Both her dining table and chairs are made from thick wood which, although rustic, is uncomfortably hard. In the middle of the table, next to a plate of biscuits, is a large brown cardboard file.

She doesn't offer me a drink but pushes the biscuits towards me. I pick up a Jammie Dodger and nibble. It's stale. I look up to see her staring at me. 'I think there's been a misunderstanding,' I say, readying myself to get back up.

'Please don't leave.' Lindsay begins to pace back and forth. 'I don't know where to start,' she mumbles.

Worry lines are already burrowing into her young face, making my training kick in. Leaning towards her, I ask, 'Take a deep breath and tell me how I can help.'

She inhales and exhales, then says, 'I am Lindsay Cross, but we are not related.'

'But DNA Hooray says we are.'

Finally, she stops pacing. 'I uploaded someone else's DNA profile, under my name. I wanted to find relatives on their database.'

I raise an eyebrow. 'Why would you do that?'

Sitting heavily onto a chair, she stares down at her fidgeting fingers for a moment, then suddenly looks up. 'I'm a junior member of the police forensic team. A few years ago, I started inputting crime scene DNA into the national database. It's taking ages. I went through hundreds of pieces of evidence bagged at crime scenes all over the UK, but then I found a small amount of matching touch DNA on random objects at two crime scenes.'

'Touch DNA? Is that like tiny pieces of skin people leave behind when they handle an object?'

Lindsay smiles. 'That's right. But touch DNA is a minute sample, so small it's destroyed when we perform the procedure on it to obtain the DNA profile. I shouldn't have done the tests, but I had to know.'

'Were the crimes related?'

She shakes her head. 'Didn't seem that way at first. I actually thought I'd made a mistake, but then last year I found that DNA again, and again. The more I looked, the more I found.'

I ask, 'What did the police say?'

She rolls her eyes. 'They said that as none of the cases appeared related it wasn't the same killer. The victims were killed in different ways, in different counties, and had no connection to one another. I tried the DNA profile against the National Database, but there were no hits, which only means he and none of his family have ever been arrested.'

A horrible feeling is gathering in my gut. I all but swallow what's left of the Jammie Dodger to appease it – a sacrifice to the bubbling volcano of worry growing by the second. 'Skip to the part why I'm here, please.'

Lindsay pulls a rubber band off her wrist, then lifts her hair into a ponytail. 'The evidence was destroyed in testing, but I still have the profile. The other week, I signed up for an account at DNA Hooray. But instead of giving them my DNA, I uploaded the profile from the samples I found. In the US they call it forensic genealogy.'

'And the profile matched me?'

Tentatively, she replies, 'Sibling match.'

The volcano erupts in my belly. I'm going to be sick. Springing to my feet, I cover my mouth.

'I'm sorry,' Lindsay says. 'But there really is no good way to tell someone their brother is a serial killer. I thought the least I could do is break it to you in person.'

Putting my hands on my knees, I bend over and take a few deep breaths. The file on the table is filled with his murders.

'Fallon, I'm trusting you. And I really hope you're the person I think you are and will do the right thing. I saw on Facebook you're friends with an Oliver Hurley – is he your brother?'

Slowly, I nod.

'Good. Can you fetch me some hair, a toothbrush – whatever you can safely lay your hands on. I can then test his DNA and…'

'Wait,' I sit down, 'Ollie and I don't share DNA. I just found out I'm adopted.'

Lindsay throws her hands up in frustration. 'How many *biological* brothers do you have?'

'Four.'

Groaning, she reaches out and grabs a biscuit. Mid-chew, she asks, 'Can you get samples from each of them?'

Narrowing my eyes I admit, 'I've never met them.'

She crams in another biscuit and I wait for her to gulp it down. 'I need to match the sample,' she says. 'If I can just do that, then I have a shot of taking this up the chain and getting a proper investigation started.'

'Shouldn't the police already be investigating these murders?'

'The crime scenes are all over the UK, so different regional forces. I pitched my serial theory to my boss, but she laughed it off. Because touch DNA is easily corrupted, she said that I'd likely transferred it onto the evidence in the lab myself. But I didn't make a mistake. I know I didn't.'

'So, how about we both go to the police in the morning and explain everything. I'm sure they'll…'

'Please, no, you can't do that.'

'Why? This is clearly a police matter.'

'I was told to drop it. It's career suicide for me to bring it up again.'

'Even with me in tow?' I ask.

'Especially with you! Using a consumer genealogy database is against data protection laws in the UK.' Her voice grows softer as she adds, 'But I just had to know.'

My eyes land on the thick file on the table: a catalogue of my brother's dark deeds. In my head, a strange tug of war begins between morbid curiosity and common sense. My fingers dance a little towards the cardboard edge.

Curiosity wins. I pull the folder closer and open it. The first photo I see is of a young woman. Unlike crime scene photos in documentaries and online, there is no blurring in this image. She is slumped against a sofa, her eyes open. Memories flare in my mind's eye – the smell of meat, the screams. A violent end of a life. I say, 'You've never been face to face with a man like this before. We need to call the police.'

Lindsay puts her palms together. 'No, please, I'll not just get the sack, but probably arrested too. Promise me you won't tell anyone.'

She's in a terrible position but wants to do the right thing. I know the feeling well. 'I promise,' I say. Then ask, 'How many has he killed?'

'Over twenty. And it gets worse.'

'How?'

'Some of the cases are considered closed. There are innocent people in prison because of this monster. Another reason why my boss told me to drop it. If it comes out both the police and CPS made not one but several mistakes, heads will roll. But *I* can't forget what I've seen.' Her eyes land on the folder. Mine follow. Shivering, I begin flicking through the thick stack of papers again. I stop midway. Twenty, probably more, people have died at the hands of someone whose DNA I share. Deep down, I know it's not my fault, but so much else is… Cat Hall

– even thinking the name punches me in the gut. Right here and now, I could help put away a serial killer, but what about Cat Hall? If I lose focus on that, could Tyler and the others get away with their crimes? It's a Sophie's serial killer choice.

'I can't be involved in this,' I say steadily. 'I'm giving important evidence in a trial. If it could bounce back on you, it could hurt my reputation and hinder the case.' The thought of the three men who committed those crimes being free is terrifying. I close the folder, then rise and walk towards the door.

'I'm sorry. I'm so sorry.' Lindsay sighs.

Stopping dead, I look back. Her tall frame has curled in on itself, making her appear child-like. Soft whimpers escape her mouth, and tears glaze her eyes.

My head and heart lock in battle. My mind wins, so I head straight out the front door.

After two panicked attempts, my car starts and I'm back driving the dark roads. My eyes flick to the rear-view mirror too many times, and with not knowing the country lanes, I swerve suddenly, almost hitting a tree. Parking up, I rip my shaking hands from the steering wheel and think through what just happened. My brother is a serial killer. But do I trust this woman? I only have her word that she is part of the police and what she's found is true. The familiarity of the situation slaps my face, making me chant a string of swear words beneath my breath. I should just drive home. Forget this little illegal game of subterfuge. But then what if it's true? Without having the courage to delve further, I might never know if the new brother sitting across the dinner table from me is capable of unspeakable acts. And worse, that I'm leaving him free to commit them.

'Stop being a coward,' I say to myself.

Inching up in my seat, I clean the stray tears from my face and stare again into the rear-view mirror. 'You have to help somehow,' I add. 'You have to go back.'

Turning the car around on a narrow, almost black, road is a mission impossible worthy of Tom Cruise, but I manage it. In silent thought, I drive back to the cottage. The light is still on. Knocking on the door, my hand feels steadier. When Lindsay sees me, she almost lunges in for a hug, but stops herself just in time.

'Don't get too excited,' I tell her, 'I'm no criminologist, but the least I can do is look at the cases, try to profile the killer for you. Maybe find connections in the murders. It could be enough to get at least one police officer on your side.'

It's not the answer Lindsay wanted, but she still smiles. 'I knew I could count on you.'

-

My brother's file now lurks on my coffee table at Poppy Fields. A sick conversation piece waiting to blow up what little I've scraped back of my normal life. I didn't even think police kept hard copies like that anymore; Lindsay must have printed off documents and photos to build it. I imagine them taped across her living room wall linked with coloured string; something a hard-boiled detective would do. Cheap whiskey in one hand, a cigarette in the other, she'd stare at the gruesome collage until her eureka moment. Only it never came. Now it's been passed onto me, like some sick craft project.

I need air.

Pulling on a coat, I pocket my stun gun then walk to the lake by the light of my mobile. Once I am looking out across the dark, rippling waters, I take a breath. My brother is a serial killer. He steals lives and hides in shadows. At this moment, he could be anywhere, hurting anyone. How could this be?

The thought of the lake teeming with life, even in winter, humbles me. I'm not the only person who matters in this world, and I'm certainly not the only one with trauma to work through. I would never have wanted this killer mission, but this time I'll do the right thing.

As I stare at a duck carefully swimming across to the edge, I hear something. Spinning around, my eyes strain as they search the darkness. Is that movement? Without a second thought, I sprint towards my front door but drop my phone midway. Cursing, I stop to pick it up. Now still, I hear boots on branches and ragged breathing. Having had enough of surprises for one night, I pull the stun gun from my pocket.

'Who's out there?' I yell.

The crunching gets louder.

Chapter 9

Fallon

A shape emerges from the shadows, I recognise it. Grant. 'What are you doing here?'

'It worried me when you didn't text back. I came to check on you.' He steps forward, rubbing his hands together. 'It's cold, can we go back to the lodge?'

Staring at the man I was in love with for over a decade, I realise my heart is no longer broken, just silent.

'We're not together,' I tell him. 'I don't need to reply to your messages.'

'Please, let's just go inside?'

I narrow my eyes. 'No. We've been apart for over a year. You have to move on with your life.'

'You're killing me. I said I was sorry. Why can't we move past it? We can make a fresh start.'

'What about your girlfriend? The one you were seeing when you were with me?'

'I dumped her. Look, I made a horrible mistake but I know better now.'

'Please go.' Bending, I lift my phone from where it fell. The torch is still on so I highlight him and, as I do, raise my other hand so the stun gun is more obvious.

'You're going to attack me with a Ladyshave?' Grant laughs. 'Kinky.'

He steps towards me. Infuriated, I press the button to ignite a stream of electricity as a warning.

My ex noticeably jumps back. 'Christ's sake! Where the hell did you get that? Wait, let me guess, Ollie.'

'Please, go,' I repeat. 'I can't deal with you right now.'

Rolling his lips under his teeth, Grant sniffles. 'This isn't like you, Fallon. You're different now.'

Different. And his tone tells me it's not for the better.

'Trauma changes people,' I say.

'I'm not asking for the world. I just want some help.'

Help. That one word drains my anger. 'Help with what?'

Looking away, he shuffles his feet like a schoolboy. 'Mum's sick.'

'What's wrong?' I ask, dreading the answer. I always liked Dorothy.

'Can we talk about it inside?'

'Okay, you can come in for ten minutes.'

'Thanks. I knew you were still my Fallon.' The smirk creeping across his face reminds me of the Grinch.

We end up talking for an hour about his mum being in hospital and the doctors not knowing what's wrong. When I ask which hospital, so I can visit her, he switches subjects telling me how, as much as he hurt me, his biggest regret is not being at Cat Hall, when I needed him most. His declaration makes me uncomfortable, so I tell him to leave. As I do, my eyes find my brother's file.

'Work to do, eh?' he spits. 'Some things never change.' As he strides out the front door, he slams it behind him, shaking the lodge.

After digesting his words, I realise how badly I handled the situation. With everything that's happened these past months, am I losing my psychology mojo? First, how naively I acted at Cat Hall, and now living with the knowledge of what Mum did, and not talking it through with her like I've been trained to do. How many times do I get to screw things up before I admit I'm useless? Do I even deserve this life? What would have happened if I had died and the other Fallon lived? Would she have been a better person than me? Made better decisions?

As I curl up on the sofa, I scoop up my brother's file and begin leafing through its blood-soaked pages. Too many victims already. I hesitate at another crime scene photo. In it is a man in his twenties propped up on a chair, hands bound with blue rope sporting purple patches where it met and soaked up his blood. What did he do to deserve such a cruel end? Wrong place, wrong time? Just as Tyler and the others didn't choose me as their victim; I was simply convenient. How big would their files have been? Or could still be, if I hear three not guilty verdicts.

I'm only a fraction of the way into the folder when I see a familiar name. Ryan Preston. The newest grave to rest near Ollie's real sister. Turning the photo face down, so as not to see the poor young man's final moment, I Google the name again. There's a new article declaring that the killers have been found. Two robbers known to work the estate have been arrested. Both claim innocence. Lindsay was right, it's not just the dead and their families my brother is hurting, it's those who'll be falsely convicted of his crime. He needs to be stopped.

After reading so much horror, falling asleep proves difficult. Over and over I think, *I'm warm. I'm healthy. I'm safe.* But my mantra is cold comfort against my brother's deeds.

–

Early the next morning, Tina video calls me for a session. As soon as her kind face appears on screen, I want to blurt out everything Lindsay said, but I don't. Not just because it could get my boss in trouble for helping, but also because I'm used to bottling things up now.

'You okay?' she asks, eyebrow raised.

'Course,' I lie. I have to protect her from this illegal mess.

She cocks her head as if to challenge me, so I change the subject to the one I know she wants me to talk about. 'Have you heard anything about the Cat Hall case?' I ask.

'A Paul Travis, from the Crown Prosecution Service, has been in touch to ask about our sessions.'

'What's he like?' I ask.

'An arrogant twat, but most good barristers are.'

'I like Joel, and he's a barrister,' I say.

Raising an eyebrow, Tina smiles. 'Yes, and it's rare a barrister like Joel would be involved in a case this much. Usually they just appear in court.'

Quickly, I explain, 'He's new to this region's CPS, and wants to make a good impression on his first case here.'

'And it is a high profile one, what with all the press coverage.'

A mind's eye flash of all those accusatory articles makes me look away.

'Are you ready to continue, pet?'

Noticing my brother's file is in view of the camera, I say, 'One minute.' Then, as casually as I can, I move it out of Tina's eye line. As I do, its heft makes me realise this is now the nearest fire I need to put out.

'Actually, Tina, can we do this another time?'

My boss stares at me. 'What could be more important than prepping for your testimony?'

'It's just I've… I've got a lot of work to do.' The words sound ridiculous. Tina's expression tells me she's thinking the same.

'I'm going to have to insist, Fallon. As much as you don't want to talk about this, you're going to be on the stand soon. Come on, they took your bag from you, what happened next?'

–

Before I knew what was happening, Tyler's gloved fingers had gripped my hand. The warm material, tight against my skin, felt like a vice trapping my fingers. Effortlessly, he pushed me towards a staircase. There was scaffolding, but no backs to the steps. It looked just as dangerous as the man behind me. My legs locked and I stopped dead. The realisation settled in my chest like a weight. If I went up those stairs, I'd never come back down.

'Don't make this harder than it needs to be,' he whispered, his mouth too close to my face.

My mind raced. There had to be a back door. If I wriggled free, I could run. No time to retrieve my bag and car keys, I'd have to keep running until I found help. The estate agent must have arrived by now and be looking for me.

I bucked against him, but Tyler's grip was too tight. From behind me, he wrestled both my arms into his hands, then used his body to force me up the stairs. The heavy feel of him at my back made me retch more than the smell of his breath. The stairs creaked as we moved up. On each step, I thought about letting myself topple backwards. He wouldn't see it coming, we'd both fall, but I'd fall on top of him, hurting him bad enough for me to scramble up and escape. The other two were still in the front room drinking and arguing, so I could escape before either realised I was gone. Just as these thoughts had moved from mind to muscle, however, we reached the top landing, and my chance died.

'Don't fuck with me,' he whispered in my ear, then pulled my arms back harder.

I let Tyler manoeuvre me down a narrow hall, then through the furthest plastic-covered doorway. When I entered, I saw a woman cowering in the far corner.

'Get in there!' He shoved me towards the other captive and I tripped over my feet into the room. His gloved hand then went into his pocket to pull out a serrated kitchen knife, the kind you could buy in any shop. He pulled a finger down the blade, cutting into this thick pleather gloves. I watched as blood dribbled down, exposing the sharpness of the weapon. He said, 'See you real soon.' Then left.

Slowly, I edged towards the other woman. She didn't turn at my approach, instead her shoulders lifted and fell, without a single sound.

'I'm Fallon. What's your name?'

I waited for her answer but none came. I introduced myself again, this time a little louder.

'Gayle,' she whispered back. As she moved towards me, I saw her top was soaked through with blood and her white-blonde hair was matted red.

I put my hand on her shoulder, and felt the judders wracking her body. The blood wasn't hers, or at least most of it wasn't. Although not wanting the answer, I asked, 'What happened?'

She stared at me for a beat, then said, 'Vic's gone.' Sniffling a whimper, she added, 'The man who brought you in here murdered my husband.'

That's when all hope in me died. They were capable of murder. There was no chance they were going to let anyone live.

Gayle, her stare somewhere between shellshock and the middle-distance, continued, 'I tried to stop the bleeding. All they did was laugh.'

'Where's your husband?' I asked.

She whimpered, then pointed to a door leading off from the room. 'He's in there. The en suite.'

I had to see the body with my own eyes.

Carefully, I inched towards the opening. The room was small, with just a glass shower compartment, a basin and a toilet.

'Is Vic okay?' she yelled after me.

Confused, I turned around to see a manic spark of hope in her stare.

Twisting back around, the first thing I saw was a leg poking out of the shower. I edged closer. They had wrapped him in plastic; the same kind which covered the entrance. Blood had pooled against the see-through material and, as I looked up the length of the shape, I saw a face. Eyes open, jaw slack. Reaching out, I moved the plastic away from his body, only to be hit by the salty scent of meat. I retched. Definitely dead.

Stepping back, I looked over at Gayle. 'I'm so sorry.'

'He's had worse injuries.' She then tried to laugh, but only spluttered.

'Gayle, I'm sorry, you said it yourself. They murdered him.'

Ignoring my statement, she said, 'Vic was working on the houses over the other side of the estate. He said they must work on the site too, because they knew stuff.'

On the street, Tyler had told me the truth about working at Cat Hall. 'What stuff?' I asked.

'That the rest of the workers aren't here tonight, and this is the house furthest from the road where no one would see or hear anything.'

Raised voices from downstairs then took my attention. I pivoted around to listen by the door. Our abductors were arguing over something, I just couldn't hear what.

'Can you run?' I asked her.

'I can't leave Vic.'

Shock had hold of her senses. Now, in her mind, her husband was still alive.

'We can get help, send them back for Vic,' I told her gently, grabbing her hands. I heaved her up and lead her to the open door. 'But right now, we have to escape.'

That's when Gayle's fingers slipped from mine.

-

'You're doing great,' Tina says.

'Yeah,' I mutter.

'In that moment, Gayle's mind was trying to protect her from the situation. You did all you could.'

I look down at my dirty pink slippers. 'Did I?'

'Let's pick this up again in the next session. In the meantime, I'd really like you to get some rest. Take care, pet.' She clicks off.

I know I should take her advice, but my mind is too tangled. My bio-brother is another Tyler. I need to start his profile. Picking up the file, I continue reading, making notes about my brutal sibling. After stumbling through another five awful murders, I make a coffee and try to bury my uncertain feelings deeper into my mind, like a shadowy crop I'm allowing to overgrow before a reluctant harvest. I can do this. I owe it to all the victims. I won't run away from this.

A sharp knock on my door slices through my thoughts. As I stand to open it, I catch sight of another crime scene photo and remember a common line through all the cases I've read – no forced entry. The killer was let in. Another knock, this time louder. I'm not expecting anyone. This is what all his victims did: blithely opened their door to danger.

'Who is it?' I yell.

No answer.

Stepping back, I look out the window. As I do, there's another, louder knock.

Stun gun in hand, I gather my courage and open the door.

Chapter 10

Fallon

'Thank God you're all right!' Ollie says. 'I thought something had happened.'

Hiding the stun gun behind my back, I ask, 'Do we have plans today?'

'No, but can't a brother stop by to see his sister?'

'Course you can. Come in.' Feeling awful about my reaction, I lead him into the kitchen then rustle in the drawer to fish out a spare set of keys. I hand them to him. 'Here, in case you need them.'

Reaching for the keys, his fingers touch mine, and a shiver slams against my spine. I look down and see he's wearing black pleather gloves. My arm jerks back and my little brother looks hurt.

'What did I do?' he says.

I can't admit that the feel of the fake leather took me back to Cat Hall. 'I got a static shock off your gloves,' I say.

'Christmas gift. Don't you like them?'

'They're stylish,' I lie.

Ollie slips off the gloves and puts them in his pocket along with the keys. 'It's not cold anyway. I'm starving. Got any food squirrelled away?'

I put some jacket potatoes in the oven, then rummage around in the fridge for something to cook with them. As I do, I ask, 'Have you spoken to Mum yet?'

'If she is *my* mum,' Ollie replies.

'Of course she's *your* mum. I remember you being born.'

'How do you know I wasn't another understudy baby she swapped in, like she did with you?' He pulls out his mobile and begins to play a game on it, then mutters, 'Apparently all babies look alike.'

'If I can work on forgiving her, you can too.'

'Do me a favour, Fal, put the psychologist back in the box for a bit. Let me figure this shit out on my own.'

I nod, then hug him. 'Sure, just promise me you'll start talking to her again soon.'

As we eat and chat, Ollie makes a few more snide comments. But even in a bad mood, he can tell something is weighing on me. As usual, he asks if he can help with whatever it is, but just as I couldn't tell Tina my latest family secret, I can't tell him either. He didn't take the first revelation particularly well; I can't imagine his reaction to one of my new brothers being a serial killer will be better. All gung ho, he'd confront the Kaplans, and Ollie would be no match for the man who committed the horrors in Lindsay's file.

While making coffee, I see a white van pull up outside. 'What's that doing here?'

'Surprise!' Ollie yells. 'It's the rest of your Christmas present!'

Before I can move towards the door, he's already opened it and is walking towards the driver, a wad of cash at the ready. I watch as the van's back doors open wide. There's a scuffle, and out leaps a huge German shepherd.

The driver throws me a smile, then jumps back in the van and speeds off.

'What the hell?' I ask, pointing at the hairy monstrosity pulling my brother towards my pink deck to pee.

'Told you, it's your other Christmas present!' he replies, looking proudly at the beast. 'He's a fully trained guard dog.'

'I can't have a dog! I don't even like them.'

Ollie walks it towards me and instinctively, I step back.

'Don't think of him as a pet – he's a guard. Here to keep you safe. I can't be here all the time you know. I have stuff to do.'

I hadn't realised until he said it, but Ollie is the only person I turn to when I'm feeling vulnerable. I hate being so needy and am immediately embarrassed. 'Sorry,' I say.

'It's not your fault. But ol' Harvey here should be able to help. He's not affectionate or anything, you just need to feed and water him and let him patrol the perimeter.' Ollie offers me the lead.

Harvey is huge, the size of a baby bear. His ears are almost twice the size of his head, and with all the fawn and white fur, he looks like a cross between Gizmo and a gremlin. I make a mental note not to feed him after midnight.

Gingerly, I take the lead. The dog pads up the steps to sit beside me.

'Look, if you're still weirded out after a few days, I'll rehome him. But I'd feel better with him here. You will too.'

'Thanks.' My hand hovers above Harvey's head, but I don't fuss him. If he's a guard and not a pet, then maybe I can be a dog owner.

Chuckling, Ollie gets into his car. Rolling down his window, he yells, 'But you have to let him off the lead!'

My well-meaning, idiotic, brother then drives away, leaving me with a sharp-toothed monster on a string. Awesome.

-

The next three days bleed together. Harvey and I live as lodgers. There are polite glances at one another, an appreciative tail wag when I feed him or fetch fresh water, but mostly it's like living with a hairy shark. At least he's my hairy shark. And although being told not to fuss him, now and then when he sits by me, my fingers find his furry head.

With everyone else busy celebrating the New Year, I devote my time to meeting with Lindsay to discuss her findings, learning about DNA, and studying cases in the US where forensic genealogy has brought killers to justice, as well as given names back to unknown victims.

Attempts to detach myself personally from what I'm doing, and treat it like a job, prove pointless. Murder after murder, I drown in my brother's darkness.

My creeping anxiety does lessen some thanks to Harvey. I hear the comforting clack, clack, clack of claws on the wooden floor as my new dog patrols. I feel safe, but the biggest bonus I've found is when I speak aloud, I no longer feel as if I'm talking to myself. With his massive ears, Harvey hears everything. I hate to admit my little brother was right, but having a dog is making me feel better. I could live without the drool and mud on the rugs, but it's a small price to pay.

Adjusting to life as a dog owner helps me forget about Grant's continued texts and my looming testimony. But everything I've learnt about my brother is inescapable. Stray images of crime scenes and words such as *bludgeon* and *ligature* haunt my thoughts, and my first attempt at a killer profile is shockingly inept. It would be a boon to have Tina's help with this, especially as she made her name in criminology before starting her business, but I can't ignore the risks I'm taking. I could lose my professional career if I'm caught working on an illegal case. And as much as I'm willing to do that for the right reasons, I won't draw my boss into a sticky web of legal issues which could end her career too.

Wait. I may not be able to have Tina's brain, but I can borrow her knowledge.

-

I haven't set foot in the Hawk office for nearly a year, but, this morning, it looks the same as it did the night I left to go house-hunting at Cat Hall. Soft apricot colours feature on every wall, cream furniture and carpets as far as the eye can see, and a big brown hawk in flight adorns the logo on the welcome sign. There's no receptionist at Hawk Therapy, just a circular waiting area with five office doors. It reminds me of Camelot's round table, no therapist above another, and Tina is our King Arthur. Patients come in and press the button beside their doctors' door to alert them that they are waiting. I do this with Tina's door, then sit down with a cup of water from the cooler.

Tina has a plethora of books likely to help with my profiling. In fact, she wrote the book on sick minds, literally. Published under the male pseudonym Dr Todd Hawk, her textbook became a must-have for anyone studying criminology. Although approached by several well-known academic publishers, she's always refused to write a second edition. Why? Because, in her own words, people don't change. She says there's no point in updating a book on personality types when tigers don't change their stripes. I've never agreed with her theory. People can change; it's why they come to therapy. Many a night, we've argued into the small hours about this, but to further substantiate her theory, Tina has never changed her mind.

Moments later, my boss emerges from a door on my left. 'Fallon, to what do I owe the pleasure?' she asks, looking me up and down with suspicion.

'I came in to borrow some books,' I say, getting up.

'Of course, although I could have dropped them round.' Her eyebrow arches as she waits for my response.

I take a swig of water. 'I wanted to come in. You can only stay so long at home until you go…' I stop myself before I say crazy. It's bad psychologist etiquette to use the C word.

She runs a hand over her dark hair. 'No worries, come in.'

I follow her into the office.

Tina's space is light and open. It's easy to breathe in it. As I sit on her leather sofa, I'm about to leap into a request for the criminology books when I realise she isn't going to just hand them over. She'll want to know what I'm up to and won't be happy until I admit why I need those particular books.

'You were going to say something?' she asks, sitting opposite me.

Without time to think of a good excuse, I blurt out the first problem which comes into my head. I tell her about Grant and his impromptu visit to talk about his Mum.

'He's close to his mum?' Tina asks.

I nod, then add, 'Mine too.'

She grimaces. 'Can I make an observation?'

'Sure.'

'You broke up several times because of his cheating, and yet you always got back to together when you, or he, were feeling vulnerable.'

That's one way of looking at it. 'I suppose I did.'

'Be careful. Don't allow current traumas to lead you back down a dark path. I always pegged him as a player.'

Shaking my head, I reply, 'Yeah, I know that.'

'No,' Tina says. Leaning forward she goes on, 'I didn't mean like that. Please don't take this the wrong way, and I should have mentioned it sooner, but I noted he always had some drama in his back pocket when your relationship teetered on the edge. Something to draw you back in. Just keep an eye out.'

'Thanks. I'll be vigilant.' Getting up, I head over to the bookcase. 'Can I grab those books now? They're for a new client.'

'My knowledge is your knowledge.'

Hoping my boss doesn't notice which texts I'm taking, I quickly pluck out the books I need and hide them in my bag.

-

Coffee and a date with a ton of textbooks. It's university all over again. Splayed out around me are five of Tina's books, including the one she wrote. Carefully, I read each in turn making notes. Too soon, I've scribbled a few worrying facts about my brother, all of which I write on sticky notes to attach to the file. On one I write, *little useable physical evidence* – he is forensically savvy. Not difficult with the internet showing criminals how to get away with their deeds. Having multiple Mos means he knows how the police work and can control himself in terms of ritual. I'm betting there is a signature at play, but it's hard to work out. Another reason why the police wouldn't entertain Lindsay's serial killer theory. Even if they did believe her, where would they even begin their investigation?

With no witnesses, I know he's patient – waiting for the best time to strike. But how is he picking them? His victimology is wildly varied: race, gender, age, sexuality, profession. And with no sexual assault on any victims, his motive seems simply to kill.

In big letters on the profile I write *arrogant*. He doesn't hide or dump bodies. His victims were left where they were murdered. It's classic narcissism, to leave his deeds exposed. And, as I noted before, there's no obvious forced entry. He talks his way inside. Nowadays, that kind of instant trust is a skill in itself. Tina said Tyler used manipulative techniques – does my brother do the same? Having run out of sticky notes, I reuse the one I noted Lindsay's address. On the back I write, *Charm hides the monster.*

Tina's book talks of organised and disorganised killers. Disorganised killers give in to impulse; they attack on a whim when the right person, place and time intersect. This eventually leaves them exposed to the police and, more often than not, caught. With this in mind, I can discern my brother is highly organised, and organised offenders have a high IQ.

For geographical profiling, I invite Lindsay to Poppy Fields for lunch. Together, we create a murder map with little red stickers on an A2 printout of the UK. It doesn't take long to realise the crime scenes are everywhere. London to Manchester, Bristol to York, tiny villages to massive cities. He's not operating in any one hunting ground. Neighbourhoods vary from affluent to working class. Looking at victims, the police have done an excellent job in each case of detailing their movements before death, timelines and backgrounds – but there's no overlap with a single person or place. It's frustrating. The only thing tying the crimes is minute specs of DNA.

After saying goodbye, I wonder if Lindsay might have gotten it wrong? No, I saw the look in her eyes, she's a woman on a mission. I see the same look in the mirror when I think about Tyler, Ropey and Streak.

I run through her notes again. The touch DNA was found on random objects near the victims; a wallet, a cricket bat, even an old Furby toy, but looking through the list it's clear there's not even one type of shop to connect them. Another dead end.

I then turn to the medical examiner's report of killing methods, hoping to find a pattern. But no: knives, ropes, blunt objects, even bare hands. The killer has used a wide range of murder methods. In fact, everything about this killer seems frighteningly random – he's an organised disorganised killer. My head hurts.

One thing is for certain. Serial killers are addicts, always chasing the high of their first kill. He's not going to stop.

It's approaching midnight when I finally give up and go to bed. I've stared at my brother's file for so long the photos of his victims appear when I close my eyes, flickering behind my eyelids like a sick slideshow.

–

The morning is cold and dark, so I put on the fire while Harvey and I eat breakfast. Against Tina's wishes, I then take some standing appointments with my regular clients. I'm about to log off Hawk to walk Harvey when my laptop tells me another client is waiting. It's a lady calling herself Yvonne34. When she appears on screen, I can see she's worried. Laying on a bed, her fingers fidget with the corner of the duvet.

'How can I help?' I ask.

'There's a man watching me,' Yvonne says.

I know better than most how danger can hide in mundane places. 'Let's talk this through. Why do you think that?'

'I saw him on my runs. He was outside all yesterday afternoon,' she whispers, then, leaning towards the screen, adds, 'and most of the night too.'

'Have you spoken to the police?'

'No.' She sighs. 'I might be blowing everything out of proportion.'

'Is he still there now?'

'Yeah, he's in a red Audi.'

'Are you alone?'

Shaking her head, she says, 'My husband Des is downstairs, but he thinks I'm being an idiot.'

As I pull across a notepad and pen, Lindsay's file drops off the table. The edge of a photo peeks out, daring me to remember that life isn't always safe, and strange men can walk up to you in the street and... I should alert one of the other therapists online. If they agree it's a dangerous situation, we could handle it together.

To mask my thoughts, I smile at her as best I can. 'I'm going to invite a colleague into our chat,' I say.

As I go to press the button, she holds her hands up to the screen.

'No, please. I don't want to speak to anyone else. I'm only doing this because you lot were the first site that popped up when I searched for someone to talk to. Des already thinks I'm bonkers.'

'My ex-boyfriend always laughed off my worries.' Remembering Tina's words, I add. 'But men react differently to situations compared to women. And back in the heyday of psychological experiments, the research was done on men, which doesn't exactly give us the best cross section of results for the world today.'

'So you think I should be scared?'

'You should trust your gut.'

Shaking her head, she goes to click off.

'Wait! Just to be safe, please call the police.'

Her fingers hover over her keyboard. 'The police won't help. They only care when the crime's been committed.' Yvonne's eyes widen. She really is terrified.

'I understand,' I say, then an idea hits me. 'But if he's parked in your street for a long period of time, that's loitering. Call 101 and let them know he's there and is acting suspiciously. Keep it to generic neighbourhood watch stuff.'

She hesitates then says, 'I'll do that.'

'Let's set up another appointment to talk.'

'I can only afford this one, Dr Hurley.'

'It'll be free.' I add quickly. 'Use the code Poppy when you request me and I get to set the rates. I'll set it to zero. Let me know you're all right.'

She says nothing, and suddenly her image disappears to black. She's clicked off.

After letting out Harvey, I shower, then pull on one of my Christmas jumpers just in time for Mum to arrive for an impromptu afternoon tea, complete with pastries and my favourite Pop-Tarts. I don't have the heart to tell her I haven't gotten around to buying a toaster.

Harvey barks once, but is fed a custard crown and is soon lying at her feet, covered in sugar and flaky pastry.

'Oh, he's a gem, and so much better than the stun thingy,' Mum says rubbing his belly. 'How was your New Year, love?'

'Just another day. You?'

Sighing, she looks away. 'My original plans fell through so I had dinner with the Sawyers and the Hussains. I found out both have single sons. I could set something up?'

Mum has never played matchmaker before. 'What did you really come over to talk about?' I prompt.

She pulls apart a croissant but doesn't eat it, just stares at the greasy marks it makes on her fingers. Finally, she says, 'Ollie won't speak with me. I was supposed to meet his new boyfriend at New Year, but he cancelled.'

In truth, I haven't totally forgiven Mum for hiding my heritage, but I don't want to punish her for something she did thirty years ago – something she clearly thought was the right thing to do at the time. 'Ollie will come round,' I say.

Crossing her legs to lean towards me, she asks, 'Have you contacted Siobhan yet?'

I shake my head.

Sighing, Mum says, 'Perhaps it's for the best. You can do it after this Cat Hall business is all over. That's soon now, isn't it?'

I nod.

'The jury is made up of people, and people aren't stupid,' Mum states. 'Those three hooligans will get what they deserve.'

People are not stupid, but it doesn't matter if you're a juror determined to do the right thing, or a psychologist who never thought they'd do the wrong one – everyone can be manipulated.

After we have eaten our bodyweights in sugar and pastry, Mum leaves to meet her neighbour for coffee.

Harvey trots up to me and I tickle him behind his ear. Lost in thought, I don't catch the call from my family liaison officer Patricia, only the message she leaves. She's confirming an appointment on Monday with Joel and Paul to run through my testimony. Thanks to Tina, I now feel ready to take on Tyler, Ropey and Streak. They won't get away with what they did.

Happy that Cat Hall is progressing, I begin to type up my notes on the killer profile. It's better than my first attempt, but disturbing none the less. The problem is, I'm only looking at the killer, rather than the mask he hides behind. Most people never see this side of him and live to tell. Even if I were to ask Siobhan to choose the son who fits my work, she'd falter. Maybe I need to learn more about the everyday face he shows to the world, not the one dripping in blood.

After zipping on my padded coat, I take Harvey for a long walk. We sit by the lake so I can clear my head. When we stop, I imagine passing my profile on to Lindsay. Will she take it to the police and finally be able to get on with her investigation, or roll her eyes at my efforts and wish she'd never contacted me at all?

At first, I don't spot Harvey edging towards a duck. I only catch his stalking out of the corner of my eye. How close his enormous body gets to the ground. How flat his ears become. How keen his stare. When the duck notices him, my dog suddenly springs forward and begins the chase.

'Harvey! No!' I yell.

As well-trained as he is, he's still an animal of instinct, and my shouts don't stop him catching up with the bird. One panicked cry, then it falls limp in his jaws. Tail wagging, he drops the corpse before me, then licks my hand. Before I can pull away, his tongue leaves a trail of bloody slobber. Suddenly I'm back in Cat Hall. Red stains covering me. My voice hoarse from screams. Fresh death in my nostrils.

I half walk, half jog back to Poppy Fields, and the door has barely swung shut behind me before my jeans are off and my hands are thrust under the kitchen tap. As I watch the pinkish water gurgle away, I weigh up whether I should keep Harvey. But after he lays his soft, heavy head on my foot, acting as if nothing happened, I realise I can't punish him for doing what comes naturally. Harvey was possessed by the wild, lizard brain which bullies the rational. Is this what it's like for my brother? An uncontrollable craving for murder when his own lizard slithers across his thoughts and demands satisfaction.

While I make dinner a strange sensation grips me. It feels as if I'm being watched. A few times I even check outside to see if anyone is out there. Staring out of the guest room window, I imagine a congregation of ducks suddenly appearing around Poppy Fields ready to judge and sentence Harvey for his crime. It's not long until the ducks morph in my mind into an unknown brother, biding his time and waiting for me to leave the lodge.

Chapter 11

The Brother

She knows I'm watching. I love it. This one reminds me of the good old days: tense curtain twitching and sideways glances. I'm not usually this obvious, but I'm enjoying the game too much. There's always the chance my prey will alert another to my presence, but most people wouldn't indulge their paranoia; that particular sticky wicket has a habit of multiplying if you allow it to take root.

Variety is the spice of life, and I often change cars mid-hunt. Today, I decided to drive a pink Mazda that everyone lovingly calls Mazzey. Some might view a pink car as drawing attention, but it's quite the opposite, being overt to be covert. I park Mazzey one street over, so I'm now downwind of my prey. As I patiently wait, Anna's jacket over my knee like a naughty child, I check my phone for updates on Nicole's case. There's one entitled *Caught*. With it is a photo of her sofa-loving boyfriend being manhandled out of their house. A satisfied smirk on the policemen's faces, and a terrified expression on Roddy's. The article tells me Nicole was killed in a fit of passion after he discovered she was meeting an online lover for a tryst. The whole piece is very convincing, I'd be on board with the story myself if it hadn't been my fingers around Nicole's throat.

Oddly, I don't feel the usual rush of pride that a false conviction would fill me with. Instead, annoyance bubbles in my stomach. With Roddy locked up, the case is closed. Nicole's murder was one more perfect crime that no one knows was mine. I should have sent part of Anna's jacket. At least then the police would have an inkling there is a larger game at foot. Maybe today I should leave a note scrawled in blood, like the Lipstick Killer or good ol' Jack? Something red and spicy.

Excitement fuels me as I walk across the street. Coming around the corner, I spot her locking her front door then heading towards a car. No, she won't get away that easily.

'Hey!' I shout, then jog towards her holding up the jacket. 'I have your prize.'

Recognising the garment, she stops and walks over to meet me. Her hair sparkles in the afternoon sun, like shiny scales of a freshly caught fish.

'Oh, you didn't have to hand-deliver it,' she says.

'I live nearby, so thought I'd drop it off.' I force a smile. 'I'll refund the postage.'

'That's nice of you.' She takes the jacket from me, then carelessly balls it up and shoves it in her bag. 'I'll leave you a five-star review,' she says, but then begins to fumble with her keys. She's caught my scent.

Stepping in front of her car, I say, 'I've lots of quality sports clothes for sale, want to see them?' I then look down at my mobile. 'Oh, I've run out of data. Could we go back to yours and use the Wi-Fi?'

'Thanks, but I'm not interested. I need to be somewhere.' Her voice is shaky, and she's sporting a rabbit-in-the-headlights look. She's not taking my bait. My prey did spot me.

Glancing around us, I check for witnesses. None. My hand snaps out to grab her, but she recoils just in time. Eyes wide, she clutches her bag against her chest, then staggers across the road from me.

Instinct will tell her to go to ground, to run inside her empty home. It's the wrong decision. And yet, sure enough, she rustles in her bag and plucks out some keys. As she does, the strap slips through her fingers and the bag falls to the ground with a thud. I step forward to pick it up, but she rushes back towards her house, and fumbles with the front door key. With her bag slung over my shoulder, I walk down the path. I hear a sigh of relief as she unlocks the door and falls into the threshold. But I'm on her heels. As she tries to swing the door shut, I use brute force to keep it open.

Smiling, I step inside her home.

'You dropped your stuff,' I say as I hang the bag on a hook by the door.

Finding her voice too late, she screams, 'No!'

I shut, then lock, the front door behind me. This isn't how my hunts usually go, and the newness of not knowing how this will play out makes my palms tingle.

'Get out of my house!'

I may not know what I'll do, but I know what she's thinking. In a situation like this, the familiar becomes foreign. Nothing is where you need it to be, especially her husband, who by now is at his office stirring a third sugar into his tea.

I edge forward and she makes a run for it, bolting upstairs. I smile to myself, knowing from my clandestine visit here last night, there's nothing that will help her up there, just more potential crime scenes to choose from.

As I climb the stairs, my prey darts into a bedroom, slamming the door behind her. I know there's no lock on it. Slowly, I wander in. When I do, I see her ashen face before the light of a laptop.

'That's not in the rules,' I mutter, then grab her arm and yank her across the bed. Writhing beneath my grip, she slips away and scurries into the hall. I hear a click. She's locked herself in the bathroom. There's a rummaging sound, and I imagine her searching for weapons. The best she can hope for is a safety razor and an old bottle of Pepto-Bismol.

Silence. I time it. Fourteen minutes.

I know she can't climb out of the window; it's too high up and way too small. Her phone is downstairs in the bag, I made sure of that when I picked it up, so there will be no calls for help. With a toilet and a water supply, she's thinking she can wait this out. And if I didn't know how to pop the door lock, and had a screwdriver in my jacket, she would have been right.

Movement inside the bathroom steals my attention.

She yells, 'Nothing has happened, you can just go.'

'Nothing happening is why I can't go. I have a perfect record.'

Silence.

'Can I ask you something?' I say.

Silence.

'Would you prefer people know who murdered you?'

Strangled cry.

'No one will, of course. I wouldn't still be doing what I'm doing if anyone knew about me. What are your thoughts on the police? Do you think they'll solve your murder?'

'I-I called them.'

'No you didn't. But I'm willing to leave them a note on your behalf. What would you like it to say?'

'Don't care, as long as it's signed with your name and address, you fuck!'

I can't help it, I laugh. 'You are funny. I didn't pick that up while I was watching you.'

Another bout of shuffling and a slight sob sounds through the door.

'Do *you* want to know about me?' I ask.

'Fuck off!' she yells back.

I was offering a gift: a few extra moments of life along with knowledge of me, something currently no one else has. It would have made her special. But I guess some people don't want to be special.

The lock is one of those old-fashioned ones from forty years ago. Accidents happen in the bathroom, so it's deliberately flimsy; that way people can reach you if you're hurt. Ironic. I jam my screwdriver in. There's a click and the handle flies up.

'Wait! Wait!' she begs.

'Do you want to talk now?'

It takes almost a minute to get an answer. 'Yes,' she whimpers.

Leaving the unlocked door shut with my victim clinging to the interior handle for dear life, I sit on a nearby wash basket. 'I've been killing since I was little. I'm very good at it. But a thought hit me recently and has been bothering me ever since – are you really the best at something if no one ever knows you are?'

'No. You should hand yourself in to the police so everyone knows. I'll go with you if you like?'

I grin. 'There's that funny side again.' I cross my legs to make the basket more comfortable. 'But no, that would be conceding. Now, if I'm caught, that's another thing entirely.'

'You will get caught,' she states. 'Killers are always caught.'

'I hate to be the one to break it to you, but we're not. Think of all the missing people in the world, all the unsolved murders. In truth, you only know about the killers who *were* caught. There are so many more of us out there than will ever be found, or even admitted to.'

Soft whimpers echo inside the tiled bathroom. 'You'll get caught,' she repeats, but this time without conviction. 'Someone will catch you.' The door handle then loses its rigidness; she's let go.

Once the deed is done, I use a toothbrush and blood to write on the walls. I try out message after message, but nothing seems right. Each clue, I wipe away with Anna's jacket, until the whole bathroom is smeared and bloody. This writing thing is harder than it looks. It has to be a good clue, but not too good. Annoyed, I eventually give up to allow myself time to concoct the perfect line for my next murder – something that epic needs to be thought through, not scrawled in scarlet on a whim. I'm better than that.

Before leaving my crime scene, I stalk back into the bedroom to see what she was doing on the laptop. It's open on a page for a company called Hawk Therapy, where my new sister works. Not a huge coincidence; it instantly pops up when people search for online therapists. They must have clients all over the country.

Did she speak with Fallon? There are only so many therapists on the site, so it's a possibility. As much as the news of a long-lost sister was a shock, dividing the opinions of my brothers, I hadn't given her much thought bar my initial Google searches and annoyance at Mum's orders. Siblings are not new to me, and as much as I need family to affix my mask of normalcy, their love and lives mean little to my game. A necessary façade of a normal man to ensure no one spots the real me.

Within inches of the laptop is a silver photo frame perched on a bedside table. Inside is a photo of my latest catch and a younger woman who looks like her – a sister? Together they share the same smile and doe eyes. I take it as my next bait.

-

My drive home takes me past Cat Hall. Without making the conscious decision, I indicate to turn into the new estate. This is where the bad thing happened to my sister.

The show home is open, so I park in its drive and get out to do another Google search for articles. What happened fascinates me and the details online are a tease; just the tip of the preverbal murder-berg. I need more.

Casually, I walk the bloodstained brick road my sister skipped down that night to reach the place where it happened. I imagined the house would be something out of a *Hammer House of Horror* episode, blackened and broken with large sunken windows and creepy ivy smothering the bricks. But it's nothing like the picture in my mind. It looks like any other house you'd find on a new estate. The only sign a tragedy occurred is a nearby lamppost with bunches upon bunches of flowers strapped to the stem. Roses, all different colours and in different stages of decay. There are cards too. *Sorry for your loss. I will always remember you. You shouldn't have been there. Your bravery will live on in our hearts*. None of the cards have my sister's name on, but then again, that's not surprising. She survived, after all, and the online articles I've found about her ordeal were scathing to say the least. Victim blaming gone amuck. It makes me wonder why Fallon was never interviewed, to get her side across. No doubt the police told her not to, not until the trial was over. She's strong to have sustained their slings and arrows. I stare at the house; maybe this mundane crucible forged her into someone strong and mighty. Or maybe it broke her, leaving cracks which one day soon will splinter, allowing the darkness of this word to seep in.

I've always been on the right side of the murder equation, so imagining what my sister felt that night is almost impossible. From my own experience, I know, to survive, she would have had to do some unforgivable things. I've murdered groups of people. Not at creepy cabins in the woods in slow motion, but in housing estates where one would always try to get away, rather than help their family. Legs are in motion long before loyalty rears its head.

A family across the road interrupts my thoughts. It's a mum with two kids, wrestling with the toddler's hand, holding her mobile, and pushing the littlest one's pram at the same time. I watch as the child's fingers slip through hers. Without hesitation, it races across the road, just as a car turns around the corner. Instead of watching them collide, I leap forward and snatch it out of the road. The car's driver, oblivious to the almost-tragedy, doesn't even slow down.

Wide-eyed, the child stares up at me. 'You should be more careful,' I say before opening my arms and freeing the little one back into the wild. A big game hunter never kills the young. If you accidently catch one, you throw it back for another day.

Chapter 12

Fallon

After a broken night's sleep, I slink onto my deck to drink my morning coffee in the rocking chair. The sun is already out, and, although not warm, it's bright. Closing my eyes, I feel Harvey flop by my feet and a forgotten calm settles in me. I don't deserve this. Getting up, I earn a rumbling growl from my dog for the disturbance, so make it up to him with a long walk.

After, I'm hard at work perfecting the profile – this time forcing myself to look at every single crime scene photo. With care, I place them in chronological order. Each kill gets steadily more inventive, almost as if he's a killer trying to find his feet, not a seasoned murderer – or maybe he's still trying to recapture the high of his first. He's not realised he'll never find that first dark taste again, no matter how many different tools he uses, angles he takes, or bodies he drops. All the kills are awful, but the worst happened in April last year. A man in his sixties. A philanthropist butchered in his home. The scene is so bad I have to turn its photo around to keep down my breakfast.

Lindsay emails to say she'll come over later. She has an *amazeballs* idea Her note ends with a smiley face. The emoji and word choice remind me she's barely out of her twenties. So young, so brave, and some might say so stupid. Hunting a serial killer with only his traumatised, newly discovered sister as backup. Has Lindsay considered not just the threat to her career, but the physical danger she could be putting herself in with this pursuit? And I'm in that unsteady boat too now. If Siobhan has told her sons about me, he could be outside Poppy Fields right now. People say you're never more than six feet away from a rat; what's the distance on serial killers?

-

It's dark by the time Lindsay arrives. As she slumps into the first chair she sees, I can feel something is wrong.

'What's happened?' I ask handing her a mug of coffee.

Wiping her nose with a tissue, she replies, 'I was at a murder scene today. It was one of his.'

'No,' I whisper. I let my body fall onto the sofa. This is my fault. I've been too slow. 'How do you know?'

'You get a feel for these things. Right from when I entered the house, I knew it was him. Testing the DNA is just a formality, but I'll do it anyway.' She sighs. 'At this rate, he's going to get away with it.'

'No, we'll catch him. It's only a matter of time.'

'Okay, but then how many more people will die before we do?' She drops her head into her hands. 'I can't take another scene like that one. I just can't.'

I want to hear all the gory details of what she saw, so I have to live with them forever like a tattoo on my memory, but Lindsay looks back up and speaks first.

'How's the profile coming?'

I look over at my pile of notes stacked on the table. The notes that, a few minutes ago I was so proud of, now feel ridiculous. 'It's not enough.'

Lindsay hangs her head. 'I'm being selfish. A career is nothing when lives are in danger. I should have kept pushing my superiors.'

'Nothing is ever simple. And you tried. You're still trying.'

Harvey brings Lindsay a toy to play tug of war. Before I can warn her not to, she pulls her end. With the might of a canine Hercules, Harvey yanks her clean off the chair. Landing with a bump, she puts her hands in the air as if to surrender.

'The woman I saw today, she had a husband, a career, a life, a future. What's my job, or even my freedom, against that?'

She's right. But life can't be that unfair. There has to be a solution that leaves us both professionally unscathed, while bringing my brother to justice. 'Wait, what was your *amazeballs* idea?' I ask, helping her up.

Shaking her head, she says, 'It doesn't matter now; it wouldn't have been enough. I need something big to take to Trout-face.'

'Trout-face?'

'My manager, Caroline Trout. I'll try again with this murder. But we need more.' Her eyes drift to my notes.

'I'll email you the profile too.'

'No, sit on it for now. Let me see if I can find something *science-y* in the meantime.'

I drain the last of my coffee and watch her expression. She's putting on a good show, but this last murder has gotten under her skin and buried itself deep. It's the first kill she could have prevented.

'We can do this,' I tell her.

'We can still do this,' she echoes, clearing away our mugs.

It's cold, so to wave her off, I reach into the cupboard for a coat, which I quickly pull over my shoulders. I watch Lindsay speed into the night, then say, 'I'm warm. I'm healthy. I'm safe.' But when I look down I see, in my haste, I didn't put on my new coat, but the one from that night. As if it's made of burning coals, I shrug it off and throw it onto the deck, creating a crumpled grey ghost in the darkness. Shivering from more than just the cold, I kick the lump of material inside and back into the cupboard, then shut the door tight, kicking it a few times for good measure. I almost cry, but stop myself. Harvey whines.

'I'm all right,' I tell him. 'Let's get an early night.'

During the hazy twilight time, I writhe beneath the weight of my winter duvet, trying to find a comfortable position. But each time I twist and turn, the material seems to constrict me further. Tired and frustrated, and envying Harvey's peaceful snores, I make a horrific decision – I won't leave Lindsay alone to face a killer. I have four brothers, all I need do is meet them and spot which one has pints of blood staining his hands. This isn't my first serial killer rodeo. How hard can it be?

–

Morning comes too quickly, and the day starts off badly. I can't find my favourite coffee mug. A small tragedy in the grand scheme of things, but it none the less feels as if it's setting the tone for my day.

I give Mum a courtesy call to let her know I'm going back on my promise not to make contact with Siobhan until after the Cat Hall case. The conversation is harder than I expect, and she hesitates for too long before replying. Eventually, it is Ollie's thoughts she echoes: stay away until after your testimony. I don't have the words to explain why I need an introduction to my brothers, so instead I ramble on about wanting to know my true heritage. Eventually she relents and wishes me luck.

I tap Siobhan's number into my mobile and save her as a contact. The woman who so easily gave me up. Who never wanted to know me. Who also gave birth to a monster. Mustering my courage, I call. After four rings, there's silence. My mouth dries until my lips feel like jerky and my head pounds with questions.

'Hello?' I say.

Chapter 13

Fallon

'This is Siobhan Kaplan. I'm not here right now. Leave a message.' Beep.

Fumbling my words, I ask her to call me back so we can talk about the not so legal adoption, then hang up, jabbing at my mobile's red button like it's the reason she wasn't there.

Harvey, plastic bone in mouth, stares at me.

'I'm not going to just wait for her,' I tell him, then get out my laptop and start Googling to find my brothers. The only problem is, 'Kaplan' alone turns up thousands of results, and I don't have their Christian names to narrow down the search. And of course, Siobhan herself has no digital footprint whatsoever – not so much as a Facebook profile or a Park Run entry.

After three hours, I'm almost ready to give up. There are too many Kaplans on the internet. Daves and Bens, Williams and Tonys, Johns, Jacks and Jacobs. I can remove some from my 'maybe' list immediately; the helpful ones who have their hometown in their bios or a profile photo showing they're old enough to be my grandfather. Others I waste fifteen minutes at a time scrolling through their Twitter feeds, finding LinkedIn handles and employer's website before discounting them.

The strongest lead I find is a mention of a Stefan Kaplan, who plays for a local cricket team. He's cited in a few articles about an addiction charity he helps out with, and in one grainy photo I think we do look alike. But even that is jaw-droppingly tenuous.

Frustrated, I stand up and walk a few quick circles around my living room, stretching my stiff muscles. I can do this. 'I'm warm. I'm healthy, I'm safe.'

Determination renewed, I sit back down and wrack my brain for new search options. I use Company's House to look for any businesses owned by a Kaplan. There's quite a number, but when I narrow my search to the local area, it leaves only one. Kaplan Motors. Their website is easy to find, and when I click on the 'About Us' page I am presented with a list of names, four of which are Kaplans: Simon, Stefan, Sam, and Garry. Siobhan has four sons. I email the site to Lindsay, with a message.

One of these men is your killer.

–

Although Sunday is my day off, I log on to Hawk. Yvonne hasn't contacted me. Some clients you just don't hear from after the first session. It's something, as a therapist, you get used to – never knowing how the story ends. I can only assume the man in the Audi was a misunderstanding.

The one person who does keep contacting me is Grant; four texts so far. Each uninvited message is a memory of Sundays we spent together. In great detail he laments on long lie-ins, bacon rolls, roast dinners, and watching Netflix until our eyelids drooped. I'm annoyed at myself for missing those days and frustrated that, with a few short texts, I've let my ex get under my skin. The photo on the mantel gives me the strength to delete his messages, and I realise I can still do all those things if I want to. I make a bacon roll for breakfast and a roast dinner for lunch. While spending the afternoon buried in Netflix watching true crime documentaries, something which before would have repelled me, I find myself adding what little I learn to the profile.

Siobhan still hasn't called back. No one is that busy they can't pick up the phone to the daughter they gave away. I thought being a mother meant you loved unconditionally, and if my mum's story is to be believed, Siobhan gave me up for my own good – so I'd have a better life. And she was right, I had an amazing life as a Hurley, maybe something I'd have never had as a Kaplan. But I can't help but wonder whether, in that *Sliding Doors* life, I would have met Grant? Would I have broken up with him and gone looking for a home at Cat Hall *that* night?

After torturing myself some more, I do something so narcissistic it shocks me. I Google myself. Below my Hawk profile, the results are overwhelmed with articles about Cat Hall. This is what Siobhan and my new brothers would see if they searched online for me – a series of unfair snapshots of horror, filtered through the lens of a headline-hungry media. Is this why Siobhan isn't contacting me? Because she's read about the things I did at Cat Hall to ensure I kept the life she gave me?

Chapter 14

The Brother

Anna's perfect pink jacket now appears on my Starsellers' sold items list. A bloody memory prompt I get to keep forever.

Online, the news of the innocent Roddy's arrest is predictably quiet. Few details will be given now as they'll be holding everything back for the trial. Which reminds me… Absently, I click on the Cat Hall articles again. This court case has been crawling on for the last few months. Curiosity as to how it's progressing grips me, and for the umpteenth time today, I think of Fallon. To survive her ordeal, she must have been very brave, or very lucky – which one was it? I have to know.

I email Mum and ask for my sister's contact details. Of course Mum replies, *no.* And: *none of us are to contact her until after the Cat Hall case.* Stamping my foot, I swear loud enough for those in the garage to hear me. I'm not a child. She may have spewed me out into the world but I don't have to do what she says. I type that I understand Fallon must be going through something awful, and I only want her address to send flowers, to let her know we are thinking about her.

No.

No? So, I don't even deserve a good reason, or an apology. I'm Fallon's brother, I can contact her if I want to. Mum doesn't own me – she never has. How dare she act like this! After imagining what I'd do if she were here in the room with me right now, I calm my dark thoughts, then call her. 'I want to do something,' I say as sweetly as I can. 'How about we send the flowers anonymously? It can be secret support.'

Mum exhales heavily down the phone. 'You win. I like that idea.'

'Yeah, secrets are your thing,' I say and chuckle.

'Don't give me shit. This whole thing has me walking on eggshells. Your brothers are driving me mad. And don't forget, what I did back then wasn't exactly legal. Heather could say I made her do it. I could get arrested.'

Mum has an impressive temper when she gets going and we all inherited it in some form or another. Unlike my siblings, I can control mine. From my first kill to my last, I will be in full control.

'Then I'd help you. I can't have my favourite mum in the clink. So, are you going to give me the address? Whether she realises it or not, Fallon needs her family.'

'You can't meet her now. Promise me. It'll ruin everything. We need to be smart about this and introduce her to the family slowly.'

'Like I said, I just want to send some secret flowers.'

Silence.

'You liked the idea, remember?' I whine, hoping she can hear my bottom lip protruding over the telephone.

'Let me think about it.'

'Why? You trust me.'

Mum knows better than to try to outwit me in a debate and, like always, she eventually gives in. 'Poppy Fields, Foxglove Lodges, Northants.'

–

I should be uploading the photo frame, setting up my next challenge, but instead I climb into my little pink car and take a short drive into the countryside.

Foxglove Lodges is beautiful. It has its own lake and private woods. I park up by the public entrance of the lake and walk down to the residential lodges. Fallon's home is still near town, but not too near to be wrapped up in the pollution and people – it's a Goldilocks location.

Within five minutes of lurking outside Poppy Fields, I catch my first real glimpse of my sister, diligently beavering away. Hers is a determined face framed by dark, messy hair which bounces in curls around her shoulders. We look alike. It's an odd sensation to see someone with whom you share blood for the first time. I imagine knocking on her door and introducing myself. With her psychological talents, she might be the first person to instantly sniff out my shadowy predilections.

I wonder if she has the same biological attributes as me. My doctors say I have one of the lowest resting heartbeats they've ever heard. Does Fallon have it too? I doubt it. A low heartrate makes it hard to be rattled by, well, anything. Anxious doctors gave me medication for my heart, to even me out and make me more human. To allow me to feel the mundane shit plaguing everyone else. I pay the prescription every month, but I never take the pills. Fate had me born this way, with a need to do more, to be more, to kill more. I won't let drugs steal that away.

Suddenly, Fallon looks up as if she has spotted me. I freeze, but her gaze only journeys into the middle-distance for a second, then she's back to her work.

I edge a little closer but frantic barking stops me in my tracks. I didn't peg her as a dog owner. Hiding behind a giant potted plant on her deck, I hear her shuffling around, then the front door opens wide.

She emerges with the biggest dog I've ever seen strapped to her hand. It reminds me of a werewolf from an old film I saw when I was little. It barks my way and I imagine that, at any moment, it will pull itself upright as if its lead was a puppet string. Open jaws dripping in slobber, it would stalk on hind legs towards me, outstretched claws itchy to free my blood.

It barks again, sniffing the air.

'No more ducks for you,' she says, pulling him in the opposite direction of the lake.

I take my pulse. Fifty-one. I wasn't even doing anything wrong; I could have popped up and introduced myself as her brother, to hell with Mum's wishes. But something inside of me is beginning to flourish and come alive, a feeling I thought I'd lost. I should get to know Fallon better.

One easily-dealt-with lock and I'm inside Poppy Fields. Her home is stylish, clean and smells of pine with a hint of mint; it's quite lovely. She has left a cup of coffee on the kitchen side. I touch it. Still warm. There's a few sips left, so I take one. Pale, no sugar, very strong – kind of like me. I move further into the living space. Dog hairs litter the sofa; she allows it on the furniture. I sit down and make myself comfortable, and as I do a big brown file on her desk catches my eye. It's chunky with an air of the ominous. Interesting. What has she's been beavering away on? Opening it, I see familiar faces. People I hunted stare back at me, just as I left them: bloody, pulse-less, and wide-eyed.

What the fuck? How did my long-lost sister get all this information on my victims? The accountant who suspected I didn't add up, but wanted the sports memorabilia I was selling too badly to care. The drug dealer who feverishly bartered for a Furby for her son. The fashion student too busy with his collection to notice I was dressed to kill. Not all my kills are accounted for, but it's more than enough to see me living the rest of my days behind bars.

Midway through the file is a report by some forensics expert called Lindsay Cross. She found my touch DNA on the objects I left at the crime scenes. I handled them without gloves, leaving miniscule *telltale hearts* to beat out my identity. How could I have been so careless?

Cross is part of the police. She's the villain who has given this file to my sister. So why haven't I been arrested yet? Luckily, few people ever remember tales of auctions and shopping, so it's doubtful items could be traced back to Starsellers. That's what makes my method for selecting victims so brilliant.

Included in the pages is a reference to a case from the US, one solved using something called forensic genealogy. Is that why Fallon has the file? Yes, it must be. Cross tracked her down through our sibling DNA. A flutter tickles my heart and I take my pulse. Sixty-three beats per minute, the highest I've ever known it.

I Google forensic genealogy in the UK. Hmm, it's not practiced here. Oh, Cross, you naughty girl. You're not playing by the rules. I may have made errors with my biological matter, but you have compromised police ethics and broken laws. Tut, tut, tut.

As I flick through the folder a final time, a Post-it note flutters out. Picking it up, I see a handwritten note. It reads: *Charm hides the monster.* What! She doesn't even know me! This flaccid line could describe a hundred killers from history. Not me. I'm a different animal. A monster would be a killer who takes lives for his own gratification, without thought or care. My prey choose themselves. I even level the playing field by hunting in their environment, not enticing them into a secondary location. My victims have a chance to escape their fate. Am I just some common serial killer to her? An impulsive yet charming fool, barely finishing his murder spree before he's captured for further study?

Without thinking, my hand holding the papers jerks out, and I almost throw them across the room. I stop myself just in time.

Aware my sister and her werewolf could be back any moment, I place everything back where I found it. Apart from the insulting Post-it, which I pocket. I then make my way to my car.

I slip into the driver's seat and think. Clearly, the police don't believe my big bad folder of death, or I'd already be in prison. To come close to me, Cross and my sister had to break the rules. What should I do?

Looking down I spot a long dog hair clinging to my sleeve. Plucking it up, I stare at it, imagining I can see all its follicles and molecules, right down to the very essence of the werewolf who shed it. As I move it around, it catches on my ring and snaps in two in my hands. Hair is only strong when it's all together, a single strand is weak. Without the police behind her, my sister is alone, yet she's willing to wade into the dark depths of my mind. I can't believe my luck! She's who I've be looking for. I don't need to tempt the police into my game when I have a sibling to play with. And that's what brothers and sisters do: play games together! Fallon has even made the first move. I can't wait to make the next one! She may have an education in the mind, but I have a degree in death and a masters in murder.

Pulling out my new silver photo frame, I upload it onto Starsellers with a long auction date. As I snap an image for the site, I run my finger across the cool metal borders and imagine placing a photo of myself and Fallon into its centre. No warmth. No safety. No secrets. One of us will win, and the other will lose more than just the game.

Chapter 15

Fallon

By the time I remember my car needs petrol, it's almost midnight. Working from home, I'm out of the habit of regularly filling up. My CPS meeting is first thing in the morning, so to beat the rush hour crush, I hop in my little Ford and drive to the petrol station.

When I pull into the forecourt, I'm the only car, and the night is so dark the lights are losing their will to shine. Suddenly, a white van speeds into the space beside me. In big, bold letters it declares it belongs to Howard Electricians and Builders. Its windows are black with muck and someone has written 'my other car is an Audi' in the dirt. It makes me think of Yvonne, and her gut feeling about the man in the red car.

The pump is on the driver's side so I don't see the driver get out. There's shuffling and as I lean across to get a better view, I catch sight of his trainers. Tyler wore a similar pair. A jolt of adrenaline rides my body, making me fumble my grab for the pump. Hearing a rumbling laugh from the other side of van, I slowly peer around, but see no one. Panic creeps into my chest, so I quickly pull away the pump and begin filling up my car. My eyes on my surroundings. I can no longer feel breath hitting my lungs. I don't want to be here. Having hopefully filled up with just enough petrol to last me a few days, I screw on my petrol cap.

Frustrated at my reaction, I walk deliberately slowly into the light of the shop to pay.

'You all right, darling?'

I look over to see an elderly man behind the counter, encased in a protective plastic box.

'Yes, thanks.' I say, then concentrate on taking the steps needed to pay for my petrol.

'That everything? Can I tempt you into some half-price chocolate?'

'No thanks. Just pump one, please.'

Still staring out into the forecourt, I tap my card against the machine to pay. As I wait for my credit card payment to be approved, I watch the petrol station CCTV monitors behind the counter. On them, I see a tall man loitering between the van and my car. The picture is too grainy to make out his features, but his head keeps turning towards the shop. I probably spooked him as much as he spooked me. The image flickers, breaking my thoughts. I take my card and smile at the attendant, who turns back to the screens.

'Bloody things. I wish the franchise would take our security more seriously. They only bother when something bad happens. But of course, it needs to happen first.' He bangs the TV. 'It wasn't installed right and has been messing with the electrics all month. You're lucky the card machine worked.'

As I dig out my car keys, I hmm back, then hurry out of the shop. The driver has moved to the far side of the van again. Not wanting to appear weird or suspicious myself, I walk as calmly and slowly as I dare.

When I'm within touching distance of my car door, a deep cough echoes through the forecourt. Shifting my keys around, I twist them so the jagged edge sticks out like a weapon. Suddenly, the lights flicker out and darkness envelops me. I let out a scream and stumble back, almost falling over. The shadow of the man moves towards me. My hands find my bonnet and I edge around my car. As I do, the lights spring back to life but, before my eyes can readjust, the van's door is banged shut and the vehicle is screeching out of the forecourt.

From the garage's door, the old man yells, 'Just a short power cut. Are you okay?'

I'd been holding my breath for so long that, when I finally breathe, I choke on the air. 'Did he just steal the diesel?' I push out.

The man shuffles further out. 'No, look, he left the money on the pump.' He picks up a £20 note.

'He… he came at me, then was gone when the lights came back on.'

The old man points at the petrol hoses. 'He was probably trying to stop you from falling over them. No doubt your reaction scared him away. Men can't do nothing nice for ladies anymore without being accused of somethin' they never intended.'

So some Good Samaritan saw a woman alone in the dark and tried to help her and I screamed at him?

As the old man continues his tirade about *women today*, I slip into my car and drive home. I know the builder wasn't Tyler, or Ropey, or even Streak – they are all sitting in a prison cell awaiting justice. Could it have been the newest killer to enter my life? No, my brother doesn't know I'm on to him, and perhaps, with Siobhan's silence, he doesn't even know I exist. What just happened was nothing. As much as I'm painfully aware bad things happen, I also know brains have a habit of interpreting new experiences with the same perimeters of the old – the darkness I'm battling now is bleeding into my life.

Finally home and utterly exhausted, I throw my duvet over the sofa and curl up with Harvey by my side. When I sleep, I dream of a toy white van slinking about the lodge, watching me through plastic covered windows.

–

The journey to the police station is longer from the lodge than it was from Ollie's house. All the while, I drive in silence thinking through what I'm going to say to the CPS. The thought of opening barely scabbed wounds makes me nauseous, but it is a necessary evil to ensure those arseholes are put away for life.

When I walk into the station, I do a double-take. Patricia is at least six months pregnant.

'Congratulations,' I say automatically, looking at her swollen belly.

'Happy accident,' she says. 'Listen, I booked an interview room. The CPS guys are already in there.' Then, without checking I'm following, she struts through the station, waving at people and holding her belly like a supermodel would clutch a fake fur coat down a catwalk.

Once we're through a set of double doors, she turns and asks, 'Drink?'

I feel bad asking a pregnant woman to fetch me anything, but I didn't sleep much last night so could do with the caffeine. 'Coffee, please.'

She bustles off, leaving me standing alone. The building is huge and only a few years old. Massive ceilings are held together by steel rods and panes of glass, almost like a greenhouse. The last time I was here was after Cat Hall. The feelings I had then – vulnerable, small, and that my world would never be the same – ravage my thoughts again, until a familiar face catches my eye.

Miller, the constable who took my statement. Smiling, he approaches.

'She's meant to take you into the room, not leave you stranded,' he says with a grimace. 'Follow me.' He leads me down a corridor, then gestures to a door. 'In here, Dr Hurley.'

'Thank you.'

Patricia appears at my shoulder. 'There you are. Shall we go in?' she says, giving the constable a dirty look.

Miller rolls his eyes, smiles at me, then walks off towards the stairs.

As Patricia opens the door to the interview room, I see a strange man. He is about my age, tall and attractive in a three-piece navy suit. Immediately, he reaches out his hand and my insides spin. In that moment, I am back at Cat Hall trusting the wrong handsome stranger. Swallowing down my fear, I force myself to shake his hand.

Patricia heaves herself past me and sits down. 'No one tells you how drained you'll feel when you're carrying,' she says.

Looking across at her, I almost ask if she needs a glass of water, then realise she's forgotten my coffee.

'I'm Paul Travis, from the CPS,' says the man.

'Nice to meet you.'

'You know my colleague from Chambers, Joel Smith,' he motions behind me. Joel is stood in the doorway, an iPad in one hand and a cup of coffee in the other. My barrister is a tall man, younger than me, dressed in a well-cut suit, and sporting hair too long and trendy for a card-carrying barrister.

'Everything okay?' he asks as I move aside for him to enter the room.

I nod.

'I read your police statement. You're very brave,' Paul says.

'Not really.' I shift in my seat.

'You were. I'm not sure what I'd have done in that situation,' Joel adds.

Patricia sighs. 'Shall we begin? I'll probably have to pee again in fifteen minutes.'

'Yes, let's start.' Joel sits near me, and I remind myself he's one of the good guys. Deliberately, I make the effort to lean towards him.

'Has the Witness Care Officer been in touch?' Joel asks.

A name bubbles to the surface of my mind, but I can't catch it. 'Yes, but I'm good with everything,' I say with a smile.

'Excellent, now let's get you prepped. First things first, we need to inform the court whether you plan on swearing on the Bible or affirming your testimony yourself. Which is it?' Joel leans towards me for my answer.

The question catches me off guard. Am I supposed to decide here and now whether I believe in God? 'I'm not sure.'

Patricia's impatience saves me the trouble of answering. 'Just put her down as Bible. It's the most common.'

Before I can give the matter any further thought, Paul writes Patricia's answer down. Desperate to take a little bit of control over the conversation, I ask, 'So, how's the case going?'

Joel nods. 'As expected, but your testimony will be crucial.'

I open my mouth to ask for clarification, but Patricia interrupts, 'Don't worry, Fallon, we're going to get Tyler Baker.'

'What about the others?' I ask quickly. 'Are they not all being tried together?'

Moving closer to me, Joel says, 'They both pled guilty. Only Baker pled not guilty to all charges.'

'They... What? No one told me!'

Joel looks over at a red-faced Paul.

'Apologies, we should have informed you,' Paul mutters, still staring at his iPad.

'That would have been nice, because then I'd have reminded you Tyler was the ringleader! He was the one who killed, and hurt, and lured...' My jumper feels as if it's searing my chest. My hand springs to my collar to pull it loose. 'How could this happen? You caught him at the scene with the others.'

'Baker is contradicting your statement. His barrister is claiming he's another victim you're falsely accusing due to hysteria.'

What? No. What? My brain starts to fold in on itself. Would anyone believe him?

Joel rustles some papers. 'Don't worry, Fallon. We know it's just a wild grab by the defence. His barrister Danielle is fast becoming known for them. You know, at first he tried to claim you were part of it all.'

Hot vomit shoots up my throat. I have to turn away to politely swallow it back down.

'Of course, we know you weren't.' Joel smiles, then quickly adds, 'Unless there's something you want to tell us?'

'Tyler is a liar,' I say.

'We believe you,' Paul says. 'But we have sworn statements from James Partridge and Alexander Knowles saying he had nothing to do with the events, which muddies the waters. It's why your testimony will make all the difference.'

Ropey and Streak. Who knew they had such normal names. All the memories I've gone through with Tina, and all the ones I've yet to relive, swarm my mind. Tyler bullied them both. He's a master manipulator. Who else could fall under his sway? The jury?

'Are you all right?' Paul asks.

Slumping in my chair, I'm about to answer when Patricia whines, 'Yeah. I'm just off to pee, again.' Then she heaves herself out the door.

'What about the physical evidence?' I ask.

'We have the knife,' Joel replies.

Images of pooling blood crowd my vision and I have to look away before asking, 'DNA?'

'Tyler Baker's DNA,' Joel says, staring at his notes rather than me, 'and fingerprints were hardly present at all, which is bad for us. We're living in the CSI age. Juries now place an almost unobtainable emphasis on forensics thanks to that ridiculous TV show.'

Holding my breath, I whisper, 'He wore gloves.'

Joel nods. 'Yes, the gloves are in the statement, but there were none found at the scene.' Looking me square in the eye he then admits, 'I'm sorry, this case has now become a he-said she-said.'

How could this happen? Even from prison Tyler has found a way to attack me, my reputation.

Our conversation is ended by a knock on the door. Paul answers it and I hear him apologise for double booking the room. The people outside have been waiting for us to finish, and give me evil looks as I slip past.

Joel walks with me through the station. Once outside, I take a gulp of fresh, cold air.

'I realise this is harrowing,' he says. 'But we can win. Take care, Fallon.'

As I watch him stride up the street, I wish I could have told him everything that happened at Cat Hall; guilt be damned. But there are only two people who know it all: me and Tyler.

-

Opening my front door, I'm greeted with a slobber attack by a happy Harvey. I left him with a new toy this morning, but it's me he's most bothered about. I ruffle his fur, then fetch him some fresh water.

Wanting to shut out the world, I light my scented candles and close all the curtains. As I do, I think about Yvonne34 and the man in the red Audi. I do hope she gets in touch soon.

Seeing I am online, Tina sends me a direct message, *You good?* I type, *yes*, then delete it and send, *no*. She asks if we can talk so I press the button to live chat.

The second Tina's face appears on my screen I blurt, 'Tyler Baker could get away with it.'

'What?'

Harvey barks as if to get in on the conversation. I stroke his head.

'He's claiming he was another victim.' I practically growl the last word. 'He says I'm hysterical and lying about his involvement. And the other two have vouched for him. If he's freed, he could hurt someone else.'

Tina interrupts my worry by holding up her hand. 'Look, I've got time now for a session. Let's carry on with your memory. If you're bullet-proof on the stand, there's no way a jury will side with Tyler.'

I'd earmarked this time today for my other investigation. My stare drifts across to my brother's file. All those victims. Lindsay said she'd find a *science-y* way to get him, but I can't help thinking, if there were one, wouldn't she have employed it by now?

'What are you looking at?' Tina asks.

'Nothing. Yes, let's do another session.'

'Take me back to inside the house.' She looks down at her notes. 'What happened after you and Gayle decided to run?'

Chapter 16

Fallon

They must have heard us talking as Tyler suddenly bounded into the room. I threw my body at him, knocking him down. Then I reached for Gayle's hand to lead her downstairs. She wouldn't take it. Instead, she ran into the en suite and started to pull at the plastic covering her husband's body.

Panicked and deluded, Gayle screamed, 'Vic! Get up!'

It was all the delay Tyler needed to scramble up and propel himself at me. With a dead-eyed stare, he swung his fist, catching me in the stomach. I fell to my knees, clutching my ribs, gasping for air.

In horror, I watched him stalk up to Gayle, then grip her shoulders. Without mercy, he repeatedly slammed her head into the side of the shower door. The glass didn't break, but spider-web cracks crept out from a patch of her blood. As Gayle's hands sprung up automatically to feel her head, Tyler swept her up and over his shoulder. They were gone before I could scramble to my feet.

I hadn't heard steps on the stairs, so I knew they had disappeared into another bedroom. I never saw what they did, but I heard the screams. All the while knowing, too soon, it would be my screams echoing through the half-built house.

Minutes felt like hours. I should have tried to run. But the blow from Tyler had cracked my ribs, and fear was sticking to my every thought. I remember trying to take stock of the situation.

'I'm cold. I'm hurt. I'm in danger,' I whispered to myself.

When Tyler brought in another woman, my first thought was so selfish: at least I'm no longer alone.

–

I gasp at my confession. Tina is kind enough not to catch my eye as I compose myself. After a heavy pause, she asks, 'The other woman was the estate agent, Rosie Howe?'

'Yes.'

'How did she end up in the house?'

I hesitate for a fraction of a second, then reply, 'Tyler kidnapped her from the show home.'

'What happened next?'

–

My second thought was lost in panic as I watched Tyler strike Rosie's face. Bleeding, she fell back against the nearest wall.

'See you real soon, ladies.' Then he was gone.

The second he was out of sight, I shuffled across the floor to Rosie. 'I'm so sorry,' I told her.

She hugged me, then mumbled, 'I was meeting my dad tonight. He'll know something is wrong when I don't turn up. He'll call for help.'

'We can't wait. We have to escape,' I told her.

'They'll catch us. Overpower us. Help will come,' she said.

I wanted to believe her. To think the police would swoop in and save us. But Gayle's screams were no longer coming from the other room.

No one saved her.

–

Tina coughs, derailing my train of thought. 'Let's leave it there for today.'

'No, let's carry on.' My mind is still in the house, and a sticky feeling of adrenaline is coating my limbs, getting me ready to do whatever I need to survive.

Harvey barks several times, and my head snaps towards the front door. I'm not expecting any deliveries today.

'You okay?'

My dog stands still, alert. 'Harvey, come here,' I say, then turn back to Tina. 'Let's continue.'

She shakes her head. 'No. You've remembered more than enough for today.'

Harvey's next barking fit stops my protests. Looking over, I see he's now pacing. As I get up to let him out, Tina says, 'Wait.'

I sit back down.

Tina stares at me, then remembers her training. 'Excellent progress.'

I nod, my throat raw from words I didn't want to say, and my mind impaled by a sharp memory.

'Take a few days off work.'

Days off sound great, but there's no rest for the wicked. 'I've a few appointments today, but I'll cut down after.'

Tina sighs. 'No, I'll cover for you. You need to concentrate on your testimony.'

'Do you think we could lose the case?' I ask.

'I just want you to get some rest.'

Harvey's ears prick and he lets out another massive bark.

'Hey,' I say to him, but he barks again.

'Don't take so much on,' Tina adds. 'Take some time and prepare for our next session. Agreed?'

'Agreed. And thanks for everything.'

'Always on your side, pet.' Tina clicks off.

In the sudden silence, I hear Harvey growl.

Patting my leg, I call his name, but he doesn't move. 'What's got you so riled up?' I ask. I walk over to him, scratch his head, then open the curtains to look out. 'What have you seen, you big gremlin?'

I open my front door, and there, laying on the deck, is a huge bunch of pink and white flowers. Scooping them up, I read the card, *thinking of you*. No signature. Bloody Grant!

I know I should bin the bouquet, but they are just too lovely. Bringing them inside, I arrange the flowers in a vase. I then take a coffee out onto the porch. Wrapped in a blanket, Harvey and I sit together in the star-filled winter night. With the distant sounds of bird calls, I'm lulled into another unfamiliar calm. It's so peaceful, I almost fall asleep. *I don't deserve respite.* Jolting myself from the spell, I gather up my mug and blanket and go back inside.

I undress and put on my favourite pyjamas. As my fingers stretch out across the file ready to pull it towards me, I hear creaking on the porch. Refusing to spend another moment feeling like a victim, I march to the front door and fling it open.

On my rocking chair, where I was sat only moments ago, now sits a man.

Chapter 17

Fallon

'Grant! What are you doing?' As I say this, my mind floods with reasons for his presence. Picking up the most pressing, I ask, 'Is your mum okay?'

'Yeah, yeah. She's doing better.'

'Then why the hell are you here?'

'I'm just checking in. It's not every day your girlfriend has to give evidence in crown court. It's soon, isn't it?' he asks, getting up and unbuttoning his leather jacket to reveal a jumper I bought him five Christmases ago.

'I'm not your girlfriend anymore. And you shouldn't be leaving me flowers.'

My ex's eyes widen. 'I didn't give you flowers.' His eyes flicker to the display behind me. 'Are you seeing someone else?' Stepping forward, he grabs my wrist. Suddenly, Harvey launches himself at Grant, knocking him down and clamping his jaw around one of his flailing arms.

Shocked, I heave my dog back. 'Stop it! Stop!' Harvey drops my ex's arm, then lets me yank him backwards by the collar.

Scrambling up, Grant shouts, 'Fuck sake!'

'Sorry. But you shouldn't be here. You wouldn't believe what I've got to deal with right now.'

'Does your arm feel like it's been ripped off? 'Cause if not, I've got you beat.' Rubbing his bruised forearm, he throws me a boyish grin.

My hand finds Harvey's head and I pat him. 'He thought you were attacking me.'

'Another of Ollie's gifts I suppose?'

'Why else would I have a dog?'

'I did think it was strange. You certainly weren't a dog person when we were together.'

Reluctantly, I nod my agreement. Already, Grant is calming down, and I can see from his exposed forearm that Harvey didn't even break the skin.

'Listen, Fallon. I came round to talk. We made such good progress last time, and I would never mean you any harm, if you can relay that to the hellhound.'

'He was just doing his job,' I say.

'Now it's his job to protect you?'

'Please, I don't have time for this.'

'Are you *her* again?'

'*Her?*'

Grant snorts. 'The woman who doesn't care about anyone else, just what's going on in *her* life.'

If he knew what I had going on in my life, he'd run screaming into the night. But once again, he's poking at my weak spot. 'Come in. Let me look at your arm.'

'Don't do me any favours.'

'Let's not fight.' As I say the words, a sick sense of déjà vu hits me. How many times have I uttered that request to this man?

Getting his way, he smirks and moves to walk inside Poppy Fields.

'Actually,' I say, stopping him mid-step, 'I'm tired, and you should really go.'

'Fine!' Grant knocks into my shoulder as he storms off into the dark.

It's not a good feeling, telling someone to leave, but I'm already fighting two battles, and I don't have the energy for a third.

–

'I have some bad news.'

Anyone facetiming at 7a.m. usually does, but this morning Lindsay looks particularly pale.

'What is it? He couldn't have committed another murder already, could he?'

'No.' She hesitates, guilt written all over her face. 'I did something stupid with your DNA.'

I don't like the sound of that. 'DNA Hooray let you have *my* DNA?'

'No, I stole your coffee mug the other night. Sorry, after that crime scene, I just felt I had to do something more amazeballs than my original idea.'

That's where my mug went. 'What did you do with my DNA?'

'I tried to upload it to the National Database. I thought if it showed up as a familial match to the profile of my killer it might get the police to at least admit there was an investigation to start. Then they would find more evidence connecting the crimes.'

'What a great idea!'

She huffs and the screen fogs for a moment. 'It would have been if Trout-face hadn't caught me before I could. When she realised we didn't have an arrest on the system for your DNA, I was suspended pending an investigation into misuse of police equipment, and breaching data protection.'

My shoulders slump. 'Oh no, Lindsay. Does this mean…'

'I'm benched. I can't run tests or find any more of his crimes. And I can't appear to be investigating anything, I'm in enough trouble.' She shakes her head. 'I'm so…'

'Don't say sorry. You're trying to do the right thing.'

Lindsay looks at something off-camera, then says, 'I have to go. Stay safe.' And before I open my mouth to ask what happens next, she's gone.

My nerves feel vulnerable, like bunting made of razorblades is beating in the wind above them. It's not Lindsay's fault this has happened. She did the best she could. But she is leaving me alone in this. I'm now the only person who knows about my brother, so am the only one who can do something about it. But without Lindsay and her lab, what can I do to get the police to take him seriously?

Ever since I moved into Foxglove Lodges, the sounds nature around me have helped calm my nerves. Maybe if I can stop my mind from whirring long enough, I can rally my courage and figure out what to do next.

When I stop at the lake, I spot ducks playfully swimming in circles, quacking and squawking, making me glad I left Harvey sleeping by the fire. None of them know what he did to their friend. Only if he were out here would they let worry and panic interrupt their day. I should take a leaf out of the ducks' book. Tired of feeling out of control and powerless, I renew my vow to find out which of my brothers is the serial killer, whatever it takes.

Suddenly, the ducks flap wildly and in unison shoot into the air. As they clear the lake, the reflection in the water ripples with a man-shaped blur.

Chapter 18

Fallon

'Fallon, Are you okay?'

My surprise subsides as I recognise Joel. 'Shit!' I whisper. Then louder I say, 'Yes, but you shouldn't sneak up on people.'

'Sorry. I just came round to apologise again that you weren't told about Tyler's defence.'

'Thanks, but that's the least of my problems right now.'

Shocked, he says, 'Really? You know you can talk to me.'

My head hurts. I promised Lindsay I wouldn't tell anyone, but I no longer have her help. And I don't want to be alone in this mess. She was gung ho on science catching my brother, but Joel might be able to help in another, more legal way. I don't know him well, but I have to trust someone, and I know he won't endanger the Cat Hall case. 'Can we talk inside?'

Nodding, he follows me into the lodge. 'Nice place. It's a shame about the colour of the decking. It looks like a giant…'

'I'm repainting in the summer,' I say.

Once we're in Poppy Fields, Harvey eyes my visitor with disdain. I fetch a chew treat for Joel to give him, which my dog merrily swallows in two bites, warming him to my barrister.

Joel sheds his coat and sits down.

'I think my brother is a serial killer.' I deliberately rush the words out of my mouth, so there'll be no taking them back.

'What?!'

'I can explain.'

It takes half an hour to painfully relay everything that's happened, from finding out about my adoption, to Lindsay contacting me, to what we have on my brother. I sound like a blithering idiot, upchucking the last few days' events like they're germs I need out of my body. When I'm done, Joel is silent. I can practically see the gears turning in his head as he processes the information.

Eventually, he asks, 'How many victims?'

I pass him the file. 'A lot.'

He pushes the folder back as if it were a spoiled plate of meat. 'I can't get involved with this, Fallon.'

'But people are dying.'

'What about Dr Hawk?'

'I don't want her involved.'

'But it's okay to dump it on me? Someone you've known barely a year?' He swears under his breath.

'I'm sorry. I really didn't know who to turn to. I thought you could help me with the legal issues in all this. Please.' As I hear the manipulative words coming out of my mouth, I cringe.

He doesn't speak. Instead, he pulls out his mobile.

I have visions of him summoning the police to take me away. 'Wait!' I say.

When Joel looks up, his face is flushed with anger. 'What do you expect me to do here? I can't go rogue. And I can't see why the police shouldn't handle this.'

Reaching out, I slip the phone out his grip.

'Please, Joel, my friend tried raising this with the police already. But they just dismissed her, saying she could have cross-contaminated evidence in the lab.'

'We'll get the DNA independently tested then. Prove she didn't make a mistake.'

Sighing, I admit, 'It was touch DNA. She used it all up testing it.'

With his head in his hands, Joel groans. 'Fallon, if there's no evidence left, don't you know what that is?' He points at the file. 'It's a bomb waiting to blow up your and anyone else's reputations who touch it.'

'But we still have the killer's DNA profile which links the crimes, regardless of their randomness.'

'Random? There's no MO?' Suddenly Joel is flipping through the file, studying it. 'Hang on, I can see at least three here are solved. One was my old region. Are you saying we put innocent men behind bars?'

'I believe so.'

I recognise the look passing over Joel's face – guilt. He's not the person he thought he was. His white cloak of righteousness has greyed; bad things have happened on his watch.

'My bosses are not going to want to revisit their wins. No wonder your friend didn't get anywhere with the police. The pressure to solve a serial case would be huge, and without an arrest it would be a career-ender for anyone involved.'

'In the past, what made the police accept other serial theories and start investigations?' I ask.

Joel looks away. 'I hate to say it, but it's usually the press who break serial stories and publicly shame the police into starting their investigation.'

'That's a great idea! I've got a list of reporters who've been trying to get me on the record for Cat Hall. I'll call them.'

'No! You can't. It'll come out that you're the source. Have you any idea what that kind of publicity will do to the Cat Hall case? With Tyler's defence playing the he-said-she-said game, they'll use it to say you're the girl who cried serial killer. Even after the trial, it could be enough to mount an appeal.'

Tyler could go free. And there would be no guarantee my brother would be caught. Shit. 'I understand, but please, you have to help me right the wrongs.'

Joel stares at me, then drops his gaze. 'All right. Let's think about this rationally. Do you know his name?'

'Sort of. I have four brothers and I know all their names.' I show him my list.

'Have you met them yet?'

I look down at my hands folded in my lap. 'I'm trying to make contact.'

'This is a lot, Fallon. The court case and hunting a serial killer. It's too much.'

'That's why I can't do it alone. Will you help?' I ask.

Grimacing, he finally nods. 'Okay. What's the plan?'

'If I get their DNA, could you get it tested against the DNA profile Lindsay created?'

Almost laughing, he admits, 'Yes, but with a case hinging just on DNA, any halfway decent defence barrister would ask for the crime scene evidence to be independently tested.'

'Which of course we can no longer do.'

Joel inches forward on his seat. 'DNA is helpful, but it isn't the only evidence that can be presented for an arrest and successful conviction. With a warrant, we can collect corroborating evidence such as mobile phone records to show whichever brother was in the area. In the meantime, find a way of narrowing down your brothers to pinpoint the suspect. Check out their alibis for the murders.'

'I've also psychologically profiled the killer. I can compare and contrast as I meet each one.'

Joel's smile is weak, but there. 'I know a DI who's not afraid to break a few rules for the greater good. If we get her as much evidence as possible, she'll find a way to start an investigation.'

When Joel leaves, I go to text Lindsay the good news about his help, but stop. Will she be mad that I told someone else? I promised to keep this between us. I didn't mean to betray her trust, but it's like she said – lives are in danger.

While staring at my mobile, I realise Siobhan still hasn't returned my call. When I left the message, did I say it was important? A matter of life or death? No, but after giving me up to a woman she just met in a hospital, she does owe me a call back. If I were counselling a mother and daughter in this position, what would I tell them? Probably that the mum should get off her bum and communicate with her long-lost daughter! Shit. I grab my mobile and call again.

One ring – all I need from her is an introduction to my brothers.

Two rings – she owes me that much.

Three rings – if she ditches my call I'm going round her house.

Four rings – someone picks up.

Chapter 19

Fallon

'Yes?' a man answers.

Surprised, I squeak out, 'Is Siobhan there?'

The man sighs into the receiver. 'She's eating dinner at the mo. May I take a message?'

'I'll try her again later.'

'Fallon?'

'Yes?'

The man chuckles. 'Well, it's good to finally hear your voice.'

Is this one of my brothers? Or, my stomach flips when the thought occurs to me, am I talking to my dad? In all the craziness, I hadn't even considered he could be in the mix, or even how much he knew of Siobhan's baby swap. If my dad knew nothing, he could be an innocent party coming to terms with the shock, just like me. 'It's good to hear yours,' I say.

'You've no idea who I am, do you?'

I'm about to say *Dad* when he laughs again.

'I'm your brother.'

I am on the phone with a potential murderer. And not one safely locked behind bars: a free-range serial killer.

'Oh, wow! Wonderful,' I reply too quickly. 'What's your name?'

'I'm Simon.'

'Mum, I mean *my* mum, mentioned Siobhan had four boys when she gave birth to me.'

'Yeah,' he says, the chuckle still audible in his voice. 'Mum and Dad were pretty active.'

'Is Mr Kaplan around?' I ask.

'Nah, he passed away.'

'I'm sorry.'

'Yeah, he was a great guy.'

Not knowing how to respond, I stay quiet, and an awkward silence stretches between us. Simon breaks it first. 'Yeah. So, this is weird. I mean, I'll be honest, the news of you hasn't gone down too well with the family.'

I say, 'I'm sorry,' before I can stop myself.

'Not your fault. It was just a bit of a shock, you know? And I can't speak for my bros, but I'd really like to get to know you. How about we meet up? You could come over to mine?'

There is a one-in-four chance that Simon is a serial killer. I remind myself that this is the reason I called, to meet my brothers and start a process of elimination, to collect evidence for Joel's DI. But that doesn't mean I should knowingly put myself in dangerous situations. I won't make the mistake again of meeting a strange man alone. 'Sounds great, but I wouldn't want to put you out. How about the Blue Sky Coffee Room in town? Tomorrow at eleven?'

'Perfect. See you there.'

Putting my mobile down, I realise that I've just arranged coffee with a potential murderer. At least this time I'm going in eyes open. I'm no longer the naive idiot from Cat Hall.

Curling up with Harvey on the sofa, I try to plot out my interview with Simon: what I need to ask, what I need to observe, what I need to do if he suddenly produces a knife and chases me screaming into the street. No, there's not a reason in the world he would suspect I know about him, if indeed he even is the killer. And it's only a one-in-four chance he is. Grabbing Tina's books, I take notes on the traits to look for and questions to ask. I can do this.

-

The Blue Sky Coffee Room sits in the centre of town. In the summer, they open their windows wide like translucent butterfly wings. But with it being winter, today the windows are shut. To make up for it, they have painted glittering snowflakes across the glass which, although beautiful, are stopping me from seeing who approaches the cafe. Each man who enters, I have to make a quick judgement on as to whether or not we're related. When a bulky man of the right age walks in, I catch his eye. He looks confused, but gives me a nervous smile before moving over to greet a woman near the bar.

'Fallon?'

Suddenly, a man is looming over me. Extending a hand, I get up to greet him, but he pushes it away with a grin and pulls me into a tight hug.

'Nice to meet you, Simon' I say, my words smothered by his shoulder.

'Who's Simon?' he says, pulling back slightly to give me a quizzical look.

I stagger backwards, my eyes scanning for the nearest exit.

'I'm just playing with you. Of course I'm Simon. But I got you, didn't I?'

'Yeah, you got me.' The breath I was holding comes out as a whistle, and I manage to choke out a small laugh for his benefit. Then a thought hits me – being in a public space with crowds was supposed to protect me, but when I panicked, not a single person noticed.

'Sorry, I have a wicked sense of humour. We all do. Bet you do too,' Simon says.

'Not that I've noticed,' I mutter.

'Want another drink?' he asks, spying my empty coffee mug. 'Same again?'

More caffeine probably isn't a good idea. 'Decaf latte, please.'

'You got it.' Simon then strides off to join the queue by the bar. As he waits, I examine his body language and posture. My new brother is broad and tall, but has a casual slouch in his shoulders, quietly confident. He's second in the queue just after a young woman, and I watch as a man tries to push in front of her. Simon only has to glare at him for the defeated pusher to fall back in line. When it's his turn, he doesn't moan about the wait, but smiles when he gives the server our order. He chats to her as she makes the coffees, their conversation light and casual. As Simon pays, I wonder if the man I'm watching could be capable of so much death.

'Decaf latte,' Simon declares as he places the steaming drink in front of me. He then sits opposite with a mug of tea. As he gently picks up the cup in his large hands, he says, 'I'm not much of a coffee drinker.'

'Are you all tea drinkers?' *Dumb question.*

'Mostly. It was the only thing Mum could make. She can't cook for shit. It doesn't stop her inviting everyone and their dogs round for dinner though. She's big on family.' Realising what he's said, he blushes and looks away.

As casually as I can, I ask, 'So, tell me about yourself?'

Simon shrugs. 'Not much to say. The family own a garage, we all work there. I'm the big boss though. I practically live in that office.'

'Married? Am I an auntie?'

'Nah, not yet. But Stefan got married last year.'

'What are my other brothers like?' As the question escapes my lips, I realise how much I don't want the killer to be Simon. Although a bit imposing, he seems nice. His eyes, hair colour, even his skin tone are the same as mine. If I'd been born a boy, I'd have looked like him.

'Dare I say we're all pretty decent guys. Well, except Garry. He can be a bit of a weasel. I'm sure the first words out of his mouth when he meets you will be to ask for money.'

I laugh at his joke, but he doesn't.

'You only just found out about us then?' he asks.

'Yeah, Ollie, my little brother, did this DNA Hooray thing.'

'Ollie? Don't tell me I have another brother! It wouldn't surprise me.'

'Oh, no, he's a Hurley.'

'Well, not everyone can be a Kapper.' He shrugs.

'A Kapper?'

'Us Kaplans.'

I'm a Kapper, part of an *us*. That's kind of nice. I'm about to comment when he rustles in his pocket and brings out a folded piece of paper.

'Was this you?' Simon asks, offering it me.

I know what it is: one of the many stories featured in the papers last year. The headline reads, *Attack at New Cat*

Hall Estate. There's a photo of me in it, one stolen from the Hawk website. I'm dressed in a suit and smiling. I forced myself to memorise all those articles, so I know what this one says. 'Yes, it's me.'

Simon purses his lips. 'Sam Googled you. We were fascinated to have a little sister, but then we found these stories.'

'You might not want me as a Kapper then,' I mutter.

'Are you joking? You did the right thing. You had to run.'

'That's not what everyone else thinks,' I say, waving the printed article.

'Well, they can all go fuck themselves. You were brave.'

I take the compliment, as I try to swallow down my rising nausea. 'Thanks.'

'We Kappers stick together.' He smiles at me again then drains his hot tea as if his throat is lined with asbestos.

Even though I know my relationship, or lack thereof, with my estranged bio-mother is not the nearest fire, I can't help but ask, 'Even Siobhan?'

Simon strokes the dark stubble lining his jaw. 'The Kapper siblings stick together,' he says, 'but loyalty isn't part of Mum's branch of our family tree.'

I'm about to press for more details when Simon takes the article back and changes the subject, 'So, they going down?'

'Pardon?'

'The fuckers who did it to you – they're going away for life, right?'

'Two are. But one, the ringleader, he's lying about what happened.'

'Are you taking the stand?'

'I'm the last prosecution witness.'

Simon lets out a long sigh from between his teeth. 'Intense. I've never been to court before. Can I sit in the gallery? It might be nice for you to have a friendly face to look at if you get nervous.'

It's a lovely offer, to have the support, but looking out at a potential serial killer isn't going to ease the situation. 'Best not. I really have to concentrate when I'm up there. I can't let Tyler get off. Let's change the subject. Tell me more about you.'

Simon chuckles. 'You are a wily one. Look, I've no doubt he'll be sent down,' he says, 'but if he does pull one out of the bag… Well, there are other ways of dealing with him.'

I balk at his declaration. Violence is never the answer, but it's usually the first impulse for killers. I'm about to clarify Simon's thoughts when I remember Ollie saying almost the same thing after Cat Hall.

With limited time, I manage to steer the conversation back to my other brothers. We talk for over an hour. I learn Simon is the eldest and not currently in a relationship, though he's really into online dating and checks his phone a few times during our coffee. Newlywed Stefan is next, then Sam, who is a mature student at university. Garry, the youngest, does odd jobs from car repairs to looking after the garage's website. They all sound normal and busy, and every one of them has some role to play at the family business. While we talk, I pretend to be checking my phone too, but secretly I'm writing notes.

After we've drained our second round of drinks, we swap mobile numbers and Simon walks me to my car. When he hugs me again, I'm ready for it, so relax a little into his grip. Upon letting me go he tells me to call him

Si – 'everyone does'. I almost say to call me Fal but stop myself at the last moment. Only Ollie calls me that.

Before leaving, he hesitates.

'Si?'

Hands up, he says, 'Like I said, Mum's bombshell about you hasn't landed the same with all of us.'

'Surely your mum expected it to explode at some point?'

Cocking his head, Si nods. 'Fair point. And to be honest, I've not really spoken to her about it to get her side, but hey, I've always wanted a sister. I'm old enough to remember the funeral for…'

'The Hurley baby,' I offer, the little overgrown grave springing into my mind's eye.

'Yeah. It's going to be a hard road to navigate to bring the family back together, but hopefully not an impossible one, what with you being a psychologist and all.'

'I'd love to meet all my brothers and at least start the conversation,' I say too quickly.

'Cool. Hey, we're having a birthday party for one of the guys at work. Why don't you pop along? Everyone will be there and I'll introduce you round.'

A party could be a perfect, very public way of quickly interrogating as many brothers as I can. 'Great.'

'Sorted then! I'm due in work now, but I'll text you details later.'

–

Back at home, elated with how I got through meeting Si without vomiting or bolting, I text Joel to let him know what's going on. He calls me instantly.

'Meeting them all at a party sounds ideal. If you can find out dates and alibis for the murders, then we can narrow down four to one. Couple that with a compelling profile and a splash of DNA, and my DI can take it from there.'

Taking a deep breath, I say, 'Sounds like a plan.'

'Good, let's have a drink on Friday and we can discuss your findings. Meet me at the Crown Court first. It would be good for you to get a feel for the building before you take the stand.'

I agree and hang up.

People are dead, so it's selfish of me to look forward to having my life back. I'm not even sure I deserve it. But I could be just one social gathering away from putting a killer behind bars, and one testimony away from doing the same to another. A strange sense of calm finds me. I should be curled in a ball on the sofa, eternally in PJs rocking back and forth as I eat apple sauce laced with sedatives, but I'm not. I feel more in control now I can do, and am actively doing, something. If all goes well at the party, I can simply pass on my findings to the police, leaving everyone's careers intact.

My stomach rumbles, making me realise food shopping has been way down my to-do list recently. So, I slip into my car, crank up the music, and drive to the nearest supermarket.

Without a list, shopping takes longer than planned. Comparing steaks, choosing dessert, picking up treats for Harvey. In the safety of the mundane, it's easy to relax. I almost fall asleep waiting in line at the deli counter. As I'm queueing up at the till, my phone beeps with a message from Si: *Your car sounded rough. Want me to look at it?*

I didn't notice anything weird with my car driving here, although the music was so loud I wouldn't have heard a brass band playing in the backseat. My first instinct is to decline his offer, but Si is my ticket to three other brothers; I don't want to upset him. I reply, *great, thank you* and add a smiley emoji. He says he'll pick it up from my house. At this, I hesitate. Do I trust Si enough to give him my address? No. I tell him I'll drop it round to his garage instead.

As I'm loading groceries into the car, a cool breeze tickles my hair and, for the first time in a long time, I take a moment to feel the freshness of the winter air on my skin.

'I'm warm. I'm healthy. I'm safe.'

Suddenly, the wind whips at me, lifting the side of my jacket. I imagine I'm wearing it; my coat from Cat Hall. The grey woollen reminder that, just when you think you're in control, something or someone comes along to prove you're not. Mentally, I shut the cupboard door, zip up my jacket, and climb into my car.

On the drive home, I turn off my music to listen to the engine. It doesn't sound different. Maybe Si is just being extra cautious? Or maybe it's an elaborate trap, to lure me somewhere remote and... No, my killer brother has no clue I'm on to him.

As I pull up to Poppy Fields, I see Ollie's car outside. Did we have plans today? Opening the door, I tease, 'Using your key so soon?'

But Ollie doesn't answer me. He's sitting at my dining room table, a brandy in one hand and the big brown file of my bio-brother's murders in the other.

Chapter 20

Fallon

'What the fuck is this?' he asks, then downs the rest of his drink.

'A case I'm consulting on.' Not a total lie.

'You're a therapist, not a criminologist, Fal. And I'm not an idiot.'

When I snatch the file away from him, some of the photos slip free and flutter to the floor. Quick as I can, I gather up the horror show and shove it out of sight. 'Tina asked me to.' Oh, that's a proper lie. Fortunately, Ollie rarely speaks to my boss so it should be a safe lie, for now.

'There's some really scary shit in there. Why would she want you to see this kind of thing after what happened to you? Especially when you're days off taking the stand.' He gets up and refills his glass, then pours a second and offers it to me. 'We agreed you'd only concentrate on Cat Hall.'

Shaking my head, I say, 'I wish I didn't need to do it, but it's important.' Then I add, 'and time-sensitive.'

Putting his hand up, he says, 'You can't save the world, Fal. And this shit,' he points at the file, 'isn't down to you. Tina is the criminologist.'

Huffing I say, 'If I'd have known you were coming round, I would have tidied it away.'

Finishing the brandy in one gulp, he sits with a thud. 'I didn't know I needed an invitation to see you. I'm still your brother, aren't I?'

I reach out to him, but he jerks back. 'Of course you're my brother. And Mum is still *our* mum.'

'Urgh, I don't want to talk about *she* of the massive lie.'

'It was an omission of truth rather than a lie,' I admit.

'Forget it. I'll just go.'

I can tell from his snappy tone that my brother has drunk too much to drive. 'No, stay. I could use the company. And you came here for a reason. Let's talk.' I walk over to the kitchen, pull out the chips from the supermarket bag, then slide them on a tray into the oven. I then salt a couple of steaks.

Once the meal is cooked, Ollie opens a bottle of wine, then sits down.

'What's the Macdonald triad?' he asks.

He really did get some serious time with my brother's file if he managed to read all my profile notes too. 'It's the three traits of a killer. Tina included it in her book.'

'What like burger, milkshake and fries,' he laughs.

Bad jokes are a good sign. Ollie has calmed down.

'Not that kind of McDonald's. The signs are wetting the bed into teens, setting fires and torturing animals.'

'Well, that's useless. Who's going to admit to any of that? Did Tyler Baker introduce himself as a fire-starting, animal-killing, bed-wetter?'

I roll my eyes. 'Most psychopaths can pretend to fit in. They develop a rudimentary type of charm.'

'Probably why his victims let him in,' he says, eyeing up the folder.

Grabbing it before he can, I tuck it out of sight, into a drawer. 'Yes, the killer doesn't outwardly appear dangerous.'

Scoffing, Ollie drains his glass of wine. 'What does that mean? The man in the dirty mac isn't how real monsters look. We don't live in a film where characters are gifted with a healthy dollop of foreshadowing. I'm betting most criminals fly under the radar presenting as normal.'

Knowing from experience that some of my 'normal' clients have the darkest pasts and motives, I nod. 'Of course I know that,' I mutter.

Not long after dinner, Ollie's shoulders start to slump, so, like he's a child, I send him to bed in my guest room.

Even though someone else is in the lodge, I still can't sleep and, deciding there's no point in wasting time just lying there, I grab a glass of milk and check my emails. There's something from Lindsay. She tells me that, although she's suspended pending review, she's managed to send me the case file of the most recent murder. Without thinking, I open the attachment and am presented with an array of horrific images.

A middle-aged woman in a herringbone suit is sprawled on her bathroom floor, her face tilted to the side. There is so much blood smeared over the walls, it blends into the room like a design feature. Just as I'm about to click off and read the report, I see something odd – a bloody sports jacket. Why would it be in the bathroom? Expanding out the image, the pixels take a moment to unblur and realign themselves. When they do, I recognise the victim – Yvonne. Can it be?

I load up the copy of our chat to compare it to the details in the file. It has to be her. The woman I spoke to just days before is now dead. She reached out to me for help, and I failed her. She has been murdered by my own flesh and blood. How much pain did he cause her? If it were half as much as I felt at Tyler's hands… Without thought, my hand flies out and I throw my glass against the wall. My dog barks and bounds up to me. Milk and sharp shards of glass are everywhere.

'Well, that didn't help, did it?' I sarcastically say to Harvey.

Grabbing a sponge to clean up the mess, I notice red dots in the stains. I cut myself. A short but deep slice sits in the palm of my hand. For a moment I watch my blood slowly weep out, dripping down my skin. I close my eyes and I'm back at Cat Hall. Pain. Fears colliding in my brain. Adrenaline feasting on my thoughts. Her desperate stare holding mine for what feels like eternity.

'Fal?'

I open my eyes and see Ollie next to me. A towel in his hand to press against the cut.

'Sorry. So sorry,' I mutter.

'Accidents happen,' he says.

Nodding, I smile at him. He doesn't know I wasn't talking about the glass.

-

Ollie has to be in the office by seven, so leaves early with toast hanging from his mouth. He yells, 'Text me later,' before I hear his car screech out from the back of the lodge.

Si has already texted the details for the party. My stomach is in turmoil. Without question, I will be the same room as a serial killer tonight. Although, looking back over my client file for Yvonne, maybe I don't have to be… The man in the red Audi. He could be my brother, the killer.

I ring Joel and tell him about Lindsay's discovery, and that Yvonne contacted Hawk before her murder. I explain how I advised her to tell the police about a man loitering on her street. If the police spoke to the red Audi driver, then they will have all his details, and can question him about Yvonne's murder.

Within minutes though, my plan is thwarted. Joel makes a quick call to his DI friend and learns the police were never contacted. Yvonne didn't listen to her gut, or to me. Cinderella still has to go to the murder ball.

Dressed in jeans and a sparkly top, I take the time to curl my hair and apply make-up. Not trusting myself to drive, even after just one drink, I take a taxi. The driver pulls up at the pub and although I reach for the handle, I can't seem to bring myself to open the car door.

What the hell am I doing?

I can't track down a serial killer. Ollie is right. I'm a therapist, not some flash criminologist with a police badge. And only *one* of my brothers is a killer. The others are innocent, and yet I'm jeopardising my chances of having a good relationship with them by meeting them for the first time armed with a series of harsh questions and even harsher accusations. Everything they do and say tonight will be filtered through my suspicions.

'You getting out?' the driver asks between taps on his mobile.

Am I getting out? Yes! I'm only here to ask questions, that's it. I'm not going to try for a citizen's arrest or challenge him to a street fight. This is purely a reconnaissance mission – nothing more.

After reaching for the handle again, I pay the driver and stride into the party.

The pub is one of the oldest in town. An odd mix of style and dilapidation, the brass fittings are dull and the red velvet seats are threadbare. The bar is made of thick wood stained with a hundred sticky rings, above which are balloons and a banner which reads: *Happy 40th, Miles*. I spot Si. Waving at me, he walks over.

'Fallon, glad you came! Don't worry, Mum's not here,' he says.

It hadn't even crossed my mind how awkward it would have been if she were. Have I really thought this through?

'You okay?' he asks.

'Yeah, course.' I look around the room. 'So, who's the birthday boy? I'll buy him a drink.'

'Over there talking with the other guys from the garage.' He points at a group of laughing, tall, well-built men. 'He's a beer man, like all of us.'

Grateful for the extra time to think through tonight's plan of attack, I queue for a pint and a brandy for me. My killer brother is in this room, breathing the same air as me, drinking from the same glasses, maybe even looking at me right now. Just my luck, I'm served before I can even count my thoughts, let alone untangle them. With unsteady hands, I grab the drinks and turn to see Si standing behind me.

'Let me help,' he offers, then carries the pint over to the group, where he presents it to a man while declaring proudly 'A present from my new sister.'

As I approach, all the men stop talking, but their mouths remain open.

'Thanks,' says the one who takes the beer. That has to be Miles.

'Happy birthday,' I say.

After a long gulp, he replies, 'Nice to meet you.'

What. Am. I. Doing? It's one thing to profile a killer on the page, another entirely to do it within stabbing distance. *Pull yourself together, Fallon.*

'You all right?' he asks.

A nervous giggle escapes before I can stop it, and I follow it with, 'You don't look forty.' Each word spoken an octave higher than the last.

Even though I meant it as a compliment, everyone laughs.

'Maybe this is too much. I can take you home if you like?' Si asks.

'No. I'm just a bit overwhelmed. Last week I only had one brother and one mum.'

'That's enough to turn most people into gibbering wrecks,' says one of the men.

'Meet Freddy,' Si says motioning to the man who just spoke. He then points to each of the other men in turn. 'And that's Mikey and Jason.'

All the mechanics surrounding me are good looking, muscular men with dark hair. It makes me wonder whether Si's garage has the side hustle of a Chippendales troupe.

'Sam mentioned you the other day,' Jason tells me with a smile.

Casually, I ask, 'Where is he?'

'He's messing with the food in the function room,' Freddy answers, pointing in the direction of a door behind the pool table.

Si is busy making old man jokes with Miles, so I decide to try for Sam, but as I move through the crowd, a woman cuts me off. She's tall and sporty looking with shiny red hair in a sharp bob cut to her chin.

'Fallon, right?' she asks.

'Yes,' I reply.

'I'm Susie, Stefan's wife.'

As we shake hands, I scan around us for a man who could be Stefan.

'He's here,' she says, then adds tentatively, 'but doesn't want to meet you. Sorry.'

'Why not?' I ask.

'He didn't take the news of a new sibling very well. He needs a bit more time to get his head around it.' She pauses to take a sip of drink. 'And Siobhan didn't exactly help. You know she told him about you over text.'

'That's bad,' I whisper.

'That's your mum for you. I'm actually surprised she's not here to cause a scene.'

Siobhan sounds like a treat. 'So, Stefan doesn't want to meet me, eh?'

'Nope. I thought I'd warn you before you tried to corner him or something. Si said you were real curious about the Kaplans.'

Susie is looking at me intensely and as I return her gaze, it occurs to me that she could be an ideal, and safe, interview subject. After all, she's definitely not the killer. 'Can I buy you a drink?'

Nodding, she leads me to a quiet table. Wobbling a little, I can see she's had too much already, so I order her a lemonade, which she sips through a smile.

We chit-chat a little, and when she hears I'm a psychologist, she opens up about her marriage. This conversational kneejerk is the psychological equivalent of medical doctors who, once their profession is announced, are exposed to a parade of suspicious moles. Normally, at this stage with a stranger, I'd back away, but not tonight. Instead, I give Susie room to admit her worries: Stefan's late nights, long trips with his cricket team, distant moods and easy agitation into arguments are causing her concern.

'Lately, he barely acknowledges I exist. I think he's having an affair,' she confesses.

It's a possibility, but he also has a one-in-four chance of being a serial killer, and everything she's telling me fits the profile. Murders all over the country would explain the trips and, remembering Tina's book, some serials get trapped in a pattern of craving the thrill of the kill, not getting the fix they imagined; depression then sets in, which would explain the mood swings.

'I shouldn't have said anything.' Susie shakes her head and drops her gaze to the bubbles in her drink.

'You're my sister-in-law. I'm here for you. You can talk to me anytime you want. In fact' – I retrieve my phone – 'let's swap numbers.'

'Thanks.'

After she inputs my number, she accesses her photo library to show me an image. 'This was us on our wedding day. He looks happy, doesn't he?'

'Yes, he does,' I reply, and mean it. His smile is broad and showing just enough teeth. Dressed in a black tuxedo with a red bow tie and matching cummerbund, he has the same dark hair and eyes as all the Kaplans. With tender comfort, he rests his arm around the waist of her satin wedding dress. In his other hand is a half-drunk champagne flute. Pure happiness caught with a click. However, a number of killers have appeared to be happily married. The photo isn't evidence of Stefan's innocent, it's simply a buoy for a worried wife to cling to during a storm in her marriage.

Just as I'm about to ask another question, a booming voice interrupts us.

'There she is!'

Two men flank our table. One, the shorter of the two, holds a half-empty pint glass in each hand.

Susie rolls her eyes and gets up. 'I'd best find Stefan. Catch you later.'

'Tatty-bye, Susie Q. Nice of you to stop by,' says one of the men sarcastically.

Feeling vulnerable sitting when the men are standing, I rise.

'I'm Sam,' says the taller of the men. 'Sorry about him.' He nods to his companion. 'Garry's a prick.'

'Thanks for the introduction, bro.' Garry nudges Sam, and manages to spill beer down his baggy tracksuit. Putting the glasses on the table, he then runs his hands over his dark, slicked-back hair.

Sam has a darker skin tone than Garry. He wears a designer jumper and has his chin-length hair scooped back into a neat ponytail. His eyes are softer, more hazel than brown.

'Great to meet you both,' I say with as much excitement as I can muster.

'You're not what I expected,' Sam remarks offhand.

'Should I take that as a compliment?' I ask, instantly regretting my tone. For all I know, Sam is the man who left Yvonne sprawled in blood in her bathroom.

Garry laughs, then punches Sam's arm. 'Told you she'd be a Kapper through and through.'

An odd look passes across Sam's face, then he mutters, 'Yeah, you told me.'

Awkward tension stretches between the brothers. I blurt, 'So, you both work with Si and Stefan at the garage?'

Huffing, Garry just stares at me.

Sam pipes up. 'Family business. We all help out. I enjoy it, but it's not what I want to do with my time. And time is precious. None of us know when it'll run out.'

'Guess we don't,' I say.

'I'm gonna get in a round,' Garry says. 'Baby sis, you got a card I can use? You're drinking brandy, right?'

Looking down, I note Garry already has two half-drunk pints. And I'm certainly not giving him my bank card. 'No, sorry.'

'Christ sake, here.' Sam hands him his Visa.

'Be right back,' Garry says. Taking the card, he then wanders off to join the queue at the bar. As he does, I notice him limping a little.

'Pay no attention to him. Like I said, he's a prick.' Sam gives me a wide, reassuring smile. 'You know, it's been a lot for us to wrap our heads round these last couple of days. I can't imagine what it must be like for you, discovering there's four of us.'

'It's pretty overwhelming.' I admit.

Raucous laughter then erupts from the mechanics and Sam moves closer to me. 'I'd love to get to know you better. Could we meet, just the two of us?'

'Sure, let's check diaries,' I reply, trying to act as if he were a colleague asking me to lunch rather than a potential killer seeking to get me alone.

'Good stuff. There's a lot we need to talk about.'

A shiver runs down my spine. *We*, just like Tyler used. Tina said it's a technique to create a quick bond with someone you want to trust you. And the killer is charming, having talked his way inside his victim's home – their safe place.

'Sure, I'd like that,' I robotically push out.

Lightning fast, he sweeps my phone from my hand and inputs his number, then rings his own phone. 'There, I'm forever in your contacts.' He beams a smile at me. 'No getting rid of me now.'

If my suspicious mind wasn't on overdrive, I'd easily be sucked in by Sam's charm. Turning away, I gulp down the rest of my brandy. 'Awesome,' I say. I can do this. God knows how many potential victims are counting on me.

After settling into a conversation, I try to provoke Sam to reveal something useful. It's not as if I can just blurt out all the murder dates and demand to know his whereabouts on each one, so instead I carefully probe him as I would a client who has come to me with a dark secret he wants to bring into the light. A nudge here, a reflection there. Has he always lived around here? How long has he worked for the family business? I listen and subtly take notes on my phone.

Through the night, I bounce between Si, Sam, and Garry, hoping to glean something, anything, that might profile their personalities. Out of all of them, Garry displays more than a few psychopathic tendencies, including a bad temper and impulsiveness. I watch as he goads Jason into a pushing match, which is broken up by Miles, who Garry then tries to punch. Fortunately, the birthday boy easily avoids further confrontation by buying a round of drinks.

Another hour ticks by and I feel as if I've stumbled into a reality show, *The Real Mechanics of Kaplan Motors*. My brothers and the lads they work with exhibit the dynamics of a tribe. Laughing and joking and continually addressing each other as *bro*, and as they get drunker, *dude*. It's surprising any one of them could hide such a bloody secret from the rest.

Looking at my notes, I realise I've learnt little of real value. None of the three brothers I've met have let slip anything which I can connect to any murders, so my attention begins to turn to the one brother who isn't partying, but lurking. I take a turn around the pub to see if I can spot Stefan, but there's too many men I don't recognise. Susie said he didn't want to meet me, but surely he'd want to hang with his 'bros'. Is he staying apart from his tribe tonight for another reason?

Cutting through my thoughts, Garry loudly challenges Freddy to a game of pool by shouting, 'Dude, you scared or something?'

Seeing the look on my face, Jason steps over to me. 'You need to watch Garry. He can be a calculating shit.'

'Why do you say that?'

'That prick's nowhere near as drunk as he's making out.'

'He's hustling his friend?'

Jason sneers. 'Not exactly subtle is it. But that's Garry all over. But hey, Freddy's no angel either.'

I go to ask another question, but he's already sauntering with purpose towards a woman at the bar. I turn back to look at Garry and, now I know what to look for, see that Jason is right. Garry might be slurring his words and stumbling into people, but his eyes are sharp.

Even when I'm not with him, I catch Si watching me. It's hard to tell whether he's being overprotective or studying me. Mostly he helps Miles drink his birthday shots and laughs loudly at jokes I don't understand.

Of all of them, Sam gravitates towards me most. As the party draws to a close, he asks about Cat Hall and how the case is going. Trying to dodge his questions, I counter with, 'How'd you know so much about the case?'

Shrugging, he points to his head. 'Up here for thinking' – then wiggles his fingers – 'down there for Googling.'

Finally getting a joke, I can't help but giggle. As I do, I glance down and notice something strapped to Sam's belt. Unconsciously, I lean forward to see it: a sheathed knife. Not hidden, but not obvious. He catches the look on my face.

'I fish and hunt.'

'Oh, interesting.' It's not interesting, it's worrying. Who brings a knife to a birthday party? Is it even legal? I start to edge back from Sam, slowly with small movements so he doesn't notice my discomfort.

'Are you against hunting or something?'

'Noooo,' I say drawing out the little word in an attempt to mask my feelings.

'You okay?'

To not have to lie, I ask, 'Do all the Kaplans go hunting together?'

'Nah, it's not in my brothers' blood, like it is mine.'

I know I should press this topic, but my heart feels as if it's about to leap up my throat.

Sam steps forward to put his hand on my shoulder to say something, but as he does, Garry circles back to us. Grabbing my arm, he yanks me towards the bar. 'Don't hog the sister,' he says.

'Sorry, bro,' Sam mumbles.

I spend the rest of my night talking with the mechanics from the garage, drowning my sorrows, and wishing one of my brothers wasn't a serial killer.

-

After gulping a pint of water back at home, I sit on my sofa and write up my brother notes. With hope, I check the odd dates they mentioned – a rock concert Si went to last month, a trip to Glasgow for Sam, Garry complaining about having to attend car auctions up north – I find none correlate to murders, so can neither rule in or out any brother.

Stefan is still an unknown, but he is acting weird, and Miles told me he's had to cover more than few shifts for him at the garage without warning or explanation.

My investigation so far is depressingly thin. What if there's another murder before I can collect what I need? Another death on my conscience. One more life snuffed out. It's torture. Then a weird thought hits me: did I die at Cat Hall? Is my body buried beneath a concrete drive? Has everything that has happened since been some sort of hell? Annoyed for thinking something so stupid, I slink off to bed. As I drift off, a dream so raw and vivid grabs me. It's a year ago, and I'm dressed in an uncomfortable paper gown, which routinely flaps open exposing my skin; just like the grey coat I wore that night. In my room is a woman with her back to me – a nurse.

'Why you?' she says. 'What's so special about you?'

'Excuse me?' I ask approaching her. As I get closer I can see who it is. Gayle. Blood-soaked through what should be a pale blue uniform and a scarlet slash across her throat. I know I'm dreaming; blood doesn't smell here.

Gayle turns to look at me and spits, 'Twice someone died when you lived.'

Red spittle hits my face. 'I'm sorry,' I splutter.

'Twice!' she screams.

Apologising again, I tell her I'm trying to make up for it. I didn't mean to run. But I don't hear my words.

'Twice!'

I feel cold.

'Twice!'

I wake with a start to find Harvey staring at me. His muzzle lowers and he licks me from chin to eye socket. Too grateful that he woke me from my nightmare, I don't yell at him for slobbering me. Instead, I let him jump up onto the bed. Eventually, I fall back asleep listening to his snores.

-

First thing in the morning, I walk Harvey and try to devise a plan to meet Stefan. By the time I get back to Poppy Fields, I've decided to call Lindsay and update her on everything. She may not be able to actively investigate, but that doesn't mean she can't talk things over with me, and spitball a few ideas as to how I can get the information Joel needs quicker.

As the phone rings, I pray her boss has dropped the suspension and she can get back to running the science side of our killer hunt. After seven rings, I wonder if she's back at work already so can't answer. Just as I've decided to text her, the call is suddenly answered.

'Hello?' comes a woman's voice.

'Hi. Is Lindsay there?'

'Who is this?' she asks.

'Just a friend. Who are you?'

'I'm Caroline Trout. I'm afraid I have some bad news.'

'What's happened?'

'Lindsay is dead.'

Chapter 21

The Brother

What a dead-end party! I've been to some dreary occasions, but this one really took the biscuit. At the end of the night, I was glad to be back in my favourite armchair mentally organising my bloody thoughts. I can't believe my sister spent all night in the same pub as me, yet didn't have a clue who I was. Have I misjudged her? Rather than make her, did Cat Hall break her?

I watched as she spoke with Susie. Women cackling together is never a good thing. Did they talk about me? Probably. Our game was the reason Fallon came to the party. Without knowing my dark tastes, I doubt she'd have bothered to get to know her new family. We Kappers are a wild, unpredictable bunch; certainly not the type a posh doctor would choose to mingle with.

And, just because we share DNA, it doesn't mean she's up to the challenge. I only need to look at my brothers to substantiate that theory.

This thought about my sister's skills played on my mind all evening. A good game requires players of equal ability. Anything less is simply slaughter, and that's no longer what I crave. It was when everyone began to give up and go home that I thought, maybe Fallon just needs a push in the right direction. I pulled out my sister's Post-it note.

After smoothing down its creases, I read her insult again: *Charm hides the monster.* I'd heard this same description about other killers. She thinks I'm the same as them. To her, I'm like those half-arsed idiots from Cat Hall. She doesn't know me, not really. Making assumptions about people is childish. For a moment I imagine what it would have been like to have grown up with Fallon. Fights and playtimes. Sharing social circles. Blaming each other for misdeeds. Mum would have preferred me of course. After all, I'm her favourite child, and in every argument she would have taken my side. All Fallon's toys would have been mine to break. Her friends mine to play with.

Charm hides the monster.

Infuriating! But, on the back of her insult, I found something useful. Something I could use to truly start my game with Fallon.

I'm never as drunk as I make out, so at 5.a.m I jumped into my car. An hour, and a few wrong turns, later I arrived at my destination. Parking up the road, I spied a lonesome country house with an old bicycle, complete with pink wicker basket, propped up against its stones. No neighbours for miles. The perfect remote location. As she was too young for Facebook, I couldn't tell if she lived alone, so I scouted out the place before I knocked on the door, which was then opened wide. The silly girl had no fear of strangers. After all, she didn't know that I knew her crimes against me. Cross didn't know there was anything *to* fear.

Dressed in jeans and a jumper, she still had a toothbrush artfully protruding from her mouth and sleepy dust crusted in the corners of her eyes.

'Sorry to bother you so early, but my car broke down at the top of the road,' I said, studying her thin frame and delicate features. 'My phone's out of battery. Can I use yours?'

Springing into action, she removed the toothbrush from her mouth and asked, 'I've my phone here. Do you want me to ring someone for you?'

Oozing charm like the monster I am, I said, 'Great. Thank you.' Then watched as she plucked her mobile from her pocket. Expectedly, she looked up at me, waiting for me to rattle off the number of someone to call.

When I didn't give her a contact, she asked. 'Do you remember any numbers?'

'Didn't think of that,' I admitted. 'They're all locked up tight on my very dead phone.'

She laughed then. 'Yeah, technology can help us, but can…'

'…make us dumb,' I said finishing her sentence.

Nodding, she looked behind her. I knew there was no one there. She did too.

'Would you call Roadside Assistance for me?' I asked.

Not wanting to insult me by showing she had, just for a moment, been afraid, she sighed and said, 'Sure. I'll look up the number online.'

Her phone lit up her face in such a lovely glow. I remember thinking what a perfect scene this was: The comforting darkness of a winter's morning. The witness-free location. The victim who dared to try and hunt me.

Seasoned hunters take down deer, foxes and pheasants, all of which give a certain thrill level, but hunting a bear or a tiger – prey that could turn the tables on you and have you arrested – now that's the stuff of bloody dreams.

While she starred down at her phone screen, I lunged forward. Her neck fit perfectly between my hands.

Dropping her mobile, she struggled, but I was too strong. I always am, even against tigers and bears.

'Can you guess who I am?' I seethed.

Instantly, she stopped flailing and an eerie calm crept over her body. I released her so she could stagger backwards.

'Get away from me.'

'Guess!' I snatched at her again, this time pulling her body against mine.

Gasping, she shivered, but I held her tight.

'Let me go!'

I needed to hear her say it. 'Tell me.'

She pushed out, 'You're the killer.'

'The police didn't believe you,' I stated. 'But here I am in the flesh.'

'I was right.'

'Does it help? Knowing you were right?' I asked.

'It helps knowing they'll believe me when they find me murdered.' Cross wriggled; her sharp elbows dug into my ribs with every squirm. This one was going to bite me as I put her down. I couldn't help it. I smiled.

'If you're smart, you'll let me go.'

I thought about it, letting her go with a warning, leaving Fallon her sidekick, and therefore weighing the odds in her favour for fun. The police didn't believe the evidence Cross gave them before, and her continued investigations into me would add to my challenge. But even as that idea slithered over my brain, I knew it was too late. I'd gone too far.

She was right though; I couldn't *murder* her. It might add credence to her theories and attract more players into the game. So, as she struggled in my arms, I thought about this new challenge. It was magical. A spilt-second of almost worry then gave way to euphoric cunning. A plan formed. It came to me in my mind's eye riding an old bicycle with a twee pink wicker basket.

She whispered, 'If you do this…'

'What?' I asked. 'What will happen when I do this?'

'She'll catch you.'

Snap. One single note of breaking bone and I was staring at a fresh corpse. Not a purposeful link in my chain; in fact, some might say an accident.

After I finished up, I found a packet of Jammie Dodgers on her dining room table. They were stale, but still tasted good.

Chapter 22

Fallon

Lindsay's neck was broken. She was found early this morning by a jogger a few miles from her house. Bicycle accident. For some unknown reason, she had set off while it was still dark, lost control and fell, breaking her neck on impact. There will be an investigation, but Caroline told me it seemed an open-and-shut case. Her conviction that it was a tragic accident was convincing, and I tried to believe it. But something in my gut told me otherwise; a rat nibbling at my innards. And I need to start listening to my gut. My brother knows. I'm not sure how, but he knew Lindsay was looking for him, and he killed her for it. Does he know about me too? Whichever brother he is, he definitely knows I exist, and there's a chance I spoke with him last night. Hours before Lindsay's murder, I could have been chatting and drinking with her killer.

I try to keep Caroline on the phone to ask more questions, but she tells me she has work to do and hangs up.

I hardly knew Lindsay. I shouldn't call us friends, but in our short time together we shared the same conviction and goal. She was a vibrant, intelligent person, and the world is poorer for her loss. Now she's gone, there's so much she'll now never get to do. Never get the promotion she deserved. Never have a brilliant career. Never catch the killer everyone told her didn't exist.

My nightmare was right. Twice I could have died and didn't. Fate could have chosen the first Fallon to live, sentencing me to the little grave in St Maude's. At Cat Hall, it could have easily been me chosen before Gayle to be carried off screaming into the kill room. Why did I get to live? I'm only a façade of a good person; Lindsay was the real deal. She risked everything to unravel twenty people's deaths. I can't let her death go unsolved. And maybe if I can convince her boss that she was murdered, it could be the catalyst to a proper police investigation.

After changing into jeans and a shirt, I grab the folder, then jump in the car. It takes two attempts to start it, but eventually my little Ford roars to life. I speed off to the police station.

I'm no stranger to this building, but today it feels different. The glass is murkier, the people inside sharper, the smell muskier. Knowing the forensics team share this location, I approach the desk and ask for Caroline Trout. The kindly officer at reception makes a call, then tells me where to find her.

Lindsay's boss is younger than I imagined. Petite and pretty with a tight blonde bun and fashionable glasses. She doesn't smile at my approach. Instead, she places her hands on her hips and cocks her head.

'I'm Dr Hurley. We spoke on the phone,' I say by way of greeting.

'Yes, Lindsay's friend. Sorry for your loss. She will be missed.'

I stare at her too long trying to find the right words.

'Can I help you with something? We're rammed today.' She lets out a humourless chuckle. 'Actually, we're always rammed.'

'Can we go somewhere to talk?' I ask, noticing the officers milling around the corridor.

'Here is fine.'

Looking around again, I find even more stragglers. Are they close enough to hear?

'Dr Hurley?'

I blurt, 'Lindsay was murdered.'

Caroline almost sighs, but stops herself before the sound escapes.

'I'm serious,' I tell her.

'Sometimes it's easier to have someone to blame when something senseless happen, but I can assure you, it was an accident, I was at the scene and saw the body. Lindsay broke her neck falling off her ridiculous antique bicycle. I'm sorry it happened, and I'm sorry for your loss. Now if that's all, I need to get on.' She turns to leave, but I grab her arm. 'Release me, doctor.'

I let her go. 'Sorry, but please, you need to listen to me.'

Snorting, she rolls her eyes. 'Tell me, why do you think Lindsay was murdered?'

'She was investigating a serial killer.'

Caroline sighs. 'Of course, she told you about that. Even when I specifically instructed her to leave it alone. What she told you was in direct violation of our data protection policy.'

'But aren't people's lives more important than policies?'

'Policies also protect people. It's why they're there.'

This is getting me nowhere. I change tactics. 'Hand on heart, I'm telling you there is a serial killer.'

'And that's who you think killed my technician?'

I nod.

A thoughtful expression spreads across her face. 'The same killer she tried to sell me on. Then, when I told her to back off, she went over my head and tried to sell to my boss – that killer?'

Oh no. I didn't know Lindsay went over her manager's head. No wonder she's standing her ground.

Caroline then smiles at me. 'Actually I think you could be right.'

Finally! 'I have information I can show you. I've made a profile and—'

Holding up her hand to stop my explanation, she states, 'Of course, her mind was too busy on her silly theory, so she didn't pay attention to the road.'

'Please. You're not listening to me.' I can feel the heat on my face sizzling my cheeks like bacon in a pan. I can almost smell it.

'I am listening to you. I hate to speak ill of the dead, but Lindsay was sadly inept in the lab. She did unauthorised destructive tests on crime scene evidence. So, I'm going to tell you exactly what I told her.' She leans into me, so close I can smell the last cup of coffee on her breath. 'Touch DNA isn't enough to start an investigation. All the crime scenes it was found at' – she air quotes *found* – 'were from Lindsay's desk. And with zero connections to crimes or victims, the most logical explanation is that she screwed up and put it there herself. There's no way of substantiating that theory though, as all the samples were destroyed as she tried to prove herself right.'

'I understand the position you're in,' I say. 'But I've been profiling the killer and there are similarities in the cases, if you'd just let me explain.'

Her hands curl into fists by her sides. 'Lindsay was wrong. And you are wrong.'

Keeping her stare, I reach into my bag to grip the edge of the folder. 'Please, just let me show you this.'

'Doctor, you know better than anyone what it's like with cognitive bias; Lindsay wanted to find a serial killer, so she did. From that point on, all evidence she found was filtered by her need to substantiate her theory. And it looks like you've followed her down that same rabbit hole.'

'I don't need you to explain cognitive bias to me, but I would ask you to take another look at Lindsay's notes, and the ones I've made.' I struggle to release the brown folder from my bag. As the contents are packed too tight, when I finally free it, it comically explodes out and flutters to the floor like a cheap firework. I bend to pick up the pages. 'There's more about his DNA, Lindsay uploaded it...'

Caroline's eyes take on a wild sheen as her stare lands on a stray photo. 'Not another word. Some of those cases are already closed. The killers have been caught and are serving their punishment.'

'Is that why you won't even entertain the idea? You don't want to admit your own guilt?' I gulp my last sentence back down.

Stepping towards me, she whispers, 'If you make this official, you'll ruin Lindsay's reputation even more than she did herself before her death. And let's not forget about killing my career as her boss, and yours to boot. This' – she points at the papers as I'm scooping them up – 'is bullshit. My advice is to bury it. I'm sure you have better things to do.' Huffing like a tired mother, she then crouches beside me to gather the file up quicker. Once it's all hidden back in the folder, she says. 'Don't contact me again.'

'People are dying, Ms Trout,' I tell her.

After meeting my eyes for a moment, she looks away. 'People die every day, Dr Hurley,' she says, then stalks off behind a door marked 'Private', where I can't follow.

She's right, people do die every day – it's everyone's fate. But how and when they die should not be up to a sick psychopath who views society as his plaything. Caroline Trout should be ashamed of herself.

Back in the car, I try to concentrate on driving, but visions of Lindsay, and what happened to her, invade my thoughts. I can't believe she's dead. Pulling off the road, I park in a layby. Closing my eyes, I put my head in my hands. Before meeting Lindsay, when I shut my eyes, my mind would routinely drag me back to Cat Hall. Cowering into my grey woollen coat, clinging to a stranger, knowing we were about to die together. Now, although I'm back in that same room, I'm clinging to Lindsay. But it's not Ropey and Tyler pulling her away from me, but the hands of an unrecognisable shadow. My grip on her fails and she's dragged into the darkness.

-

Halfway home, I remember I'm supposed to meet Joel, so turn around and drive to the Crown Court's car park.

Once inside, I'm checked by the guards then asked for my ID. All the while I feel weird, suspicious almost, as if when my bag is scanned they'll discover a bloody knife nestled between my book and lipstick. Everything about this place has me on edge. High ceilings that make you feel small, statues whose eyes follow you through the halls. It's overwhelming and I'm glad I took this dry run before my testimony. At least now I'll know what to expect.

Waiting on a lumpy seat in the lobby, I watch people walk through the security gates. It's easy to spot the barristers; today is like any other to them. The victims and accused are obvious too, and strangely look the same: concerned and uncomfortable. When Joel comes in, however, he doesn't sport the determined mask the other barristers wear. Instead, when he sees me, worry passes across his face.

'Court starts in half an hour.' He pauses, then adds, 'You remember you can't come in?'

'Hello to you too,' I snap, getting to my feet. I then say, 'Sorry.' My residual anger has no place with Joel. Lindsay's murder isn't his fault.

'That's okay. Tense times all round.'

'I need to tell you something.'

'What's wrong?' Joel asks.

I'm about to blurt out the news of Lindsay's death when Paul approaches us, making me hesitate.

'Tell you later,' I say.

Paul looks from me to his colleague. 'Have I missed something?'

'Nothing,' Joel tells him. Looking at me, he says, 'I'll see you in a few hours at the coffee place down the road.'

'Of course. I brought a book. I...' I trail off when someone catches my eye. It's Tyler Baker, flanked by police. For a moment, my mind fogs. I'm breathing the same air as him – again. Shaking off this thought, I then notice how different he now looks, hair cut neat and clean shaven. He looks normal, not a would-be serial killer. Horror washes over me. This new Tyler can't be who the jury see – it's not right.

'Fallon?' Paul asks.

Tyler hasn't seen me. He's too busy grimacing at everyone who walks by. Acting the innocent man accused.

'Fallon?'

If things had gone differently, could I have killed him that night? Murder is in my DNA. If I had ended his life, would it be me in handcuffs today?

'Fallon!' Paul is staring at me.

'Sorry,' I say. 'What?'

'You should go.' Joel gently grips my elbow and turns me towards the exit.

'Sure,' I mutter, but as I turn back to see the new and improved Tyler again, I find he's gone.

Chapter 23

The Brother

Know your opponent. These are the wise words which find me, for the first time, sitting in a courtroom waiting to hear about Fallon's last brush with death. In the air is a distinct smell of BO and cheap furniture polish, and the wooden bench I'm sat on is bum-numbingly hard.

Being in the pulsing heart of the UK legal system makes me think about what would happen if they caught me. How packed the gallery would be. How many journalists would want my interview. How the bewigged idiots in black gowns would begin. 'This man hunted and killed people in a sadistic game of chance, arbitrarily, like God.'

My barrister would rebut: 'Yes, but wasn't it a fairer way of choosing his prey? To allow them to bid for the honour?'

Logic wouldn't matter of course. I'd still be convicted and live the rest of my days in a cage, waiting for my chance to escape back into the wild.

The gallery for the Cat Hall case is crammed with journalists and random thrill-seekers, so I end up uncomfortably pinned between a trainee solicitor and an old woman who keeps offering me boiled sweets. Gormless faces eager to be entertained surround me. I feel as if I'm the only one here seeking the truth of what happened that night. Only with this knowledge will I truly know my sister and how best to win against her, now I've laid down the gauntlet.

The defence barrister appears worried when she nears her client. She has the look of a doe with nowhere to run. The defendant, Tyler Baker, is large, but no taller or broader than me. Arrogance holds his head up high. He thinks he's above everyone else. If he were free, I'd prove there's someone better than him with a flick of my knife.

When a uniformed policeman struts into the courtroom, I hold my breath. For a spilt-second I think he's here for me, that Fallon has figured out Cross' death and set the dogs on me. But he doesn't even glance my way. Instead he climbs into the witness box and declares to tell the truth. The CPS gently interrogate him as one of the first officers on scene. They tease out the information they need, then volley him to the defence.

'Constable Miller,' she begins, 'you were the first person to see the survivor Fallon Hurley?'

'Yes, I arrived at her car just outside the Cat Hall estate.'

'And what was her condition?'

He hesitates, as if it's a trick question, then replies, 'Distraught, as any victim would be.'

'And you have witnessed many distraught victims?'

Before Miller can answer, the CPS yell out, 'Pardon me, but relevance?'

She takes a breath. 'In your opinion as a police officer, was Ms Hurley in a state consistent with other victims you have experienced?'

Where is this going? I look over at Tyler. A smirk flashes across his face.

Miller rolls his eyes. 'There's no one state. And if you'd had spent even a second with a victim, you'd know that.'

'Apologies,' she says quickly, but then throws a knowing glance at the jury. 'When you arrested my client, did he seem upset?'

'He weren't happy.'

'Didn't he, at the time, say he was a victim too?'

'Mr Baker wasn't acting like a victim.'

Dramatically, the barrister whirls around. 'But like you said, not all victims act alike.'

The constable exhales deeply and I, along with the whole court room, lean forward to hear his thoughts. 'Your client continually told Dr Hurley he'd "see her real soon." Does that sound like a fellow victim to you?'

'Actually yes, in his statement he said he was comforting her, letting her know she wasn't alone. That they'd see one another again.'

'His tone wasn't comforting.'

'Good job tone of voice isn't a criminal offence.'

'Pardon me, but, argumentative,' says the CPS.

The judge raises an eyebrow and weighs up his decision. 'I agree.' He looks at the defence. 'Careful as you go.'

'Apologies,' she says. 'Now, going back to Dr Hurley, I think we can all agree on the fact that she ran away.'

'She escaped,' interjects Miller.

'Indeed, she escaped leaving the victims to be murdered by the hands of Knowles and Partridge.'

The policeman shakes his head. '*Who* killed those people is why we're here today.'

Unperturbed, the defence continues, 'But the fact she ran is not up for debate. I think it would be fair to say that that action would bring with it a certain amount of guilt.'

'That would be fair to say.'

'Have you ever seen guilty people act out? Perhaps blame others to soften their conscience?'

'Pardon, but' – the CPS barrister rises – 'Constable Miller has no background in psychology and should not be submitted to such ridiculous questioning.'

'I have to agree,' says the judge to the defence. 'Perhaps you can hold off on this line of questioning for the *right* witness.'

She nods, but dares a look at the jury. Their piqued interest makes her smile. She's piqued my interest too. Guilt is an interesting motivator. When I read that Fallon had run, I didn't even consider it an unusual reaction. When my victims get a whiff of me they try to bolt; it's a natural instinct to get away from the danger. Who cares who you leave behind, you have to look out for number one. My sister isn't like me though. Her job is to care for people, so this act would have left her questioning herself. And that guilt can be exploited.

Proceedings swiftly move from hearsay to evidence. It's like watching an unscripted, overly polite, TV show. The defence has almost no narrative framework for the story she's weaving, that Tyler Baker was a victim rather than a perpetrator. With pathetic panache, she flails whenever her wild statements are contradicted. Having gotten all I need, I get up to leave, but am ushered back down by my elderly gallery neighbour. It seems I have to wait until everything is done for the day – I'm trapped. A tight, blistering feeling steams through my body, which I suppress with the memory of Cross' throat between my hands and the snapping sound which followed. How thin and light she was when I carried her across to the twee bicycle. Finding the picture-perfect hill was the key. One push and over the bicycle and body went. If she'd been part of my chain I'd have left her on her doorstep, but she wasn't officially killed by a hunter. On paper, she was ended by a steep bit of grass.

How much longer is this session going to be? Reaching into my pocket, I pull out my favourite pen and chew the top. My teeth ever-so-slightly sink into the orange plastic. These people are now wasting my time. I have such a long to-do list. Yvonne's silver photo frame has almost chosen the next victim in my murder chain.

After another twenty minutes of arguing over evidence, it's revealed Exhibit H, a knife covered in the victim's blood, was recovered from the scene. There were no fingerprints anywhere and, with a lacklustre monologue, the defence explain when a victim is stabbed, the stabber will often cut themselves. With no such wounds found on Tyler, it couldn't have been him wielding the blade.

The CPS appears flustered for a moment, then rallies. 'But there were wounds found on Tyler. Scratches made by the victims.'

That volley is met with an objection. The defence barrister argues the wounds were caused when Tyler was attacked as he heroically tried to save the victims. Lies.

While the barristers argue, I get another good look at Tyler Baker in the dock. Such a careful mask covering the monstrous face beneath. It really does take one to know one. He catches me staring and we exchange a glare; it's delicate despite the connotations slithering beneath. A serial killer caught on his first tentative dark steps – it's embarrassing really and, in fairness, he should have admitted everything when he was caught. Some people just don't play by the rules. If I had feelings, I would feel bad. The outcome of this legal battle will be determined by whoever is the best liar. Justice shouldn't be so twisted.

As they escort Tyler Baker away, he looks back at me. I bare my teeth. If we were dogs meeting in the wild, he'd roll over to expose his belly. Instead, he's escorted back to his safe little cage.

I've crossed swords with other killers before. The first time was when I was barely thirteen. We met on a school trip. The entire class was made to rough it overnight and camp in the woods. Roughing it was putting it mildly. I was so irritated by not having access to my TV, video games and well-cooked food, I would have merrily murdered the teacher to get back home. The boy was from another school. He was older and taller than me. He thought he was *better* than me.

In a pathetic attempt to keep track of the kids, the schools on the campsite had sign in books. That way, if you didn't return from your orienteering, they could organise a suitable search party.

One evening, seeing me sitting alone, the boy approached.

'Come for a walk,' he said. 'We can scout out the best trails for tomorrow. Or are you chicken?'

Curious about his intent, I signed my school's book, and then walked away with him.

'Hang on, let me just grab something,' he said, then disappeared for a moment. When he re-emerged, he looked flushed.

For a while, we walked together. He had the same smile as Tyler Baker, practised rather than real. You can't fake sincerity. Even I rarely manage it.

Ten minutes of inane chit-chat later, he disappeared into a nearby bush, as if abandoning me. Having a great sense of direction, I was unperturbed, so pushed on alone into the dark forest.

My would-be killer then had the cheek to stalk me. With so many crunching branches and trampled brushes, it was comical. At first I thought he only meant to scare me, but then I saw the knife, dull yet scabby with dried blood. Finally swaggering up to me, he quoted some B-movie line about not taking it personally, I was just in the wrong place at the wrong time. His knife was all but useless; I had to beat him to death with a thick tree branch. He may have been bigger and older, but I was better.

It wasn't till I got back to my school's campsite and went to sign in I saw he had ripped out the page I signed out on. Fortunately, he'd neglected to sign out in his book at all. Funny how things work out. To all the teachers, I had never left the camp, and he had simply disappeared.

Chapter 24

Fallon

While I wait in the coffee shop, I spend time writing profiles on my brothers. Did one of them kill Lindsay? Or is cognitive bias affecting me, connecting a twist of fate to a theory I'm already wedded to? Maybe I overreacted with Caroline. People have accidents every day. And yet I can't shake the horrible feeling in my gut that this is more than coincidence. After all, what are the odds? And for someone in law enforcement, such as Trout, to not even stop to give the killer theory the once over, is abhorrent. My brain is so addled with frustration, I take out a piece of paper and compose an email to her bosses. Everything I wanted to say at the police station surges out of me and onto the page. I then edit it down, and by the time I'm finished, the bubbling pot of anger inside me has simmered. I have no intention of sending it. But the exercise has calmed me enough for my talk with Joel.

Walking across the road with a cigarette hanging from his lip, my barrister looks defeated. But as he grinds the butt beneath his foot and looks up at the door, his expression morphs to a smile, as if he's wearing one of those sad/happy acting masks.

'Hey, how's the coffee?' he asks, stepping up to my table.

'Hot and crammed with caffeine,' I say.

'Just the way I like it.'

As he queues, I finish my drink in two gulps. If Lindsay's death wasn't an accident, I need to admit I may have put him in danger too.

Moments later, Joel sits down with a huge mug. I'm about to launch into a sorry-laced speech when he says, 'So, I shouldn't be doing this, but there's a lot of *shouldn't-be-doings* going around lately. On the stand, we need to make a point about Tyler's knife.'

Jolted by his words, it takes a second for me to change my train of thought. 'What's happened?'

'Tyler's barrister is putting forward a better case than expected. Paul presented the knife evidence this morning, but you need to state Tyler had the knife on him first to prove intention, and also to state he wore gloves. Make sure it's on the record.'

'Of course,' I reply.

'In our earlier talks you mentioned gloves on Tyler's hands? You definitely remember them, right?'

I'll never forget them. 'Yes.'

Sitting back in his chair, Joel says, 'I need you to be very specific about what happened. Don't leave anything out which Tyler can contradict later.'

Staring at the gathering queue for coffee at the counter, I nod.

Joel puts his thumbs up. 'Now for our other project. My friend, DI Worth, is looking into Yvonne Lowry's case, but we need more. There are a lot of red Audis in the world.'

'And my brothers all work at a garage. It might not have even been his car.'

'Understood,' he says. 'How's it going with your brothers? What are your thoughts?'

I have thoughts, I just can't seem to get them past my lips.

'What's wrong?' he prompts.

'The forensic scientist who put the file together, she died this morning.'

'What?'

I squeeze my eyes shut in response. 'I was told it was a bicycle accident, but I think perhaps…'

'Your brother?'

'Any one of them could have committed the murder, they were all in the area for a party.'

Joel raises an eyebrow. 'But then… that would mean he knew she was tracking him.'

I bow my head as he realises the truth. 'By dragging you in on this, I've put you in danger too. I'm so sorry,' I say. My hand springs out to touch his arm but, instead of recoiling or yelling at me, he rolls his eyes.

'I'm a barrister for the CPS, I've got any number of gangs, murderers and lowlifes gunning for me at any one given time. What's one more serial killer?'

His words ease my guilt, but only a little.

Edging forward, Joel says, 'Give me her details so I can ask around about her death. But promise me something, Fallon.'

I nod.

'Right now, concentrate on your testimony. We need you clear-headed on the stand. Once Tyler's convicted, we can delve deeper into your family tree.'

It's almost the same advice Ollie gave. Nearest fire first. But my brother is burning too bright now, and he's so near, it's blinding me.

-

After making the long walk back to my car, I climb in and turn the key in the ignition. There's a loud popping sound. I try again, nothing. I could text Ollie, but I've dragged him into my dramas too much recently. My finger hesitates for so long on my mobile, the screen turns black. 'Shit,' I say, then call Si.

'Ready for your MOT?' he laughs.

'You were right about the car. It won't start at all now. I'm stranded.'

'Where? Are you alone?'

'I'm in the Crown Court car park.'

'Don't worry, I'm in the area. Be there in mo.'

He hangs up, leaving me uncertain as to how long a *mo* is, and if I've just asked a serial killer to rescue me.

Chapter 25

Fallon

'You were quick,' I say to Si as he strides up to my car.

'Told you, we weren't far.'

I follow his eyes to see Garry crossing the road from my left, limping a little. Putting his hand up, he says, 'Got your message, Si. I just called Sam to say we're bringing in her car and to meet us at the garage.'

Two potential serial killers for the price of one. Awesome.

'Thanks, bro,' Si replies as he takes my keys from me, but instead of trying to start the car, he pops the bonnet.

'I called Stefan to come in too,' Garry says offhand, 'but he said he's too busy.' He says the last two words as if in air quotes.

Si purses his lips. 'I told you to let him be.'

I watch as my eldest brother curls his fingers into a fist. Feeling uncomfortable, I ask, 'Is everything all right?'

Garry leans against my car. 'Stefan's been a nightmare recently. Missing shifts, lurking at the party rather than socialising, and he's been asking weird questions about you.'

'I'm sorry,' pops out before I can stop it.

'Not your fault,' Si says, bending down to open my petrol cap. 'It'll get better when he meets you properly.'

I'm about to air another question about Stefan's behaviour when Si asks, 'Did you put diesel in the car?'

'No, why?'

'I reckon that's why it won't start. There's diesel in with the petrol. I can smell it.'

Garry edges round me to stare at the engine. 'When did you last fill up?'

'The last time I was at the garage was… Oh, a couple of nights ago, when the lights went off and there was this guy, and a van, and…' The quizzical looks on my brothers' faces stop my story. I sound crazy.

'You're positive you put petrol in?' Garry asks.

My memory spits out what it can of that night, but the colour of the pump is absent. 'I didn't pay attention. I might have used the wrong pump,' I admit. 'I was distracted.'

'Well, after running for a while, the diesel has now clogged the fuel line. Probably the filters, too,' Si says. 'But don't worry. We can flush it, but not here.'

I smile up at them gratefully, although as I do, a sickening feeling settles in the pit of my stomach. What if I didn't make a mistake with the diesel? What if one of them spiked my tank while I was having coffee with Joel? It's a classic serial killer move, to disable a car to strand a victim, then act like a Good Samaritan so they willingly leave with you. I'm sure I've read about cases in Tina's books where murderers used this very technique. Could it be one of them? Or has my paranoid mind raced forward at a hundred miles a minute only to reach another wrong conclusion.

Si is still looking at me. I drop my gaze and begin to feel around in my bag for my mobile. Joel's not too far away.

'We'll wait with the car while you grab a taxi home. I'll call you once it's fixed,' Si states.

Suppressing a relieved sigh, I say, 'Thanks. How much do I owe you?'

Without waiting a beat, Garry says, 'You can treat us to dinner.'

-

Once I'm safely in the taxi, I take a deep breath and relax into the backseat. The driver turns around to look at me. 'Where to?'

I pause. I should say Foxglove, but instead I give him another address, St Maude's. My head is muddled and I need to talk to someone who won't be put in danger because of my selfish confessions.

When I arrive, I walk towards the Hurley baby's grave. The words I want to say stampede through my mind like a herd of elephants. Cat Hall, my killer brother, and now Lindsay's death – more than likely at his hands. I'm so distracted it's not until I'm feet from the headstone that I notice someone else there already.

As my shadow falls on him, he spins around to confront me. Stefan. I recognise him from Susie's wedding photo, albeit today's Stefan is lither and more muscular than the man in the tuxedo.

'What the fuck?' he breathes.

I stare at him. Part of me wants to run screaming out the church gates. The other part of me can't believe my luck that he's here – the last brother I need to question. He denied me the opportunity at the party, but now I've accidentally cornered him.

'Why are *you* here?' he demands.

I tell him the truth. 'I didn't know you'd be here. I only wanted to speak with her.' I nod at Baby Kaplan's grave.

Snorting, he replies, 'She's not *your* sister.'

I want to reply, *she's not yours either*, but I don't, because it's then I notice his right hand is clutching something behind his back. I step to the side and see it glint in the late afternoon sun. Whatever it is, it's metallic.

Catching my look of horror, he grimaces. 'Leave me alone. I only just bloody got here.'

I should step away, but instead I move forward. Edging closer to spot what's behind my brother's back.

'Si told me not to blame you for what happened, and as much as I get it wasn't your fault, I can't help it.' He brings his right hand forward and my stomach lurches… but it's just a can of beer. After taking a long gulp, he looks me up and down with a smirk. 'Jumpy are we?'

Something clicks in me. I take another step towards him. He could be the man who murdered Lindsay and Yvonne, along with countless others, but this niggling thought does nothing to stop me moving closer. I need information for the investigation, and this might be the only chance I get before the killer strikes again. If I push his buttons, will he remain calculating and cunning like the killer in my profile? Or will he lose his rag and go on the defensive? Only one way to find out. I take a deep breath, then let loose. 'You know nothing about me. And clearly you don't want to. And that's fine. Why don't you take your beer and fuck off out of this churchyard before I fetch the vicar.'

Before I've even finished my tirade, he bursts out laughing. 'Fuckin' hell, you've got some lady balls on you. Well, I don't need a DNA test to know you truly are a Kapper.'

Frustrated, I turn to march into the church, but he lurches forward and grabs my wrist. The deafening rhythm of my heartbeat supresses my hearing, so I only catch half of what he says, something about siblings and guilt. Then, as quick as he grabbed me, he lets me go, and backs away.

'Sorry, I shouldn't have said that,' he mumbles, then looks down at his shuffling feet.

In a short amount of time, Stefan has exhibited so many moods, I've got mental whiplash. The psychologist Fallon aches to get to the bottom of it, but the other me, the one birthed at Cat Hall, is unsure what to do next. Am I pushing my luck? If the killer is Stefan and he murders me as he did Lindsay, I have people in my life who won't let my death go. I profiled this killer as not leaving witnesses. Because of their love and tenacity, people I care about could end up on his hit list. No.

'I have to go,' I state, then slowly step back.

Ignoring my words, Stefan says, 'I'm being unfair. You don't really know me.'

'That's okay, we can get to know each other. I just have something I need to do now.'

Turning tail, I powerwalk out the gates, leaving Stefan to haunt the graveyard alone.

Angering a potential serial killer was stupid. What would I have achieved? Knowing for sure it was him as he plunged a knife into my chest?

Catching a taxi at the top of the street, all the while chiding myself for my dumbassery, I make notes on my phone about today's encounter.

Back at home, with Harvey, I stare at my profile. Stefan was certainly the odd mix of impulsive and reserved – the organised disorganised type. Could he be charming enough to talk his way into victim's homes? He was charming enough to marry Susie. I reread her words from the party: distant, easily agitated. A lot of people act out when they are under stress, or suffering mental breakdowns. If I'd known for sure then and there at the grave that Stefan was the killer, what would I have done? Still run? Citizen's arrest? I should have tried harder today. I owe it to Lindsay to finish what she started before he drops another body. But my only helper now is Joel, who is busy with the Cat Hall case – rightfully so.

Frustrated, I go to bed early and lie awake, listening to the house creaking. Harvey, a hairy weight across my feet, steadily snores, his massive legs kicking out as if he's dreaming of chasing ducks.

'I'm warm. I'm healthy. I'm safe,' I whisper, although I realise now that I might only be two of those things. If my brother knew about Lindsay, he surely knows about me too.

Hours slip by while I catastrophize my life: the clients I could be letting down, Tyler Baker escaping justice, the worry my brother might now be hunting me. My thoughts smash together like stars in my mind to create a new universe of thought. I'm so deep into it, I don't register the noise at first. It's not until Harvey sits upright, huge ears pricked, that my adrenaline kicks in. I spring out of bed and rush to the front door.

Tired of feeling like a victim, I fling open the door to confront whatever it is. Barking, Harvey dives out. The thought of losing my hairy friend suddenly seems worse than challenging whoever woke me.

'Harvey!' I yell, stumbling through the door after him.

With trembling fingers, I reach for my mobile and use the torch to light my deck. Harvey looks out across the darkness towards the lake.

'Who's out there?' I call.

No answer.

'I've called the police!'

Nothing.

Taking another step out, I scan the sides of the lodge, trying to make out any shapes in the darkness. Perhaps it's my Christmas fox come back for a visit? Or Tina for an impromptu face to face session? Or a knife-wielding maniac I'm related to?

My phone beeps in my hand, making me jump. I look down to see a message from Grant, *Can I come over?* Before I know what I'm doing, I text back a relieved, *Yes.*

Within ten minutes, my ex-boyfriend pulls up. 'Everything okay?' he asks.

'I think I have a prowler.'

'You want me to take a look?'

'No, just come in.' It's only then that I realise I'm in a nightdress, so I grab a coat to pull around me as Grant walks into the lodge. Harvey trots in after him and, eyeballing my ex, sits down beside me.

'Could you put *him* in another room?' Grant asks, inching back.

'No, he stays,' I say firmly. He can't protect me if he's locked up.

Shrugging, Grant takes off his jacket and sits down.

His eyes land on the photo on the mantelpiece. 'You still have that awful photo up.'

'Sometimes you need to be reminded of bad days,' I say.

'Wow, that's dark. Not like you at all.'

'People change,' I whisper.

'Let's sit down,' he says motioning to my sofa.

Staying standing, I ask, 'Why did you text me? It's late.'

'I was just thinking about you. I think about you a lot. What you went through. I should have been there to protect you.' He gets up and walks towards me. 'But I'm here now.'

I step back out of his reach. Staring into his face, I remember Tina's words about my ex, and a truly horrible idea hits me. 'Was it you before, out there?'

Ignoring my question, Grant pleads, 'I've changed, Fallon. Let me protect you, like I should have done at Cat Hall.'

'You've not...' I want to say he hasn't changed, but it would rock my psychology ideals to the core – he knows that. People can change, but only if they want to, and I'm not seeing that here. Not sure I ever did with Grant.

'I love you.' He leans forward, eyes closed and mouth open.

I push him back. 'No.' I then walk across to the guest room and pick up his box of old stuff. 'You need to leave and take this with you.' I thrust it out at him, but he shoves it from my hands and the contents, a psychical embodiment of our life together, spill across the floor.

'Fallon, I love you,' he repeats, moving closer.

Recoiling, I step back too quickly. Standing on the scattered junk, I lose my balance, then fall backwards to the floor. Pain sears through the base of my skull as my vision blurs. Then, blackness.

Chapter 26

Fallon

I wake to Harvey barking.

Holding onto the sofa, I pull myself up and scan my now empty lodge. What happened?

'Grant?'

No reply. I check each room and find Harvey trapped in the guest bedroom. There's no one else here. Finding the front door closed but unlocked, I lock it quick.

What was my ex's plan? I can't believe the man I spent all those years with, in his arms, in his bed, would leave me injured. No one would do that to someone they love. Heat trickles up from my feet to my head, making my vision swim in coloured dots. I feel the back of my head where a lump is forming. For all he knows, I could have concussion.

I ruffle Harvey's fur, and when we both head to the sofa, I notice he's limping. Grant hurt my dog, then trapped him in another room. As I rub Harvey's leg, he curls his huge hairy body around me.

Grabbing my phone, I check it to find a text from Grant apologising for my 'accident' and asking to try again. My head aches and I don't need this stress. I reply that I hope his mum gets better, but he shouldn't contact me, or ever come back to Foxglove.

In the morning, I call Ollie about Grant. Patiently he hears me out, then offers to stay with me for a few days. For too many reasons, I can't accept. So, he settles for the offer of a dinner to celebrate the end of the court case. He even promises to bring his new boyfriend so I can finally meet him. Ollie still hasn't even offered a name. He's secretive, always has been… except when it comes to telling Mum on me. Barely five minutes after I put the phone down on him, she calls. At least they're talking now.

'Hi, Mum.'

'What's this about Grant? He told me he was going round yours last night to…'

I push the phone to my shoulder and squeeze my eyes shut. Her voice becomes a squashed sound. My heart is so heavy I have to sit down. Mum goes to bed early, so for Grant to have called her and given her the good news that he was coming to see me, it would have had to have been before I texted he could come round. My ex planned the whole thing.

'Please don't talk to him again,' I say dryly.

'Oh, honey. Have I done something wrong? I thought it would be a nice surprise, especially with everything going on.'

She doesn't know the half of it. 'Mum, when he calls you again, please ignore him.'

'Of course. Oh, I've been meaning to ask if I could come to court to watch you give evidence.'

Thinking of my Mum in the gallery, face eager, hands poised to clap like I'm in some bizarre school play, is borderline harrowing. 'I'd prefer you didn't,' I tell her gently. 'But I'll call once it's over.'

'Come on, love, let's just talk about it.'

'When it's all over. Please, I just need space right now.'

'Understood. And I promise to ignore Grant.'

'Thanks,' I say and hang up.

Harvey pads up to me and I throw my arms around his neck. Turning, he slobbers over my cheek. After washing my face, I decide to block Grant's contact on my phone. It won't stop him coming round, but at least it's one less thing to worry about. As I'm updating my phone settings, a text comes in from Sam asking if we could meet today at a diner called The Hungry Piglet. I text back a thumbs up. I need to know more about my charming, knife-carrying brother. It's high time I put on my big psychologist pants and started narrowing down my suspects.

-

The Hungry Piglet sits in the middle of Maple Industrial Estate. It has the look of a child's plastic toy. It vaguely smells of plastic too. When I walk in, everyone looks over at me, like we're characters in a Western. I wish we were. At least in a gun-fight there are only so many bullets. Right now, all I can think about is if Sam will bring his knife with him today, and if he's used it on more than just animals.

Arriving early, I sit by the window and watch him park up. As he climbs out of his car, he stretches, then appears to smell the air and look around. Taking out his phone, he checks it then, noticing me, waves before stepping inside. After making himself comfortable in the seat opposite me he asks, 'Did the garage not give you a courtesy car?'

'I just got a taxi,' I reply.

Sam types something on his phone, then asks, 'You been here before?'

'No, but it seems nice,' I say, looking around at the laminated, red gingham tablecloths and menus.

'Don't let it fool you. They source ingredients locally and have a killer chef.' He picks up a menu. 'And that's what I want to be.'

My eyes widen. Killer? He didn't mean to use that word, did he?

Ignoring my reaction, he tells me, 'You should order the full English lunch.'

Staring down at the menu I see the lunch is a play on the breakfast, with multiple common lunch items packed together on a plate. Unsure I can eat anything right now without throwing up, I opt for a loaded bacon roll and a pot of coffee. Sam orders the lunch he recommended and a beer, then sits back in his chair. I speak first.

'So, you want to be a chef? Is that what you're at uni for?' I ask.

'Yeah. It's a pretty cut-throat course.'

I'm about to leap in with another question when his words sink in. Is he playing with me? Slipping dangerous, inciting words into the conversation to gauge my reaction?

'Why do you say that?'

Grinning, he leans forward and I see a hint of his perfect white teeth. It's probably what Little Red Riding Hood saw just before the wolf ate her. 'The food industry is competitive. Is it the same for psychologists? Is there some leader board for those who save the most people?'

My fingers find the edge of the menu. Without thinking, I slip my nail into a gap between the paper and plastic, and begin to pick.

'Sorry, that was a dumb question. I'm not handling this very well.'

Carefully, I drop the menu, then bend and scoop it up. As I do, I check to see if a knife is strapped to his jeans.

I can't see one. Once I'm back upright, I say, 'People all react differently to life's upheavals.'

'Cat Hall must have been a real eye-opener for you.'

Just like clockwork, the horror of that night drops into my stomach, taking my confidence with it.

'Did you really run?' he pushes.

All this time I've dealt with reporters' accusations and half-truths, too scared to tell them what happened for fear of judgement. I want to snap back at him, but defending myself is not what I'm here for.

'Yes. I ran.'

Inching forward on his chair, he says, 'I read stuff online. Sounded brutal. You did the right thing.'

I need to keep him talking, and as uncomfortable as the topic of Cat Hall is, it could be a litmus test of sorts. 'What would you have done?'

Without hesitation he replies, 'Beat them senseless.'

'You'd have taken on three men?' The killer is arrogant and violent. 'How?'

He looks thoughtful. 'Not all at once. I'd have separated them, fought them one at a time.'

'What if one of them beat you?'

Shaking his head, he crosses his legs and sits back in the chair. 'I grew up with three brothers. I can handle myself.'

It doesn't even enter his head that he could have lost a fight; with all those kills behind him, the serial's arrogance would be off the charts. Was it Sam's hands around Lindsay's throat? Not being able to hide the flash of fear on my face, I watch his expression soften.

'Hey, but no one would have expected you to do that. Girls should never have to fight. They deserve to be protected.'

Before I can comment, the waitress arrives with our order. I watch Sam carefully dissect his food into mouthfuls, then begin to eat. I tear off a piece of the roll and devour it. He was right, it's amazing. A cross between culinary excellence and the kind of comfort food that makes you warm inside.

'This place inspired me to become a chef.'

Happier to have more mundane conversation I admit, 'The roll's delicious. But why does this place look…'

'…like a greasy spoon roadside diner?'

I nod.

'Because the unexpected adds flavour.'

'You like surprises?'

'Doesn't everyone?'

I shake my head. 'Not everyone.'

-

Back at Foxglove Lodges, I update my notes on Sam. Thinking back, apart from the Cat Hall jibe and potential for him to be a serial killer, it was a lovely lunch. My brother was sweet. He paid for the meal and left a generous tip. Even walked me to the taxi. Creating and using a profile is more difficult than I thought. No one is just one thing, and all the attributes I have down for the killer are sinister. For all I know, after each murder, he donates to charity or adopts a stray cat. John Wayne Gacy was a clown at children's parties – wait, that is creepy!

Sam's hunting makes me uncomfortable, so much so I didn't quiz him much on it. What sort of hunting could he possibly do in Northamptonshire? I Google hunting clubs he could belong to, and although I find a few, I don't see his name or photo on any of the member lists. Of course I don't; this killer doesn't kill in a pack. The websites I find mention a few hunting terms and techniques, so I make a note of them on Sam's profile.

The shrill ring of my mobile tears me from my work. It's Tina.

'Where have you been? You missed our final session.'

Shit! I was supposed to speak to her today. 'I'm so sorry, I forgot. I've been busy.'

'What's more important than your testimony?'

I can't answer her question. Before Lindsay, Cat Hall was the most pressing thing in my life. How could I forget my final session, especially after what Joel said about the defence's case? Time is running out and I feel as if I've barely thought about my testimony since my killer brother entered my life.

'Fallon?'

'I'm still here.'

'We both know it's easier not to face up to certain situations in life, but I expected more from you.'

Events from the last few days spike through my thoughts. I don't even know where to begin. 'I'm sorry, Tina. Really. I'm letting everyone down.' I admit.

'Come on, pet. If people didn't have psychological problems we'd both be out of jobs. Are you free now?'

'Course,' I say, ashamed at my behaviour.

'Take your time. Let's go back. Rosie was in the house with you.'

Closing my eyes, I tell her how Cat Hall ended.

Chapter 27

Fallon

As we awaited our fate, I held Rosie and told her, 'It'll be okay.'

I knew it was a lie.

'Someone will come,' she muttered over and over, as if she were chanting a spell to keep us safe.

When all three men came back into the room, we both knew there was no hope. Still, Rosie fought. Her left eye had swollen shut, but she pushed me aside and barrelled into them, trying to knock them over. Anger flared across both Tyler and Ropey's faces. Streak merely backed away, declaring, 'I'm off for a fag.'

I heard his quick steps downstairs as Tyler punched Rosie's stomach, just as he had mine, and she stumbled back.

Leaping up, I tried to shield her. The words, 'Don't' and 'Stop it' snapped out of my mouth, but they just laughed.

'I like their spirit. In another world we could have all been friends,' Tyler said. 'Do you think all serial killers feel like this about their victims?'

Unsure as to who he was talking to, I replied, 'No.'

Ignoring my response, Ropey whined, 'Let me play?'

'You're not ready yet. I'll take this one too.' Tyler pointed at me. 'Then we'll both do the estate agent together.'

Rosie opened her mouth, but I'll never know what she would have said as Ropey struck her face, splitting her lip. I hugged her as she doubled over, but rough hands gripped my shoulders and yanked me away. With Rosie still attached, we fell as a jumbled lump of limbs.

'It'll be okay,' I whispered to her. There was that lie again.

Tyler wrapped a beefy arm about my neck and another around my waist. 'Come on, be the good girl I know you are.' As he hauled me out of Rosie's arms, his expelled breath forced its way into my lungs, making me splutter.

I flailed, screamed and writhed as he continued to pull me backwards down the stairs. I saw Rosie trying to stand, then falling down onto the floor before Ropey. For what felt like forever, our eyes locked. As I was dragged out of view, she craned her head to keep my stare. Rosie then silently mouthed one word, run.

Holding me with one arm, Tyler yanked open my coat, then pulled out his knife. Fast as he could, he sawed through the wool of my jumper. Because of my winter layers, the cuts to my skin were shallow, but the blood that dripped down my wrists felt like fire. Suddenly, a cold rip exposed my skin. For a split-second, I thought he'd plunged the knife into my chest and was sawing at bone, but, when I dared to look down, I found only my clothes were pulled apart and splayed open.

'Fight,' he whispered as I felt the cheap pleather of his gloves groping my exposed skin. His body pressed me to the ground. Frantically, I bucked to dislodge the weight. Before I could react, his hands wrapped around my throat. Panic rode my body as I clawed at his face. My feeble attempts to stop him drew a growling laugh from his lips. Then the small bones in my neck crunched as pressure built behind my eyes. As my face burnt, his snarling smile blurred before me. The pain was excruciating. I just wanted it to end. But suddenly, he released my throat.

Gasping, my relief was short-lived as he went back to his attempt to undress me. Wheezing, I coughed as the room spun in my peripheral vision. When I felt his gloved fingers on my bare leg, energy I didn't know I had leapt into my muscles. I pushed and punched. As I heard my bra rip, I kicked out, catching him in the crotch. Yelling in pain, he fell off me. I was free. Springing up, I looked around. Neither of the other men were in sight.

I ran to the bottom of the stairs, calling out, 'Rosie!'

No reply.

Swearing, Tyler scrambled up on all fours.

I took a running kick at his face. My foot collided with his nose, sending him reeling as blood poured down his top.

I scanned the room for my bag. It was where they left it. I scooped up its contents, then raced to the front door. Through the plastic, I ran into the night. Thinking he was behind me, I didn't look back. Couldn't. I just kept my eyes on the street ahead. My feet were heavy and the icy wind was forcing its way through the rips in my clothes, but I kept running.

Following the half-made road, I sprinted towards my car, fumbled out my keys and threw myself inside just as Tyler limped around the bend. When he saw where I was, he sped up. I put the keys in the ignition and paused. If I drove away, I'd be leaving Rosie. But if I stayed, I'd be risking my life and the chance to get help. Run.

Quickly, I locked the car doors. When he reached me, he slammed his fist against the passenger window, banging like a demented ape. Eyes wild and inhuman, he pounded, then suddenly stopped and stepped back. 'See you real soon,' he shouted, then winked as he blew me a kiss. In horror, I watched as his blood-laced spit landed on the thin layer of glass between us.

I twisted the keys. The car stalled, then started. I put it in gear, crunching it a few times as I did. Suddenly, I was driving and, with every frantic check of my rear-view mirror, Tyler was disappearing.

Miles ticked by with my fingers locked on the steering wheel. Once I felt safe, I pulled over. My body slipped from the car like water and I groped for my bag. I found my phone and dialled 999. After crying the address down the line, I stared at my tan suede boots. They were covered in blood.

The rest blurred until a police officer was helping me up, telling me the familiar lie that everything would be okay. I yelled at him to check the house at the end of the street. I screamed there were two more victims in there who needed help. Lots of talking into radios. Lots of nodding. Lots of sullen looks.

'Rosie!' I yelled at one officer. 'Is she all right?'

He radioed my question to the police at the house. I heard a garbled response, then saw his lips tighten.

'We caught the three men. They're in custody,' he told me. 'But I'm afraid the women in the house were deceased.'

–

There is a pained expression on Tina's face. Quickly, she corrects it. 'I'm so sorry, Fallon. That poor excuse for a man can't walk free.'

'Do you think, if he's released, he'll kill again?' I ask.

'In real life, serial killers are not as calculating as the ones we see on screen. They're more impulsive.'

'But he's had plenty of time awaiting trial to…'

'Change his impulsive nature?' Tina raises an eyebrow. 'Look, I'm not saying people can never act differently. A killer could, in theory, train himself to be less impulsive, but it won't be a lasting change. Eventually, something will go against his plans, and his base nature will step in.'

Slowly, I nod, making a note to research impulsive killers later.

'So you feel guilty about Cat Hall,' Tina says, 'but let's explore what you could have done. You wrestle yourself free from Baker, then what?'

I take a minute. In all my personal guilt trips, I have never indulged in a *what if* fantasy. All my energy went on torturing myself for fleeing when I should have fought. 'Um, I guess I would have knocked him out.'

'Right, you've got him on the floor. What about the other two men?'

'I would have attacked Ropey.'

'And Streak?'

'His heart wasn't in it. He might have just let us go.'

'Maybe. He certainly comes across that way in your recollections. But could you have really taken on two violent men? You know, Fallon, I've known you for years, and I don't remember you taking a boxing class or gaining super-strength from a tricked-out radiation experiment. If you did, you kept it all very quiet.'

Frowning, I say, 'You're making fun of me.'

'No I'm not. Indulge me a moment and let's get this straight. With no fighting skills or superpowers, you'd have fought off both armed men, carried out an injured woman, then drove off into the sunset.'

My face screws up in an unflattering look of annoyance. 'No, but I could have done something... different.' I could have thought things through more, stopped myself from doing the one thing I shouldn't have.

'Without your quick thinking, both of you would have been lost and those monsters would have been free to kill again. At least two of them were serial killers in the making. Have you ever thought about all those you saved by calling the police in time to arrest them?' Not waiting for my answer, Tina continues, 'I hate that you're in pain, but you know the score. How many people have you counselled in the past who blame themselves for events out of their control?'

Part of what happened was in my control. 'I had some control.'

'Put the blame where it needs to be – squarely on the shoulders of those arseholes.'

'Thanks, Tina.'

'Pointing out the obvious is not a gratitude-demanding task. Do me a favour, pet?'

'What?'

'Stay out of the way of killers for a bit.' She chuckles.

We say goodbye, then, to ease my thoughts, I grab Harvey's lead. A walk to organise my thoughts is what I need. I hate to admit it, but Ollie bought me another great present.

'Only a short one today, Harvey. There's lots to do.'

Chapter 28

The Brother

After accepting my bloody destiny, I devoured everything I could on my kind. Books about them. Books on how to hunt them. Books on what it's like to be them. Fallon has a lot of books. Which is why I'm sitting in Poppy Fields with a mug of her coffee and leafing through a few while she's out. Funny how she's using them to catch me, while I used them to stop my would-be captors realising I even exist.

All these years I've been a shadow, an imaginary bogeyman, a fleeting thought to police officers which never took root. Cross found me though. Now she'll never find anyone else again. Shame really, perhaps I stole some other killer's perfect opponent, and they will never feel the sweet, just sensation I had when I read about her *accident* online.

My file is chunkier than when I saw it last. Fallon has added to it. Walkies usually last an hour, so I've enough time to get myself up to date, then slip out without her, or her werewolf, being any the wiser. Some might say these clandestine visits are cheating, and that I'm peeking at the cards my sister holds. But it's only cheating if you get caught – otherwise it's strategy.

As I move through the lodge, I spy the flowers I left for her. A few of the heads are drooping and browned petals have gathered around the foot of the vase. It looks like a bedraggled mess of little corpses. Carefully, I deadhead the worst of the blooms, then refill the water. To keep them alive longer, I drop in a penny. The dirty, metallic smell reminds me of good times.

It's chilly in here. Leaning over, I flip the switch on the electric fire, so it'll be nice and warm for when Fallon comes back in out of the cold. Watching the glow of the metal bars, I imagine what would happen if she arrived early to find me drinking coffee by her fire. At Cat Hall she trusted a stranger, but she's met me now. And it would be that familiarity which would make her hesitate, giving me the time needed to make the first move. Stretching my limbs one by one, like a lion, I bask in the sudden warmth for a moment, until I remember my file. Upon opening it, the first thing I see is a handwritten note. Fallon has spoken to a woman called Caroline Trout. Displeased with how their conversation went, she has composed a complaint ready to be emailed to management. Words like *incompetent*, *rude*, and *downright bull-headed* are all crossed out and replaced with *over-worked, under pressure*, and *in need of a fresh pair of eyes*. It goes on to talk about Cross's death not being an accident... and that there's a serial killer on the loose. No! She can't bring in more players! That's not how this game is played. Bad sport. It's me versus Fallon, not me versus the whole Northamptonshire constabulary; they already had their chance to catch me when I killed on my home territory last month. With the note not being finished, I can only conclude it's not yet been sent. Cross's death should have taught her we are playing a two-person game, but clearly I wasn't specific enough. Not to worry, I still have time to set my sister straight on the rules.

Screwing up the note, I walk into the kitchen and turn on the stove. I placed it in the flame and watch it curl, blacken and die. I then wash the remaining ash down the sink.

The rest of the file is average to say the least. Arrogant, predatory, ah yes – and intelligent. A profile that could speak to any serial killer. Now I'm reading it with the fresh eyes she asked for, I can see the file is pathetic nonsense. Did I expect more? Hoped for, but never expected. It's taken years for me to perfect my skills. What's she been doing all this time? My sister has frittered away her free time reading books written by 'experts' who've never once come face to face with someone of my calibre. Laughable.

I look over at the wall behind her desk, heavy with certificates and qualifications. She's spent her time earning a degree and a masters, then a PhD at Oxford University. With each level of her professional development, there are framed photos. Fallon with her fake Mum. Fallon with her fake brother. Fallon with good ol' Dr Hawk who wrote the book on killers. Hmm. Maybe I choose the wrong opponent. It happens. In life we all trust people who let us down. Those we misjudge as equals who turn out to be unworthy of our time. An awful feeling, but a common one none the less. Perhaps I should finish my game with my sister here and now? Find a good hide-and-seek spot, and patiently wait to gift her a tragic accident.

Chapter 29

Fallon

Once we're home, I swear I can smell fresh coffee; it makes me fancy a cup. First, I give Harvey a bowl of water, then grab my new mug, which isn't where I left it. Lindsay couldn't have taken this one. It's also warm in here. When I find the fire on, I start to worry. I don't even remember using it this morning. Stress must be getting to me.

Harvey sniffs around the lodge for a bit, then follows me outside to sit on the deck. The dreaded folder of death before me, and Harvey nudging a slimy ball into my lap, I throw the ball and watch how happy my hairy shark is chasing it down.

According to Tina's books, the key to a serial killer's profile is victimology. But try as I might, I can't work it out. No matter how many times I read the victims' details, I can't see a link.

After about the fiftieth ball throw, my arm aches, but Harvey is still as happy as ever. The next time he rolls the slobber-covered ball towards me, I hide it in my coat. Flummoxed, Harvey snuffles around for a bit, but he doesn't give up. Within seconds he's nudging a rubber bone towards me.

'You don't care what you're fetching, do you? You just love the game.' I ruffle Harvey's head and throw the bone.

Wait, no, could that be it? Is my brother playing a game? What if there is no victimology, because he's not choosing the victims himself? Something or someone else is.

Pulling out my mobile, I call Joel to tell him my theory.

'That is a great way of ensuring no connections between victims. Your brother is clever.'

'And resourceful. Random targets means he has to think on his feet. Apart from opportunists, that's rare for killers. Most kill victims of their own choosing, it's part of the...' I gulp. 'Thrill.'

'And that's what gets them caught.'

I nod, then realise I'm on the phone, rather than a video chat. 'Without knowing how he's choosing victims though, I'm not sure how useful this information is.'

'Every theory can help. Profiling is more of an art than a science at times.'

After hanging up, I put my dinner in the oven and feed Harvey. Joel is right, profiling is more art at times, *facts* drawn by subjective interpretation.

With this in mind, I pour through the file again, adding more notes. As the minutes tick by, I become convinced my brother is playing a game. Lindsay said his DNA was found on items near the victims. Could these things be important to him? If so, why does he abandon them? From reading Tina's books, I know some serials take trophies – they don't leave them behind. But maybe I'm missing something?

In an attempt to straighten my theory, I write a list of characteristics I think my brother has: cunning, above-average intelligence, arrogance, physical strength, a hyper-competitive drive and charm. He has oodles of charm. Looking at my brother notes, I tick off the traits: Simon has already exhibited many. Stefan definitely has too. Garry is violent enough and Sam is… Wait. I stare out the window; is that Sam outside my lodge?

Without thinking, I fling open the front door. Shock passes across his face. 'I… I was just going to knock,' he says, climbing up the deck towards me.

'How did you know I lived here?'

'Mum told me.'

I open my mouth, then shut it quick. If she told him, then she told all my brothers. The killer knows where I live.

Jangling keys, he says, 'I brought you a courtesy car to use while we're working on yours.'

I peer behind him to see a white Honda on my drive. 'Thanks.'

'The garage is sending a car to pick me up in about half an hour. Can I come in and wait?'

Harvey barks. My dog is right, I shouldn't let this brother in, but it would be too weird not to now.

Sam leans past me and spots Harvey. 'He's a big lad. Is he friendly?'

My stare slowly slips towards Lindsay's folder resting on the table. Whether it's him or not, he can't see what I'm doing.

'Sure.' I grab Harvey's collar, pulling him in behind me. Sam follows. When he shuts the front door, I free my dog. Two barks and Sam has Harvey on his back, tickling his belly. As they play, I quickly shove the file under a sofa cushion.

'I love dogs,' he says. 'Always wanted one growing up, but we couldn't afford it.'

'You could get one now.'

'Nah, I'm out too much. Wouldn't be fair.' Standing up, he wipes Harvey's slobber and hairs down his jeans. 'Well, there's a lot of DNA.' He laughs.

There's that weird sense of humour again. Like he's taunting me. I shouldn't have let him inside. My stun gun is in my bedroom, I just need to grab it.

Sam steps towards me. It takes everything I have not to recoil. 'Your car is coming along nicely. Jason flushed it, and Miles has given it a tune up.'

'Thanks. Sam, can you play with Harvey while I pop on a jumper?' I say. 'Today feels colder inside than out.' Smooth.

'Feels pretty warm in here, but okay.' He leans across and tickles Harvey's ears.

Once inside my bedroom, I pull on my Christmas jumper; the one with pockets so I can conceal the stun gun.

'Getting to know each other will be awkward at times.'

I spin round to see Sam standing in my bedroom doorway. 'Yeah?' Did he see me hide the stun gun?

'But I promise we're good guys. Well, Garry can be a prick. But he's all right once you get to know him. And, well, Stefan is Stefan.' Sam's hand drops to his waist to fiddle with the hem of his jumper. As he does this, I catch a glimpse of it – the knife handle. 'Si seems excited to have a little sister.'

I can't escape. He's standing in front of the room's only door. 'That's nice,' I mumble.

He steps towards me. 'Family is everything,' he says and winks, just like Tyler, sending a judder up my spine. Still, I hold my ground. His tone then changes, making his next sentence a deep whisper, 'So, there's something we need to talk about.' I watch in horror as his fingers slither towards the knife. 'Something I think you already know about me.'

Shit! I thrust out my stun gun and press the button. It hits Sam square in the chest. Groaning, he collapses to his knees.

'Jesus,' he mutters, rolling onto his back.

'Stay where you are. I'm calling the police.' I rush into the living room and grab my mobile.

I dial two nines, then see Sam staggering towards me. 'Fallon?'

Thrusting out my weapon again, he snatches it before I can press the button. 'Stop it!'

Harvey trots up to us, whining. Putting a hand on my dog to steady himself, Sam drops the stun gun onto the table, then holds up his hands. 'Fuck sake! Why'd you do that?'

'Get out now!'

Sam's expression is pain, shock and bewilderment. Then, slowly, a shade of understanding comes into the mix. 'I'm so sorry, I should have realised you've got hella PTSD. No harm done, other than my heart racing. Fortunately, my jacket bore the brunt of the shock.' He looks down at his belt. 'Were you triggered by the knife? Like I said, it's just for hunting. I want to specialise in cooking what I catch. Gourmet sustainability.'

If I can unlock the window quick enough, I could fit through…

With Harvey by his side, Sam walks away to slump down on a nearby chair. 'It's now or never,' he whispers.

Frantic, I look at the front door. If I can just barrel past him I could escape.

'I'm your half-brother.'

'You're my… what?'

'Half-brother. I thought, with all the odd questions about my childhood, you had already guessed.'

I force a smile. 'I had an inkling something was up with one of you.'

Thinking we are on the same page, Sam continues, 'Mum had an affair. Mr Kaplan was a great guy; he just adopted me. I didn't know how you would react, that she kept me in the family, and not you. Never thought you'd electrocute me, though. Bravo for being unpredictable.'

Relief bubbles through my body, leaving me to all but fall down onto a nearby chair. Sam can't be the killer. His DNA wouldn't match Lindsay's sample. Then, the realisation of what I've done catches up to me.

'I'm so sorry. Are you okay?' I rush forward to check his pulse. 'Should I call an ambulance?'

'Nah, I've had worse injuries out on the town with Stefan. Where did you get the stun gun?'

'My brother Ollie.'

'Sounds like he'd fit right in as a Kapper.' He smirks then quickly adds, 'Not that you don't.'

'Thanks. Sorry, again.'

'You're forgiven. But let's not tell my bros about this, eh? I got knocked on my arse by my little sister, they'll tease me into eternity.'

'Works for me.'

Knowing Sam is definitely not the killer, I relax. After fully recovering from the shock, he plays with Harvey some more, then leaves with the promise we'll catch up again soon – without weapons next time.

One brother down, three to go.

Chapter 30

The Brother

No matter how good you are, there's always someone better; that's what my mother used to tell me growing up. So, after tasting my first kill, I learnt all I could about the bloody arts. With the internet still a glint in a geek's eye, it was the crime section at the local library which introduced me to my teachers. Gein, Bundy, Gacy, Sutcliffe, Berkowitz, and Kemper. Of course, the books I found were not true representations of my killer guides; they were events filtered through a rational mind trying to understand what went wrong with these men. Bumps to the head came up a lot. I asked my mother if any childhood accidents befell me.

'None. You were a careful child,' she told me. 'Always thinking two steps ahead of where you were going and what you were doing.' And that's why I left Poppy Fields without killing Fallon. I'm not a fool. I got lucky with Cross. She'd already cried wolf too many times, so no one would, even for a second, believe that the wolf finally got her after they'd denied its existence. No one wants to admit they're wrong. I need my sister in the same state as Cross. Pressure and paranoia piled up so high she can barely see over it. Not a difficult feat. Poor little Fallon has taken on way too much. She's like a sponge soaking up everyone else's tragedy. Was she like that before Cat Hall? Or is her sanctimonious nature born more of bloody nurture? I often wonder that about myself. Was I born to kill, or was I driven to it? Growing up, I don't remember bruises from anything other than fighting and sports. I do remember Mother's little talks though, the times she'd pull me aside and whisper, 'I had such great hopes for you.' And I'm sure she did; working at a garage is certainly not boasting material for afternoon teas with friends who have doctors for children. Would discovering her son is a serial killer, the successful kind, be a badge of honour to crow about over scones and jam?

After learning all I could from my contemporaries, I started to fish further afield for information. There's no handy distance learning how-to courses for serial killers. The closest I found were true crime magazines. Deconstructing the unsolved murders trapped in their pages helped me on my way to becoming the best. That's how I learnt forensics and how to cover my tracks. Textbooks helped too. There was one I saw at Fallon's by a Dr Todd Hawk. There can't be many Hawks knocking around, so I'm assuming he has something to do with Tina Hawk. Googling, I find it is her. Originally, she wrote it under a male pen name. Sad really, that she felt she had to write as a man to discuss such dark subject matter. It's not like murder is only in the male domain. There are female serials – they're just harder to find. Their methods more subtle. Most women will never know the joy of slicing through human skin, apart from Lizzie Borden of course, although I have serious doubts those kills belonged to her.

During my tea break, I decide to pay a visit to the local bookshop. First thing I do, what I always do in shops like this, is check for my favourite book. *The Most Dangerous*

Game by Richard Connell. I found my copy at the age of thirteen in the local library. I read it cover to cover thirty times. The story now is imprinted on my memory: a remote island, a big-game hunter's party, and a strange count who makes them his prey. It was everything my hormone-addled imagination needed. From then on my murders made more sense. Shame, I don't find it here. I often lament on the fledgling murderers that it won't get the chance to inspire.

Moving into the non-fiction section, I search for a copy of Dr Hawk's opus on sick minds. I track it down easily enough, and as I flick through the pages see a chapter on 'The Hunt'. Instantly drawn in, I sit on the floor and read. Twenty pages of unfounded, pompous assumptions. It's utter nonsense! No wonder Fallon is struggling to keep up with me if this stupid woman was her teacher. I need to give my sister another chance; it's the brotherly thing to do. Perhaps I can be her teacher – send her a message, give her a clue, help her see the light, with something more personal than Cross. A thought begins to dance through my mind. I'm about to pull myself up and check my work schedule when I notice a woman looking at me. Dowdy tweed coat and clutching a romance novel to her chest. No doubt she's imagining me as her handsome leading man. That it'll be me who lifts her from the sinking mundane mud of her life like so many of her heroes did for the heroines in her books. In her pathetic romantic haze, there's something she's wilfully forgetting – those characters were written to be together. The author crafted them to fulfil their tired plots. No one has written me for her.

Before finding my game, I used to kill at will. Victims of chance and opportunity. Challenges I took up on the fly. And as she is deep within her daydream, it's only fair that I have mine: a faraway look in my eyes will draw her in. A brief interaction where I'll take on the mantle of a bumbling romantic lead, someone like floppy-haired Hugh Grant in his heyday. We'll laugh. We'll cry. We'll leave the bookshop to start our life together. Just like Nicole, she'll be so wrapped up in the possibilities, she'll trust me when I take her for a moonlight picnic in the woods. Candles, great food, and much-needed solitude. Why invite the world when we only need one another?

Mother told me to never meet a lady empty-handed, so I'll bring her a gift. A soft, bright red shawl to shield her from the chill of the dark night. Ah, then the real hunt begins. She'll run. She'll die. I'll carefully hide the body. All evidence of our encounter will be disposed of and I'll be back home in time to have a beer and watch *Match of the Day*. Less like her romance novels and more like my kind of story: Boy meets girl, Boy hunts girl, Boy buries girl.

Focusing, I see she's still staring at me. A sigh on her lips to match her gormless expression.

'Can I help you?'

Clutching Dr Hawk's book, I turn to see a gangly shop assistant has sneaked up behind me.

'No thanks,' I squint at his name tag, 'Gavin.' Smiling, I add, 'I'm not the one who needs help.'

Chapter 31

Fallon

As I drink a morning coffee on the deck, I spot my Ford coming round the corner. Si parks up, then a second car pulls up behind him with Garry and two other lads from the garage. Both I recognise from the party.

'Hey, nice place you have here,' Si says, getting out. The other driver, Miles, stays in his car. Tentatively, I wave at him. He waves back. Then the passenger doors open and Jason slides out along with Garry.

Harvey barks.

'What's his name?' Si asks, staring at my dog.

'Harvey!' I yell over the barking as both brothers move in to fuss him. 'Thanks so much for helping. How much do I owe you?' I ask.

'We told you, dinner.' Although talking to me, Garry is checking out my lodge. 'Wow, this must have a cost a bit,' he adds, stepping back to take in the private woods behind my house. 'Although maybe a bit too remote. All things considered.'

Smiling, I say, 'I'd ask you in, but I have a client soon.'

Si nods. 'No probs. How about we do our brother-dinner together on Wednesday?'

Hearing the day makes my cheeks burn. 'That's when I testify,' I say.

'Thursday then?' Garry suggests.

It could be the perfect opportunity to get know both brothers. 'Sounds like a plan.'

'We could do the Wool Pack pub,' Garry says.

'You sure you don't want us in the gallery when you testify?' Si asks.

Too quickly, I say, 'I'll catch you up at dinner.'

He moves closer to me. 'I'm really glad we're getting to know each other, Fallon. I've always wanted a little sister.'

'I always wanted big brothers.' I smile again, although I can't feel the gesture making it to my eyes.

'Awesome.' Si takes the Honda's keys from me and throws them to Jason to drive the car away.

Still staring, Garry cocks his head then asks, 'Um, you know your decking looks like a giant prick wrapped around your house, right?'

'I'm well aware.'

Garry snickers, earning a sour look from Si. Composing himself, he then says, 'All right, we've got more cars to pick up. See you real soon.'

My knees won't hold me up any longer. I stretch my arm out towards the bannister and use it to keep me upright. Limited sleep, and the responsibility of putting away two killers is stressing my already jagged nerves.

Without noticing my odd reaction, my brothers both walk over to the waiting car and, even though he is just as big as them, Miles all but scurries out to let in his bosses. After folding his large frame into the driver's seat, Si waves out the window, and they all drive away.

When I can no longer hear the engines, I slip down to perch on the deck. Harvey nudges me, and I hug him close. 'Did you get vibes off either Si or Garry?' I ask him. My dog snuffles my ear, then slinks off to pee.

-

I spend most of the day on Hawk Therapy, speaking with my regular clients. After dinner, while I'm eye-deep in my brother's profile, my mobile breaks my thoughts. I glance at the caller ID – it's Susie.

'So sorry to call out the blue like this,' she says.

'What's wrong?'

'Stefan's acting really weird. Well, weirder.'

'Do you need help?'

'No.'

She says no too quickly, and I'm about to ask the question again when she adds, 'He was going on and on about *you* needing help.'

'That's odd,' I mutter.

'I wouldn't have bothered you with this, but he told me I had to let you know.'

'To let me know he was being weird?'

'No, that he *now* wants to talk to you. Will you?'

I need to determine if Stefan is the killer, but the thought of being alone with him again is frightening. *I can do this*. 'How about we all go for coffee tomorrow morning?'

'Fallon, please, it has to be now.'

'All right, I'll call him.'

'He left his mobile here.'

My fingers, curling around the phone, suddenly feel numb. 'I can't,' I whisper.

'You said you'd be there for me, remember, at the party? I think he's going to do something stupid. Please, don't let me down. Meet him.'

The words I spoke to Susie boomerang through my creeping panic. I look at the clock, 7 p.m., most of coffee shops are already shut. 'Okay, how about at the pub where Miles' party was held?'

'No, he's already there, waiting for you.' I can hear it clearer in her voice now – desperation laced with love.

'Where?'

'I'm so sorry,' she sobs.

'Tell me where he wants to meet me,' I repeat.

'Cat Hall.'

Chapter 32

Fallon

I know I shouldn't go. Anyone with a rational thought left in their head would lock the front door, climb onto their sofa and ignore such an obviously stupid invitation. But I'm fresh out of rational thought; it's been bled out of me. If Stefan is the killer and I don't show up, he could choose another target for his deadly attentions. That's how I've profiled this killer; he won't stop killing. I should tell the police, but what would I say? Without evidence there is nothing they can do. And if he's just an innocent brother, I'd have ruined my relationship with him before it's even started. I have to do this.

I tell my clients that, to move forward, they must face their fears. If I'm honest, I haven't done this with Cat Hall. Since that night, I've never set foot back there, and even avoided driving past it. But suddenly after rushing out the door, here I am, parked in the same spot I did over a year ago, and possibly heading off alone to meet another serial killer. History repeating itself. It certainly does have a sick sense of humour. I wish I'd brought Harvey with me, but everything moved so fast, my rational mind has only just caught up, and I've no time to go back for my hairy shark.

After taking a long deep breath, I pocket my freshly charged stun gun, then walk towards the place Stefan is bound to be waiting. Maybe this time, my Cat Hall confrontation will be different. *I* will be different – better.

Builders have now almost finished the new estate. Gone are the diggers and dusty barriers; in their place are small, colourful houses neatly grown in rows. Families have moved in. I see lights and hear TVs pumped up too loud. If needed, there are potential witnesses, but also potential victims; I can't forget that.

Too soon, I reach the house at the end of the road. It's also complete now. Facing my fears sounded like a good idea, and even though, deep down, I know it is just a house, it was the men in it who were the danger, it doesn't stop panic scuttling up my skin when I spot him lurking by a lamp-post. Stefan hasn't seen me yet. I could still run back to my car, just like I did that night. I can't.

'Why here?' I shout over to him.

My brother turns around, a weak smile creeping over his lips. 'Glad you came. Susie said you wouldn't. But I knew you would.'

I stop a few metres away, my hand in my pocket. 'You didn't answer my question.'

Scoffing, Stefan moves a little closer. When he sees me flinch, he stops. 'I just want to talk.'

'And we couldn't do that over the phone?'

'I needed to see you. I've brought you a present.' He pads his jacket down until he finds what he's looking for. Initially, he struggles to free it from his pocket, but then he brings out a small box.

'What is it?' I ask.

Extending his arm, he offers it to me. To collect it, I need to move closer. Fat chance.

'Stop being cryptic, Stefan. Why are we here?'

'It's the perfect place to talk.' He looks around us.

My itchy finger caresses the button on the stun gun. 'What's on your mind?'

Stefan takes one step towards me, box still outstretched. 'It's a gift. Take it.'

He has a one-in-three chance of being the killer. I can't risk my life just to be polite.

'I don't want it.'

Throwing the box at my feet he yells, 'Don't be rude, Fallon.' He then holds his hands up and takes another step towards me. 'Sorry, just listen for a minute.'

Fear pours through my thoughts. My stun gun took down Sam long enough for me to get a head start, it'll do the same to Stefan if he's the killer. I just need the courage to move close enough to use it. 'I'm listening,' I say. Then, as calmly as I can, I take a step towards him.

'I wanted to talk with you because...'

'It's okay.' I say taking another step forward.

He nods and looks away, then mumbles a sentence I don't quite hear. One word in it rings loud and clear, though – *killer.*

Shit! Am I within zapping distance? How quickly could the police get here?

Stefan continues, 'All my life... I...'

I'm close enough to do it now. To take down a man who committed unspeakable acts.

'...I thought I'd killed you.' Stifling a small whimper, he retrieves a hip flask from his pocket. After taking a swig, he offers it to me.

Shaking my head, I stand my ground. 'You thought you'd killed *me*?'

His once irate expression has now morphed to sorrow. After taking another swig, he says, 'I'm old enough to remember the baby who came home with Mum from the hospital.' He takes a final gulp, then continues, 'The first night you were home, I was so obsessed with being a good brother, I-I…'

'What did you do?'

'I've never told anyone.'

He turns away from me and I step forward to grab his shoulder and twist him back around. 'What happened?'

Now I'm closer I can see the veins in his nose are burst and blooming, and his bloodshot eyes are filled with tears.

'I thought you were cold, so I gave you extra blankets. I spent ages tucking you in so tight… But then the next morning you and Mum were gone and when she came back alone and told us you'd died, I thought…'

The realisation of what he's saying snaps me into psychologist mode. 'You thought the blankets suffocated me.'

'Mum said you'd stopped breathing. I thought she'd hidden that you'd died at home to cover for me. All these years, I believed I'd killed my own sister.'

'I'm so sorry you shouldered that guilt. Your mum should have said something sooner.'

Scoffing he pushes off my hand. 'She's *your* mum too, remember.'

'So she is.'

Looking down at his empty flask, he asks, 'Want to come back to mine for a drink. Talk for a bit?'

Decades of guilt could explain his drinking and behaviour. Psychologically, his false belief would also explain his adverse reaction to me suddenly showing up in his family's lives. Believing I was dead, and he was to blame, for so long would make it hard for his mind to make sense of this rewrite of his history; something that defined him throughout his whole life. All this aside, none of it exonerates him from being the killer. For all I know this is a clever lure to lead me to a secondary location.

'We all have demons,' I say.

'It's why I picked this place to meet you; cause of what happened, you know how I've felt all these years. The guilt.' Bending down, he scoops up the box he tried to give me. From inside, he pulls out a rose-coloured ribbon. 'I thought it might help you a little if you could tie it to the memorial lamp post or something… it was stupid idea.'

Actually, it was a lovey idea, but I can't get distracted, and I can't just ask if he's *the* killer. If he is, he could easily strangle me at this distance. If he's not, the accusation could cut his emotional wounds even deeper. If I can just find out what he's been doing with his time… 'Are you cheating on Susie?'

'No! Fuck. Is that really what she thinks?'

'How could she not? You're out at all hours, distant and moody.'

Closing his eyes, he wobbles a little. He's already had way too much to drink today. 'Believe it or not, I'm trying to get sober, if you must know. And I was doing all right until you showed up.'

A familiar wave of guilt washes over me. I ruined my brother's sobriety. 'You were going to meetings?' I ask.

'Yeah, I'd even stayed at a few detox facilities. I told Susie I was playing cricket. I didn't want her to find out I'd been drinking again.'

Wait, this could help. Rehab clinics are almost as secure as prisons. 'When were you there?'

'Why?'

'Indulge me.'

'First two weeks in December, then before that over Easter last year.'

There was a murder at the start of December. 'Which facility in December?'

'Burnt Oak, up in Scotland.'

An alibi! Stefan can't be the killer. I know Burnt Oak. There's no way he could have escaped such a secure facility, then made it down here in time to kill Ryan.

'Why is all of this making you so happy?' he asks.

My hand finds my mouth. I'm smiling.

'Are you enjoying this? Me airing all my beer-soaked laundry?'

'No, not at all.' I lunge forward and embrace him uncomfortably.

'Get off,' he says and pushes me away.

'Look, I know people. If you really want to get sober. I'm here for you and will set something up. You didn't kill anyone, Stefan.'

Reaching his hands to sit behind his head, he smiles at me. 'Yeah, I know that now.'

'Maybe don't be so hard on yourself going forward,' I say.

Standing up straighter, he looks me in the eye. 'You got it, doc.'

For a brief moment, I envy Stefan. All his life he believed he had done something terrible, and now he knows for sure he didn't. After this revelation, he can move forward into a brighter future. There is one thing he needs to do though.

'Stefan, Susie deserves to know about everything.'

He shakes his head. 'I couldn't.'

'When my mum told me about the baby swap, I saw a weight lift from her. Subtle at first, but she's gotten lighter every day since. You deserve that feeling. And your wife deserves to share in it with you too. For better or worse, remember?'

'Man, you're good. One small speech and I want to spill my guts,' he says with a laugh. 'You really are Super Psychologist.'

'Yeah, I left my cape at home,' I joke.

Knowing it'll be a difficult conversation. I offer to drive him home.

Before we leave, I take the time to tie the ribbon to the lamp-post so it sits with all the other tokens of sadness. When the bow looks as good as I can get it, I stand back and silently take it in.

'What really happened here?' Stefan asks. 'Personal demons can spot each other from a mile away.'

Not wanting to answer the question I say, 'Right, let's get you back home. You've a worried wife you need to explain a few things to.'

'Will you stay with us for a bit? Referee?'

'Of course. You're my brother.'

Chapter 33

The Brother

My pulse sits at a rare fifty-three as the evening draws in and I double back to Foxglove to stand outside Poppy Fields. The Ford is gone, so I know she is out.

Suddenly her dog's angry face appears in the living room window. His eyes filled with rage, hackles stiff, and a growl rumbling through the glass. I get it, I'm on his territory. The thing is, I need to give her a little nudge. Help her. And I can't do that with this thing nipping at my heels.

Bark. Bark. Bark!

Fortunately, I've brought just the right silver bullet for the werewolf. I pick the lock and open the door. Slowly, I reach into my bag, then call out, 'Oh, Harvey!'

–

Dog dealt with, I check her file's progress. She has eliminated one of my brothers. Sam is no longer in the running for Kapper Killer of Year – the award I win, hands down, every year. My sister *is* closing in. Fallon is better than the Hawk. Instead of help, I just need to take the game to the next level.

I scan the lodge and see a photo on the mantel of her and some guy. There's an honesty to it. No photoshopped faces or half-arsed smiles. I know he doesn't live here – an ex she's never gotten over perhaps? I don't understand love – an unnecessary feeling destined to become ridiculous masochism. Who in their right mind would chain their self-worth to another? I remember a Starsellers sale of binoculars to a woman who had recently been dumped by her boyfriend and had taken to wailing through tubs of ice cream and gin each night. An avant-garde kill, I stalked her while she stalked him. It's one of those experiences which could be recalled as either sad or funny depending on your mood. We spoke before she died, more in depth than the conversations I'd had with the others. In her loveless despair, she asked the right questions and got to know me – a little.

What would a fictional villain do in my position? I think, my hand finding Harvey's fur. As I run my fingers through it, they come away covered in dead hairs, making me wince.

She left in a hurry. Her laptop is still on and the Hawk logo fills the screen. Staring at the outspread wings, hungry eyes, and open talons gives me an idea. Something to strike at the very heart of her guilt-ridden psyche birthed at Cat Hall. Death is inevitable, but it hits harder when it's preventable. I open Starsellers and bring the frame's auction date forward, then mark the item as 'collect in person'. It will earn me a digital slap on the wrist by the site, but I don't care. What I'm doing will be epic.

'I think I might have cracked the perfect challenge for my sister,' I tell Harvey.

Urgh, when I look down at my trousers there's more hair on me than on the dog. Why do people love pets? Something dumb and smelly that relies solely on you. And he does smell. Knowing where she keeps her pet supplies,

I decide to dig out the thing's brush. I then set about making him look pretty for when she comes back and our game together truly begins.

-

When I get home, I shower off the gag-worthy dog smell, then settle in my chair with a beer.

The silver photo frame's end time is fast approaching. A hot seething steam whistles between my flesh and bones, aching for release. Suddenly, one bidder makes me a private offer – three times what the frame is worth. I immediately take it off auction and accept the offer. £200. That's how badly she wanted to win.

After I explain to the buyer over email that I'm away for the next two days, and that she can collect the frame when I get back, I casually ask how local she is. The address is too perfect. Within fifteen minutes, I get my first look at the new owner of Yvonne's photo frame. Young and pretty. Without a care in the world, she walks with her dog alone towards a nearby park. Her dog is not a werewolf like my sister's. It's mid-sized and only has three legs. Patiently, its owner slows her pace to accommodate the thing's hobbling. As I follow them, I have to weaken my stride too.

As I watch walkies, I wonder why the silver photo frame was so important to her. Who would she have used it for? Who in her life is important enough to warrant such a spend? It doesn't matter now. Her prize can frame her final photo. Taken by the morgue, it'll capture her expression of horror as I squeeze her trembling throat like a lump of clay. She will be a petrified portrait, cadaver couture, the ultimate still life – that is, if Fallon can't save her in time.

Chapter 34

Fallon

When I pull up outside Poppy Fields, I find it unusually quiet. Harvey isn't barking to welcome me home.

Opening the door, I prepare myself to be Harveyed with slobbery kisses. Instead, it's as if he's not even here.

'Harvey?' I call.

I walk from the living room to the kitchen and as I do, I get a whiff of a meaty smell I can't put my finger. It turns my stomach. Where is he? Did he get out?

Bending, I grab one of his favourite toys, a squeaky chicken. I press it a few times, hoping the sound will see him bounding over to me. Nothing.

As I move further into the lodge, the weird smell is everywhere, making me gag. What the hell is that?

The bedroom and bathroom doors are all closed. Could he have gotten into one of them and trapped himself inside? If he did, why am I not hearing him scratching to get free? I open the door to the guest room but find it just as I left it. The bathrooms are also Harvey-free.

The last room I check is my bedroom. As I open the door, the meaty smell becomes stronger.

Sprawled across the end of my bed is Harvey, merrily gnawing on a huge bone. He's so happy eating his meaty meal, he barely acknowledges my presence.

'Where did you get that from?' I ask. As I stroke his head, I find his fur brushed to the point it's almost silky – odd.

Looking down, I see he's made a horrific mess of marrow and bone bits on my sheets. Where did the bone come from? Quickly, I wrap it in a towel and pull it away from him. It could be poisoned. He whines but allows it. Next, I check him all over for signs of poison, dull eyes, lolling tongue, but there's nothing. If anything, he's more playful than usual.

How could this happen? Wait, is this a warning? The killer is one of the two brothers who dropped my car off here today. The message is loud and clear: I'm on to you, and could have killed your dog if I'd chosen. He's now playing his game with me.

In a panic, I call Joel, but get his voicemail. I leave a garbled tirade about my brother. What he's done, and what he could do. When I hang up, I think about calling the police, but I still don't have any real proof of any of his crimes.

After I air the lodge and light scented candles, the horrible meaty smell dissipates. But my fear remains. How did he get inside? When I check my front door, I find criss-cross scratches around the lock. My brother picked it. It was that easy for him. Waggling metal tools in the lock rendered the barrier to my safe home redundant. I feel sick.

Si or Garry? Garry or Si? Usually, when a killer is unmasked, it's the person everyone least suspects. The friendly neighbour hoarding too many power tools. The dedicated scout leader too good at knots. The loving husband and father who no one saw coming, not even his own family.

When Joel texts to say he'll be over first thing in the morning, panic creeps in. A whole night alone with Harvey, who is now best friends with the killer thanks to the bony gift. I have the stun gun, but when I used it on Sam, it only took him down for a moment. Would it buy me enough time?

Lindsay didn't have a dog to bribe; she didn't get a warning that he was onto her. I guess I'm lucky. Although, *lucky* feels an odd choice of words.

Phone still in my hand, I call a twenty-four-hour locksmith and ask for an emergency appointment. After checking the lock on my front door, he admits there is no such thing as an unpickable lock, but tells me the new ones he fits are harder to crack by normal people. As my brother is not a normal, I invest in a deadbolt too.

–

When Joel arrives the next day, he immediately clocks the new deadbolt.

'Are you and Harvey all right?'

Upon hearing his name, my dog bounds into the room and practically knocks Joel down. Manoeuvring the hairy beast out of the way, my barrister sits.

'He was sending me a message,' I say.

'Don't get lost in your brother's games.'

'It's not exactly a conscious decision. That's like saying don't be afraid of that tall building to an acrophobic.'

'Fair enough.'

I sit beside Joel. 'At least now I've exonerated Sam and Stefan, there's only two brothers left.'

'Make a point of telling both you've changed your locks and say you have a security company watching your lodge. That should stop whoever did this coming back. What are your thoughts on them?'

I can't afford to make assumptions. 'It could be either. But I'm having dinner with both on Thursday. I can use the time to press for dates, compare them to the profile.'

'You only really catch a killer when he's behind bars for life. Cross was right, the DNA will help, so let's still try for that too.' Joel lets out a deep sigh.

'Thanks again for helping with this,' I say.

'It's okay. But I don't want you to forget about your testimony tomorrow.'

I've been dreading this day for so long, I could have never forgotten it; pushed it to the furthest recesses of my mind, yes – but never forgotten.

When I don't reply, Joel continues, 'In court, there is more than one version of the truth. When Baker testifies, he'll tell his version and if his is better, the jury will believe him. We have the benefit of putting our case forward first, so if all goes well the jury will side with us and it won't matter what Baker tells them.'

Remembering the smug look on Caroline Trout's face, I say, 'Cognitive bias.'

'Right. It takes a lot to steer a person from the first thing they hear.'

'Their psychological anchor for the events.'

'Exactly, but we can't rely on it. I've met Baker, he's oddly charming and has a clean record. With the other two confessing, the jury already have someone to blame for the murders.'

'I'm ready to prove Tyler a liar,' I declare.

'Good to hear. Remember to tell us everything. All Baker needs is something to contradict in his testimony, and make it look as if you're lying. Let's not give it to him.'

I say, 'Agreed.' But the tone in my voice is not as resolute as the thought in my head.

Once Joel's gone, I lock the door, then make a coffee. To occupy my mind, I research 'best DNA samples' and learn I ideally need something with my brothers' salvia on. A cup or a glass from dinner should do the trick. I then read and reread the folder and my profile between walks with Harvey.

Crawling into bed for an early night, I try to tame my thoughts. One problem at a time. The nearest fire is my testimony. Closing my eyes, I feel Harvey jump onto my bed. He scratches the sheets a little, then settles in the crook of my legs. 'I'm warm. I'm healthy. I'm… wasting time!'

Throwing off the duvet, I get up to practice what I'll say on the stand. Second-guessing everything the defence might ask me, and mentally preparing myself to take on Tyler, again. I have to make him pay for what he did. Prove that the world is just by having him spend the rest of his best killing days in prison.

-

Today's the big day. I try on five different outfits for court. Nothing seems right, and I kick myself for not thinking about it last night. I'd love to just pull on one of my Christmas jumpers and burrow into the soft, warm wool, but it wouldn't be appropriate attire.

Finally, I give up and text Ollie. Instead of replying he speeds round and throws himself into my wardrobe. A few minutes later, he hands me the perfect outfit. 'You ready?'

'I hope so,' I mutter.

'Hey, Fal. I know there's something you've held back about Cat Hall.'

In weak protest, I open my mouth to reply. He beats me to it.

'And I don't care. Even if you told me, I wouldn't care. The world isn't always fair. You know that now. So I'm not even going to say tell the truth today, or any other bullshit. Lie on the stand if you have to. Do whatever it takes to get that arsehole put away.'

'The ends justify the means?'

'Every fucking time.'

'He did it, I don't need to lie.'

'Even better. Now get dressed.'

With renewed rigor, I wrestle myself into a pink satin blouse and grey pencil skirt.

Ollie drives me to court, all the while quoting inspirational lines from Gordon Gekko and, God help me, Patrick Bateman. By the time we park up, I'm ready to put out the nearest fire.

The CPS team meet us outside. After one last good-luck speech from my little brother, I walk in with Joel. Once we make it through the metal detectors, he plants me in the witness suite ready to be called. As he leaves, Patricia waddles over.

To distract myself, I ask, 'How many more weeks?' nodding towards her baby bump.

'Five. I can't wait to get it all over and done with.'

'I know the feeling.'

I'm then treated to half an hour of complaints about the baby shower her best friend threw her, and how lazy her boyfriend has been. Her baby's father is Paul from Chambers. I let her drone on about their relationship, her voice skimming my mind like a flat rock across a still pond, until a thought slaps me – Tyler is in the next room. He'll be sitting down with his barrister, smiling and chatting and acting the innocent man. Minty breath and no hidden knives. The perfect picture of a man accused of a crime he didn't commit. He's probably already got a Netflix documentary lined up to take on the mantle of his innocence with a one-sided narrative and million-pound marketing campaign. Me? I'm like a can of pop, with small tingling explosions in my chest sending numbing heat through my body. The feeling is familiar. I had it at Cat Hall; desperation driving me to seek out any means necessary to win back my life.

Suddenly, the clerk beckons me. The walk to the courtroom is short. I'd imagined a seemingly endless corridor leading to a chunky wooden chair, the electric kind they used for executions. I'd sit in it, then grow small, like Alice in Wonderland, shrinking until my legs barely reached the edge of the seat. The judge would loom over me, scowling. Each time I'd open my mouth to speak, no sound would come out until eventually the guards would lift me up, as if I were a child, and carry me to a cell.

When the doors open, I walk into court. Murmurs sound from the gallery. As the clerk manoeuvers me onto the witness stand, I glance up, but all the faces looking my way blur into a fleshy mass. I wish I hadn't told everyone to stay away; maybe I'd feel less like a tiny boat among a sea of warships. It's then I see Tyler Baker in the dock. Wearing a suit, and with his hair cut and chin shaved, he looks like any man you'd see on the street. He stares straight at me. How I keep my face blank, I'll never know. On a table nearby, a woman, his barrister, shuffles her papers – her gender an obvious ploy to prove to the jury women are not afraid of him.

The clerk shoves a Bible in my face. Placing my sweaty palm on it, I recite that I'll tell the truth.

Joel stands, his face void of emotion. It's as if we've never met, let alone spent hours together as co-conspirators in an illegal serial killer investigation.

'Dr Hurley, can you please tell the court, in your own words, what happened that night.'

I knew this was coming, it's what I've been preparing for with Tina, but what I wasn't ready for is how the request hits me square in the gut. Everything I want to say, and everything I don't, floods my mind and mouth, mixing together so I can no longer distinguish one from another. I can't bring myself to look up at the faces in the court, so cast my stare down to my hands laying limp in my lap. Slowly, I then repeat the events as best I can, and as close to the police statement that they have already read.

When I'm finished, I dare a glance up to see Joel give a quick and comforting nod. He then asks, 'The defendant claims that he was a victim in these events. Can you clarify that for the court? How did he represent himself that night?'

'I met the defendant Tyler Baker.' As I say his name, I can't help but look over at him. A soft smile is playing on his lips, as if he's concerned for me. 'At Cat Hall. He led me to the house.'

'The house which held both Gayle and Victor Steiff?'

'Yes.'

'So in that act he showed participation in the crimes.'

'Yes.'

Joel moves closer to the jury. 'Dr Hurley, did Tyler Baker in any way act or appear as a victim that night?'

'No. In fact, I quickly realised he was in charge. The others were under his control.'

'Can you elaborate on *control*?'

Remembering my sessions with Tina, I reply, 'Yes, he openly threatened and bullied Streak, and goaded Ropey.'

'Knowles and Partridge,' Joel corrects.

I nod. 'Tyler even told Knowles that if he didn't participate his sister would be next.'

'Excuse me, that's hearsay,' says Tyler's barrister.

'Dr Hurley witnessed the events first hand,' Joel replies.

'But none of these supposed threats were in the sworn statements by the other men present at Cat Hall.'

The judge looks over to me. 'Let's move on to another subject.'

Nodding, I take a deep breath, knowing from this moment on the questions will get even harder.

'When was the first time you saw Exhibit H, the knife?' Joel asks.

'Tyler pulled it from his pocket and showed it to myself and Gayle. He even cut his gloves to show how sharp it was.'

'To your knowledge, were all the victims murdered with a knife: Gayle, Vic and Rosie?'

The defence rises to object, but sits back down. Joel's not saying it was Tyler's knife but *a knife*; she can't argue against causes of death.

I confirm with, 'Yes. I saw Vic's body.' A torrent of sense-packed memories threaten to take me. To stop them, I think back to my talks with Tina. I can do this. 'And the police told me that was what happened to Gayle and Rosie.'

Joel takes a moment to look across at the jury for their reaction, then continues, 'With the Steiffs already present, tell me about Rosie Howe. How did she come to be in the house?'

The witness stand sways beneath my feet. Heat from a hundred staring eyes scalds my soul. My story must be consistent. 'Tyler took her from the show home.'

Waiting a beat to let my answer land with the jury, Joel then approaches me. 'And why was Mr Baker there that night?'

'He said he worked at the site. They all did.'

'We have statements from several builders, and work contracts for all three men, to back this up.' Joel moves to his table and retrieves some papers. 'Permission to approach with the statements?'

The judge nods, then takes the papers off him to check, like a teacher reading homework.

'One might then surmise this obvious connection with the convicted criminals who freely admit their crimes, along with Dr Hurley's testimony, shows Mr Baker as a willing participant rather than a victim at the tragic events at Cat Hall.'

'Excuse me!' Tyler's barrister yells. 'If my colleague is taking the stand, shouldn't he be sworn in?'

Before the judge can rule, Joel throws me a look.

Quickly, I add, 'It was clear to me they were all friends.'

After a few more questions, Joel sits back down.

I move to climb down from the stand, but the judge waves me to stay. The defence barrister rises and, smiling, approaches.

I try not to focus on her, so instead look out across the gallery. It's then I see him. Staring right at me, mouth twisted and cheeks red with rage.

Chapter 35

Fallon

Rosie's father doesn't blink when our eyes lock.

'On the night in question, were you frightened, Dr Hurley?'

I recognise him from the news articles.

'Dr Hurley?'

'Sorry, can you repeat the question?'

Huffing at my lapse in concentration, she says, 'The night it happened, were you scared?'

'Terrified.'

'Have you ever been *terrified* before?'

'Afraid, but not terrified.'

'You say my client was the ringleader. Is that your professional opinion?' She cocks her head.

My psychologist brain knee-jerks through my Cat Hall memories, 'Looking at the dynamics between the men, it was easy to see Tyler was in charge. When he told them what to do, neither questioned his instructions, no matter how' – I hesitate and look over at the jury – 'violent they were. Streak even appeared reluctant to take part, but that didn't stop the defendant making him. Tyler was not another victim.' Good response, maybe I'm doing well.

'But you just said you were terrified. Can you honestly say you were calm enough to psycho-evaluate three men?'

I turn to look at the jury. 'I didn't need a masters in psychology to see what was happening.' An old woman in the second row stares at me intently. Is everyone looking at me like that?

The defence edges nearer. 'In your *professional opinion*, would a traumatic event make someone less or more attentive to details?'

'Trauma could impair a person's cognitive functions, but I remember everything in vivid detail – thanks to the defendant.'

'Let's talk about the knife. You claim only you and one of the deceased, Gayle Steiff, saw it in the defendant's hand?'

'Yes,' I reply. Covertly, I glance at my watch. The longer this goes on, the greater the odds of saying something to turn the jury away from me.

'But you could be mistaken?'

'No. He cut his hand with it. Sliced right through his gloves.'

'The infamous gloves, which were not found at the scene.' The barrister waits a few seconds, allowing her statement to sink in.

'Just because they were not found, doesn't mean they did not exist,' I say.

She smiles at me. Have I fallen into a trap?

'Dr Hurley, are we to believe that you, throughout this' – she looks down at her notes – 'awful attack, remembered every single detail?'

'Your Honour, please,' Joel yells. 'My learned friend is badgering the witness.'

'Actually I'd like to hear the answer,' says the judge.

My stare swings from one barrister to another. I do remember everything now, but did I at the time of giving my statement? The statement she clearly has a copy of in her hands. During my sessions with Tina, my narrative wasn't being questioned or judged, so I spoke freely.

'Dr Hurley?' prompts the judge.

'Can you repeat the question?'

'Can you confidently say that you remember every detail of your attack?' she repeats.

She'll test me on something if I say I do, but if I admit I don't I'll appear unreliable in the jury's eyes.

'Not every single detail,' I admit. A murmur reverberates around the court. Quickly, I add, 'But the important things, like who attacked me and with what, are trapped in my memories forever.' At this I dare another glance into the gallery. Rosie's father still has his eyes locked on me. Heat rises through my body to settle in my cheeks. Am I sweating through my satin blouse?

'So, in that moment, you could discern the important facts, from the non-important facts?'

I nod.

'Three murders were important, yes?'

'Of course,' I reply. She's still smiling.

'And punishing the guilty party is important to you, yes?'

'It's important to everyone.'

'And as you admitted that you don't remember everything that night, I put it to you that, when the police told you Rosie and Gayle were dead, you created a false memory, then convinced the same of all around you? Thus satisfying your important memories.'

Joel stands up. 'Your Honour, badgering!'

The judge ignores this and lets her continue.

'I mean, you ran leaving those helpless women to suffer their fate. And let's not forget you are the only witness contradicting events. This accusation of my client could even be born of survivor guilt.'

Under the stare of not just Rosie's father, but the whole courtroom, I narrow my eyes and spit back, 'I'm the only witness because I escaped that' – I point over at Tyler – 'monster!'

The judge waggles his finger at me. 'Control yourself, Dr Hurley.'

'Sorry,' I say, but I'm not looking at the judge, my eyes are on Rosie's father.

The barrister shrugs at my outburst, then says, 'No further questions.'

'Does the Crown wish to redirect?' the judge asks.

Joel shakes his head.

Waving a robed arm, the judge declares, 'The witness may step down.'

When the court door closes behind me, I tell the guard I need the toilets. He points in their direction and I run. The moment I'm locked in the stall, I sit down, put my head in my hands and think back over my testimony. Important memories? My opinion? She set me up to look unreliable, and I just arrogantly fell into her trap. I hadn't prepared enough for today. This is all my fault.

After spending over an hour in the ladies, I edge out and look both up and down the hall to see if the coast is clear. I then quickly make my way towards the main doors.

As I get to the metal detectors, I'm waved aside by a guard.

'Dr Hurley!'

Turning at my name I see him. Still red-faced – still angry. Rosie's father heading straight for me. Now my testimony is over, I can talk with him, but instead of waiting, I rush out the door.

'Dr Hurley!' he calls after me.

When I reach my car, I promise myself that I will speak with him, just not now. I have a serial killer to catch.

-

Back at Poppy Fields, I painstakingly text Mum, Ollie and Tina about my testimony. Wanting more detail, Ollie invites himself round for a late night brandy. Not feeling up to it today, I suggest we do it tomorrow instead. Tina then calls and instructs me to rest, but working, helping people, is taking the edge off the dank well of despair my life is quickly tumbling down.

What if Tyler is released? What if my brother comes after me? What if – two of the worst words to be haunted by when you're hunting one serial killer and trying to put another behind bars.

At three in the afternoon, I ignore my boss's advice, and click onto Hawk. After watching the familiar bird fly onto the screen, I immediately get a message from another psychologist online: *Client waiting who will only speak with you.*

The virtual waiting room shows a single username, Im_Next123. Not a user I recognise, but some clients do change their handle mid-therapy. I open a chat with them, but see only darkness. There's no video recording from their side. I turn on mine to encourage them to do the same. They don't, instead a direct message appears on the screen.

Dr Hurley?

'I'm here. Do I know you?'

Yes.

'To whom am I speaking to?'

A laughing emoji appears on the screen.

Annoyed, I say, 'I'll help you if you need help, but if you're playing games, you need to log off this site.'

Don't you want to save me?

'Of course I want to help you. Turn on your camera so we can speak face to face.'

You've already seen my face, but I'm not ready for you to know who I really am – not yet.

I'm about to log off when a thought hits my mind like an icy wind. I'm talking to *him*. He's on the other end of this laptop. 'Brother?'

Yes! You do know me. Just thought I'd check in with my sister, see how your testimony went today?

Shit! My hand lifts to slam down the laptop lid, but I hesitate. This could be my chance to get under his skin, to ask the right questions and dig up the answers, maybe even a confession, which could lead the police to his door. Both Garry and Si knew I was in court today. 'As expected.'

I do hope Baker is punished. I didn't like him one bit.

He's been to court. 'Have you met others like him before?'

More than you'd think. But let's not talk about them.

I look around my lodge. Harvey is snoring by the fire. 'Did you enjoy being in my home?'

> You did get my message! I wasn't sure.

Remembering Joel's advice, I say, 'I've changed the locks and have a security company watching this place, so it was the first and last time you'll be here.'

> Wasn't the first. Won't be the last.

How many times has he been in my home?

> How's your hunt for me coming along?

'Fan-fucking-tastic. How are you doing?' I ask, masking my fear with anger.

> You seem upset, sis.

'No, I'm sad. My friend Lindsay was murdered. I also lost a client called Yvonne.'

> My, knowing you is dangerous.

I wait for him to add to his sentence, to admit he killed them both. Most people, when faced with a lull in conversation, will speak to fill the void. But not my brother. Three minutes tick by without me even seeing the word *typing* on the screen. Eventually my impatience gets the better of me. 'Why are we doing this?' I ask.

> I'm here to give you a clue.

'A clue to your identity?'

> A clue to my next victim.

Chapter 36

Fallon

Knowing he's watching my reaction, I smile as if he'd just offered me help on a crossword, not put a person's life in my hands. Through clenched teeth, I say, 'That's kind of you.'

I'm a peach. But I need you to play by the rules.

'What are the rules?' I ask.

This is a two-player game. You can't bring in any of your little helpers. If you do. You'll lose and I'll take my prize right then and there; fair's fair. Deal?

What can I say? I open my mouth, but nothing comes out. He's challenging me, and I can't back down. I nod.

Excellent.

'How do I win?' I ask.

As you know, I enjoy a homely crime scene, so as long as the victim is outside their house by the time the clock strikes murder, I'll walk away. But if you do not manage to entice her outside before then, well, you know what will happen.

Her; it's a woman. 'You swear you'll play by that rule?'

> Of course. You have my word. Would you like me to tell you about her?

Calmly, I say, 'Please.'

> Barely out of her teens. Lives near you. Plays guitar in a band. She likes silk scarves, and silver photo frames. Owns a three-legged dog. Her favourite colour is blue.

Young and kind, living her life to the full, yet now my monstrous brother is in her shadow. And it sounds like he's already been in her home. 'What's her name? Where does she live? Why her?' I ask, my voice betraying me at every trembled question.

> So many questions. But you're not asking the right ones.

'What are the right ones?'

> It's no fun if I tell you. But, since you're flailing, and I'm a good sport, I'm going to educate you. Unlike Yvonne, she's not seen me watching her.

He knew Yvonne contacted me. It's why he's taunting me through Hawk.

> You look constipated when you're thoughtful, sis.

'I'll eat more fibre,' I say offhand.

The laughing emoji appears.

Tell you what, let's play three questions. But, let me be clear about the rules. I'll answer truthfully, scout's honour, but you can't directly ask me who she is or which of your brothers I am – agreed?

I nod. Questions are good. Even if he lies he might expose a fact that narrows down my search. Being on camera, I can't flick through my profile in front of him, and I can't shut down the camera in case it spooks him. I'll need to go from memory – something, anything to give me a lead, or at least confirm some suspicions. 'How did you pick her, your next victim?' I ask.

Thirty seconds ticks by. 'You know, it smacks of lies if you take too long to answer.' Am I pushing my luck? This could be the best chance I get to identify him. It's either Garry or Si, and I might soon have enough syntax from this game to narrow it down to one before our dinner.

A complex question deserves a complex answer.

'So, what's the answer?'

She chose herself.

'That's not an answer.'

Then ask better questions. Two more left.

How can you win at a game when your opponent is making all the rules? Conjuring the profile in my mind, I mentally flick through the pages. He's both organised and disorganised, knowing which he favours could help. I also need to know if she's still alive, and I'm not on some fool's errand. He might have already killed her and, rather than a game I have a tiny chance of winning, this is some sick prank. But that's two questions. Wait – two birds, one stone. 'How are you going to kill her?'

> I don't decide until the moment is upon us both, but I always carry a good selection in my kill kit.

The moment has yet to come upon them; meaning he's not killed her yet. And he's organised, he brings weapons with him; but he also has a hint of the disorganised as he picks a method of murder on a whim. Shit, this poor girl is going to die because I'm a terrible psychologist. Another innocent life to add to my growing list of failures.

> Tick tock. Last question.

'You say you'll back off if I get to her first, but I don't trust you.'

> You can trust me. Like I said, fair's fair.

It's hard to believe words on the screen, but right now I have no choice. 'How long until you kill her?'

> Sorry, little sis. You've already asked all your questions.

'Technically, not trusting you was a statement that you simply confirmed.'

A laughing emoji appears again, its yellow and white mouth looking strangely sinister.

> Clever.

'What did you expect, we do share the same DNA,' I say, cringing.

> Touché… I've been challenging myself with 24 hours, so it's only right that you play by the same rules. Happy hunting!

And with that, a message appears saying, *Im_Next123 has left the chat.*

'Yeah, see you at tomorrow's dinner, you murdering prick,' I spit at the blank screen.

Twenty-four hours from now to find and save her. I barely enjoyed a single relieved breath after my testimony and now I'm responsible for another life.

–

Fair's fair. That's what he said. I know he's playing a game, but it would appear he has rules. I make a note of this in his profile.

I think about reporting Im_Next123 to Tina as a client endangering a life, but if my brother finds out, he'll make good on his promise of a swift death. I can't let a young girl be murdered – not again. I have to play his game.

Rolling around the answers he gave in my mind, I start Googling. Silk scarves and silver photo frames are not going to help me, so I try to find local bands with a young female guitarist. After clicking through a few dodgy sites, I finally have a shortlist of three bands. Two are playing tonight. Am I really going to march up to each woman playing a guitar and ask if her favourite colour is blue and if she owns a three-legged dog? You bet I am!

I arrive at the first pub early. The band are only just setting up so I corner one member and ask if any of them own a three-legged dog, as I saw one in the car park. They all shoot me faraway looks of disdain. She's not here.

It takes me an hour to drive to the next pub and, by the time I arrive, they are in full swing. Two girls on guitar, neither wearing a scarf or anything blue. Worrying I'm doing the wrong thing in believing my brother, and I should be asking for help, I drink a lemonade and I wait for them to break their set. As soon as they do, I approach the band with the same lie about the stray dog. No one bites. She has to be in the last band.

Exhausted and angry I get back home and shoot off an email to the third band, Jumpin', who seem to be more of a collective of DJs, musicians and singers. I write that I have a dog who's just had his leg amputated and a friend told me to speak with someone in the band about their pup who has the same affliction.

Then it's a waiting game. I turn on the TV but can't settle. I watch show after mindless show; everything from the latest reality twaddle to soaps I've never watched before, all the while my attention crucified to one thought – I'm going to fail her.

–

Past two in the morning, with Harvey a hairy weight across my legs, I check my emails for the fiftieth time and find one from Jumpin'. *You have the wrong band – no one here has a three-legged dog.*

Eleven hours gone, thirteen left. I want to call Si and Garry, to see if whoever it is slips up as their mild-mannered normal alter ego, but it could spook him.

Due to the vague clues he gave me, another hour is lost to falling down random rabbit holes, and triple-guessing every idea and action I take, or don't take.

While eating breakfast, I flick through the file once more. I reread the information I've collected on Garry and Si. As I do, Harvey drops his ball expectantly at my feet. I should take him for a walk, but it seems such a mundane, frivolous thing to do while a girl's life is at stake.

Harvey whines and another guilt trip takes me for a ride. He depends on me too. Being a dog owner is exhausting, I can't imagine the issues a three-legged dog has... Wait, finding a girl amongst hundreds is a statistical nightmare, but how many three-legged dogs can there be in the area?

I make a note of twenty-five vets within a thirty-mile radius of Foxglove. Grabbing Harvey's lead, we go for a walk and I start calling the geographically nearest, then working out from there. I use my previous rouse about finding a three-legged dog and asking if they know who it belongs to. It's a tricky tightrope what with data protection laws the way they are. With careful lies, I stumble across two owners of three-legged dogs, but one is a man and the other an elderly lady. It takes hours. All the while I watch the clock count down. Finally, just past 2 p.m. I deliver my practised lie to Paws & Tails and the receptionist gasps. 'Poor Peggy, is she hurt?'

'Peggy is fine. I'd just like to get her back to her owner.' Lying is becoming shockingly easy for me.

'Oh, well I can give her a call for you.'

Her – it's a good start. 'The thing is, I'm a doctor and I see patients at my home and with client confidentiality, I can't have strangers visiting the premises. But I can drop Peggy off.' Harvey, rubber bone in mouth, stares at me while I continue my deceit.

'I'm not sure I should give you Casey's address.'

Casey – I have a first name. 'Actually, I think I might have seen her out when I walk my dog at Foxglove – young, pretty, plays in a band, wears a lot of blue?' I grind my teeth at the sheer absurdity of my words.

'That's Casey! So you do know her.'

Thank God! I now just need her address. 'Peggy is becoming agitated. I'd really like to get her home.'

The receptionist thinks too long on this, so I snatch the bone from Harvey's mouth. He whines at its loss, and I mouth the word 'sorry' to him.

'Oh dear, Peggy does sound in distress.'

'Casey wouldn't mind you giving me her details,' I fish.

'I really shouldn't. My boss would kill me.' I hear movement on the other end of the phone. Is she hanging up?

'Wait, I have a vague idea of where she lives. I just don't have time, as a doctor, to go walking Peggy down every street. I won't tell Casey you gave me the address. I just really want to get this poor girl home.'

Silence. Have I pushed her too far?

A whistle of air hits then hits the phone. 'She lives at...' There's a clicking sound as she types. 'Nineteen Rutland Road.'

Yes!

'That's not far, I'll nip her over now. Thanks.' I hang up quick.

3 p.m. is fast approaching. There's only twenty minutes left on my brother's deadline.

Chapter 37

Fallon

Rutland Road is a ten-minute drive from Foxglove, but every red traffic light and twenty-mile-an-hour zone feels like it extends my journey by hours. I can't let Casey down.

Harvey whines in the backseat. I try to soothe him, but it doesn't stop his constant fidgeting. I couldn't leave him behind this time. If my brother is there already, I might need my hairy shark.

I pull onto the road, only to find that it's huge. Rutland winds around a roundabout and house numbers can't be seen from the road. After spotting a place to park, I free Harvey, then we run from house to house counting them down to find the right one. Cars are everywhere, and with my brother working for a garage, he could be lurking in any one of them. He might even be inside her house right now, his hands around her throat like Lindsay. A bloody screwdriver in his hand like with Yvonne. Or wielding any other dark weapon which takes his fancy.

Looking at my watch, I still have seven minutes. He has to be here too, waiting for the clock to run out so he can win the game.

Suddenly, I spot number eighteen. Harvey and I bound across the road to nineteen. I bang on the blue door. No answer. I bang again, the side of my hand numbing with each knock. If he's lied and lured her someplace else, this was all for nothing.

'Casey!' I yell.

Six minutes left.

'Casey!'

There's movement on the other side of the door.

'Who is it?' a female voice asks.

'My name is Dr Fallon Hurley. Are you Casey?'

'Yes.' A horrible thought hits me. 'Is there a man in there with you?'

'No, why?'

I'm in time. 'Please, open the door. You're in danger.'

Harvey barks as if to second my statement. The door opens slowly. It's Casey in a blue jumper, a three-legged collie behind wagging her tail at the sight of Harvey.

'Why am I in danger?' she asks.

'I'll explain everything. But please you and Peggy need to come with me. I promise, I'll keep you safe.'

'Nah, I'm good. Thanks.' She moves to shut the door.

Jamming my boot in the way, I stop her. 'Please, look here, I'm a psychologist.' I rummage in my bag then show her my Hawk ID.

Staring at it she shrugs. 'So?'

Was it in the rules that I couldn't tell her about my serial killer brother? 'I spoke with a client yesterday who said he's going to hurt you. Please, you need to trust me.' I look down at my watch, I only have five minutes to get her out of the house. 'Please!'

'Who's your client?'

'Someone very dangerous.'

She has the bored look of a girl just out of her teens. She doesn't believe me. If some mad woman knocked on my door the night of Cat Hall and warned me not to go, would I have heeded her advice? Probably not. No one expects bad things – they rarely see them coming. What could have been said to stop me?

'Perhaps I should just call the police?' she offers.

Four minutes. 'They won't make it in time. Please, just come outside.' Frantically, I look up and down the street. I know he's here. He might already be inside her house. If she shuts the door, she's as good as dead.

Harvey barks. Casey peers out at him. Desperate, and with time running out, I make a decision. I'll use the same techniques Tyler used on me.

'I could get in trouble for coming here and telling you this. We should go for a quick walk and talk. You don't want to be *that* girl who didn't heed a warning, do you?' I hold my breath.

'Hang on.' Casey closes the door.

No!

I'm about to bang on it again, when she emerges with her coat, and Peggy on a lead. Within three minutes we are outside, and my whole body unclenches as Harvey pulls us towards a nearby park.

When I tell her what could have just happened, she doesn't believe me, but she still answers my questions as I try to figure out how my brother chose her. The thing is, all her latest activities are so mundane, eating out, playing guitar in a fledging band, walking Peggy, shopping and hanging with friends, her answers don't help much.

When we get back to her house, I help her check it. No sign of my brother, but the back door is open when she swore she locked it. I bend down to examine the lock and see familiar criss-cross scratches. At this, Casey's expression changes from dubious to freaked out.

Someone, uninvited, entered her home; I understand this notion all too well. After a quick text to her boyfriend, I leave her packing an overnight bag.

My brother doesn't always talk his way in; sometimes he sneaks inside like a crafty shadow – like he did with me. But I have confirmed one thing about him: he did play by his own rules. Casey is alive.

As I walk back to my car, I scan the neighboured for Si or Garry, and even though I don't spot either I still feel eyes on me. I ruined his game. Did I quench his thirst for excitement, or, frustrated, will he lash out at someone else?

Thankfully, Casey is safe, and with a renewed sense of worth, I get ready for dinner. Whichever brother it is, I'll be eating with him soon. Perhaps I can get under his skin and he'll make a mistake. Or perhaps, as I just foiled his plan, I'm already under his skin and he'll be itching to dig me out.

–

The Wool Pack pub is a pleasant bistro sitting in the middle of town. Humming with people, and smelling of spices and herbs, it would be a wonderful place to eat, if I wasn't breaking bread with a serial killer. When I arrive, I find Si already at the table. Garry is running late so, carefully, I ask about Si's day and he tells me about a fuck-up at the garage. Clients often speak in metaphors without realising, and, as I listen to how the tyre delivery was too early and they'd not had a chance to make room for the stock, I wonder if the anger dancing behind his eyes is for me rather than the tyre man.

Garry doesn't apologise for being late, just heads straight to the bar. Si excuses himself and follows his brother. When they come back, both have a pint of beer and a shot of brandy in their hands.

'Here,' Si says offering me his shot glass. 'Congratulations.'

'For what?'

'Getting through your testimony,' he clarifies.

'Oh, yes. Let's not dredge that up.' I scan the table, trying to spot a good source for their DNA. The pint glasses both are drinking from are too big to subtly steal.

Narrowing his eyes, Garry glares at me. 'You okay?'

'Fine,' I say. 'You been up to much?'

Garry takes a swig of beer. 'Nothing much.'

One of these two men just pitted me against a ticking clock to save a girl's life. I ask, 'Do you play any competitive sports?' Smooth.

Neither man has the annoyed look of being beaten at his own game.

Si answers, 'We play cricket. The garage has a team. Do you like games?'

Garry leans in for my answer.

'Not really,' I say, then try to gauge their reaction. Si shrugs and Garry gulps down half his beer.

Si then asks, 'You travel much?'

'Yeah, Super Psychiatrist has to be able to fly, right?' adds Garry.

'Psychologist,' I correct, then regret it as he eye-rolls me. 'Not so much.'

'You look pale. Have another drink.' Garry slides his shot across to me, like a challenge.

Peer pressure hits me like a ton of bricks and I down the shot. Looking at the menu, I check for something bland and filling which will be easy to vomit up later.

We order food, and Si tells me Siobhan now wants to meet. It's a big deal: the mum who gave me up to a woman she'd just met wants to get to know me. Perversely, this makes me realise how deep I'm in to catching my brother. Instead of wondering about what I'll ask her and what she'll tell me, I'm thinking what information I can glean from Siobhan about her sons to separate a killer from just another big brother. Does she have suspicions about Si or Garry? Did either of them torture animals or set fires when they were young?

'You know, you don't have to meet her if you don't want to.' Garry tells me. 'If I could get out of all the family crap, I would.'

Shaking off my thoughtful silence, I gush, 'I'd love to meet her.'

Si nods and arranges it for us all there and then on his mobile, for Tuesday.

When the food arrives, Si flirts with the waitress, making her giggle. Watching, Garry snorts, then takes out his phone. I use the time to casually check my mobile too; as I do, a diary notification reminds me Ollie is coming round later to discuss my testimony.

When I hear the waitress give Si her number, I think through my knowledge of serial killers. They play at being human and doing human things, and yet Si's ease and charm appear natural. Garry, on the other hand, is withdrawn and sullen, but that doesn't mean to say he can't fake it when he needs to.

I push out, 'Tell me about your childhood?' then cringe at the cliché.

Leaning back in his chair, Garry picks up a chip then dunks it into a dollop of ketchup. 'You didn't miss much. Never seemed to get anything I wanted.'

'Garry had to dress in our hand-me-downs,' Si adds.

'It's hard to develop your own style when you're wearing everyone else's,' Garry says grudgingly. He then drags the whole plate of communal chips we ordered towards himself and protectively puts an arm about it. Prisoners do the same with their food, as if to ward off potential thieves. Not a surprising trait with him growing up with three brothers.

'School wasn't pleasant for any of us, but we had our good looks.' Si laughs. 'Well, all of us except Garry.'

Narrowing his eyes, Garry snorts again. Tiny pieces of blood-red chips splatter out of his mouth. 'Hard growing up competing with you lot. Always trying to be the best. No wonder...' He trails off with a sneer.

'No wonder what?' I prompt.

'Drop it,' he spits. 'I'm not in the mood to be profiled.'

Si leans over and punches his arm. 'Quit being a prick. I can't take you anywhere.'

Tension suddenly descends to laughter. I laugh with them. A little too manically though, as they both stop and stare at me.

'Don't be nervous, it's not the final lap just yet,' Si tells me.

What does that mean?

'Yeah, there's plenty of time for us all to get to know one another, we're family.' Garry nods as he speaks, then his fingers creep over and steal a little food from my plate. Our eyes meet, and he smiles as if to challenge me to say something.

'I'm going to pay the bill – I need to sort those tyres out at the garage. You good here?' Si asks, staring at me, then glaring at Garry.

'Of course.'

Garry smiles. 'Yeah, it'll be nice to get some alone time. There's things we need to discuss.'

As Si leaves, Garry's smile grows into a grin, the kind I've seen before. Bile bubbles up my throat.

'I need the toilet,' I say, then head straight for the bathroom. Weaving through tables and customers, I try to get a hold of myself. Garry has a fifty per cent chance of being a killer, but he also has a fifty per cent chance of being just another brother. When I reach the ladies, I look back at our table. No longer stuffing his face with food, Garry stares after me. When our eyes lock, he slowly lifts his hand and bends his fingers up and down in a creepy wave. Bursting through the toilet door, I scare a woman touching up her lipstick. Swearing at me, she grabs her bag and hurries out, leaving me alone.

In the mirror, I see a haggard fool of a woman. 'Pull yourself together,' I tell my reflection, but my words are lost in the loud pop music being pumped into the toilet. If I were a betting woman, my money would be on Garry over Si. Psychologically, he fits the profile. I just need science to confirm it. Once I'm calmer, I'll saunter back to the table, and make an excuse to leave. Then, as Garry heads off, I'll double back, grab the cutlery off his plate, and run like the wind to my car. One quick lab test and it'll reveal the killer's DNA either belongs to Garry, or doesn't. And if it doesn't, then it's Si.

At first, I'm too distracted to notice the door opening, but then I catch a glimpse of him in the mirror. No hesitation in entering a women's toilet, he strides in, then moves the bin to block my only exit.

Chapter 38

Fallon

'Garry?'

'I came to check on you. I thought, if you were being sick, you might need your hair holding or something.'

The information I learnt at dinner spins around my head. Garry is unpredictable, he has a chip on his shoulder, and all the ones we ordered in his belly. I already knew he had violent tendencies after witnessing his actions at Miles' party. And now I'm trapped in a toilet with him.

'Why block the door?' I ask, edging towards a cubicle. I might be able to lock myself in and scream until someone finds me. But would I attract help quick enough over this bloody music?

Garry looks back at the bin. 'Weird force of habit. Growing up with three brothers, the toilet was the only place you got some alone time. And that was only when you barricaded the door.' He follows up his answer with a goofy grin.

'A lady might need the loo, perhaps you can take the bin away and wait outside?'

But he doesn't do it. Instead, he steps towards me. Recoiling, I catch my side on a basin. Dull pain shimmies through my ribs, kickstarting a familiar feeling.

'Whoa! Sorry, Fallon. I just can't have anything happen to you on my watch. What if you'd passed out and choked on your own vomit? That shit happens you know. People die in the weirdest ways, especially when others *aren't* there to save them.'

A collage of all the murders collected in the file floods my mind. It ends with an image of a bicycle with a pink wicker basket covered with blood.

'Look, I'll go. Don't have a heart attack.' He bends to move the bin. 'You know, Fallon, I can't quite work you out at times.'

Narrowing my eyes, I ask, 'Why are *you* trying to work me out?'

'You're my little sister. I've always been the youngest, having to compete with my brothers, and now there's perfect little you.'

'Perfect!' I laugh. Wait… 'What?'

Garry shakes his head, then casually stands with his back to the Tampax machine. 'It's the same in every family. Your little brother knows what it's like. The things you have to do to prove yourself worthy.' He pats his leg.

'What have you done?'

'Oh, you wouldn't believe it.'

'Try me.'

Garry walks over to me, his limp more pronounced. I back away from him. The stall is just behind me now. But instead of reaching me, my brother awkwardly slides down onto the floor, his back against the tiles. 'The most recent debacle was when Stefan got drunk and jumped off the roof.'

'Recent?' I edge over as I speak, angling myself nearer the door.

'Yeah, believe me. I wish I hadn't been stupid enough to go up there after him. I broke my leg. Only got the cast off a couple of weeks ago. I can walk okay, but it hurts sometimes and I still can't drive. It's why we had to rope Miles and Jason into dropping cars off the other day.'

A broken leg would have taken at least eight weeks to heal. Which means... Garry would have been on crutches. There's no way he could have killed Ryan, or committed any of the murders in the past few months.

Spluttering out a relieved sigh, I slip down onto the floor to sit beside him. However weird his appearance in this bathroom is right now, he's not a killer. He's my brother.

'Are you better now?' I ask.

Garry chuckles. 'Yeah, but Si wasn't too happy with Stefan. I dropped like a rock and that prick just bounded off the roof like some sort of superhero with barely a scratch. Said if he caught him doing something stupid like that again, he'd kill him.'

'Risking his life?'

'Nah, risking arrest. It wasn't one of our roofs we jumped from.'

'Why would he say that?'

'Come on, Super Psychologist, you must have figured it out by now.'

I raise an eyebrow. 'Figured out what?'

'Why we call Si, Si.'

'His name is Simon?'

Garry laughs. 'Si is short for psycho.'

–

By the time I get back to the table, the waitress has cleared away our dishes, along with any of Si's DNA I could have taken. Shit.

But at least now I know who the killer is – Si. Charming, protective and ultimately evil, it was Si who broke into my home. Si who killed Lindsay and made it look like an accident. Si who I need to catch before he kills again.

Chapter 39

The Brother

Do most brothers hate their sisters? Only tolerating them on special occasions. Are they rivals from birth to death, first for their parents' affections and then for who can win at the game of life? Do they always play fair with one another? No, they don't. Fallon cheated. It was me who knew Casey's house and routine. Me who had chosen one of her pretty blue silk scarfs to take. Hell, I'd even played with Peggy while Casey was out. Fallon should never have been able to beat me.

I was there, ready and waiting. I'd watched for over half an hour from the kitchen pantry as Peggy had been groomed and pampered, then had her photo taken in several kitsch poses. I was going to print one out on Casey's posh computer and stuff it into the frame to leave behind. It was going to be epic. I'd have known that perfect feeling once again – I knew it. Then, there *she* was. Gushing at the door. Using her mind tricks to lure out my prey. The werewolf panting beside her. I imagined Fallon failing, my victim closing the door, leaving us alone together. My sister would have broken the rules then, called the police. Not that that would have mattered. It would have been all finished by the time they showed up.

But it never happened.

All the dark energies I'd conjured left my body as Casey left her house. My beloved murder chain has been broken, and it's all *her* fault. The silver frame sits on my sold items, but will never hold one of my bloody memories. When Fallon drove away, my temper almost got the better of me. I stood on Casey's street and stared at her blue door. But I couldn't do it. My limbs screamed yes, but my mind calmly told me no. I'm a lot of things, but I'm no cheater; not like my little sister.

Driving back to the garage, I realised then, as the older brother, I needed to strike back. Part of meeting challenges is being adaptable. I had to find a way to resurrect my game; add a new link to the chain – one which would punish Fallon for her treachery. I would take out one of her pawns. Sink one of her battleships. Guess who? Her false victory will be short-lived. With a good dollop of dark, thought-out intent, I could still make it work. Mentally I retraced my steps, thinking back to my time in Poppy Fields. That's when I realised who'd be my next victim…

-

It was too easy to find the house. When will people learn to turn off their online locations on social media? Parking up the street, I stalked closer to my new prey's home. Smothered with ivy, it sported quaint wooden windowsills painted pink. Although the location was not as remote as Foxglove Lodges, it was still set back far enough from the road to afford privacy.

Before arriving, I'd dressed in a green electrician's outfit, complete with toolbox and baseball cap. Even if someone saw me, they wouldn't question my presence. A dog may be man's best friend, but assumption is a serial killer's.

After a quick look around, I noticed the logo for a doorbell camera by the front door, so headed over the fence and into the garden. No cameras there. Within minutes, I'd picked the lock and was inside. I looked around, then chose the perfect blind of a wardrobe in which to hide.

The slick tension I'd lost at Casey's began to build once again. I released the stolen silk scarf from my pocket, and slowly began to slip it through my fingers. I could still smell her perfume, the house's incense, even the scent of the dog. Again and again, it touched my skin until it became a part of me; an extension quickened with murderous intent. My prey would be back soon.

Chapter 40

Fallon

Once home, I text Joel, *Can we talk?*

His reply is a question mark.

I type an epic message detailing all my other brothers' alibis and explaining that now leaves only one who could have possibly killed all those people: Si, and he's out there right now gearing up to kill someone. Yet, when I reread it, it all sounds like conjecture, just ammunition for a half-way decent defence barrister to parade in front of a jury like a line of cancan dancers. Delete. Instead, I call and start the conversation with another question which has been festering inside me all day.

'Was it bad after I left court yesterday?'

'You were a victim of a crime, not an expert witness as the defence tried to twist you into. Juries are not idiots. I watched their faces. They didn't like the way Danielle bullied you on the stand. It's still all to play for.' He sighs. 'Hey, how's the family investigation going? Did you pick up anything at dinner we can test?'

I take a deep breath. 'I know which brother it is. It's Si. Garry broke his leg a month ago, he couldn't have committed the latest murders.'

Too quickly he replies, 'Great news.' Then adds, 'Well, not so much for you and your family, but that we have it narrowed down. Get me a DNA sample to confirm; if it matches we just need an excuse to arrest him and make everything official.'

'You said your DI doesn't mind breaking the rules?' Cringing, I continue, 'Si has a temper. All she needs to do is tease it out.' Hating myself for uttering the horrific idea aloud, I quickly add, 'I've never met DI Worth so maybe that's a bad idea. He could hurt her.'

'Don't worry about Worth, she's had dealings with serials before. She enjoys confrontation. If anyone can get the drop on a killer, no matter how clever he thinks he is, it's her.'

'Wow, I hope I get to meet her soon.'

'I'm sure you will.'

–

Looking at my watch I see Ollie is late for our catch up drink. He's never late. Worried, I leave my third message of the evening on his voicemail, then call Mum. She says they spoke yesterday, and they're getting on better, but she doesn't know where he could be.

My thoughts darken. What if Si has him? Grabbing my stun gun, I speed over to my little brother's house. When I reach it, I see a strange red Audi in Ollie's drive. Shit! Not even taking the time to shut my car door, I run for the porch. The last time I felt like this I was running away from danger, not bolting towards it. Out of breath I go to knock, but the door opens before I can touch it.

Chapter 41

Fallon

'Fal?' Ollie says.

'You're okay!' Lunging forward, I hug him.

'Um, you could have called ahead, I...'

'You didn't answer my calls. You were supposed to—' I'm about to yell at him for standing me up when the door falls open further and I see a man.

Constable Miller is sitting on Ollie's sofa.

'Dr Hurley?' he says, then gets up to join Ollie at the door.

The penny drops. '*You're* the new boyfriend,' I say. Relief grips me and I awkwardly hug him too. Not only is Ollie alive, but he's dating a policeman who can keep him safe.

Miller pats my back, then politely pushes me away.

'Come in.' Ollie motions for me to join them inside.

I blush furiously. 'No, I can't right now.'

'Sorry, Fal. I really wanted to tell you. We met end of last year. He interviewed me.' Ollie then laughs. 'It got pretty in depth.'

Miller laughs too. They seem good together. 'It's my fault Ollie stood you up tonight. I caught him just as he was heading to yours, and we just lost track of time. I'll let you two catch up.' He leans in to kiss my little brother.

I smile. 'Don't be silly. It was just my turn to worry. You guys stay here together. I'll get out of your hair.'

Ollie's grin almost covers his surprise. 'You sure?' he asks.

'Course. Constable Miller should stay as long as...' I almost say possible, but catch myself just in time to say, '...he likes.'

'Ray,' Miller says. 'I think you can call me Ray now.'

'Excellent. Right then, Ray, keep my little brother safe.'

As I say goodbye to Ollie, I fight off a pang of jealously. How much easier would my life be if I had a boyfriend whom I trusted? Who I could tell everything to. But I brush the selfish thought away as quickly as it came. This whole situation would be so much worse if I had a partner. If I am in danger, he'd be in danger too.

As I'm nearing the A road to take me back to Foxglove, my phone rings. I pull over to take it and cringe to see the caller is Grant's mum. I blocked him, so he must have decided to use her phone to hassle me. It's as if he psychically knows whenever I feel vulnerable.

I answer with, 'I blocked you for a reason.'

'Hello?' It really is his mum.

'Sorry. Hi. Is everything okay?'

She sniffles.

'Dorothy?'

'Oh, Fallon.'

'What's wrong?'

'Grant committed suicide.'

I drop the phone, and scramble to scoop it back up. Heat builds in my cheeks, radiating up my face and stinging my eyes. What? How could Grant commit suicide? Dorothy goes on to tell me that he hung himself in our old garage. When they found him, there was an apology note addressed to me pinned to his chest. I listen to her anger and pain, then try to calm her down. I say how sorry I am and talk about how he was a good man. Lies blend so seamlessly that in the end, even I believe them.

When she hangs up, I drive, like an automaton, back to Poppy Fields. I then sit on the sofa, phone in hand, and try to make sense of it. How could this have happened? Because I blocked him, my only link to Grant was my old Facebook account, so I log on. On the second attempt I remember my password and I'm in. It's then I see it. My timeline is one long post-athon by Grant – public to all. Pleas to get back together, reminders of photos we shared and trips we took; it's a desperate digital love letter. It ends with a post on my timeline this afternoon; the photo he clocked at the lodge. Under it, there's a message: *Your move.* He expected me to respond, and I didn't. If I hadn't blocked him, he could have sent this to me directly and I'd have seen it in time.

Curling up on my sofa, Harvey taking up all the leg room, I realise my triumph in unmasking Si is lost in Grant's suicide. My ex's actions were extreme, but I should have been kinder. I'll never see him again. Another needless death that's all my fault.

I'm worse than Si.

Chapter 42

The Brother

After a lovely dinner, I relax in my favourite armchair and think back over my latest victory against my sister…

Grant was a wriggly fucker. It took several attempts to wrap the scarf around his neck.

'Stop! Who are you?' he spluttered as I dragged him across the carpet towards his back door. Too many questions then spilled from his lips; all I could have answered, yet chose not to. Once we were in the garage, I sat him on a chair. Pushing a piece of paper and pen in front of him, I said, 'Write what I tell you.' He nodded. With my silky noose tight around his trembling throat, he wrote his own suicide note. The proverbial Monopoly Get Out of Jail Free card for me, and the cunning clue, slash punishment, for Fallon. I'd win this round. Steal her hope of a future with this idiot.

To ramp-up the guilt, like Casey was meant to, I told him to apologise for everything he had done to her in the past, all the lies he unsuccessfully wove, all the times he'd cheated, and all the promises he'd broken; basically all the sappy shit women want to hear. Closure is important.

When we were done, he asked, 'Are you her new boyfriend?'

This assumption made me uncomfortable. I'd have punched him, but the injury would have appeared out of place, so instead I gripped the scarf's slack around his neck, giving it a good yank. A strangled spray of spit shot from his mouth.

'What do you want?' he begged through unmanly tears. Ignoring him, I used his pathetic face to unlock his mobile and access his social media. A few bleak posts here and there about how sad he was without Fallon would cement my story. That's when an idea hit me. One so daring, it made my fingers tingle as I searched through Grant's photos for just the right one. I remembered it from Poppy Fields's mantel. In it, they didn't look very happy, but then again, in truth, that's what relationships are – unhappiness maintained by hope. I posted the photo on her timeline with a two-word challenge, *your move.*

To strangle a grown man, you need strength, persistence, and material which doesn't snap off mid-murder. Fortunately, I had all three. After five minutes of struggling, Grant's shell of a body became a heavy weight in my arms; a meat puppet with its strings cut. At this point in a murder, my thoughts normally morph from red to philosophical. All those special things which made him who he was, were now absent from the world. My hands took them. There will never be another Grant, or another of any of my victims. Some killers are arrogant enough to think they make a positive difference with their death dealing – snuffing out those less-dead, like prostitutes and criminals. I like to think there's a little darkness in everyone. A red-tinted cloud that, on certain days, gathers in their mind ready to drip blood. It could be a flood or a drizzle, dependant on those other factors studied by psychologists like my sister.

Gifting Grant a length of string – blue twine you can buy in any shop – I fashioned a noose and hoisted him up the garage's main beam. As I folded Casey's scarf neatly into his pocket, the body swayed a little like one of those crystals on leather thongs that idiots dangle over pregnant bellies to guess the gender. As I watched gravity play with the corpse, I thought, if he spins right, I'll win my game with Fallon, if he twists left, I'll lose. With barely any movement, I almost pushed him myself, but it would have been cheating.

Looking up at his slack face, I couldn't imagine anyone other than debt collectors and subscription channels would truly miss him, but you never know. I once killed a man whose obituary listed a hundred good deeds to help him through the pearly gates. I couldn't have been the only one to spot his collection of torture devices in the basement, some adorned with fresh blood. It's always the one you least suspect.

Chapter 43

Fallon

The winter sun is poking through the living room curtains, daring me to mistake it for spring. For a moment I think I dreamt last night's news. But my real life is so much more frightening now than nightmares. Grant is dead. And with the morning comes an awful thought – did my brother kill him? I need to know more about what happened, find out if this is Si paying me back for saving Casey.

Driving to Grant's childhood home transports me back in time. We were always round his mum's house. Dorothy baked great cakes and sewed dresses from patterns. Her arms were always welcoming and warm. Grant was her only child. And now he's gone, leaving her alone.

When I get there, I see her car is parked in the drive, so I know she's home.

'Hello?' I call through the letterbox.

The door flies open. Grant's mum, red-faced and broken, stares back at me, her appearance reminiscent of Rosie's father.

'I'm so sorry,' I tell her, then lunge forward for a hug. We stay that way for a long moment before she invites me inside. I make her a cup of tea and we sit down.

Remembering her illness, I ask, 'Are you feeling better?'

Her eyebrow raises. 'Whatever do you mean?'

'Grant told me you had been in hospital.'

Dorothy looks confused. 'I'm healthy as a horse. Why ever would he tell you that?'

Why ever indeed. I was right about him, the conniving… no, as bad as he was, he's dead because of me. I can't forget that, and Dorothy doesn't need that parting information about her son. 'Nothing,' I say.

That's when I see it crumpled in her hand. Without a word, Dorothy passes me Grant's suicide note. Not the real one, but a photocopy. I read it, then reread it. The handwriting is his, but shaky. He says sorry too many times. To be fair, one time is too many for Grant. A shiver runs down my spine when I note a few deliberate words: arrogant, charm, narcissist – all of which appear in my brother's profile – which he clearly found and read after breaking into my home. And, most oddly, there's no mention of Grant ending his life. When he wrote this, he didn't know he was signing his own death warrant.

'He wasn't always a good man, but he loved you, Fallon.'

In his own way, Grant did. It just wasn't in the way I wanted or needed. 'Yeah,' I say, 'he did. I'm so sorry' – I sob – 'it's all my fault.'

She puts an arm around my shoulders. 'There, there. You didn't put the rope around his neck,' she says. 'You know, even in his despair he needed to be close to you. He died with your scarf in his pocket.'

Scarf? I don't wear them. 'What did it look like?'

'A beautiful blue silk one. I can get it back from the police for you, if you like?'

A blue silk scarf. I remember Si touting Casey as liking silk scarves and the colour blue – clues I could never have used to find her. I shiver at the thought that, even then, he was thinking two kills ahead. However am I going to beat him?

'Oh dear, you've gone so pale. This whole... thing is such a shock. Can I make you some lunch or something?'

I'd love nothing more than to sit down to a wonderful meal with this equally wonderful lady, but now I know for sure Si killed Grant, I need to act. Sweet as she is, I can't tell Dorothy the truth. I won't put that horrific knowledge on her until Si is in handcuffs and answering for his crimes.

Waiting for my Tuesday tea with the Kaplans is not good enough. I need the DNA sample now. But how can I get it? I can't just wander into the garage and demand something adorned with Si's saliva.

And yet... Si *is* the boss, so is the only one with an office. If I can think of an excuse to get in there, I could bag something of his. But just randomly stopping by is too suspicious and Si can't realise what I'm doing; it'd no doubt be considered against his rules. I need an excuse. The last time the car was there, I had accidently put diesel in the tank – that could work again. I don't mind looking scatty if it saves lives.

Driving to the petrol station gives me the time to convince myself I'm doing the right thing. How many more people have to die before my brother feels as if he's won his game? Five, fifteen, fifty? Without stopping him, it'll never end. Countless people will lose their lives, and he's now shown he doesn't mind killing those around me. Ollie, Mum, Tina – any of them could be next.

I put in over half a tank of diesel. Unlike before when it was a small amount, this time there's a scary judder when I turn on the ignition. I just hope the car makes it to the garage. And, if Si is there, I make it back out alive.

Chapter 44

Fallon

Kaplan Motors is homely for a large building. There are five car bays, a reception, an office, and a waiting room. As I walk in, I don't see any of my brothers but instead two mechanics hard at work, who I recognise as Jason and Miles. They don't look over to me, so I approach Miles.

'Hi,' I say. 'Is Si here?'

'Not yet. What's up?'

'My car's acting funny again, I was hoping you guys could check it out.' I try for a doe-eyed flirty look, but clearly don't manage it as Miles appears borderline horrified.

'Jase!' he yells.

The other mechanic saunters over. 'What's this? Can't keep away from us, eh?' Jason says wiping his hands on a cloth.

'She's a Kapper, remember?' Miles whispers to him.

'I remember,' Jason replies, then turns to look at my car. 'What seems to be the problem?'

Miles takes my car keys and pops the bonnet. After a quick assessment, he takes a deep breath. 'Diesel again.'

'Someone doing this on purpose to you?' Jason asks.

'No,' I say too quickly. 'I'm dealing with a lot now. I must have done it by mistake.'

'You can tell us if someone is doing this to you,' Miles presses.

'Yeah, what's the point in having four strapping brothers with sexy friends if they can't protect you once in a while,' Jason says and winks.

I take a few steps back, but quickly get a hold of myself.

'Si will wallop you if he catches you talking to his sister like that,' Miles says, punching Jason's arm. He then looks at me. 'Sorry about him.'

Jason blushes. 'Yeah, Si has a temper, but I think I could hold my own.'

Si has killed men bigger than Jason. Would he hesitate to hurt someone he knew? When killers attack those in their social circle, it's easier for the police to connect the pieces of the murder puzzle. I suspect Si knows this, so in theory both Jason and Miles would be safe from him. Being new to his life, would I?

I need that DNA sample.

'It's fine, really. Could I leave it with you and just wait in Si's office?'

'The waiting room has coffee.' Jason motions to a door on the other side of the garage. 'There's free Wi-Fi too.'

'Thanks,' I say, then reluctantly head towards the door.

The waiting room is wall-to-wall glass. Although cold outside, it's stifling in here. There are two large sofas with an odd array of scatter cushions – none matching. It's also annoyingly far away from Si's office, so there're no DNA samples on offer. Shit.

Taking off my coat, I grab a coffee from the machine, which doesn't taste nearly as bad as I expect, then begin to causally meander towards the back door. Before I make it, Miles comes in and asks, 'What's your favourite colour?'

'Excuse me?'

'For the courtesy car. We're gonna need to keep yours to flush it.'

'Oh, pink, but I don't think you'll have a pink car hanging around. The white one I had before is fine.'

'The Honda is out, but...' he beckons me to follow him. Parked outside the garage is a Mazda in a beautiful shade of fuchsia.

'I can use this one?' I ask.

'For insurance purposes we need a dashcam installed. But we'll sort that out, then drop it round yours later.'

'What happened with Mazzey's other dashcam?' says Jason, reappearing.

Miles shrugs. 'Si took it off, not sure why.'

Feeling awful that I'm making them do all this work, I say, 'How much do I owe you?'

He groans as if I'd offered to give him a pedicure. 'No charge.'

'Yeah, Si would kick our arses if we didn't look after you,' Jason adds. 'Mazzey is a good runner. She won't let you down.'

'Let me have your mobile. I'll load the dashcam app and input the login details. Just in case someone is targeting your car,' Miles says.

'I doubt they are, but thanks anyway.' I pull out my mobile, unlock it, and offer it to him. He scrolls through the app store and downloads the right one, then shows me how to use it.

Looking back at the little car, he adds, 'we'll give Mazzey the once over and drop her off later for you.'

'Thanks again. I really appreciate it.' I need to get into the office. 'Hey, can I just nip up to Si's office? Leave him a note?'

'Or you could just text him,' Miles says.

'I like the personal touch.'

'Whatever makes you happy.' Jason waves me in its direction.

As quick as I can, I sprint across the garage. The door is shut but not locked. *Simon Kaplan* is embossed on the glass, reminding me of something from an old-timey detective film. Like the waiting room, his office is also a glass box, so both men watch me as I sit at his desk and smile as I write a quick note:

Thanks for your help. Catch you soon. X

The bin is empty. There are no stray cups – Si is the cleanest man I've ever known. I'm just about to give up when I spot a pen on the desk. It's orange and has Kaplan Motors engraved on it. The plastic is shiny and new, but its top is chewed. Teeth indents cover the lid. Quickly, I pull out one of Harvey's poo bags and scoop it up, then pop it in my pocket. I run across the garage and all but yell, 'Well, I've taken up enough of your time.' Before Miles or Jason can reply, I'm out the door and hailing a taxi.

Chapter 45

The Brother

Even though she left hours ago, Fallon's perfume still lingers in the garage. It's sickly and sticks at the back of my throat like a cough I can't quite clear. What made her come here? Perhaps she now knows about my little dig, the swinging boyfriend, and it was anger at my brilliance which drove her here. People say us Kappers have wicked tempers. I don't, I just don't take shit. A normal person, living a normal life, will internally process their anger. They'll nod, take their medicine, then complain ad nauseam to everyone around them. But they don't react, thus letting the original shit-slinger get away with their behaviour. I admit, I find that difficult. So when a man swaggers into the garage, nose in the air and pathetic designer labels drenching his body, I am fully prepared not to take his shit.

'My car's still making a tapping noise,' he tells me, throwing his keys against my chest.

As not one of three qualified mechanics could hear the noise, one would be forgiven for thinking the car was fine, and said noise was in his head – a screw loose perhaps? Bending down, I pick up his keys, then casually put them in my pocket. 'There's nothing wrong with your car,' I tell him. 'We didn't even charge you for looking.

Remember?' I reach across to a nearby clipboard to fill in his customer form, but my favourite pen is missing; I must have left it in the office.

'I'm telling you, the noise is still there. It sounds like it's coming from… Look at me when I'm talking to you!'

My stare lifts. Eyeball to eyeball, he tries to square off against me. In the annals of my lizard brain, toothy bubbles burst across my vision, devouring rational thought.

'Who the fuck do you think you are? You—' I don't let him finish the sentence. My fist collides with his stomach. He doubles over. Silently, I step behind him and place my arm across his windpipe. I'm lucky fate is on my side and it's just me and him here. The other guys have gone to the deli in town for lunch.

The customer struggles a little, but nothing too impressive. Bullies are not prepared for a fight. When he wakes, I will tell him he passed out. Even if he remembers my actions, he'll be too ashamed to retaliate.

Frantic fingers claw at my arms, so I tighten my grip. As I do, I imagine it's Fallon struggling to free herself. The smell of dog on her clothes, that cunning little brain ticking like a clock counting down my demise. Laughing at my latest effort, yet another perfect murder I can't take credit for. And in that sappy, pathetic therapist voice declaring herself the winner of the game. Breaking my chain!

One swift snap.

What have I done? This murder is far from perfect; not planned, no gloves, and certainly not part of my game. No, this was the most reckless kind of kill: a temper-driven one. A bloody act so quick, I didn't even have time to enjoy it. I haven't committed anything like this since I was a teenager.

Staring at the mess and self-analysing isn't going to get me back on track. Picking up his legs, I drag the dead body through the garage. His car is conveniently parked by the entrance, so I open the boot and throw him in. Once he's inside, I lean in to double-check there's no pulse. After a liberal splash of bleach to remove DNA, touch or otherwise, I change out of my dirty overalls, then drive the car into a nearby estate. All the while I listen for the noise in the engine. I'd hate to leave a job unfinished. Zero tapping.

Parking in a rough part of town, I leave the keys in the ignition and walk to the garage, head down, all the while chiding myself for my reaction. Fallon is getting to me. She's proving more cunning than I gave her credit for. I thought killing her ex-lover would have her a gibbering wreck, not propel her straight into my domain to hunt me!

Could she beat me? Yes, if I do something as impulsive as that again.

This game has to end.

Chapter 46

Fallon

As I'm walking Harvey back to the lodge, the fuchsia Mazda pulls up with another car behind it. I expect to see Miles and Jason, but Si slides out and walks towards me. He's dressed in garage overalls, but unlike the other two mechanics I met today, his don't have a spot of grease on them. Smiling at me, he saunters over to my home like he hasn't just murdered my ex. Psychology is all about rooting out your true feelings, but if Si's victims are to get the justice they deserve, I can't tip my hand or challenge him yet. Let the dance of lies begin.

'Sorry I missed you earlier. I had some business to take care of,' he says, then bends down to ruffle Harvey behind the ear. 'Miles said they sorted you out?'

'Yeah, you've got some good guys working for you.'

'You don't know them that well. They can be a bit of a handful.' He laughs, then hands me the car keys. 'Here. We installed the dashcam. Miles left instructions in the glove compartment, but I think all you have to do it turn it on. I also gave her the once over, tyre pressure and the like.'

'You're a good' – mentally, I stumble for the word to end the sentence: liar, killer, murderer – 'brother.'

'I've had a lot of practice.' Cocking his head, he asks, 'You okay?'

Is he expecting me to tell him about Grant's 'suicide'? To cry on his shoulder? 'Never better.'

'If you say so. Hey, keep Mazzey as long as you need her. Wouldn't want you left stranded, again.'

Thanking a killer who has murdered two people in your life is hard work, so the word comes out more as an insult. 'Thanks,' I spit.

'Remember, I'm here if you need any help.'

'Okey-dokey.' Did I really just say okey-dokey?

'Seriously, you're real pale.' Si reaches out a hand to me, but I jerk back. It's the hand that wrapped around Lindsay's throat, and snuffed my ex-boyfriend out of this world.

'Fallon?'

'I'm fine. Just need to crack on. I have a client appointment.'

'Sure.' He turns to walk away, but stops. Looking back at me he says, 'By the way, I got your note.'

'What?'

'The thank you note you left in my office.'

'No worries.'

'I'll catch *you* later,' he says, then slips into the other car. I squint to see its driver is Mikey. I wave and he gives me a thumbs up.

When they leave, I sit in Mazzey and look through the camera instructions. I go to turn it on, but I find it's already running. And as I access the app on my phone, I see the camera is transmitting. There's no sound, only images. There's a rewind button so I take it back to the start of the recording. The garage is framed at an odd angle; it must have been recording while being installed.

Time lapses and nothing out of the ordinary happens, however, viewing something like this, something I was never meant to see, is strangely addictive. I keep watching until the screen frames a dark figure. I can't see a face, just garage overalls.

Another man walks in. He's shorter, so I can at least see his face. They talk for a moment, then, without warning, the mechanic's arm snakes around the man's throat. The mechanic must be Si! In horror, I watch as my brother strangles a man right there in his garage. One second ticks slowly by before my brother jerks up his bicep. The victim shudders once, then drops to the floor. Shit! Shit! Shit! In panic, I fumble my phone and it falls down the side of the car. Miles must have left the camera running, and Si hadn't known. I have a kill on tape. Frantically, I shove my fingers between the seat and door, then wiggle them around until I feel my phone. As soon as it's back in my hand, I call Joel. Please don't let him still be in court.

'Fallon?' he answers.

'You won't believe what I just saw,' I splutter.

'What?'

'Si's garage fitted a dashcam on the car they've given me. It was turned on and caught my brother strangling a man.'

'You saw Simon Kaplan kill someone?'

'Yes,' I say, then quickly correct it to, 'Well, no, you can't see his face. But it has to be him. I saw him wearing the same overalls just now when he dropped the car off.'

'Was his name visible on the overalls?'

I think about this. 'No.'

'Do all your brothers wear the same uniform at the garage?'

'Yes, but Si is the only brother I now haven't cleared.'

'Can you send me the video? I can try to identify the victim.'

'Hang on.' I flip back to the app, but as I do, the word deleted flashes onto the screen. I press to rewind the recording, but it's gone. The video now starts when the car pulls up in front of the lodge. 'Shit. He's deleted it.'

'Already? How?'

'It's their camera, the garage has the login to the app. Si must have realised what he did.'

'Could you identify the victim if you saw him again?'

'Maybe.' He was so plain looking, and even now when I try to summon an image of him in my mind's eye, it's lacking useable detail.

'Did you see the number plate of the car?'

'No,' I all but whine. I was in such shock, I never even thought to jot it down. 'But I do have a DNA sample. I collected a chewed pen from his office.'

'Good, I'll come over now and pick up all the information you've got, along with the pen, then I'll contact DI Worth. Be careful. We're close to catching him, and that's when these guys devolve.'

Devolve? I don't like the sound of that. Did the man in the garage die because Si is devolving?

Joel arrives with a professional looking baggie and takes the pen. As the chewed orange piece of plastic slips into a bag marked evidence, I let out a sigh of relief, one which deepens when I hand him Lindsay's folder and my profile. This will soon be over. I can then start to deal with the fallout.

'When will Worth arrest him?' I ask.

'She'll find a way once we've tested the DNA. Bear in mind this isn't official. It could take a few days.'

'Days?'

Joel's face flushes with anger. 'Do you know how much trouble I could get in if any of this comes out? I'm doing the best I can. There's a host of reasons why this' – he waves the file – 'was not taken seriously by the police. And my friend is going to have to bend the law to make an arrest.'

'But when she does, that's it, right? It's over?'

He doesn't answer, just carefully places the folder in his bag.

'Joel?'

'There are legal procedures in place for a reason. We currently have the theory of a dead forensic technician, hearsay evidence, illegally obtained DNA and a profile by a family therapist. Worth's one of the best investigators I've ever worked with, but she's not a magician. I'll let you know once we've tested the DNA. For now, just act normal. We don't want to spook him.'

-

Holed up for the weekend at Poppy Fields, I keep busy with Hawk Therapy. Every now and then I catch myself itching to pick up my profile, to add the odd note here and there, only to remember it's gone.

I speak to Sam, who tells me they are short-handed at the garage and everyone is busy. Partly they blame me, as I pulled some strings and got a place for Stefan at a detox facility. Garry texts, asking for us to spend some time together. And Si – Si is deathly quiet.

Feeling like the world around me is teeming with danger is not a new sensation, and its odd familiarity brings some comfort. You don't need to get scared if you stay scared.

Although worry over my brother's intentions stopped me from attending court these past few days, Joel tells me it's going well and nearing the end. Upon hearing this I realise I owe it to all the victims to attend at least one session before it draws to a close.

-

On Monday morning, hyper-aware of my surroundings, I drive to the Crown Court, park up, get patted down by security, and then slip into the pews. I don't see Rosie's father or anyone else I know. Under my breath I whisper, 'I'm warm. I'm healthy. I'm safe.'

The gallery is filling up, but no one sits near me. I try to make eye contact with the growing audience to show I'm earnest, but to no avail. Is it a sign that my testimony didn't go as well as I thought? If random gallery-goers didn't believe me, does it mean the jury are feeling the same? As if on cue, the twelve are brought in, smiling and nodding as if their job isn't harrowing. Well, maybe one of them should be attacked by a gang of killers, then we'll see how seriously they take today. Embarrassed by the thought, I stand to leave before they close the court down, but there's a man blocking my exit. Si.

He spots me, then shuffles up the aisle to sit beside me. Wearing a weak smile, he pats my leg. Gagging at his touch, I turn away, and as the doors of the court close, I resign myself to spend the next couple of hours within touching distance of a serial killer.

Si easily conceals his emotions. I can't read him. I can, however, read Tyler Baker as he's marched through court and into the dock. The evil grin carved into his face, the kind belonging on a Jack-o'-lantern, dissolves into a look of concern when he notices the jury watching.

'Prick,' Si whispers.

Expecting me to say something, my brother shifts his gaze to me.

'Indeed,' I say, then kick myself. Indeed, I sound like an idiot.

A hush falls over the court as the judge takes his seat. Tyler then moves to the witness box.

'Is he testifying?' Si whispers.

Ignoring the question, I watch the man who tried to kill me put his hand on the Bible and swear to tell the truth. As he says the words, his eyes find me in the gallery. Quickly, he bows his head to hide a smirk.

'Mr Baker,' begins his barrister. 'Can you tell me why, on the night in question, you were at Cat Hall?'

Leaning forward, he says, 'I worked for Simpson Builders, one of those contracted to build the houses at Cat Hall.'

'Do you still work there?' she asks.

'Not anymore now, thanks to this debacle. But I loved my job. I enjoy doing things with my hands.' He says this to the jury with a smile. 'On the night in question, I was working late. A family was moving into one of the three-storeys the next day so I wanted to ensure everything was just right for them.'

'What a guy,' Si sarcastically whispers.

'Ropey and Streak…'

'James Partridge and Alexander Knowles,' the barrister corrects.

'Yes, they worked with me. I was checking up on them as I hadn't heard from either all day. When I reached the house they were working on, I noticed blood, so thought there'd been an accident.'

'What did you do?'

'I ran inside and saw they had killed Victor Steiff and were holding his wife hostage.'

'Gayle Steiff?'

'Yes. She was putting up a good fight.'

An image of Tyler's face looming over me clouds my mind's eye. The gloved hands groping for the buttons on my coat feel as real as they did that night. I swear I can even smell his breath.

'You okay?' Si asks.

I lie with a nod.

'Then what happened?' asks Tyler's barrister.

Sighing, he wipes away a crocodile tear. 'I tried to stop it, but there were two of them and only one of me.'

'When did you come across Dr Hurley?'

'I met her by the show home. I tried to send her away, but she was raging about how her estate agent was late. She headed straight for the house. That's when Ropey and Streak caught her and put her upstairs with Gayle.'

His lies know no bounds. How can he sit there spouting nonsense and not expect God to strike him dead for lying on the Bible?

Si shifts forward in his seat, his palms, curled into fists, rest on his knees.

'What was Ms Hurley like at this point?'

'Freaking out. She kept talking about running; how she wasn't injured so could make a break for it. I didn't want her to. Ropey and Streak were acting crazy. I thought they'd kill her if she ran.'

'They both testified as much in their sworn police statements.' The barrister holds up two pieces of paper from her folder. I wish I'd read their statements. What fiction had they told?

'And what about Rosie Howe?'

Bile bubbles in my stomach like a boiling water. Lurching forward, I grip the back of the pews in front.

'Fallon?' Si leans too close to me.

I push him back out of my personal space.

Tyler stares at me. 'When Ms Hurley was in the house, she told Ropey and Streak she had an appointment with Rosie; that she'd be missed, so they had to let her go.'

'Then what happened?' his barrister prompts.

'They let her go.'

A gasp shoots through the jury.

'She was let go,' the barrister repeats.

Joel flashes me a quizzical expression, then looks at his notes.

'Ropey said if she gave them the estate agent, they'd let her go. So, she went to the show home and fetched Rosie. Like a lamb to the slaughter.'

The silence in the room is heavy as she lets the statement sink in. I don't need to look up. I can feel all their eyes, waiting for me to react.

'But they didn't let Ms Hurley go after she brought them Miss Howe?'

Huffing, Tyler sits back in his seat as if he was watching TV, not giving testimony. 'They were never gonna let her go. She's a head-doctor, how could she think they would?'

Finally, I glance up. Even Joel has his eyes on me. Shame and regret slam into my chest, because Rosie's death being my fault is the first thing Tyler has said which is true.

Chapter 47

Fallon

My psyche had buried parts of that night so deep, even now, it takes a moment to fully conjure the memory.

–

After hearing Gayle's final scream, I knew I didn't have long. So when Tyler strolled back up the stairs and opened the door, I fell back into the corner of the room, and put my hands over my face. Everything I'd ever done, and everything I would never do, raced through my mind.

'Don't be a bitch about this, Fallon.'

'Get away from me,' I yelled, then flailed out at him with my arms and legs.

Laughing, Tyler caught one of my ankles and began to pull me across the floor, then down the stairs. Each step hit my back and head as he dragged me like a caveman towards the living room, where the other two were waiting.

When my legs were finally dropped, and I was free of his hands, I scrambled up.

'I like you. You're plucky,' Tyler said. 'I wonder how long it will be before you're missed.'

Panic swarmed my brain. Missed. Would I be missed soon enough to save me? That's when I remembered what brought me here, what I was supposed to do. And it's when I said the words I have regretted every day since. My knee-jerk cross to bear. 'I was meeting the estate agent. She's probably already called the police.'

'She?' Ropey repeated.

I realised my mistake instantly. If only I had edited my thought and said 'he' or even just kept my stupid mouth shut.

'We should go,' Streak said.

'No, I've got a better idea. Let's pay the show home a visit.' Tyler then grabbed my arm and marched me back into the street.

In the cool air, I thought I could get away from him while the others were still in the house, but the fear was too intense; it dissolved every escape plan that dared form. I complied.

The walk to the show home felt like miles, yet we were standing outside within minutes. Every step, I prayed Rosie was still in traffic and the door would be locked. But the door opened. Before stepping inside, Tyler pulled out his knife and weaved it under my coat and jumper, so the bloody blade was touching my bare stomach.

'Go along with everything I say, or I'll gut you where you stand.'

I nodded.

Rosie was sitting at the dining room table. She had her mobile to her ear and smiled when she saw us enter.

Tyler grinned back. I felt the tip of his knife nip at my belly.

Cradling her phone between her shoulder and ear, she said, 'Dr Hurley, I won't be a moment.' Rosie finished her call with a 'See you later, Dad'.

I pushed out, 'Maybe…,' but my words stopped as I felt a trickle of hot blood on my cold skin.

'So sorry I kept you. Have you spotted something you'd like to take a closer look at?'

Tyler edged forward. 'Yes, there's a house at the end of the street. Can you walk us over?'

-

The barrister's voice brings me back into the courtroom, 'So, you were not party to any crimes at Cat Hall?' she asks Tyler.

'No. I was even injured myself.'

'Confirmed by blood found on your clothes, and the various cuts and bruises on your body.'

Bottom lip trembling, he leans forward to lock eyes with the jury. After a few seconds he says, 'I'm a victim too.'

I knew this was his defence, but hearing him say it aloud makes me gasp, and the entire court looks over at me again. As all eyes are on me, they don't see Tyler give me a quick wink, only my shudder.

Si puts an arm around my shoulders. It's heavy and meant to be supportive, yet feels suffocating. I shrug it off and catch a strange look passing across my brother's face. Hurt?

Joel rises, ready to cross-examine.

'Mr Baker, was anything you just said true?'

'Badgering, Your Honour,' calls out the other barrister.

The judge sighs and tells Joel, 'Careful, Mr Smith.'

Joel looks over at the jury. 'Apologies. But I can't be the only one wondering that.' Scooping up his notes, he then says, 'Mr Baker, would it be fair to say you are close friends with James Knowles and Alexander Partridge?'

'I hung with them a few times.'

'As we've discovered through numerous Facebook and YouTube postings of you all together. Looking at your posts, you all liked the idea of murders' – he looks down at his notes – 'and serial killers.'

'It was only for a laugh,' Tyler corrects.

'Ah, yes, serial killers are funny,' Joel says glibly.

'It was all just pretend. I'd have never done anything like it for real. It's against my morals.'

Joel smiles. 'But your friends confessed as much.'

'Yeah, but *I* never hurt anyone.'

'Did you suggest they do what they did?'

Tyler feigns shock. 'No.'

'Can you please explain your relationship with Knowles and Partridge.'

Tyler huffs. 'We're buds.'

'We have witnesses that claim you bullied and controlled both of your *buds* through intimidation and violence. Would that be a fair assessment of your friendship?'

'What witnesses? That doctor who couldn't remember what really happened? Didn't remember that I tried to save her?'

'We have other witness statements too,' Joel says, then hands sheets of paper to the judge.

'Answer the question, Mr Baker,' the judge says.

'I never made Ropey and Streak do anything they didn't want to do. I don't have X-Men mind control abilities.'

Soft chuckles sound through the court.

'Did you know both have police records?'

'Yes.'

'For assault, amongst other things.'

'Excuse me, but,' says Tyler's barrister, 'Knowles and Partridge are not on trial here.'

'Withdrawn,' says Joel. 'Mr Baker, as your barrister so painstakingly put forward in her opening statement, you do not have a criminal record?'

'No, I'm innocent.'

'Not quite what I asked.' Joel shrugs. 'So, will you deny you bullied your friends into taking the blame for your part in the incident, so you can remain innocent?' He air quotes *innocent*. Three jury members lean forward for the answer.

I can see Tyler thinking through his response, but Joel beats him to it. 'It's not a stumper of a question.'

Usually, I hate to see anyone stressed or cornered, but the look on Tyler's face is delicious. 'I plead the fifth,' he finally says.

The judge turns to the witness stand. 'Mr Baker, you are not in the USA. But you can remain silent if you do not wish to answer the question.'

Slowly Tyler says, 'No.'

'Maybe *good* friends don't need to be asked,' Joel adds.

-

As court draws to a close for the day, I move as quickly as I can to the exit. Si calls my name, but I keep walking until I reach the foyer. As I do, a hand grips my wrist from behind. I whirl around to confront Si, but find Joel still in his wig and gown.

'What happened in there?' he asks.

'Tyler was lying,' I say.

'About everything?'

I want to say yes, but instead I reply, 'There were some truths littered amongst the lies.'

'Did you bring Rosie into the house?'

There's the question. The one I should answer yes to, then rush to explain how I was terrorised and forced and not thinking straight. That I then tried to help her. But whatever way I tell the story, it ends with me running and leaving her behind; the action everyone thought was bad enough without knowing the full extent of my panicked treachery.

'Yes,' springs out before I can stop it.

'Fallon!'

'I'm so sorry.'

Joel shakes his head. 'Tyler now has a truthful contradiction to your statement. You should have told me.'

I have no excuse. 'Sorry.'

'We'll talk later,' Joel says, then disappears into chambers.

I'm so upset, I don't notice the skinny man with a mobile phone in his hand as he rushes towards me. 'Just a few questions,' he yells.

'No comment,' I say, then sidestep him to jog towards the door.

Si strides past the reporter, throwing him a look as he does. When he reaches me, he says, 'Intense stuff.'

'I want to go home,' I mutter.

'It was all lies, right?' he asks. 'You didn't do what he said.'

I shake my head. Even in the presence of a sadistic serial killer, I'm the worst person in the room.

'Shit, there really isn't a single reason for Tyler not to have his neck broken.'

My eyes widen at Si's statement.

'Remember, Mum wants to meet at her place for tea tomorrow.'

'Pardon?'

'The meeting we arranged at the Wool Pack. You remember?'

'Oh, yes. Are the other Kappers going?'

'Sure.' Si nods. 'I'll text you Mum's address and meet you there.'

'Sounds like a plan,' I say – a plan I need to keep to appear normal, and not to raise Si's suspicions.

'Try to stay out of trouble.' He leans down and hugs me. It takes all the effort I have to lift my arms and pat his back.

Back at Poppy Fields, I text Mum that I'm meeting Siobhan. She calls, but I don't have the strength to talk, so tell her I'm working. Lies get easier the more you tell.

-

That night, I should be welcoming a good night's sleep, but I can't – not now. I couldn't stand to dream of Rosie like I did Gayle, especially now everyone knows what I did to her.

After three morning coffees, I pull up outside the Kaplan's house to finally meet my bio-mum. The estate isn't as rough as I expected, and I chide myself for thinking in stereotypes. Constructed in the 1970s, the houses all look the same. If the buildings were people, each home would wear bell-bottom flares and love beads.

Si pulls up a moment after me. He climbs out of his red Audi, waves then walks up to greet me. A sick feeling creeps around my stomach as he approaches. Stepping back, I hit my bum on the open car door. Rosie didn't sense I'd betrayed her, but will a serial killer sense I've betrayed him?

'You all right?' Si asks.

'Sorry, I…' Not being able to explain the feeling to myself, let alone him, I abandon my sentence. It's then I spot he's carrying a bag. A black plastic one bulging with an unknown something.

Catching me staring, he lifts it. 'It's a cake for today.'

'Oh, should I have brought something?' I ask.

'You're nervous. I get it. It's not every day you meet your bio-mum who said you died.'

'So weird, right?' Oddly, finally speaking with Siobhan Kaplan doesn't faze me. This part of today's meeting will be a breeze – it's the other part where at any moment a SWAT team in matching black outfits, led by DI worth, could propel from the side of the house and arrest Si, which has me twisted.

'Come on then,' he says, backing away to let me move ahead of him and through a wooden gate towards the house.

'Who else is coming?' I ask.

'The others can't make it today. So it's just the two of us.'

I stop walking. 'I thought all the Kappers were going to be here?'

'With Stefan gone, the garage needs all hands on deck.'

As I edge my way further up the path, a thought hits my mind, cartoon-anvil style. He knows I know. This is a trap! He said *the two of us*. Who's to say Siobhan Kaplan is even here? Without any of my other brothers present, I've only got Si's word she wanted this get together in the first place. I could be about to wander into another house of horrors with a madman. He'd be able to murder me behind closed doors, then claim I never showed up today. My car, my actual car, is sitting in his garage still. I came in *his* car, which wouldn't look out of place on this street.

No one else knows I'm here. It would be as if I drove off, never to be heard from again.

Stopping dead, I say, 'Maybe we should do this another time. Like in town. We could have dinner together?' I take a step back, ready to retreat.

'But Mum's made sandwiches. She's real excited to see you.' Si puts his heavy hand on my shoulder. 'C'mon, Fallon. Kappers don't puss out.'

'But I'm under so much stress right now.' I whine, then realise I should just flatly refuse, get back in the car and drive away. Rudeness might lose friends, but it could save your life. 'Today wasn't a good idea. You can explain it to her, right?'

'Let's just talk inside,' he says, then grabs at my arm.

Jerking out of the way, Si stumbles back to sure up his footing. As he does, the plastic bag sways against the gate and clunks. Cakes don't make that sound.

My brother's eyes darken.

'You said it was a cake,' I say nodding to the bag.

'There's a knife in there too.'

'Siobhan doesn't own knives?'

Cocking his head, he chuckles. 'Not like the ones I have.'

Shit! To escape, I'd have to jump over the little fence and make it back to the car before he catches me. Not happening. I scan the neighbouring houses. No one there, and no guarantee they are even at home to run to for help. What do I do?

Chapter 48

Fallon

'There you are,' comes a female voice from the door. I turn to see a woman who looks just like me, only older and thinner. Her brown hair is streaked grey and her make-up is too heavy for daytime.

Hesitating, I say an awkward, 'Hi.'

'Don't linger outside, come in. I've made sandwiches.' Siobhan smiles at me.

Si holds up the black bag. 'Mum, Fallon's not feeling well at the moment, perhaps we can do this another day?'

'Oh, bless.' She says to me. 'Why don't you just sit down for a bit? Let your family take care of you.' Siobhan ventures down the path in her slippers, takes my hand, and leads me inside. As our skin touches, I want to ask her if she ever loved me. If, when she looked at me just then and saw how alike we are, she felt something. Did she ever, through the years, have a twinge of regret at giving her only daughter away? Questions like that have crowded my mind since Boxing Day, but right now there's something more important than my feelings at stake. So, I let her silently lead me inside. Like an ominous shadow, Si follows us.

The house is an odd mixture of styles. Siobhan clearly picked furniture and ornaments which caught her eye, rather than anything matching. Looking around, I find each wall heavy with photos. All my brothers at various milestones in their life. Stefan with his cricket club. Si with the lads from the garage. Sam in a chef's hat. Garry fishing with a man I'm assuming was my dad.

Mixed among the photos of the men is a baby-laden Siobhan at various ages.

Catching me staring, she explains. 'I took one photo for each pregnancy.'

I scan the line of images. In one she's straddling a motorcycle, in another she is cuddling a golden retriever. Apron wrapped tight around her bump, she mans a BBQ outside a caravan. In another she lays across the bonnet of a soft-top car in a kaftan. Wearing a daring bikini, she sits before a half-fallen sandcastle. In the last she is holding up her O level results. She had her babies early. Then I realise, I'm the bump in one of those photos. All this time, I've been on my family's wall.

I perch on a large fake suede sofa and Siobhan sits next to me. Si settles into an armchair opposite.

'Just the two of us today, Mum. Everyone else is working.'

'That's all right. And thanks for the cake.' She pulls a box out of Si's bag, then a metallic cake slice – a kitsch weapon no self-respecting serial killer would wield. He was teasing me.

'Tea?' Siobhan asks, holding up a bucket-sized teapot.

'Thank you.'

She leans across the table, and it's then I notice the mountainous plates covered in foil. After fiddling with a cosy, she pours tea for all of us. 'So, I bet you have questions.'

I have a lot of questions, but I start with, 'How are you?'

Siobhan smiles. Her fingers, still warm from the teapot, encloses my wrist. 'I'm good. I always knew I'd made the right choice all those years ago, but seeing you here, so smart, a doctor, and so sweet; Heather brought you up good.'

'I had a lovely childhood,' I say.

'Every Christmas we sent cards. As long as I got the card, I knew you were okay.' She looks down at her slippers. 'I'm sorry if you think what I did was wrong. But I saw the hurt in your mum's eyes when her little girl was taken from her, I knew what she was feeling. It seemed the right thing to do for everyone. Our wages were already spread so thin and we could barely afford the boys we had.'

'We didn't have it that bad,' Si cuts in, leaning forward to free a lump of sandwiches from under a tinfoil dome.

'It sounds awful, but what little we had was *because* we had one less mouth to feed. Four was already too many.' She whispers the next part, as if to convince herself rather than us, 'I did it for all of you.'

Ever since I learnt of my true heritage, I'd wanted to ask Siobhan why she'd done it. I was so sure there was going to be an extra secret why she hadn't wanted me. But sitting with her now, the answer really is what everyone said. I wish all answers in life were as simple.

I take a sandwich, not out of hunger, but politeness. Like a rat, I nibble its edges as I look around the room for tell-tale serial killer paraphernalia Si could have left. There's nothing.

We talk for a few hours and Si doesn't leave us for a second. Instead, he haunts the armchair in the corner, eating sandwiches, then the cake he brought, nodding where appropriate.

I mention leaving first. Reluctantly, the two then get up and walk me to the door.

As no SWAT team catapulted through the front window on my visit, I suspect the lab hasn't finished their analysis – or perhaps Worth is still getting her head around my garbled profile.

Outside, Siobhan lurches forward to hug me. I'm rigid in her embrace, so she pulls away quickly. 'I'm so glad to finally meet you, Fallon. I often think about my wayward babes,' she says.

'We're all back together now, Mum.' Si puts his arm around her and I shiver to think of how many hugs he's given with the same hands which took so many lives.

'Thanks for having me,' I say.

Siobhan steps back inside to let Si and me walk to my car.

'Went well, don't you think?' he asks.

'Yeah, your mum is great.' With the security of having one leg inside my getaway vehicle, a sudden bout of courage hits me. 'By the way, I'm loving the camera app Miles put on my phone.' I watch his face carefully. If he knows I saw the murder at the garage through the app, I should see a reaction. I don't.

Without a beat, he replies. 'I'll tell him. Hey, I cook a mean steak. How about you come round mine next time?'

I nod yes, but inwardly promise myself I'll never be alone with this psychopath ever again.

–

Joel calls in the afternoon. He's still pissed with me. I apologise again for not telling him about my part in

Rosie's abduction, but his reaction is stunted and our conversation strictly business. He tells me the defence have rested and the verdict could be as early as tomorrow. Soon, I'll know for sure if Tyler will be walking the streets; if a jury of my peers have decided I'm lying, and that monster of a man is telling the truth. Changing the subject, I ask after Si's pen.

'The lab have it. I'll let you know as soon as I have news.' Joel's tone is snappy and our conversation doesn't last long after that.

As night draws in, Harvey pads about the lodge as if he's pacing a cage. I know exactly how he feels.

–

Today, I could find out if I caught one or two, or no serial killers at all. What twisted road led me here? Can I ever make up for the mistakes made along the way? Snuffling my hand, Harvey licks my fingers. It's the jolt I need to get up, wash my hands, and finish what I started. Mistakes can be valuable when they are learnt from, when they gift strength. The least I can do is make mine count.

Determined, I open my cupboard door and pull out my grey wool coat. With all my Cat Hall secrets laid bare, it somehow feels right to face my anxiety head on and wear it today to court. In my mind I reframe it from what I wore that night to soft woollen armour which tried to keep me safe, and will hopefully do the same again today.

Patricia meets me outside the courthouse. We sit down and I buy her a bottle of water from a nearby vending machine. I'm about to ask about her thoughts on the case when I receive a text from Ollie. It reads, *We're all dressed up and ready to meet you at court if you need us.* A huge part of me wants them to be here. But another, darker side, couldn't take their reaction if something goes… wrong. I text back thanks, but I'll see them both later. Instantly, I get an agreement from Ollie and another text from Mum with a heart emoji. I'm about to reply when I spot Joel barrelling towards us.

'We have a verdict,' he yells, out of breath.

'The jury didn't deliberate for long. Is that a good sign?' I ask.

'Hard to tell.'

Joel's words punch me in the gut. Was Tyler more convincing than me?

'It only takes a few strong-willed people to see through him,' Patricia assures me, but her words don't stop my stomach gurgling. Joel worked hard, and the only Achilles heel in the case was me.

As Patricia makes her way over to the vending machine to buy some crisps, I pull Joel aside to ask, 'What about the pen? Does the DNA match the killer?'

Sighing, Joel motions for me to sit down. 'I heard back this morning.'

Inhaling deeply, I hold the air.

'It's a match.'

Even though I knew it would be, the answer still hits me like a slap to the face.

'This is a good thing. DI Worth will tail your brother, and find an excuse to arrest him so we can officially get his DNA. You said he has a temper, maybe she'll even catch him in the act or…' Joel stops talking and I follow his eye line to Si being frisked by a court guard. He waves at us, then strides over. At least I know he doesn't have any weapons, although he snapped the man's neck in the video as if it were a crayon; he doesn't need weapons to be dangerous.

'You're here again,' I state, wondering what his angle is.

'I'm your big brother, course I'm here. What's going on?'

As he gets closer, I sway towards Joel.

'The verdict is in. We're waiting to be called into court.' Joel stares at Si with a better poker face than me.

'Isn't it a bit soon?'

Joel shrugs. 'Juries can take between six minutes and eighteen days. Let's not read into it.'

'Really? It's still a hella quick deliberation. I hope justice prevails,' Si says, giving me a gentle nudge. 'You wanna grab lunch after, just the two of us, to celebrate the end of all this?'

He's still trying to get me alone. How much can he possibly know? Did he clock the missing pen? Will his last act as a free man be to kill me?

Si cocks his head. 'You're worried about the verdict.'

'We're all worried,' Joel jumps in.

'Well, I guess it should be fine, as long as you did your job properly, eh, super barrister,' Si says, his tone dropping into unfriendly.

Joel, although a tall, well-built man, visibly shrinks under Si's gaze. 'I've got to get ready,' he says, flustered. 'Will you be all right, Fallon?'

He means with Si. 'Of course.'

'See you both in there then.' And Joel disappears through the gathering crowd.

It's only then I realise how many people have swarmed into court. Flinching as I'm repeatedly barged by passing shoulders, I think, what if I can't get into the gallery? I'll not hear them say Tyler is guilty and being locked up forever. As if reading my mind, Si grabs me and, like a steamer ship through an angry sea, moves us through the crowd depositing me into the best seat in the house.

'There are some familiar faces here to support you,' Si whispers as we settle in our seats.

I don't even look up. Support won't help. What if Tyler is acquitted? The man who killed Vic, Gayle and Rosie. The man who tried to kill me, and will, I'm sure, kill again if he is free to walk the streets. I finally look out at the people waiting for justice and spot the Kappers, some of the guys from the garage, Rosie's father, and even the estate agents from Cat Hall. I'm drowning in people I've let down. Bowing my head, I say, 'I'm warm. I'm healthy. I'm safe.' And pull my coat tighter about my chest.

Tyler Baker is the last person before the judge to walk in. He's dressed in another new suit, clean-shaven and hair slicked back. The very image of a 21st-century psycho. As he enters the dock, he scans the gallery. His eyes stop on me. A familiar grin spreads across his face like a virus.

'Has the jury reached a unanimous verdict?' asks the judge.

The forewoman stands up. 'We have.'

'What say you in the case of Tyler Baker in the charge of the murder of Rosie Howe?'

Chapter 49

Fallon

'Not guilty.'

Blood rushes to my cheeks, burning me from the inside out. Tyler sighs and wipes away a non-existent tear.

'What say you in the case of Tyler Baker in the charge of the murder of Gayle Steiff?'

'Not guilty.'

The heat of my anger boils my innards; imagining the smell makes me gag.

'What say you in the case of Tyler Baker in the charge of the murder of Victor Steiff?'

'Not guilty.'

My coat, the one I was so proud to finally put back on, tightens around me like an iron maiden.

That's all the charges. My body trembles and I can't speak. Abductor and murderer Tyler Baker punches the air as if he won the lottery.

My breath stops midway up my throat. The room erupts into chaos, so much so that the judge holds up his hands to stop the noise. He tells Tyler he is free to go, and suddenly my already pounding head feels like a balloon rising into the air. I close my eyes.

Three not guilty verdicts.

Three slaps across the faces of the victims.

Three wrongs not righted because of me.

I don't realise I'm shaking until Si's hand lands on my shoulder, holding me still. Redemption is lost to me in the Cat Hall case, and the only tiny comfort I have is that the murderer beside me is potentially hours off being arrested. A killer for a killer.

As I think this, Si gets up and pulls me after him. Dazed, I flop along behind like a ragdoll as he makes his way to the exit. Once we're in the lobby, he props me on a chair and kneels before me.

'I'll drive you home.'

'I have a car.'

'You can't drive in this state. Give me the keys.' Si reaches for my bag but I swing it away from him. Tutting at my childishness, he shakes his head. 'Wait here,' he instructs, and then is gone.

I'm so numb I can't even feel the chair beneath me. My eyes burn with tears that won't fall. The wool of the coat is itching me down to my bones. What just happened?

'There you are!'

I turn towards the voice and see Joel. My mouth won't open. Even if it could, I wouldn't know what to say.

'You need to leave. There are reporters everywhere and they're looking for you to comment.'

'I'm so sorry,' I mutter. I need to get myself together. 'I'll go home.'

Behind the shock, I know I should ask questions of Joel too. Why didn't he push Tyler harder on the stand? How could one mistake set a murderer free?

Joel's face is blank but I can tell he's trying hard not to show his anger. As much as I'd like to blame someone else for this travesty, it was me who caused the jury to side with Tyler.

Through the crowd, I spot a pack of reporters heading my way, so rush off towards the exit. Too busy looking back to see if they are following, I don't spot him in time to change direction. Rosie's father. All but smashing into him, I mumble a string of apologies. It takes him a millisecond to recognise me.

'Is it true?' he asks. 'Did you do that to my daughter then blame everything on that innocent man?'

I can't speak. Words swirl about my head like blood gurgling down a drain.

'Answer me!' he demands, eyes wild.

'Tyler killed Rosie and the others. Please, let's set something up to talk. I'll help you.' I want to add, *I owe it to you*, but stop myself.

Scoffing, he grips the sleeve of my coat and pulls me towards him. 'How can I believe anything you say?'

I never did fix that missing button. In one swift motion, I undo the only other fastening and, turning, slip out of the coat, leaving Rosie's father holding it. I run for the exit, yelling an apology behind me.

When I'm finally in the car, it takes three attempts to put on my seatbelt. Numbly, I shove the key in the ignition, but don't twist it. Instead, I fish out my mobile. Garry has texted suggesting we meet, and there are messages from Tina and Ollie, both asking for an update. For a moment I question whether I heard the jury's words right. Not guilty, three times, plain as day. Ignoring Garry, I text Tina and Ollie the horrifying news then turn off my phone and sit in the car for the next few hours, long after my parking ticket has run out. Staring into the space ahead, any cohesive thoughts are strangled; murdered before they can fully form.

At first, I don't hear the taps on the window. They're light and tentative. Focusing is not an option, so I can't register who is outside my car.

The rapping becomes louder.

The handle moves.

Did I lock the car?

Chapter 50

Fallon

The car door swings open. Lunging to hold the handle, I almost fall out, but am saved by the seatbelt.

'Do you need help?'

Glancing up, I recognise the voice before the face. Si.

'Why are you here?'

He pushes me back inside the car. 'I told you to stay put. But when I came back, I couldn't find you. I waited at Foxglove but you never showed up. I got worried, and tried calling, but I think your phone is off. Let me drive you back to mine.' He moves to undo my seatbelt, but I slap his hand away.

'You're in shock. For fuck's sake, let me help you,' he says.

Without realising, my anger from court bubbles back up. I turn to face him and spit, 'I know.'

With an arched eyebrow, he steps back from the car. 'You know what?'

What am I doing? Joel said not to spook him. Quickly, I backtrack, 'I know you want to help, but you can't right now.'

But Si is stubborn and leans towards me. 'We need to talk. It's only fair I give you' – he looks around us – 'a warning.'

Instinctively, I edge back, but the seatbelt stops me from gaining any real distance. He's so close I can't even shut the door. 'Warn me of what?' I splutter.

'Garry. He says he wants to talk with you, but I think he's going to sell your story to the papers.'

'He... What?'

Si rises and crosses his arms over his chest. 'You didn't do any interviews when it happened, and your words are now worth a lot of money. Garry's been following your case. He was here today too, even though he was supposed to be out delivering a car. Just thought I'd do the brotherly thing and give you a heads up.'

Delivering a car? 'Hang on, I thought Garry couldn't drive because of his leg?'

'What's up with his leg?'

'He told me he broke it.'

Narrowing his eyes, Si stares at me. 'When was this?'

'The other day after dinner. He told me that he'd broken his leg jumping off a roof with Stefan a few months ago.'

'What a load of crap. Garry has never broken a bone in his life.'

'Are you sure?'

'Positive. He rubbed that fact in my face last March when I broke my arm. He had to drive me everywhere. Little shit never let me forget it.'

'But he's limping.'

Si rolls his eyes. 'Little prick's always been a good actor.'

Garry lied to me. And, with a broken arm, Si wouldn't have been able to kill the philanthropist in April. Which means... It has to be Garry. *Garry*, not Si.

Ignoring Si's question I ask, 'Why would Garry lie about something like that?'

'He says all sorts of shit to gain sympathy. And you clearly care about people. He was playing you to get close.' Si shakes his head. 'I'm sorry I didn't warn you earlier. I just hoped I was wrong about his intentions. My little bro was always a bit…'

I'm barely listening to Si now, my mind is reeling. The pen – how could the pen have been a DNA match if the killer is Garry, not Si? 'Do you own an orange pen?'

'An orange pen? Fallon, what's going on?' Si asks, but when I don't answer he continues, 'We had a load of promotional ones made up for the garage a few months back.'

'Do you chew your pens?'

Si raises an eyebrow. 'You're sounding weird. Can I call someone? Ollie?'

'Do you chew your pens?' I ask again, my tone firmer.

'No, I don't even use pens. I prefer pencils.'

'Does Garry use your office?'

'Everyone at the garage does.'

Shit! Cognitive bias. I thought the killer was Si so just picked up the pen from his office to prove my hypothesis.

Si isn't the killer.

In a fog, I drive out of the car park, leaving my big brother staring after me. Using my hands-free, I call Joel.

Voicemail.

I leave an urgent message telling him the pen belongs to Garry, not Si. How his broken leg was a lie. I sound like a crazed idiot, but it's all my mind will allow me to be right now.

Chapter 51

The Brother

What a fucking stupid verdict.

After Baker grins his way out of the courtroom, I think of a hundred things to tell my sister. But none of them will help. He didn't deserve the win. I'd heard justice was blind, but apparently she's deaf too. How could such a pathetic killer, one who pales in comparison to me, be allowed to go free? What would happen if I lost the game and stood trial? Would the DNA be enough to see me spending the rest of my life behind bars – publicly declared a loser? Would it be my face in Hawk's next book? My wily deeds drummed up into unsubstantiated psycho-babble? That would be a fate worse than prison. I'd be a laughing stock to my kind while Baker is held up as an idol. No. No. No.

It was fun while it lasted, but this game with my sister needs to end sooner rather than later. Having already played the suicide and accident cards, the only other option left is murder, but this death can't appear to be mine, or officially be part of my chain. I've put too much effort into creating my mask for this life, I refuse to give it up. I've not come this far to fall at the final Hurley.

I need… wait, I know exactly what to do. There are already lesser men in prison serving my time for me, and who better to throw into the police's crosshairs than a lacklustre, lying prick who doesn't play by the rules. Two birds, one sharp stone.

Adrenaline quickens my limbs, saturating my brain, as I take the first step on my penultimate round: hunting a predator.

–

Three hours out of prison and Tyler Baker is watching TV, laughing so loud I can hear him from outside the house. Peering through his curtainless window, I scan the room. With both of his killing buddies in prison, I'm happy to see he's alone. As I move towards the door, something black in Tyler's hands catches my eye. It's the missing gloves. He does have them. Whilst his eyes are latched to the TV screen, he threads the cheap pleather through his fingers again and again. The gloves are his trophy. Disgusted, I watch him raise them to his nose and inhale. My sister's blood is on them, a DNA mirror of my own. He might as well be slapping me with those fucking gloves.

I ring the doorbell, not once, but three times in quick succession.

Opening the door, Tyler snaps, 'Hold your horses.' Upon seeing me, he asks, 'Who the fuck are you?'

Deep in the recesses of his tiny, dark mind, he knows who the fuck I am. Our eyes locked on more than one occasion in court. 'Do you want to do this on your doorstep?'

'Do what?' He moves to close the front door on me.

'I'd have thought you'd have had enough of locked doors by now.'

He grins at me. 'Who are you again?'

I mirror his grin. 'I promise I won't hurt you.'

'Not what I asked,' he says, narrowing his eyes; those deep murky hollows where his sharp-toothed animal hides.

'Then I don't have to keep my promise.' Swiftly, I punch him in the stomach. Winded, he stumbles backwards and I enter his house, locking the door behind us.

Catching his breath, Tyler stands up. 'You're gonna pay, you—'

I headbutt him. The blow breaks his nose, sending eye-watering pain through his skull and blood pouring down his face. His meaty hands dive upwards to assess the damage.

As I take off my jacket and lay it over a nearby chair, I tell him, 'I'm Fallon Hurley's brother.'

'Shit,' he says, seeing the blood on his fingers. 'I saw you in court.'

'Guilty as charged.'

His eyes then swing to his mobile on the dining room table. Artfully, I step between him and his only way to call for help.

Tyler grunts. 'So what? You're gonna kill me for what happened at Cat Hall? You heard the jury, I'm innocent.'

I pull out my knife and let its heft settle in my hand. Moving closer to him, I shake my head. 'Not why I'm here.'

His eyes dart around the room, but he's not seeing anything useful. 'I'll admit everything!' he suddenly says. 'I'll go to the police.'

'Pinkie swear?' I laugh. 'I think you've already proved yourself a liar. And a shit serial killer to boot.'

Scrambling, he reels away from me, pushing a nearby hall table into my path. I'd love to be the silent, slow-walking slasher hunting him down, but I don't have time. Jumping over the table, I catch him up in a dirty tackle, kicking at his shins.

Collapsing to the floor, he holds his hands up in surrender. 'Please, stop!'

He thinks he can talk his way out of this, like he did in court, poor fool. In a jerky grab, he pulls a bag from a nearby chair. It's zipped up tight, so he struggles with shaking fingers to open it. Bless, it's his amateur kill kit. I slap it out from his grip, and it tumbles to the floor.

Eyes wide, he pleads, 'No! Please no!'

'Isn't that what they said, those you killed. *Please, no.* Did it stop you?'

An odd calm settles over his face. I get the same look when I'm scrolling through my sold Starsellers items.

'Wait,' he says again. 'Can we…'

I thrust the knife into his gut and pull it down a little, just a hint of evisceration. Moaning, he tries to hold in his bowels, but with the blood loss, his hands quickly weaken. Between his drooping fingers, I catch the hint of shiny innards. I love their pink shade; it reminds me of Fallon's decking.

As he slowly dies, a blast of nostalgic euphoria sweeps into my brain. Twirling and whirling in a feverish dance. Light-headed, I sit down to greet my old friend. My sister did cure my dulled senses. A perfectly executed plan is impressive, but there's a simple joy to an impulsive hunt – and that is what has eluded me for so long. This morning, I had no intention of ending this worm, but now, here I am covered in his blood, enjoying every minute of it. Nothing and no one told me to do it. He bid on nothing. He saw nothing. He isn't part of my murder chain, although he will play an excellent pawn in Fallon's game.

Tyler's eyes dull. Everything that made him the idiot he was disappears, leaving me with a wonderful, bloody prop.

I reverse the car up to the door. Unceremoniously, I shove the corpse into the boot, along with his kill kit and the infamous gloves. Truly, I may have made mistakes here and there, but redemption is just a dead sister away.

Once parked by Foxglove's lake, I check Tyler's kill kit. Ski mask, rope, and knives. Yawn-worthy content, but if I'm to pull off this kill-illusion then these are the bland items I'll have to work with. The last round with my sister is now murder misdirection. I top off the kit with the gloves. For once, the science will work in my favour. When they test them and find the DNA of all the Cat Hall victims, it will be the perfect gift for the police wrapped in a fake leather bow.

My sister almost got me. And she did reinvigorate my game, making me appreciate what I am and how clever I can be when challenged. Everyone should have a nemesis. Yes, I've made a few errors along the way, and although the knowledge I'm not perfect threw me off my game for a hot second, I'm now here, enacting the best plan I've ever conjured. Cool, calm and collected. As usual. Tonight, I'm going to be the victor – I can feel it in my bones.

Ready to play my final bloody hand, I lay in wait for just the right moment to make my way inside Poppy Fields one final time.

Chapter 52

Fallon

Safe back at Poppy Fields, I call Tina.

She answers with, 'I got your text. What happened?'

The question feels so big, I only mutter, 'I didn't tell you everything.'

'Was it something Tyler used in court?'

'Yes. But it was a truth wrapped in a lie.'

'Will you tell me now?'

Through tears I flush out my buried memory. I tell her about Rosie, and what I did. Once finished, I daren't even look up.

'Everything you just told me, the threats, the panic – anyone would have done the same. Yes, you should have told the police, but you know how tricky the mind can be.'

'I let Vic and Gayle down. I let Rosie down… her father…' I sniffle.

'We'll talk with Rosie's father together. Everything will be all right.'

'But Tyler is free.'

'The police have him on their radar, pet.'

'But he could hurt someone else.'

'That's his choice. It's the same choice every human has within them. As much as you've been trying to lately, you can't save the world. It's over now, get some rest.' As Tina clicks off, I try to let her words sink in. *It's over now.*

But it isn't – not yet.

Joel texts me to say he's heard my message about Garry. He writes that DI Worth has slyly checked medical records at the general hospital and found Si is telling the truth; he really did break his arm last March. Garry, on the other hand, has a clean bill of health. Convinced that Garry is now our man, she will begin her surveillance of him tomorrow. Without solid alibis for the murders, she'll build a case against him.

Although hesitating at first, I reply with a thumbs up emoji and then text, *I'm sorry about the verdict.* Joel lost his first case, a high profile one, in his new job because of me. I just hope that being involved with catching a prolific serial killer helps his reputation recover, rather than burns him again.

It's getting late, but I'm still wide awake. Nervous energy dancing through my body, I'm reaching for Harvey's lead when there's a knock at the door.

'Who is it?' I call out.

No reply. I know I locked the door, but a sudden creeping dread still eats away at my thoughts. Edging forward, I reach out to check, but as I touch the handle, my letterbox snaps open and something is slowly fed through. Jumping back, I watch in horror as black pleather gloves fall to the floor.

Harvey barks by my side. I try to pull him backwards into another room so we can lock ourselves in, but he's too strong. His collar slips through my hands, and he bolts towards the door. Once there, he sniffs the air.

'Harvey,' I whisper, but he doesn't move. Bending, I retrieve my stun gun from the table where I left it.

Silence stretches on for what seems like forever. Did Harvey scare my impromptu visitor away?

There's another knock, gentler this time. 'Fallon? Are you in there?'

It's Garry's voice. Shit! 'Go away!' I yell.

'You need to let me in.'

'No, I don't.'

'Why not?'

What do I say? The truth. 'I don't trust you.'

'That doesn't matter. You're not safe.'

'I've called the police,' I lie.

There's another knock on the door. I hear him breathing on the other side. 'Please, let me in. It's not safe out here for me either.'

'Why?' I ask.

'Because there's a dead guy on your deck!'

I'm not falling for that. 'Go! Away!'

'Fallon!' Garry yells.

There's a loud bang, and in horror, I watch my door vibrate.

The deadbolt. Lunging forward, I try to pull it across but I'm too late. My front door explodes inwards and I'm knocked to the floor. Holding his shoulder, Garry barges in.

Scrambling to my feet I yell, 'Get out!'

Harvey trots over to Garry, but instead of biting him as he did Grant, he just sniffs his hands and waits for a head scratch. Of course, he had won my dog over with a lamb bone.

'Jesus, Fallon, did you not hear me? There's a fucking dead body on your porch!'

'Leave!'

'Are you being held hostage?'

Ignoring his bizarre question, I call Harvey back to my side.

'Did you kill the guy on the deck? Is it Tyler Baker?' Garry asks.

Edging around him, I peek out the front door. As I do, I see blood dripping off my rocking chair, staining the pink wood beneath. Slowly, my stare rises to a fleshy, broken lump.

It is Tyler. Did Garry kill him?

I have an open door, I should run. Harvey will follow me. If we make it to the neighbours, we can call the police. DI Worth could arrest Garry quite literally red-handed.

Inching out the door, I repeat, 'I've called the police.'

'I heard you the first time. But don't worry, I called them too when I saw the corpse. I don't think you should go anywhere. Whoever did this could still be here, somewhere.' He peers outside as if to scour the treeline for the real murderer; it's a good act. Palms up, Garry then asks, 'Do you have any weapons?'

I shove my hand holding the stun gun behind my back. 'Nope.'

'Shit,' he whispers, then strides into the kitchen to pick up the biggest knife from my block.

I know I should run. But I've had enough. Enough of being scared. Enough of facing off with psychopaths. Enough of complying.

With tight-lipped defiance I tell him, 'I'm not going to make this easy for you.'

Cocking his head, Garry puts a hand up to silence me. 'Did you hear that?'

'Hear what?'

Garry edges further into my home. 'Is someone else here?'

Harvey's ears prick. It's then I hear it too. Shuffling in the guest bedroom. Someone else *is* here.

Chapter 53

Fallon

The door opens and a shadow steps into the light. Standing before me is not one of my brothers, but another man I recognise. Miles. Dressed in black with a bag slung across his shoulder.

'Surprise,' he says, waving a gloved hand.

'What?' I stumble back over Harvey.

'Let's keep the werewolf out of this.' Grabbing Harvey's collar, Miles pulls my dog back into the guest bedroom, then shuts the door to trap him.

'What the hell are you doing here?' Garry asks.

'I killed the prick on the deck,' he says calmly.

In shock, I look from Miles to Garry. 'But… Why?' Nothing about this makes any sense.

Smiling, he says, 'You're both gonna laugh when I tell you.'

Edging in front of me, holding his knife aloft, Garry says, 'Try me.'

Taking a deep breath, Miles looks at both of us in turn, then exclaims, 'I'm your brother!'

My jaw drops. What? *How?*

'You're having a laugh,' Garry spits.

'Is it that hard to believe Mum gave me up too?' Miles' stare lands back on me. 'Although I found out about it way before you did.'

Shaking his head, Garry steps forward. 'What the fuck are you on?'

My arm springs out to stop him from moving any further forward. 'I'll handle this,' I say. Garry doesn't know what Miles is capable of.

Sidestepping my attempt to stop him, Garry takes out his mobile. 'I'm gonna call Si and get this sorted…'

Before I can say another word, Miles throws down his bag, then pushes me out of the way to tackle Garry.

In films, fights last minutes. Each fighter gets the upper hand then loses it, until there's a winner. What Miles does is nothing like the movies. Once they're on the ground, he beats Garry's head against the floor until I hear a sickening crack. Without thinking, I jump onto Miles' back and shove the stun gun into his jacket. Trembling, he falls away.

I check Garry. He's still breathing. 'You're going to be okay,' I tell him.

Before I know what's happening, a hand grabs my neck and pulls me backwards.

'Nice try, sis. But my jacket took most of the charge.'

Scrambling up, I beg, 'Wait, please.'

Lunging forward, he slams into my shoulder. I lose my grip on the stun gun. It falls from my hand and slides into the kitchen. Pain is eaten by panic as Miles snatches a handful of my hair and swings me back against the kitchen counter. The force slides me down to the floor. Winded, I splutter, 'Miles. You know me.'

'Yes, I know *you* very well. And you now know me. Well, the parts of me most don't see.'

At that moment, I remember Garry called the police. Any minute now they'll come through my door to save us. In the meantime, I just need to keep everyone alive.

Quickly, I ask, 'But how can you be my brother? And the other Kappers didn't know?'

Darkness leaves Miles' expression as he offers me a bloody hand. 'You want to know how I stayed hidden. How I won?'

Won? He's won nothing yet. Tentatively, I take his hand and he pulls me to my feet. It's more terrifying to feel his hand in mine than it would be if he'd yanked me up by the hair.

'No one knows, except Mum.' He motions for me to sit down.

Carefully, I perch on the edge of the chair nearest Garry's unconscious body. Miles' sudden change of temperament is perplexing, but I'm going to make the most of it.

'Five sons.' I state. 'What happened to you?'

'My mother told me the story when I turned eighteen. Seven months into her pregnancy, she had a miscarriage. Fortunately for her and my father, their cleaner was the ever-pregnant Siobhan Kaplan. I was her first baby. She was a teenager doing her O levels, and had just started dating Daddy Kaplan. They weren't ready for me. Given her track record, I reckon you can guess the rest.' He sits down on the sofa. 'Odd, considering she was ready for the other four who came along, but then not you either. We've a lot in common, Fallon. We're the book-end-babies mummy didn't want.'

'So, Siobhan knows who you are?'

'I tracked her down a few years ago. She said she'd made a mistake in giving me away and wanted me to be a part of her life. She even got me a job at Si's garage so I could get to know my brothers organically. You've not seen it yet, but Si does have a wicked temper. We weren't sure how he'd take finding out he had an older brother. Weak reasoning. I always did question it – until you. Now I know why I had to be kept in the shadows. To stop everyone finding out about you too.'

'That's not my fault,' I say.

Ignoring me, he continues, 'I wasn't shocked when Mum admitted I had a sister, but I was intrigued when I looked you up and saw what happened at Cat Hall. And then, fuck me, I found your pathetic file on me. You know you didn't catch all my kills.'

He's wearing an annoying, smug expression. 'I guess Lindsay won't make it into the file now,' I say.

'Cross? She was an accident,' he replies through a smile.

'And Grant.'

Laughing he puts his up hands. 'Now come on, sis. I did you a favour there with that simpering little prick.'

Dryly I state, 'Casey won't be in your file either.'

In an instant, his arrogant expression vanishes leaving behind a flush to his cheeks. 'Now that was pure luck on your part. Admit it.' He steps towards me. 'Admit it was pure luck you won that round.'

If I challenge him more, will he enjoy it or will his temper end me right here and now? My profile flashes before my eyes. Competitive, yes. Superficial charm, yes. Organised – mostly. I can do this. Pushing my shoulders back, I ready myself for his attack.

He bursts out laughing. 'I love it. My little doe sister at bay. The perfect end to our little game.'

At bay?

'Tell me,' he says leaning forward. 'Did you suspect mild-mannered Miles, even for a second?'

I shake my head.

Garry then groans, snapping both our heads towards the sound.

'Are you planning on killing your own brother?' I ask.

'I don't mind a brace of victims every now and then.'

Brace? That's a hunting term. Wait, so is at bay. It's how he thinks of himself – a hunter. I can use that.

'Killing an unconscious man isn't worthy of a hunter, certainly not very sporting.'

Grunting, he steps over and gently kicks Garry to see if there's a reaction. There's only another weak groan.

'I can wait until he wakes up.'

'Seriously, you'd kill you own brother?'

'We're only DNA related.'

Bile catches in my throat. I told Joel that Garry was the killer. Would he and Worth still test the DNA? Or believe that, with Garry dead, justice was served and shove this whole thing under the carpet?

'Please don't hurt him,' I beg.

'Don't spoil my big ending with tears.' A wistful smile plays across Miles' lips. 'You know, this game with you has been quite the challenge. You were a worthy adversary. I choose well.'

Were – past tense? I have to say something. If I catch him off-guard, the organised killer morphs into the disorganised one, and it's that killer I stand a chance against. 'Wait, what about your game? You're *choosing* to kill Garry and me. Your other victims were chosen for you.'

He looks thoughtful. 'What's your point?'

'It's not much of a challenge if you pick prey yourself.' I cringe as I speak. 'That just makes you like all the others – an average, boring killer.'

'You've seen what I've done!' He strides towards my desk, then straddles my chair. 'Now, where's that profile you're so proud of?' In long sweeping motions he pushes books, papers and even my laptop off the desk.

'Didn't like what it said, eh?' I push.

I don't even see him run at me, just feel it when he grabs my wrist. With one yank, I'm off my seat. I pull back, but it's like trying to break free of a python.

Please let that be sirens I hear in the distance.

Miles pulls me into the kitchen, then gathers my wrists into one tight fist. With his free hand he scoops up his bag and turns his attentions to riffling through it. I struggle, but I'm not strong enough to escape. I need to think of something quick. I can use his arrogance against him. 'You know, getting away with what you did probably makes you the greatest serial killer of all time. Maybe you could tell me why you did it?'

Glancing back at me, he narrows his eyes. 'You wouldn't understand. People like you don't play by the rules.'

Obsessed with rules and games, he's childish in his thinking. Think, Fallon! I blurt, 'Did something happen in your childhood?'

Pulling a knife out of the bag, he says, 'Tell you what, let's play who has the biggest issues.' Gripping my arm tight, Miles drags me across the room. Dumping me before the broken door, he says, 'Run.'

'What?'

'It's what you did at Cat Hall. Run.'

'No, I won't leave my brother.'

'Fuck him, he'd run given half a chance. Head towards the lake. It's peaceful there. A good place for the game to end, don't you think?'

'So you can hunt me down like an animal? People are not playthings, Miles.'

'Then what good are they?' He lifts the knife.

Rising, I lunge forward and slam my fists against his shoulders, making him step back.

Easily regaining his balance, he spits, 'I imagined this differently.' He points the knife at me, disappointment colouring his face.

With practiced calm, I reply, 'Still chasing that first kill's high?' I open my mouth to expand on my question, but stop when his eyes blacken. Our conversation is over.

No more running.

I body tackle Miles. He's heavy and strong so doesn't fall down. But, in the confusion, the knife escapes his grasp and falls to the floor. With a laugh, he twists one of his arms about my neck in a chokehold. Lindsay's neck was broken, just like the man in the garage, I need to do something quick. Struggling for breath, I stamp hard on his foot, and he lets me go. I bend to retrieve the knife and swing it wildly at his face. He catches my wrist, then punches me in the stomach. Doubling over, I gasp, but don't drop the knife.

'That's the spirit.' Miles circles me.

We move in our dance again, only this time my back is to the kitchen. If I can just get to the stun gun… 'Tell me how you imagined this?' I risk a glance behind me and see pink plastic poking out from beneath the cooker.

'As an epic showdown I inevitably win. Or maybe you kill me. Perhaps you'll realise it's in your DNA and I'll start your game.' Charging forward, he grabs my hand holding the knife. I surprise him by dropping the blade, then use the distraction to pull myself free. Falling to the floor, I scoot backwards on the linoleum towards the cooker, then reach behind me for the stun gun. It's cool against my fingers, solid in my grip. But it's too late. Miles has the knife and is looming over me. The blade poised to plunge into my chest.

Chapter 54

The Brother

What did I do?

Standing back, I watch Fallon slump over. Thirty-nine people brought me here, all killed with deathly precision, yet instead of stabbing my sister's heart, I aimed for her shoulder. From the kitchen floor, she looks up at me with such defiance, it makes me feel warm inside. Is this sensation pride?

'Why didn't I kill you?' I ask.

Holding her shoulder to stop the bleeding, she snorts. 'Freudian slip?'

I can't help it, I laugh. She laughs too. Siblings having fun together.

'Have you played your game against someone else before?' she asks.

'No.'

'Did it make it more exciting?'

My heartbeat has trundled up to a good sixty-six beats per minute. 'Yes.'

Nodding, she adds, 'Solitaire can be fun, but ultimately a little sad, don't you think?'

Bending, I help put pressure on her wound. 'Why don't we play a little longer, just the two if us.' Why am I saying this? I could snatch the win right now. Tyler would easily get the blame for both murders.

'What about Garry?'

'I can get rid of him,' I say and watch her flinch.

'Please don't. He's our brother.'

Shrugging I state. 'We have three others.'

'Miles, you're an amazing serial killer. It's such a shame only me and you know. If you let Garry live, we can play the next level all together.'

What is she on about? This game is played by my rules. There's no next level, just the next kill. I shake my head, then turn to sort out Garry.

'Wait.' Her hand leaps up to stop me. 'He's still unconscious? Remember, you're better than that.'

She's right; hunters don't sulk in the shadows slaughtering sleeping prey. I need to wait until Garry wakes up, then I can kill him. Turning towards my sister, I shake the knife at her. 'Clever little vixen aren't you? Twisting me around and around, making me hesitate like this. You may have gotten in my head, but you can't stay there.' I edge closer to her.

She blurts, 'You don't want to do this. It's why you gave me so many clues with Casey. Deep down, you want me to win. You want to be caught. All serials want to be caught.'

Before I can catch myself, I smile, a real honest-to-goodness smile. 'Last chance, Fallon. Run.'

Lurching forward, she falls against my chest, catching the zip on my jacket. It opens to reveal my T-shirt covered in Tyler's blood. She gasps.

'Murder's a grubby business, sis.'

Suppressing a shudder, she straightens her spine.

I twist the knife's hilt in my hand. 'Ready, steady, go…'

Chapter 55

Fallon

Miles thrusts the knife. As he does, I twist from his reach to catch him full in the chest with the stun gun. This time, there's no padded jacket to subdue the voltage. I push the button several times against his t-shirt. With a sudden jerk, he drops with a thump to the floor.

Blood is streaming from my shoulder, so I grab a nearby tea-towel and wrap up my wound as best I can. The knife is lying nearby, so I kick it away from him. I then bend and zap Miles again for good measure.

Sirens finally sound. My shoulder feels on fire, but I manage to stagger to the front door. Opening it, I see two police cars and an ambulance pull up. I fall onto the deck in relief and watch my blood ooze out across the shadowed pink slates. Tyler's corpse is still sitting on my rocking chair, mouth slack and splattered with blood. It's a horrible thought, but it's the one good thing Miles did – taking a fellow predator out of this world.

'Fallon!' a policeman shouts. It's Ray. Behind him a woman sprints towards Poppy Fields. I don't recognise her, but from her determination and worry I guess it's DI Worth.

'The killer is Miles – he's by the cooker,' I tell them. 'And Garry is hurt. Please help him.'

Garry is swiftly pulled onto a stretcher and taken away by the ambulance.

Holding onto Ray, I hobble back inside to watch Worth roll Miles over. Like a horror film villain, he's already coming round, ready to attack again. But there are too many police officers. Handcuffs click around his wrists as they tell him he's being arrested on suspicion of murder.

Chuckling, he looks over at me. 'Hey, sis.'

I step closer to him. 'Miles?'

'Good game. I nearly had you there, didn't I?'

'Yes, you almost had me.' Struggling with my shoulder, I kneel down so I'm on his level. 'You lost, so you're going to admit all your crimes, aren't you?' I ask. 'You didn't lie to me before when you said fair's fair.'

All the police stop what they're doing and remain silent and statue-like around him.

Rolling his eyes, he echoes, 'Fair's fair.'

I watch DI Worth bundle him into the back of her car. The DNA profile Lindsay had will match, but it won't matter; Miles has rules. He stood by them with Casey, and I have no doubt the killer I profiled will do as he says and confess his crimes now I've won the game.

Chapter 56

Fallon

Although I try to hibernate my latest trauma away, it doesn't stop me getting visitors.

My new family take it in shifts to stop by. Sam cooks me delicious meals. Susie takes me shopping. Garry, fresh out of hospital for a concussion, offers to walk Harvey while my shoulder heals. Apparently, he's looking for an investor to start a dog walking business. Even from rehab, Stefan FaceTimes me to talk.

When Si drives me to Siobhan's, I take time to really look at her photo collection. There are six pregnancy photos – Miles was always on her wall too.

Whilst drinking tea and eating cakes, she admits, 'He sought me out years ago. I should have told everyone, but that would have meant admitting I gave Miles away – and if everyone knew about him, they'd perhaps find out about Fallon, too. Nothing was legal back then.'

'That's no excuse, Mum,' Si snaps.

'I know. And the longer I hid his identity, the worse the thought of telling everyone got. I'm so sorry.'

A feeling I know all too well. I lean forward. 'Did you know what he was?'

Shaking her head, she says, 'I'd be lying if I said I never sensed a wrongness in him. But you always want to think the best of your kids.'

'I wished you'd at least told me about him, Mum. Christ, I worked with the guy for years.' Si says, shaking his head.

'I just couldn't.' Siobhan pats his knee, but he jerks out from under her touch.

'He could have killed Fallon and Garry. Some things are more important than your secrets.' Si's face is red and his fingers are curled into neat fists.

'It's going to be all right,' I tell him. 'We'll work through it together.'

Siobhan then looks at me with such kindness and pride. I still haven't completely forgiven her for what she did, but I know she meant well, and, like Mum said, it counts for something.

-

Sitting in Tina's office, a glass of water trembling in my hand, I blurt everything out about my new family, along with my serial killer hunt. Once I'm done, she takes a full minute before saying, 'I can't believe your biological brother is a serial killer. You protected me, which is lovely, but it was my decision whether to be involved. I'm not saying I could have spotted Miles – it sounds like this forensic genealogy thing isn't as straightforward as it appears – but I could have helped.'

'I'm sorry. There's so much I'd wish I'd done differently.'

Tina shifts in her chair. 'I know it's a sore subject, but one good thing came out of this. Tyler is no longer a threat, and with the gloves found at the scene he's been outed as a liar.'

'At least Vic, Gayle and Rosie got justice,' I say.

Tina nods. 'I spoke with Rosie's father.'

I hold my breath.

She reaches behind her chair and pulls out a bag. 'He left you this.'

Instantly, I see what's in it. My coat. I pull it out.

'He fixed the missing button,' Tina explains.

My fingers follow the grey wool down until I find the perfectly sewed on button. 'That was sweet of him.'

'You can tell him in person. I offered some complimentary sessions. It would be great if you can join us.'

Nodding, I say, 'Of course I will.'

'He's not ready to stay it aloud yet, but he does forgive you for your part in Cat Hall.'

'I don't deserve that.'

'Yes, you do. We shouldn't be defined by panicked mistakes.'

I'm about to ask if I can speak with him alone, when I hear Tina's bell. Someone is in the waiting room. I don't expect to see Ollie at the Hawk offices, but there he is, bottle of wine in the crook of his arm and Mum trailing behind him.

'Sorry for the ambush, I asked them here.' My boss nods to my family who sit beside me.

Ollie hands Tina the wine, then pulls out a newspaper from his bag. 'I picked this up.'

Tentatively, I take the paper and read the headline: *Cat Hall Victim Catches Serial Killer.*

'They're calling you a hero, love,' Mum says taking the paper from me. She reads aloud, 'Dr Fallon Hurley, survivor of last year's incident at Cat Hall, caught the serial killer now known as the Starsellers Slasher. Once in custody, he confessed to killing nearly forty people using the popular auction app to choose his victims.'

An auction site! That's how he was doing it.

Over her shoulder, Ollie continues reading, 'He also confessed to murdering budding serial killer, Tyler Baker, who escaped justice for his part at Cat Hall. Miles Loughlin, who was unavailable to comment, is now residing at Her Majesty's pleasure awaiting sentencing.'

Loughlin. He isn't even a Kaplan. With no obvious surname connection, it appears as if we're not even related.

'I'm so proud of you, pet,' Tina says, clapping her hands. 'And, I hate to bring it up, but I'm getting quite a few requests for Hawk to consult on murder cases.'

Could I fall down another bloody rabbit hole? Before Miles my answer would have been a resounding no. But now, I think I understand his need to play and win games; the righteous buzz it leaves in its wake. 'We'll see,' I tell Tina, who rises an eyebrow at me.

After talking for hours, we all say goodbye and I find myself with only one more thing I have to face.

-

Tina offered to visit the prison with me, but I thought it best to meet Miles alone. When he sits opposite, he smiles as if we're old friends.

'Shoulder feeling better?' he asks.

Pleasantries were not my reason to come, but I indulge him all the same. 'It's healing well. You didn't do any permanent damage. How are you? How's the food?' Urgh, how's the food!

'Nothing like Sam's cooking, but better than expected. Apologies for the whole trying-to-kill-you thing. I've seen the error of my ways. Killing is not a game.'

'You're taking the piss.'

'Course I am.' He laughs. 'You can never go back after your first blooding.'

Suddenly, I imagine my big brother as a little boy, a smear of scarlet staining his face. Who was his first kill?

'Have you told the police about all the murders? Even the ones not on the system?'

Rolling his eyes at me, he snorts. 'You caught me, of course I fessed up. And before you ask, yes, I gave them the details of Lindsay and Grant.'

My shoulders drop a little. Lindsay's life and work will now be seen for it really it was and Grant's Mum will know her son didn't take his own life. I'm not sure being murdered by a serial killer is a better legacy than an accident or suicide, but at least Miles gave them their truth.

'Thank you,' I tell him, 'you're a good sport.'

'Is that why you came? To make sure the police got their prize?'

'No entirely. I want to help you.'

'Are you going to bake a cake with a file in it?' Throwing his head back, he laughs.

'I mean therapy. Tina encouraged me to take you on as a client. She thought it would be good for both of us.'

'No offence, but therapy is for pussies. Talking about feelings I don't have won't get you very far. Besides, you shouldn't listen to her. Dr Hawk's infamous book was narrow in its scope.'

'How so?' I ask.

Leaning forward, he beckons me to do the same, but I stay put.

'There are more types of killers out there than you could ever imagine. Her highly esteemed theories barely scratch the surface.'

His face is mischievous, like *A Midsummer Night's Dream's* Puck in a prison jumpsuit. Before I reached the visitors' room, the guard told me Miles had taken to playing another game: how many punches will the walls of his cell take before they crack. Looking down at his hands, I see new and old scabs dusting his knuckles. What little part of my heart I'd locked away for this brother aches at the sight.

Breaking my thoughts, he says, 'You're doubting me?'

'I'm not.'

'You are. I've met other killers in here. They all need to tell their stories. I don't want to set you up as the psychopath whisperer or anything, but you should spend some time with them.'

'You're trying to help me?' I search his face for an ounce of love, something I can work with.

'Can't have you blindly wandering into another Cat Hall,' he replies.

A twitch of his lips, an unsteady undertone in his voice. He's saying the words, but doesn't mean them. No, he's not looking out for me, he's training me to be a better opponent, someone to play against next time.

Smiling, I say, 'Sure. I'll let you and your friends educate me.'

'Excellent decision, sis,' he says, with a murderous twinkle in his eye. 'Game on.'

Epilogue

To: Fallon Hurley
Poppy Fields
Foxglove Lodges
Northants

Dear sis,

You're probably wondering how I got this letter to you, past prying eyes. Well, it was simple really. I dictated it on a visit to a lovely lady, and she posted it to you. Now we have that out of the way, I wanted to thank you for coming to see me last month. None of the other family members have come, not even Mum. But I've made a friend in here. Billy. He's been confined for decades, so bit of a dab hand at the system now – taught me everything he knows. We play chess every Wednesday. Sometimes he even beats me. The prison has made him a custodian, so he knows all the secret nooks and crannies and has access to some splendid chemicals.

Last we met you saw the injuries on my hand. Don't worry, I'm not trying to hurt myself the way your little psychologist mind thinks. I'm enjoying my trips to the infirmary. I've worked out it's one of the most interesting parts of the prison, what with it doubling as the morgue. Corpses are transported from it straight to a rather unsecure hospital. Prisoners often mention how they'll only escape when they're dead. And with my low heart rate, I'm good at playing dead. All I need is a fresh corpse whose body bag I can borrow for the ride.

I have my eye on a prisoner who looks near to death. Ricky is in his twenties, dumb as a post, and raped three teenagers. Should have been put in with all the other kiddie fiddlers, but he pled out so they only charged him with assault; I don't need to tell you about the flaws in our legal system! At lunch he blabbed with pride about what he'd really done. Billy confirmed his story, saying he'd said as much to him too, so I'm not alone in thinking Ricky should die sooner rather later. Really, it's a public service. One push down a tall staircase and the world is free of one of its many burdens.

My friend has even offered to dispose of the body; he wants the bones for something fun. I think this a highly successful partnership. See, I'm not a lone hunter anymore, but co-operating with others. I'm not going to tell you the full plan. I'll let you piece it together like Cross did with my kills. It'll be the start of our new game.

Well, must dash. The postal system is rather slow, so by the time you read this I'll be well on my way. We won't be disturbed this time, so can have a proper catch up. Not to steal a line from that idiot Tyler, but, *see you real soon*, sis.

Or, then again, maybe I'm just playing with you.

A Letter from N V Peacock

Dear Reader,

We haven't spoken for a while. How are you? I hope you're well.

At this point, you might wonder what made me write this book. Well, with what you already know about me, you've probably summarised that I own a very twisted imagination and revel in the darker side of life. Growing up, I was always reading horror books and watching films that's recommended age was way beyond my own! This trait drew me to ghost stories, true crime and psychological discussions. I've always felt an instant kinship to others with the same minds. If you're reading this letter, I bet you have a curiously dark mind too!

Throughout my life, I've become obsessed with the *what if* question? Sometimes, it's a good obsession as it can help me be innovative and imagine solutions to problems. But sometimes it's a bad one, leaving wild, unchecked thoughts to fester in my mind. *The Brother* was born from one of the latter thoughts.

I have an older brother. Lured in by a DNA genealogy offer online, he sent away to find out where he comes from. There wasn't much in the way of surprises there. We already knew our family was descended from Vikings – both of us being tall and blonde, as children we would often go marauding through sweet shops and libraries.

But, when he showed me the DNA results, I still got that *what if* sensation. Sections noted relatives we could contact, and it made me think, just because you share blood with someone, doesn't mean to say they are good person to have in your life.

I've always loved true crime, and during Lockdown I was glued to podcasts. When I heard the US case of the Golden State Killer was finally closed using forensic genealogy, I thought that crime investigations had turned a corner. Tracing people through their family DNA via commercial genealogy databases meant that killers who thought they had escaped justice should now sleep with one eye open. And not only was this new technique catching criminals, but it was giving names back to those poor unidentified victims too. John and Jane Does were finally being identified, and their families were being gifted closure for their missing loved ones. Eagerly, I looked online to find the cases that the UK had employed this method on, but found we didn't do it here! Shocked, my mind whirred with the questions I pose throughout the book – what would you do if you knew your brother was a killer – and without the same freedom as the US, how far would you go to stop him? Would you break the law? Put yourself in danger?

As a writer, you're told to write what you know, and I always embed an aspect of myself into each protagonist. In my debut book, *Little Bones*, Cherrie had my dark sense of humour. Fallon, in *The Brother*, inherited my love of psychology and my impulse to understand and help others. Like her, my advice might not always be taken, but I pride myself on always be there for my family and friends whenever they need a shoulder to cry on, a listening ear, or a pair of hands to help bury a body – too far?

Northamptonshire has always been my home, so I usually set my books in my local area, but names and descriptions have been changed, so although The Hungry Piglet might sound like a great place to stop off for a spot of lunch, you won't find it – sorry!

You can, however, find me on Twitter @Nickyp_author and remember to follow me on my Amazon author page for book updates and more. Please do also check out other books from Hera by my talented sister and brother authors.

www.herabooks.com

Thank you for buying my book, reader. If you enjoyed it, please take a few moments to write a review, and of course give it a shout out on social media. As you discovered in *The Brother*, untold secrets can fester inside your soul, so don't keep it to yourself. Tell everyone you meet about my books!

It's been lovely to have this time with you. Hope you feel the same way. In the future, let's not leave it so long between talks. Speak again in early 2024 when my next book hits shelves.

Take care of yourself and those you love.

Until we meet again,

N V Peacock

Acknowledgments

Even as an author, I find it hard to write this part of the book. There are always so many people to thank, that I'm paranoid I'll miss someone out! But of course, I couldn't just list everyone I've ever known down for fear of getting the proverbial hook off the stage for droning on too long! So, here goes…

The Brother is my second full-length novel, and the journey it took me on is very special to me. Not just because of how proud I felt when I finished it, but because of the people who I found along the way, and of course those who have been in my life for quite some time.

The first person who needs a huge thank you is my lovely literary agent, Maddalena Cavaciuti. It means a lot that she was there with me when I needed help, that she encourages and appreciates my dark mind, and of course that she took the time to help mould this book into the twisted tale it became. Being an author can be fraught with many challenges, from procrastination, to juggling commitments, to the dreaded submission process, but having Maddalena as a constant cheerleader throughout has been amazing. I feel very lucky that she is my agent.

Thank you to Keshini Naidoo and Jennie Ayres of the amazing Hera, who have embraced my dark side and given me a home for my thrillers. Their support and attention to detail is second to none, and with the Peacock being the goddess Hera's sacred animal, it feels fated that I found my way to them. And not to forget the cover designers and scores of dedicated sales and marketing professionals who work tirelessly to ensure the success of the book. And I should really mention my copy editor Phil Williams for his efforts in taming my punctuation (sorry about all the semi-colons, Phil!).

I wouldn't be where I am now without my fellow author Jane Isaac, whose wise words and patience with me, at times, borders on saintly. Our carvery and catch up meals are something I cherish and always look forward to – as well as getting an early read of her thrillers too! My friends are all very special to me. Carole Goodley, my unofficial life coach, who always gives the best advice. Shusha Walmsley, who has the best laugh and warmest hugs. Julie Kendrick, a fountain of knowledge regarding books and police procedure. Karen Rust, who I can talk to about anything from writing to true crime to Marvel films – and whose book I'm certain one day you'll be reading too. And Jean Miller, who regularly accompanies me for cinema visits, murder mystery games, bingo nights, and talks on serial killers; regardless of the potential nightmares. Yes, bingo can get scary!

Writing can be such a solitary vocation, so I need to mention my local writers' group, which is brimming with so many wonderful people, all with a story to tell and a generous spirit to share their time and talents with fellow writers. It's often forgotten that authors wouldn't be where they are today without the support of local libraries and bookshops who give the gift of the written word to the world, so I'd like to thank them too. I also need to highlight Writing East Midlands, who provide courses, events and organise workshops for writers in the region.

There's also my wonderfully weird family, who has now put up with me for quite some time. My nieces and nephews (big thanks for the new laptop, Harrison!) My big brother and his better half. My dad, who has now stopped rolling his eyes when I say I'm an author, and my mum, who reads every read I write.

Last but not least, you the reader. Without you buying, reviewing and recommending my books, I wouldn't have my dream job.

Thank you all.